A Resolution at Midnight

FORGE BOOKS BY SHELLEY NOBLE

Ask Me No Questions
Tell Me No Lies
A Resolution at Midnight

SHELLEY NOBLE

A Resolution at Midnight

A Tom Doherty Associates Book · *New York*

A RESOLUTION AT MIDNIGHT

Copyright © 2020 by Shelley Freydont

All rights reserved.

A Forge Book
Published by Tom Doherty Associates
120 Broadway
New York, NY 10271

www.tor-forge.com

Forge® is a registered trademark of Macmillan Publishing Group, LLC.

The Library of Congress Cataloging-in-Publication Data is available upon request.

ISBN 978-1-250-75026-6 (hardcover)
ISBN 978-1-250-75027-3 (ebook)

Our books may be purchased in bulk for promotional, educational, or business use. Please contact your local bookseller or the Macmillan Corporate and Premium Sales Department at 1-800-221-7945, extension 5442, or by email at MacmillanSpecialMarkets@macmillan.com.

First Edition: October 2020

Printed in the United States of America

10   9   8   7   6   5   4   3   2   1

To Irene, Nancy, and Yvonne—best of the best.

A Resolution at Midnight

1

Philomena Amesbury, Phil to her friends, the Countess of Dunbridge to everyone else, handed her armful of packages to the footman of the Plaza Hotel and stepped out of the red Darracq taxicab.

"Lovely day, isn't it, Mr. Fitzroy?"

The doorman, dressed in the full fawn-and-gold braided livery of the Plaza, smiled and looked dubiously at the gray clouds that overcast the sky.

"Indeed, Lady Dunbridge. Did you enjoy your morning of shopping?"

"I did. Everyone is so festive." Of course there had been that unsightly shoving match between two ladies over who went first up the escalator at Bloomingdale's and the disappointing moment when the proprietor at the little bookstore across the street had informed her that he'd sold his last copy of the latest Arthur Conan Doyle novel, which she had been hoping to buy as a present for her butler, Preswick.

A misstep on her part. She shouldn't have waited until ten days before Christmas to reserve a copy. But after six months in Manhattan and three at the Plaza, she was still learning her way in a place where countesses did things for themselves.

"There are more packages in the taxi and even more being delivered, if you'd please have them stored until I call for them."

"Yes, Lady Dunbridge." Mr. Fitzroy nodded to the bellman,

who reached into the taxi and took the remaining packages into the hotel.

The taxi drove away, and Phil took the opportunity to look across the street to where a small boy hawked his newspapers at the entrance to Central Park. He had designated himself as her small but vigilant lookout, and who went by the soubriquet of Just a Friend.

Phil waved, though he wasn't looking her way. He was wearing a new scarf and mittens to add to the winter coat Preswick had bought him a few weeks before. Her butler might be a tad old-fashioned in his ways and a bit long in the tooth, but he had a heart warmer than the bag of chestnuts nestled inside her purse.

Oh the freedom of leaving England, with its peerage and restrictions, for America where she could come and go as she wished at any time of the day and be whatever she wanted. If it hadn't been for the earl dying and leaving her a dowager at twenty-six, and her last rather public indiscretions with a certain Frenchman, she would never have known the excitement of life in Manhattan.

Well, to be honest, there had also been that little incident of a murder that she'd inadvertently solved and that had made all the major newspapers—much to her father's chagrin. Her father might look the other way at *affaires de coeur* and other minor eccentricities by his daughter, but he wouldn't stomach her hobnobbing with the metropolitan police. He'd intended to pack her off to Great-Aunt Sephronia in the wilds of Yorkshire, hence Phil's quickly organized trip to the New World.

And as it had turned out, that one little involvement with the London police had done much to ensure her success in New York. For there was no one people admired more than someone with a title who could solve their most dastardly crimes while keeping their family secrets locked in her breast—and a few others locked in the safe in her apartment upstairs.

Phil headed toward the bank of bronze elevators where

Egbert, her favorite operator, nodded and gestured her inside the cage.

"Lovely day, Lady Dunbridge," he said in a melodious voice that always sounded like a song.

"Indeed, Egbert. Do you think we'll have snow for Christmas?"

"Perhaps."

Phil opened her handbag and pulled out a brown paper cone of chestnuts. "I thought you might enjoy these."

"Ah, roasted chestnuts. Thank you." Egbert quickly slipped off one white glove and took them from her.

"Make sure you enjoy them while they're still hot," Phil said.

He slipped them into his pocket and slid his hand back into his glove just as they reached the fifth floor.

He opened the gate and waited for her to reach her door and let herself inside.

All was quiet. She'd given her maid, Lily, and Preswick the day off to do their own shopping and to enjoy the festivities of the city. This would be their first Christmas as a household and they were all looking forward to it.

Preswick, after a rough start, had taken to life in Manhattan, and Lily was thriving.

At least Phil thought she was. Phil actually knew very little about Lily before the day Phil had first encountered her as she fought off several sturdy British customs officials who had discovered her attempting to stow away on the ship to America. Recognizing a kindred spirit, Phil had paid her passage and hired her as a lady's maid, her own maid having refused to board the ship at the last minute. When she refused to give her name, Phil called her Lily because of her porcelain complexion. Preswick had done the rest.

They'd become quite a team, the three of them.

Phil unpinned her hat and tossed it and her handbag onto the occasional chair set next to the hall table. A white envelope lay on the floor by the door.

Strange. Usually when there was a message, the concierge, a kind but inquisitive creature, made sure to stop her on her way upstairs.

She picked up the envelope and read one handwritten word. *Countess.*

There was only one man who called her that, a deliberate misuse of proper address. She was certain he knew better. Perhaps he was letting her know his opinion of titles. A form of challenge? Or, dare she hope, a term of affection? Whichever, it sent a thrill of excitement through her.

She ripped open the envelope, let it fall to the ground as she perused the single sheet of paper. *Theatre Unique. 1:15. Last Row.*

It was written in the bold classic script that she knew well. She glanced at the Ormolu clock on the mantel. Twelve forty-three. She'd never make it. She didn't stop to equivocate, but grabbed her purse and hat from the chair and hurried back down the hall to the elevator.

It was infuriating, Phil thought, looking out the passenger window of the taxicab inching its way down Fifth Avenue. The streets were congested with holiday traffic. Pedestrians clogged the sidewalks, jostling each other as they hurried from one shop to another.

The subway would have been much faster, though there wasn't a station near the hotel and she'd as yet never taken one of the underground railways, something she should probably remedy as soon as the weather was better.

She checked her lapel watch. Almost one o'clock. He could have given her more notice, or left the note with the concierge and saved her several lost minutes of going upstairs. But that was not Mr. X's way. *Mr. X.* She still didn't know his name or what he looked like, since he always appeared in disguise, when he bothered to appear at all.

But though she might not know what he looked like, she

knew how he felt, every luscious contour of him—until he'd disappeared, always before the light of dawn.

She leaned forward and tapped on the glass window that separated her from the driver.

"It's most urgent that we hurry," she explained.

"You shoulda left earlier. It's Christmastime."

It wasn't like she'd had a choice. Though she enjoyed the excitement of notes slipped under the door or left on pillows, and chance meetings at balls or in dark alleys, it just wasn't efficient. They needed a better system of communication.

She could imagine him sitting in the theater, dressed as who knew what, waiting for how long? He was taking an awfully big chance if it was something urgent.

And things always were with him.

"I'd be ever so grateful, if you could see your way through this traffic."

The driver turned around long enough to scowl at her.

She lifted her eyebrows and clasped her handbag suggestively. "Very grateful."

Almost immediately the taxi swerved out of line and swung around the truck in front of it, nearly coming to blows with another taxi attempting the same thing in the opposite direction.

The taxi lurched and swerved back to its side of the street. Phil adjusted her hat, which she hadn't secured properly in her haste to get into the taxi. A block later he turned in front of a trolley and headed toward Park Avenue, which was not quite as heavily trafficked. It took them straight down past Union Square to Fourteenth Street, where he turned and stopped at the curb.

Phil tipped him generously and the taxi squeezed back into traffic. Across the street the Academy of Music, now no longer the center of the arts, stood shoulder to shoulder with Tammany Hall, headquarters of the most powerful politicians in Manhattan.

The Theatre Unique was located on the south side of the street, sandwiched between a row of small storefront businesses, several theatrical agencies, an oyster bar, and a cigar shop. THEATRE UNIQUE was picked out in the new electric lights across a curved arch that led to a rather byzantine-looking ticket kiosk. Above the arch, nude gods held up garlands of flowers, while above them, cherubs played a fanfare on plaster trumpets.

There was no end to excess in America, even in their theaters, Phil thought as she headed to the kiosk.

She handed over fifteen cents, snatched her ticket, and fairly ran to the entrance.

Only as she stepped into darkness did she realize that she was entering a nickelodeon.

She couldn't begin to guess why Mr. X wanted to meet her here. But he must have had his reasons. He always did and she never questioned him. At least not out loud.

She stood just inside the door, silhouettes of seated people coming in and out of focus as the moving images cast them in flickering exchanges of light and dark.

Still, she didn't venture farther, but swept a look around the perimeter of the room, peered into the dark corners, along the back wall to the square of light through which the images were projected. She perused the rows of seats, picking out as many details as possible, as Dr. Gross in his handbook *Criminal Investigation* had recommended.

Everyone seemed mesmerized by the screen, which was showing speeding race cars that normally would have interested her. But not today.

She was intrigued by her summons, and just a little wary. Anticipation tickled the hairs on the back of her neck as the cars silently raced across the screen and an unseen pianist plunked away at a tinny rendition of Scott Joplin's popular "The Entertainer."

Really, life had been much easier when gentlemen callers

appeared at the door with a card and a bouquet of your favorite flowers. But so much less interesting.

A single gentleman sat alone at the near end of the back row. He appeared to be asleep. There were no other people sitting in the last several rows.

Taking a final quick look around the flickering room, Phil pulled her skirts back, eased into the row, and sat down.

He didn't greet her. Didn't even appear to wake up. Purposely ignoring her? She felt a little niggle of irritation.

Though perhaps they were being watched. She leaned back, gave her outward attention to the screen.

"I'm here," she whispered, keeping her eyes focused on the racing cars.

No response.

She risked a sideways glance. He'd gone all out today. And, she had to admit, she was impressed.

He seemed shorter, more heavyset than usual, almost paunchy. Dressed in corduroy trousers and nondescript jacket. No hat that she could see, just thinning hair that was slicked back except where several strands fell over his forehead. He looked the epitome of a middle-aged working man.

And still he ignored her. He was obviously perturbed that she was late.

Well, really, was she expected to sit quietly at home waiting for instructions?

"You've made your point," she whispered. "It's the holidays. I was out shopping. I came immediately upon returning home, but traffic is particularly heavy this time of the year."

Nothing from her companion.

"Don't you think you're taking this a bit far? I apologize. It won't happen again, though I don't know why you just couldn't have skulked around the hotel dressed as a shoeshine boy and told me what I needed to hear. Why are we here?"

Nothing. They were definitely being watched or he would have acknowledged her by now.

She turned her head slightly, pretending to look in her bag. She was certain no one had been behind her when she sat down.

And she was filled with an unnamed dread.

She touched his shoulder. He slumped forward. She leaned closer but couldn't see his face or smell the faint aroma of the exotic pipe tobacco he favored. But she did smell something sickly metallic, and her stomach heaved.

With a herculean effort, she pulled him upright; his head rolled, then snapped back over the seat back.

The race continued inexorably on the screen.

The gash where his throat had been slit, and the black stain, soaking his collar and spreading down his woolen jumper, appeared and disappeared in the flicking light and dark, light and dark, of the moving picture.

Her mind—and yes, her heart—reeled, as logic fought for purchase.

She had learned much about the science of psychology since beginning her detective career. The mind could play tricks on you, or show you the way out of a maze. At times it was hard to distinguish which was which.

This was not Mr. X. This man was shorter, stockier, his neck thicker. Even with his talent for absurd disguises, Mr. X couldn't possibly change so much.

Besides, Mr. X would never succumb to the indignity of having his throat slit in an afternoon nickelodeon.

But whoever he was, he was definitely dead. No one could survive that much blood loss. Whoever had killed him had been efficient and ruthless—and might still be in the theater.

She instinctively reached out and touched the man's hand. Still warm. Her stomach revolted, but she felt down the rough wool of his coat and slipped her hand in his pocket. A stub of a pencil, a notebook, what felt like a smashed packet of cigarettes, and a small rectangular box. Matches?

She didn't think twice but pulled the items out and shoved

them in her handbag, knowing full well that she was interfering with a crime scene, one that might somehow involve
her.

She reached out again, slid her hand beneath the lapel of
his jacket . . . and was nearly swept away on a tide of relief.

This definitely wasn't Mr. X. Her eyes might deceive her,
but her touch never would.

But who was he? And why was she sent here to meet him?

She quickly felt inside his jacket, reached over and tried
the other pocket, and found nothing more.

A scream pierced through the music that accompanied
the racing cars—through the erratic lights and the pictures
that flashed and jumped and seemed to suddenly grow very
bright—bright enough to see a young woman standing at the
end of the aisle.

"No!" the girl cried. "No!" She turned and ran.

There was a sudden stir around the theater, murmurs as
heads began to turn, looking for the source of the scream.

Phil, suddenly galvanized into action, ducked her head and
sidestepped to the end of the aisle.

Someone yelled, "What's happening?"

A man stood and turned from his seat. "Back there, in the
last row! Call the cops!"

The girl had disappeared. Phil turned back to the suddenly
silent theater. The music had stopped. The race cars continued
to whizz across the silent screen.

Someone slipped up beside her, took her by both elbows.
She immediately tried to strike out.

"Don't turn around," he whispered. "I'm the theater manager. You need to get out of here. This way, please."

He gave her a push, then grabbed her by one arm and propelled her down the aisle toward a back door, past two other
men attempting to restore order as the patrons fought their
way to the entrance in the opposite direction.

"Hurry," he hissed. And just as the house lights came on,

he pushed her through a door camouflaged by a mural across the back wall.

Things were happening too fast. But she knew he was right. She couldn't be found here.

The door closed behind them and they sped down a narrow dark corridor. Phil couldn't see where they were going. She stumbled; he dragged her up and didn't let go of her until they'd reached the end. He unlocked a door, opened it a crack, and peered out.

"Turn right and go to the street. Be careful not to be seen." He shoved her out the door.

She whirled around just as the door shut in her face. She rattled the handle but it was locked. Pounded on the door to no avail.

"What's going on? Let me in!"

But there was no answer.

Phil turned around, senses alert. She was in an alley surrounded by trash cans and cast-off furniture. She covered her nose, lifted her skirt, and ran toward the street. She just managed to throw herself against the brick building at the sound of police sticks clacking against the wall, summoning help. Two constables ran across the end of the alley toward Fourteenth Street.

When their sticks could no longer be heard over the pounding of her heart, Phil peeked around the edge of the building. Finding the street empty, she stepped out onto the sidewalk.

Why had the manager been so anxious for her to be out of the theater? Why pick her out of the rest of the audience? Did he know who she was? She hadn't even gotten a good look at his face. Had that been on purpose? He'd stayed mostly behind her, guiding her by the arm. She couldn't have turned to look at him if she'd tried. Which she hadn't.

When she reached Fourteenth Street, instinct told her to walk in the opposite direction toward Union Square, to take a taxi home and wait to be contacted.

But curiosity propelled her back toward the front of the theater.

She kept close to the storefronts, pretending to look at the notices at the booking agencies, the menu of the oyster bar, as she slowly made her way down the sidewalk.

A black motorcar screeched to a stop in front of the theater, and two men got out. Phil ducked her head to peruse the boxes of Tiparillos and Cubans in the cigar-shop window. One of the men she recognized immediately. Sergeant Charles Becker, the scourge of the Tenderloin, known as the most corrupt policeman on the force. She had no reason to doubt that it was true.

He'd tried to railroad Phil's friend Bev into admitting she'd killed her husband, which she hadn't. He was tall, broad, and muscular, with a mean expression even when smiling. He preferred the round crown of a bowler hat, which had inspired Bev to dub him the Fireplug.

A shiver ran up Phil's spine.

What on earth was he doing here, outside his district? And how had he arrived so quickly? The Tenderloin was on the far side of town.

The mere fact that Becker had been summoned could only mean someone was trying to cover up something. And his quick arrival must mean Phil wasn't the first to discover the body.

And with Becker on the case, did that mean Detective Sergeant John Atkins would soon be following?

If she'd only been on time—which she would have been if she'd known about it earlier—she might have been able to prevent the murder.

Becker and his companion went inside, and Phil decided it would make better sense to leave them to it. She had no intention of crossing paths or swords with Becker if she could help it. Once had been enough.

Her knees were suddenly weak. Denial and fear had kept

her going. But now, the relief she felt when she realized that whoever the victim was, it wasn't Mr. X, threatened to overcome her. That and the stab of guilt for her own relief, when some poor family would not be seeing their husband, son, or father ever again.

Phil's steps faltered as much from the thought as from the pile of horse manure she had to sidestep in the street. Last year she would never have even considered the possibility that someone might murder a person in a theater. But since coming to America, her eyes had been opened. The Americans were such an ingenuous—somewhat ruthless—lot.

She reached the far side of the street just as a black morgue van drove past and stopped behind the police car. Two men jumped out, opened the back, and pulled out a stretcher before rushing into the theater.

Phil watched in dismay. Neither Becker nor the morgue van could possibly have arrived so quickly.

Not unless they had already been waiting nearby.

2

Phil loitered at the curb as long as she could.

Curiosity was urging her to return to see what was going on. Her English upbringing, which reared its head at the most inconvenient times, and her sense of survival were telling her to walk away as quickly as decorum allowed.

For once Phil gave in to good sense. There was nothing she could do here. What if she had been found sitting next to the dead man? Not even Mr. X and his secretive organization could save her from Becker.

Had he been expecting trouble? If so, why hadn't he warned her? Why not tell her what she was supposed to do? And what was she supposed to do now? She didn't even know who the victim was.

And if Mr. X was there, why did he let the man die? The uncomfortable thought that perhaps he had been the one wielding the knife occurred to her, but she refused to believe it.

Really, it was enough to make any countess tear her hair.

She stopped at a hot corn vendor's cart, turned to look back toward the theater. The morgue van and the black automobile were both gone. Odd; they couldn't have possibly examined the body and questioned witnesses this quickly. Not even five minutes had passed.

A slit throat was nothing to blink at. It was murder, pure and simple. To be whisked away like that meant either they were more interested in quelling a panic among the other theatergoers or . . .

They already knew he was dead and didn't want the body found there.

The corn seller was watching her expectantly. She smiled and moved on, followed by a few colorful epithets from the disappointed man.

The park was crowded, and if she hadn't just stumbled on a murder, Phil would have enjoyed the festive air. To walk alone through a park was delightful enough, but with the holiday bustle, the children, the ladies burdened down with packages, and the newsboys, all shivering as they hawked their dailies to the passersby, it should have been a wonderful time.

There were handmade crafts laid out along the sidewalk as hopeful mongers plied their wares. Acorn dolls, papier-mâché puppets, bottles of homemade elixirs, and secondhand items that might bring in a few extra coins for the holidays. An artist making charcoal portraits; a one-legged man selling baked potatoes. A slightly out-of-tune brass trio blared "Good King Wenceslas."

Phil passed all these without slowing down as she made her way to the taxi stand at the north side of the park. Perhaps there would be another message waiting for her at home.

Preswick opened the door and bowed the way he'd bowed hundreds, maybe thousands, of times before—his bald head shiny as a new penny, his livery pressed and neat as a pin.

She'd never been so glad to see her stuffy old friend.

"Good afternoon, my lady."

"Martini," Phil croaked, and walked straight past him to the parlor, unpinning her hat for the second time that day.

Lily was there to catch it when Phil tossed it toward a chair, then relieved Phil of her handbag and gloves and reached to unbutton her coat.

Lily's hands stopped several inches from the ivory buttons. "What happened here?"

Phil looked down and saw several smears across the bone-colored wool of her left arm. It took a few seconds of bewilderment before she understood. "I'm afraid it's blood."

Preswick looked up from the drinks table, where a silver bucket had been stocked with ice.

"Ar-r-re you hur-r-rt?" Lily asked, rolling the r's, which she tended to do when upset or angry.

"No," Phil said, feeling an urgent need to be rid of the spoiled coat. She turned around, and Lily slid it off her shoulders.

"Not me—someone else." Phil sighed. She was about to involve them in another murder, her faithful butler, who should be living in happy retirement, and her new lady's maid, whose real identity was a mystery. Both of them were completely loyal and stalwart, and Phil marveled at how she'd been so lucky in her choice—more or less—in servants.

"Just leave that now. Come in and sit. You, too, Preswick," she said as he handed her a frosty glass of the current rage in Manhattan, a dry martini.

Lily perched on a side chair facing the settee, and Preswick pulled up a straight-backed chair—he refused to appear comfortable even in America—and sat.

Phil took a sip of the refreshing cocktail. Would have lingered over it without another thought if she didn't have news to impart.

"I arrived home earlier to find a note from whom I believed was our elusive friend. It merely said 'Theatre Unique, one fifteen,' which as it turns out is a Union Square nickelodeon.

"It was already past noon, so I was consequently late in meeting the person."

She had their full attention, but she was loathe to bring the horrific scene into her apartment, which in her absence had begun to take on a colorful holiday flair. Two red poinsettia plants had been added to the mantel, and the smell of clove and oranges filled the air.

"My lady?" Preswick encouraged.

Phil brought her attention back to the situation at hand.

"I was to meet him in the back row, which I did, only to find him slumped over and his throat slit."

Phil heard Lily's intake of breath.

"That must have been when I got the bloodstains. He was sitting to my left."

"And did you recognize the gentleman?" Preswick asked in his most even tone.

But Lily hadn't as yet learned such rigid control.

"Assassin!" She vehemently shook her head. "But not Mister-r-r-r X. He would not be so stupid."

"No," Phil said. "At least I don't think so. I didn't have time to fully investigate. I was whisked out the back door by a man who said he was the theater manager, which is remarkable in itself."

"They wer-r-re expecting you," Lily said, and got a sharp look from Preswick for her trouble.

"It seems so, but even more remarkable was that when I returned to the street, I saw Sergeant Becker get out of a black automobile and go inside."

"The Fir-r-replug!" exclaimed Lily.

"Lily," Preswick admonished.

"Sorry, Mr. Preswick."

"If you will proceed, my lady."

Phil nodded. "That was all. I decided it would be better not to be seen by *Le Grand* Fireplug." She attempted a teasing look toward her upright butler, which he rightfully ignored.

"And besides, by the time I made my way back to the park, the police had gone. Gone!" she exclaimed, and took a healthy gulp of her drink before handing it back to Preswick for a refill.

"Where did they go, madam?" Lily asked as soon as Preswick left his chair.

"That's just it. I have no idea. And to tell the truth I'm not even now certain it was not Mr. X."

"Bah."

"You're right, it's just that my mind can't quite grasp the whole situation." She had been unnerved in that one moment of discovery, not knowing for certain who it was. And rather frightened at the extent of emotion evoked when she'd thought that Mr. X might be dead.

Preswick returned with another drink. Phil already was feeling the first one, since she'd been so busy shopping and discovering murder victims that she hadn't had time to eat since breakfast.

"What would you like us to do, my lady?"

The telephone rang.

Preswick stood. "That will be Mrs. Reynolds. She has called several times to remind you of the meeting this afternoon."

"Heavens, the Christmas charity ball. I'd forgotten the committee meeting was this afternoon. I promised Bev I'd put in an appearance. It's the next-to-last meeting and I haven't been to one. I can't let her down."

"Yes, my lady. What shall I tell her?"

"Tell her that I was detained and . . . and I'll be there as quickly as I can."

"Yes, my lady." He strode away to answer the call.

"Lily, something befitting charitable works with rich patronesses." Phil started to stand. "Oh, my purse!"

"It's right here, my lady."

"I forgot about it." Phil reached for the handbag, though she dreaded touching the dead man's possessions again.

She took it over to the little table by the alcove window, just as Preswick rejoined them. He turned on the study lamp, and he and Lily gathered close as Phil unclasped the bag and dumped the contents onto the table. Compact, coin purse, penknife, hankie. She pushed these to one side, leaving the pencil stub, notebook, cigarette pack, and box of matches.

"I took these from his jacket pocket. It was all I found before some young woman screamed and I was abruptly escorted out of the theater."

Phil picked up the notebook, looked through several pages of indecipherable scratchings, then blank pages. She dropped it back to the table; touched the pencil, the cigarettes; picked up the matchbox. It was quite pretty, black shiny cardboard, with a red rose printed on the top.

"I probably shouldn't have done it, but I was afraid he would have information that might fall into the wrong hands. I managed to feel in his inside pockets, but I didn't have a chance to search further."

"This is pretty," Lily said, fingering the matchbox. She turned it for Phil to see.

"A better quality than most matchbox advertisers use, wouldn't you say?" Phil asked.

"Yes, my lady." Preswick took the box and examined it more closely. "High quality; fine restaurants and private clubs often have these made for their patrons."

"The victim was hardly dressed like he could afford an expensive restaurant, much less a private club."

"It's quite possible that he inadvertently took it from someone else. Asked for a light to his cigarette and put the matchbox in his pocket without thinking."

"And so a dead end. Unless you can find something in those few pages."

"Yes, my lady," Preswick said. "We'll endeavor to do our best to decipher them while you are at your committee meeting."

"Ugh, remind me why I agreed to be honorary hostess for this event."

"You said it was your philanthropic duty, my lady."

Phil sighed. "A moment of febrile hubris." She didn't have a penny to fly with other than the allowance left to her by her grandmother and the apartment in the Plaza in return for her services, not by a generous lover but by an entity or organization—as yet to her unknown—for her detectival skills. A talent that had been as much a surprise to her as useful to them.

There had also been a substantial but inexplicable amount

of cash deposited in her bank account several weeks ago, which she assumed was a bonus for a job well done.

Fairly well done. She hadn't been able to prevent a second murder in her last case. The frustration and, yes, the guilt of that failure still nagged at her.

"I must hurry. I just hope the ladies left me some food."

Lily took Phil's coat from the chair where it still lay, and Phil started down the hall pulling out hairpins. She was halfway to her room before she realized Lily hadn't followed her.

"What is it?" she asked, returning to where Lily was holding her coat under the lamp, scrutinizing the wool. "No time for that now, Lily."

"Yes, my lady." Though she didn't release her hold on the coat or move away from the lamp.

Phil blinked. When they'd first become mistress and servant that spring day on the Southampton pier, Lily refused to call her "my lady." So they had decided that in private Lily could suffice with "madam." "My lady" seemed like a silly affectation now that they were in America, and Lily usually reserved it for when they were in company or she was annoyed, angry, or downright cheeky. Or under Preswick's watchful eye.

"You can do that later, Lily," Phil said. "Though I doubt if the stains will come out. Lily?"

Lily slowly looked up from Phil's coat. "My lady?"

The girl must be rattled; two "my ladys" without being nudged by Preswick.

"Yes, what is it?"

"You said the man was sitting on your left."

"Yes."

"These smears are on the left side, as they should be. But . . ." She held up the coat. "But this stain is on your right sleeve. See here, on the upper part."

Phil looked more closely.

Preswick stood closer to peer at it. "It isn't a smear. It—it's the shape of a thumbprint." He turned the sleeve to catch the light. "And fingers."

It was. Good heavens. *It most certainly was.*

Then Phil remembered. "It must be from where the theater manager hurried me down the aisle to the rear exit." She touched her arm, remembering. "He held me by the arm, and practically dragged me away from the entrance. That's where his thumb would have rested. But why would the manager have blood on his hands?"

The three looked at each other, loathe to say what they were all thinking.

"Perhaps he had foreknowledge of the man's demise," Preswick said.

"He had already discovered the body and left it there," Phil said. "After possibly searching it."

"That would explain why the police arrived so quickly," Preswick said.

"But not why they summoned the sergeant from all the way across town instead of the local precinct."

"If he'd discovered the body and got bloodied, he could have passed it onto your coat," Lily suggested.

"Or," Phil said, her mouth suddenly dry in spite of the martinis, "I was escorted down the aisle by the killer himself."

3

Her announcement was met by shocked silence.

"Oh, madam, he might have killed you, too."

"But he didn't," Phil said. "I wonder why?"

"Shall I telephone to Mrs. Reynolds and tell her you are indisposed, my lady?"

"I'm not indisposed, Preswick. I am angry. This could have been avoided if we'd had proper means of communications.

"And now I must go off to do good in the world, by playing hostess to an event that probably costs as much to hold as they give to the poor. You and Lily, I'm afraid, will have to remain here and wait for any notes that might be slipped under the door, or odd characters looking up at our window. Because until we find out who the victim was and why he wanted to meet, our hands are tied."

"Perhaps we'll discover something in the notebook while you're gone, my lady."

"Please do, Preswick. Lily, my new mulberry visiting dress."

Lily hurried away.

"And Preswick, please have all the evening editions of the newspapers sent round. I doubt if there will be anything yet, but there are always reporters hanging about looking for a story; it's possible one of them heard something."

"Yes, my lady."

"I wish it didn't always take hours, sometimes days, to print the news. It's infuriating." She swept down the hall to change.

Twenty minutes later, wearing a stylish new visiting dress—part of the ensemble she'd ordered from Paris with her unexpected windfall—and carrying a new handbag, her hair miraculously revived, Phil stepped into her fifth taxi of the day.

Really, having an auto at one's disposal would be much more efficient. But where would she leave it if she had to chase criminals on foot? And what were the possibilities that Preswick would be willing to learn to drive?

The taxi stopped in front of a brownstone on West Sixty-Eighth Street, where Bev had temporarily "set up housekeeping"—an odd name for it since neither Bev nor Phil nor most of the women of their acquaintance actually knew a thing about keeping house.

The brownstone belonged to Bev's father, the respected New York publisher Daniel Sloane. But he was still in Europe after having whisked Bev out of the country to avoid scandal and for her own safety after a particularly wide-reaching murder investigation.

It was already growing dark when Phil stepped onto the sidewalk and paused to search for anyone, someone in particular, who might be waiting to make contact. But though there were a number of people hurrying on their way, she didn't see anyone who might be waiting particularly for her.

With a resigned sigh, she climbed the steps to the committee meeting.

"Good afternoon, Lady Dunbridge," Bev's butler, Tuttle, said as she stepped into the foyer, all dark wood paneling and classical paintings.

Before she'd even unbuttoned her coat, a brown tweed with mink collar and blessedly free from any stain, Bev, dressed unusually sedately in a dark gray afternoon dress, came bustling out of the parlor.

"Where have you been all afternoon?" she demanded.

"Shopping," Phil said, handing her gloves to Tuttle.

"I thought you'd never get here. All the committee heads

are here. They've been droning on for at least an hour about seating arrangements and orchestra placements and ticket sales. I may go mad before I've 'salvaged' my reputation by good works. Oh, how I miss the old gang."

By which she meant the highfliers and fringe fast set that Bev had embraced as wife of Reggie Reynolds, gambler, horse breeder, dubious businessman.

"I've served tea, but I have a new cocktail I'm dying to try as soon as the stodgy ones leave. In the spirit of Christmas, of course."

Petite and vivacious and about as subtle as a steamroller, Bev scuttled Phil into the drawing room.

"She's here, *enfin!*" Bev announced.

Phil was met by a circle of a half-dozen women of varying ages and build, whom Phil had met once when she'd accepted the position of honorary hostess, and had systematically forgotten. Mainly they wanted her title on the invitations, and her money, such as it was—though they didn't need to know about that—in their bank account.

"Lady Dunbridge."

"Elizabeth Abernathy," Bev whispered, as Phil crossed the space to shake hands with the heavyset charity-ball chairwoman.

"Mrs. Abernathy, I must give you my profuse apologies. I was unavoidably detained."

"Think nothing of it, Lady Dunbridge. We are so honored to have your participation."

Phil took and released Mrs. Abernathy's hand and said to the room in general, "I must apologize to you all for being late. I was truly unavoidably detained."

The deputy mayor's wife, a buxom petite woman with bouffant hair and a hat that reminded Phil of a treat at the ice-cream parlor, who also happened to be in charge of refreshments, clapped her hand to her chest. "We are all feeling it. Sometimes I think I must meet myself coming and going."

Phil nodded sympathetically. The deputy mayor's wife might get more done if she carried less plumage on her head. Word from Paris was that hats would be smaller next season. Phil enjoyed feathers as much as the next woman, and those large brims were convenient for disguising one's identity. But they could be debilitating if you were in a hurry.

She almost missed the next introduction.

"You remember Mrs. Trout, our subscriptions manageress." Bev beamed. "And what wonderful news she's brought us today. We've raised almost fifteen thousand dollars."

Bev was laying it on a bit thick, probably more from boredom than true philanthropic excitement.

"And Imogen has raised it almost single-handedly," added Mrs. Abernathy.

They all looked to Imogen Trout, young, tall, and remote, red hair waved back from symmetrical features beneath a stylish toque hat. Phil had seen her before but never been introduced to her. Exotic and beautiful, Mrs. Trout was impossible to ignore.

"Kudos to you, Mrs. Trout."

"It wuz nothin' really," Imogen said in the most excruciatingly thick drawl that Phil had ever heard. She had to concentrate not to grit her teeth. No wonder Imogen spent most of her time posing and looking otherworldly.

Bev whispered, "Texas Panhandle," and introduced several others, whose names Phil filed away for future use.

"And these two ladies are my old school chums from Vassar."

"Martha Rive," said a tall, spare young woman, not waiting for an introduction. "Publicity."

Bev had mentioned Martha before, and she lived up to Bev's description of her. With ash-blond hair pulled back into a low bun and a narrow-brimmed, low-crowned black felt hat perched squarely on her head, she looked fiercely intelligent and all business—the epitome of the modern independent woman.

She was expensively dressed—evidently her Knickerbocker family hadn't cut her off completely—which was surprising, since she'd flouted her family's sense of decorum and expectations and landed a job as society reporter with *The New York Times*.

"And Rosalind Chandler, another Vassar attendee. Roz's husband is building commissioner at City Hall. She got us a good deal on the Plaza ballroom and expedited the wherefores and the whatnots."

Rosalind nodded slightly, her dark brown hair making a halo between her pale complexion and her wide-brimmed hat. "It was quite easy, much less than these ladies have done."

"Maybe so," Bev said. "But we do appreciate it. Now, Phil, sit down and we'll bring you up to date. Tuttle, pour Lady Dunbridge a cup of tea."

It was an hour and several cups of tea later, after Tuttle had drawn the drapes and Phil was floating in oolong, that most of the ladies began making preparations for their departure.

"Roz, you're looking absolutely peaked," Mrs. Abernathy said. "Shall I drop you on my way?"

Roz, who had seemed to be wilting, sat up straighter. "Thank you, Elizabeth, but Jarvis is picking me up here. Dinner with his mother." She smiled, an expression that said she wasn't looking forward to the visit.

"Send Mrs. Chandler my best. And remember, ladies, we only have one more meeting to attend to any last details. The ball is only a week away, so please try to make the last meeting. Goodbye, Roz. Miss Rive. I assume you're staying also?"

Martha Rive gave her a tight smile.

"And thank you, Beverly, for lending your home for the meetings even though you're still in mourning and—"

"I'm thinking of making an exception and attending the ball," Bev said. "In the name of charity."

Mrs. Abernathy pursed her lips. "Of course, Beverly, if you think it's appropriate."

At which point Tuttle saw the ladies out and, like the consummate butler he was, returned with a bucket of ice.

"'If you think it's appropriate,'" Bev mimicked, as she crossed to the drinks table to mix her Christmas cocktails. "She thinks nothing of using me and then treats me like—"

"Like you're in mourning," Phil said. "By all means, go, show your support for the cause, just don't wear sequins."

"And don't waltz," Martha added.

Bev grinned fiendishly. "You, neither."

"Why not you, Miss Rive, if I may ask? Are you in mourning?"

"Gads, no. I'll be there covering the event for the paper; my family will be invited guests. We'll avoid each other like the plague. Poor Mrs. A. is caught in the middle, but she dare not slight me. All that free publicity from the *Times*."

"Is the paper involved in the fundraiser?"

"Oh yes, we at the *Times* take our philanthropic endeavors seriously. Still, Elizabeth Abernathy never loses a chance to try to make me feel ridiculous. A hopeless venture, but she deep down believes that it all has to do with me not landing a husband. Oh gads, the mind boggles."

"She's not so bad," Roz said. "Just old-fashioned."

"Unlike you, you dear sweet thing," Martha said, and leaned over to kiss her cheek.

"Coming from you, I suppose that means 'hopelessly dull.'"

"Not at all, just hopelessly naïve. And in spite of everything Bev and I did to corrupt you." Martha took a glass of red liquid that Tuttle was holding, looked at it dubiously before taking a sip.

Roz held up her hand. "None for me, Tuttle." She looked toward the door. "I can't imagine where Jarvis is."

"Or doesn't want to," Martha said into her drink glass. Fortunately, Phil was the only one who heard her.

"Oh, Roz," Bev said. "You have to try my new Christmas

cocktail. We deserve it after the last few hours. I thought they'd never leave."

"I really can't. I have an awful headache, and Jarvis will be here any minute."

"Jarvis won't mind waiting. Take off your hat and have a sip of this, and I guarantee you'll feel better."

Martha barked a low throaty laugh. "Until the morning anyway."

Rosalind breathed out a laugh, or was it a sigh? For a moment Phil thought she might burst into tears, but it passed. "I can't."

Bev lowered her chin and looked sternly at Roz. "There's nothing you need to tell us?"

"Like what?" asked Roz.

"You're not drinking. You're not feeling sickly, are you? Incubating a little Chandler perhaps?"

Phil thought it was incredibly ham-fisted of Bev to mention it, but Roz laughed.

"Alas, no. I can't drink because Mrs. Chandler thinks I debauch too much."

Martha groaned. "Oh spare us those middle-class morals."

"The Chandlers are not middle class."

"Just tightfisted."

"Never mind, Roz," Bev said brightly, just as Tuttle announced Roz's husband, Jarvis Chandler.

It took Phil an effort to recover her shock at seeing Roz's husband in the flesh. She'd imagined a young man, at least relatively good-looking, enamored with his wife and facing a promising future among the movers in Tammany Hall. As it turned out, Jarvis Chandler was twice Roz's age. A pleasant enough face in a fairly trim body except for an incipient paunch . . . Obviously balding and attempting to divert attention with a wide, limp mustache that made Phil want to reach for a razor.

Roz fairly leaped from her chair. "I was beginning to think you forgot me."

"Silly girl, how could I forget you?"

"Oh, that he would," Martha said under her breath, which earned her a sharp look from Bev.

Martha brandished her glass—there was no other word for it. "How delightful to see you. And—"

A panicked look from Roz brought Martha up sharp.

"—on such a lovely day," she finished.

He was introduced to Phil. He gave her a quick appraising look, then nodded over her hand. "Now we must hurry, my dear, the traffic is abominable."

Roz smiled back at him, a little desperately, Phil thought, and swore never to live under the slavish thrall of any man. Not that she ever would. The earl had cured her of that.

Roz's evident worship of her husband was more cloying than Bev's Christmas cocktail.

"Ladies." Jarvis Chandler trundled his wife away.

As soon as they heard the front door close behind them, Martha slipped off her shoes and stretched her legs out along Bev's sofa. "If that's love, I swear I'm going to become a wizened old spinster."

"He is a crashing boor," Bev agreed.

"And after Roz's inheritance. I wish the old reprobate would go to hell."

"Or to jail," Bev added.

"Well, that's never going to happen," Martha said.

"Divorce?" Bev suggested.

Martha shook her head. "But seriously, Bev. I'm worried about her."

"She does seem a little, I don't know . . . why are you worried?"

Martha cast a sideways look at Phil.

"Phil is the soul of discretion."

Martha gave Phil a skeptical look. "She's withering away.

He's making her miserable, and her health is suffering. I could have kicked you when you said that bit about a little Chandler."

"I'm sorry. I don't see her as much as you do," Bev said. "Is she hoping for a baby?"

"To keep her company, maybe. But not from him."

"Someone else?" Bev asked. "She seems to adore him."

"You adored Reggie, didn't you?"

"When I wasn't ready to brain him. But that was different. Roz is—"

"Putting on an act. You should have recognized that. That's what she always did when she was in trouble, acted flitty."

"You don't think she'll do anything rash, do you?" Bev glanced at Phil. "Maybe she will divorce him."

"Not likely," Martha said. "She's afraid to breathe wrong, now that Jarvis is being groomed for mayor."

"You're kidding."

"Afraid not. McClellan has turned out to be more civic-minded than Tammany intended. Rumor has it, they'll supplant him in the next election."

"Poor Roz," Bev said. "The three of us were best friends in school, then out of the blue, her parents took her out of school to marry Jarvis."

"Her adoptive parents," Martha reminded her. "And the powers that be are not happy that she's an orphan, but they're turning a blind eye since she's loaded."

"She's adopted?" Phil asked out of pure surprise.

"She was born somewhere out west. Her parents died in an influenza epidemic when she was a baby. The Hastingses, a well-to-do Manhattan family, were the closest relatives, distant cousins and childless, so they brought her to live with them. They doted on her, but they were older, concerned for her future, so when Jarvis offered, they jumped at the chance.

"They were killed three years ago. Boating accident. Roz has been going through the motions of living since then." Martha looked into her glass, drained it, and put it down.

"If she'd just divorce him, then maybe we could teach her how to enjoy life again," Bev said.

"Not a chance. When they handed over Roz, they handed over her inheritance." Martha sat up and reached for a beaded silver bag that Phil had been admiring. "I'm dying for a fag. You don't mind if I smoke, do you, Lady Dunbridge?"

"Of course she doesn't," Bev said.

"Oh good, I didn't know if you were a stickler—peerage and all that," she said in an exaggerated Cockney accent.

Bev guffawed. "Not Phil. Nothing fazes her."

Not true, thought Phil. She was pretty fazed, right now. A dead man in the theater had fazed her to her marrow, but she didn't need to share that with her new acquaintance.

"Now drink up. I have a whole pitcher of my Christmas cocktail."

Phil shuddered. It wasn't like Bev to be so off in her mixology. Maybe she'd like a nice drinks recipe book for Christmas.

"I'm game," Martha said on a long exhale of smoke. "Nasty habit, and very unladylike, I know," she said to Phil. "It comes from hanging around a newspaper office all day. Sometimes the air is so thick you don't even have to light up to enjoy the smoke.

"Bev did warn you, didn't she? I'm only on the committee doing penance for thwarting my family's best intentions and following my destiny into the newsroom of *The New York Times.* Oh, the scandal."

Bev *had* told her about Martha Rive, blue blood, highstrung, and twice as stubborn as all the Rives put together.

"Yes, actually she said you were a reporter."

Martha snorted. "If you call reporting attending all the fashionable weddings, soirées, and debutante balls, and writing endlessly about gauze, china silks, and the well-stocked trousseau."

"Nothing earth-shattering, I take it."

"Not as yet. Though a couple of weeks ago, I did cover a

rather interesting Chanukah celebration at the Academy of Music. Unusual, a play about the Maccabees and the lighting of candles, but Sydney pulled the article to make room for something 'less arcane.' His words."

Martha sighed, gave them a wry smile. "At least I have my own desk now. And at least, the men *do* think twice about asking me to 'type this up, doll, it's due in an hour.' You'd think with all the new typewriting machines Charlie Miller—he's editor in chief—convinced the *Times* to buy—one for each reporter no less—that a few of the half-wits would bother to learn to use more than two fingers.

"But no, better to wait for one of the few overworked, underpaid typewriter girls or an unsuspecting society columnist and have them do the grunt work. Sometimes I could commit mayhem.

"Though I shouldn't complain. I get to have a prime seat at the New Year's Eve ball drop. Because our readers will all want to know what society was wearing in the sixty seconds that it took the monstrosity to slide down the flagpole."

"The whole town is talking about it," Bev said. "It'll be exciting."

"We're hoping it will become a tradition, since the city nixed fireworks after last year's display got rather out of hand." Martha finished her cigarette and stubbed it out in her saucer.

She was obviously well-bred, and Phil thought her attitude was as much to see if she could shock Phil as it was real.

"Now I must be off, too. The Clinton-Swift soirée."

"I'm not even invited," Bev groused. "Belle Swift assured me it was only because of my status of mourning. Otherwise I would be there."

"I'm just covering it for tomorrow's edition. I shall remain inconspicuously in the background furiously scribbling who was there and what people wore, while they didn't listen to whatever soprano, pianist, reciter of poetry, or whatnot carried valiantly on.

"Then I'll rush back to the office, where I'll type it all up and shoot it down to Compositing. And if I'm really lucky, I'll be there when Tommy Green arrives with his breaking news. I hope it's good. And I hope he's okay. He's already late and it's not like Tommy to be late." She huffed out a sigh and polished off her drink.

"Well, you're the one who wanted to be a reporter," Bev said.

"Journalist," Martha corrected her. "And so I shall be, but until then I stand with one foot in each world. Rather like a governess—not one of the family, and yet not quite a servant."

Phil nodded, but she was only half listening. She must be off her game, because she was about to miss a golden opportunity. She'd just complained about the news being so slow, and here was someone, a friend of Bev's, who actually worked for the *Times*. The place where news went before it was made public.

"I think what you do is fascinating," Phil said abruptly.

"You do?"

"Yes, right in the midst of things when the latest news comes in."

Martha eyed her speculatively. And Phil realized that they had been taking each other's measure since Phil had arrived. She was okay with that. Martha thought Phil might drop some morsels of gossip her way, and in return . . . well, it wouldn't hurt Phil to have a friend in the newspaper business.

And the sooner the better.

4

"I'll have Tuttle ring for a taxi, Marty," Bev said.

"On a reporter's salary? I'll walk up to the Seventy-Second Street station and take the subway. It'll be faster anyway."

Phil, inspiration striking, followed them to the door.

"I was thinking, Miss Rive . . ." Phil began.

"Lord, call me Marty. Everyone does."

"Marty. Bev and I are planning to meet for lunch tomorrow."

Phil saw Bev blink before she said, "That's right, we are."

"Would you care to join us? We could meet you at your offices and you could show us around a bit. It sounds so exciting."

Bev bit her lip. Phil silently ordered her not to laugh.

"If I don't have to dress. I'll be in uniform, white-collared shirt and tweed skirt. No hat."

"Excellent. Shall we say one o'clock?"

"Sure. Until tomorrow, then."

Phil and Bev stood on the landing watching her walk briskly toward Broadway and the subway station.

"Brr, better her than me," Bev said. "Come back inside. Tuttle, are there some of those sandwiches left? I swear I could eat a horse, well, not a horse, I love them too much. But something. I was so busy trying to play the distinguished hostess that I couldn't swallow a thing.

"And I'll make us something to drink that's a little less . . ."

"Awful," Phil supplied.

"I was going to say festive, but it was awful, wasn't it? Thank heavens I didn't offer it to Mrs. Abernathy."

"So tell me more about your friends Roz and Marty," Phil said, once Bev had fitted them out with champagne and Tuttle had returned with sandwiches.

"Well, we met at Vassar. Marty was the bane of her family, a firebrand suffragette, justice and equality and all that stuff. They sent her to college only because she threatened to run away to California if they didn't. But, alas, breeding will out, and the more middle-class girls never warmed to her."

Bev took another sip of her champagne and rested her head against the cushion of the high-backed settee. "Roz was young and impressionable. She was certainly innocent at the beginning; still acts like it, now that I think about. It's like she's regressed into the past."

"You haven't kept in touch?"

"Not really. Her parents took her out after the second year, and after that our paths never really crossed. She married Jarvis Chandler and took up with Imogen Trout, a piece of cheap cloth, if you ask me. I see her name in the papers occasionally. Not that I really care, but it bothers Marty. They were closer at school. I rarely saw either of them until Roz called and asked me to fill in as hospitality chairwoman for someone who had to drop out."

"Which, now that I think of it, was merely a ploy to get you to be hostess. Real countesses aren't exactly thick on the trees . . . or whatever that saying is."

"You mean you weren't even one of the sponsors of this charity ball until recently?"

"Gad, no. I just write a check every year and call my duty done. But I was trying to speed along my return to society. She suggested that it would be good to have an important person to act as hostess and asked me if I knew anyone, and I guess I sort of suggested you."

Phil rolled her eyes toward the ceiling.

"Now, Marty, on the other hand . . . Lord, what a kickup when she told her family that she was going to pursue journalism. A Rive doesn't *pursue* anything; it comes to them. There was a fight to the finish between Marty and her father, who had encouraged her to go to college in the first place. She stormed out, moved out, and scrimps by on a reporter's salary, hence the subway."

"He disowned her?" Phil could certainly relate.

"Oh, he would forgive her, but she won't capitulate, though at this point her mother is so upset that she could keep her job *and* get a generous allowance if she would just apologize. Stupid, I know. Keep the job and take the money. What's she holding out for?"

"Pride?" Phil suggested.

"So why this sudden interest in journalism?" Bev's eyes narrowed, then brightened. "Are you working on a new case?"

"Heavens, Bev. I'm merely curious."

"Ha. You *do* have a new case. Tell me all about it."

"There's nothing to tell. Well, perhaps a little something, but I'm not certain yet." Phil held up a preemptory hand. "If it is something, you'll be the first to know." Of course she would never be able to tell Bev everything. Bev took too much delight in the world to hold her tongue.

"That's why you want to have lunch with Marty. To have a snitch in the newspaper office."

"I would never," said Phil. *Not exactly.* "I just thought it would be useful to know an insider who could check facts on any rumors that come our way."

"You're so clever. Marty will love it. She's dying to do something important."

"You're not to tell her. Though I have no doubt she was willing to meet us because she has similar plans for me if we continue our acquaintance."

Bev sucked in her breath. "Use your confidence? Phil, she wouldn't. Marty is totally trustworthy."

"Perhaps. But she is a journalist and she needs to further her career. It must be hard to live on her salary. Speaking of which, does she wear tweeds when covering society events? Her skirt today wasn't *port à prêtez*."

"Actually it was a Madame Laferrière." Bev bit her lip. "Her mother does slip her the odd bit in order to maintain her wardrobe. She can't have her daughter running around in rags. But mum's the word."

Easier said than done in Bev's case.

"Marty works hard, but at least she still knows how to have fun. But poor Roz married a man twenty-five years older and very particular about his reputation." Bev's eyes twinkled mischievously. "You should give her advice on how to work around that little impediment."

"I think I'll leave Rosalind Chandler to her own marriage. Now, I'd better have Tuttle telephone for a taxi for me. It's been a long day."

"You can't leave so early."

"Bev, I've had an exhausting day. I'm going to take a long soak in the tub and go to bed."

"You, exhausted? Why I remember—" Her expression changed. "You're expecting a visitor. Do I know him? I want every juicy detail tomorrow."

"As wrong as your red Christmas cocktail," Phil said with more bite than she'd intended as the day came rushing back: the discovery of the dead man, the sense of panic when she thought it was Mr. X, the despair of not knowing if she would see that particular visitor again.

"I hate to disappoint you, Bev, but there is no visitor in my evening plans. I've decided to make our first Christmas in New York the best it can be. I have a lot to do, shopping, planning, cards to write . . . Don't you?"

"Oh Lord, yes. I have to get gifts off to Connecticut." She shuddered dramatically. "Since I refused to spend Christmas with my relatives, the least I can do is overwhelm them with my generosity."

A hot soak in lavender beads should have revived Phil's mood, and it did until it didn't. She went over the afternoon's events, time after time. Remembering every detail of the dead man in the nickelodeon—an excellent title for a dime novel if ever there was one.

Only she'd been so surprised at the discovery that her escape had passed in a fog. The manager, who might not be the manager but possibly her elusive comrade in investigation, or even the killer, or . . . And there still remained a tiny, tenacious grain of doubt that the dead man had really been the ultimate disguise, and the most interesting man of her acquaintance had been hauled away in a coroner's van.

Why didn't he send her word? Chastise her for being late for her appointment, which she hadn't even known about—and may have consequently caused the man's demise?

And with that idea, tears threatened to overflow. She reined herself back in. Countesses didn't cry, not even when they were tired, hurt, or frightened. Not even in private. At least not anymore.

She just needed to pull herself together and figure out where to begin her investigations about why and who and what on earth for?

"Madam, you'll be puckered to a prune if you don't get out of the tub now."

Lily stood holding a warmed towel before her, and Phil reluctantly got out of the tub and let Lily wrap it around her.

"You can go now, Lily. I'll see myself to bed. Leave the window open a bit."

"It's freezing outside."

"I like the fresh air."

"Pfft, he won't be climbing up five stories of the Plaza for all the world to see. Not in this weather." Lily huffed out a sigh. "Why can't he use the door like a gentleman?"

Phil smiled, her first real smile since her visit to the Theatre Unique. "That would show a distinct lack of imagination." And if one thing was certain, he never lacked imagination in anything he did.

"What do we do now?"

Phil summoned up the remnants of her sangfroid. "I think the best thing we can do at the moment is to continue to check the papers on the outside chance"—a phrase she'd picked up at the Belmont track last summer—"that we receive another message."

"And if we receive no message?" Lily asked, her brow beginning to furrow.

"Then we'll improvise until we do." Phil had never in her brief career as a crime solver waited for instructions before proceeding. This time would be no different.

A stack of newspapers lay perfectly folded on the table when Phil went into breakfast the next morning. Even with Preswick's careful eye for detail, she could tell that at least some of them had already been opened and refolded for her perusal.

"So," she said. "No news of our deceased theatergoer?"

"No, my lady," Preswick said, pouring her a cup of hot coffee. "Most likely the evening posts."

"Hopefully we won't have to wait. Mrs. Reynolds and I are having lunch with a friend of hers who just happens to work for the *Times* as a society reporter."

"Indeed, my lady." Preswick's voice registered no surprise.

Lily's, however, did. "How will a lady who writes about weddings help us catch a killer? . . . My lady."

"Actually, I'm not sure she can," Phil said, suddenly feeling hungry. She reached for a piece of toast. "But it can't hurt to have a friend in the news business."

"Shall I accompany you?"

"Not today, Lily. I want you and Mr. Preswick to stand by in case something comes while I am out." Seeing Lily's crestfallen face, she added, "It's less than two weeks before Christmas and we've just begun to decorate. We shall have Christmas in every corner."

She didn't miss the hopeful look Lily shot the stolid butler. He was as enigmatic as the Sphinx, not that Phil had actually seen that wonder, but she had no doubt that she would return to an apartment filled with greenery.

Phil was waiting downstairs when Bev's Packard pulled up to the curb just after noon. And though it took nearly thirty minutes before the auto stopped in front of the *New York Times* building, it was well worth the wait.

Built at the intersection of Broadway and Forty-Second Street, which had been renamed Times Square in honor of the new building, its twenty-five stories of arched windows and Doric columns was impressive. Phil took a moment just to look up at its dizzying height before she and Bev joined the throngs of people entering the building.

They stopped at the information desk, where they were given directions to the nineteenth floor.

There were four elevators, and Phil had to admit she felt a wave of trepidation as they stepped inside. She was quite accustomed to taking the elevator to her fifth-floor apartment at the Plaza, had even braved going to the seventeenth floor of the hotel, once.

But twenty-five floors. It was rather daunting. Bev, however, was an old hand. She had grown up in publishing circles and had been to the *Times* building many times. Phil lifted her chin and prepared to stay calm, and before she knew it, they were stepping off onto the editorial rooms on the nineteenth floor.

Bev stopped at the reception desk to ask for Martha Rive.

"Marty had to run down to seventeen. You're the friends she's meeting for lunch? You're to meet her there." She grimaced. "Trouble in the newsroom, so brace yourselves. Bedlam. Carr's having a meltdown." She flashed a perfunctory smile and went back to her magazine, and Phil and Bev took the elevator two floors down to the newsroom.

Bedlam was an apt description. A sea of desks, some occupied by men in white shirts, sleeves rolled up, ties loosened, scribbling away or yelling into the telephone or across the room. Some unoccupied but for half-eaten lunches and coffee cups balanced precariously on piles of paper.

Cylinders ran up the side of the wall, transporting papers from floor to floor. A few women were clacking away at typewriting machines. A young man pushed a mail cart down one of the narrow aisles, dropping bundles off and occasionally pausing for a brief word.

The volume was almost painful.

Bev was not at all daunted. "She's probably in the managing editor's office," she shouted over the din. "Carr Van Anda, friend of Papa's, very smart. Knows the news before it's news. You'll like him."

Bev headed toward the back of the room, where several doors led to offices. Before they'd gone far, she pulled up short. "There's Marty." She changed course and veered to the right, skirting the mail boy, who practically threw himself across a nearby desk to get out of the way.

Phil hurried after her.

At the far side of the room, crammed in between a filing cabinet and a typewriting machine, Martha Rive was bent over a desk riffling through a handful of papers. She dropped those and scooped another handful, saw Bev and Phil, and waved the papers at them.

"Bit of a kerfuffle," Martha said as she continued to riffle through the sheets. "Tommy Green missed his deadline, lead story. Big exposé. Big problem. Can't find him anywhere. Carr is having a fit."

Marty slapped the papers on the overcrowded desk. "He held the presses for him last night, then had to go with a different lead. Not a happy man this morning."

The words had barely left her mouth when a door at the end of the room banged open, rattling the frosted glass, and a man stormed out. With a high forehead and rimless glasses, dressed in an immaculate black suit, he looked the epitome of a scholar.

He was followed by a younger man, tall, blond, dressed in a fashionable sack suit, his classic features marred by consternation.

They made a beeline for the three women.

"Oh, Lord," Martha said, and slapped a smile on her face.

"Carr Van Anda," Bev told Phil. "And Sydney Lord, associate news editor. Greek God unto himself. Marty's nemesis."

"Have you found anything?" Carr Van Anda demanded, coming to a stop and sliding slightly on a piece of paper that had found its way to the floor.

Marty shook her head. "We sent Eddie the mail boy down to his apartment earlier this morning, but Tommy didn't answer the door and none of the neighbors had seen him since yesterday morning. I looked in his desk: nothing intelligible there."

"Eddie, get over here!" Van Anda yelled. The mail boy left his trolley among the forest of desks and hurried over.

"No sign of him? You're sure?"

Eddie nodded. He was slim, wiry, and practically quaking in his shoes.

Mr. Van Anda waved him away, frowned. "This is not like Tommy. Not when he's working on a big story. Where's Harry?"

"I sent one of the typewriter girls to look in editorial and typing," Marty said.

"Eddie, leave the mail and go help look for Harry."

"Yes, sir." Eddie pirouetted midstep and hurried away in the opposite direction.

"Carr," Marty said. "If you'll calm down for a minute, look who's here."

Van Anda blinked as if it was the first time he'd noticed his surroundings, squinted, and poked his head forward. "Bevy Sloane? My goodness. Mrs. Reynolds. What brings you to the madhouse? How are you? Sorry about Reg. How's your father?" He swiveled his head toward Phil.

"My friend, the Countess of Dunbridge," Bev said. "Lady Dunbridge, may I present Carr Van Anda, managing editor of the *Times*."

Dowager countess, actually, but who was quibbling?

"Ah, Lady Dunbridge, I don't believe I've had the honor."

"A pleasure," Phil said, accepting his handshake.

Sydney cleared his throat.

"Oh, and Sydney Lord," Marty said, so begrudgingly that Phil wanted to laugh.

"My pleasure." He smiled and bowed over Phil's hand. A charmer for sure and very nice-looking.

Phil turned her attention back to Mr. Van Anda. "It's certainly exciting here."

"It's bedlam most days, but today is unusually so. Can I help you ladies in any way? Unless you want a sneak peek at our New Year's Eve electric ball. That I can't do. Hell, today I can't even find my ace reporter."

"We just came to claim Marty for lunch," Bev said. "But we seem to have caught her at a bad time."

"Well, I don't want to ruin your plans, but—"

"Not at all," Phil said. "We're happy to wait."

"Go ahead, Miss Rive. You've done more than your share of searching. But if you do see Tommy, tell him to get his . . . self in here immediately. Lady Dunbridge, I hope you'll come back for a tour when things are a bit calmer. Bevy, tell your father hello when you see him. Ladies . . ."

With a crisp bow, he hurried away, got halfway across the floor, and yelled, "Sydney, send Harry straight to my office."

"Of course, sir," he said, his voice tight where a moment ago it had been all smooth condescension. "Lady Dunbridge, it's been a pleasure. I'm sorry that I can't spare a few minutes to show you around, but we have a responsibility to get the news out on time. 'All the news that's fit to print,'" he added, quoting the *Times*'s banner.

"And some that isn't," said Marty, under her breath.

Sydney either didn't hear or chose to ignore her statement. "Just be sure to find Harry before you leave, Marty. To my office first." He turned on his heel and strode away.

"Like hell I will," Marty spat. "Come with me to fetch my things from the editorial floor and we'll leave these gentlemen to deal with the crisis."

The reception area was amazingly quiet. Marty pressed the call button. The far elevator opened and they hurried toward it. The door opened and two people stepped out: the mail boy who had just left them and a petite young woman, head bent, red hair twisted onto the top of her head. Her hands were clasped tightly in front of her, and Phil was reminded of a few trips to the headmistress at Madame Floret's *école* in Paris.

"Harry," Marty said. "Thank God. You were about to ruin my luncheon plans. Carr wants to see you in his office yesterday. Do you know where Tommy is?"

The young woman shook her head but didn't look up.

"What is wrong with you? When did you see him last? He's missed his deadline."

The young woman finally glanced up. Her eyes were red-rimmed, as if she'd been recently crying. Her eyes met Phil's for a mere second before she quickly looked away.

But in that brief second Phil recognized her. In the light

and dark flickering of the moving picture, Phil hadn't known the color of her hair or her eyes, but she now recognized the same fullness of lips, the pointed chin, and the boyish shape beneath her coat she'd noticed then.

It was the girl in the movie house. And Phil knew in that instant that *she* knew exactly what had happened to Tommy Green—and so did Phil.

5

"I have to go." The young woman wrenched out of the mail boy's grip and hurried away, not looking back.

"It's not your fault," Marty called after her. "But avoid Sydney. Go straight to Carr's office and tell him whatever you know." Marty turned to the mail boy who had accompanied her and who was now watching her retreat with a hangdog look.

"I found her in the toilet, bawling her eyes out. Musta had a fight with her boyfriend, poor thing. We lose more typewriter girls that way."

"Well, go after her and make sure she doesn't get waylaid by Sydney."

"Yes, miss." He shook his head and shuffled after her.

Phil stood watching. Normally she would have followed Harry and insist the girl tell her everything immediately. But Phil couldn't be certain what the girl would say, or who would be listening. And unfortunately, without further instructions, she had no idea of what to divulge. Until then, she would have to keep Tommy Green's murder to herself.

"That was Harry?"

"Alas, yes. Harriet Wells. Tommy's designated typewriter girl," Marty said, stepping into the elevator. "Stupid girl."

"How so?" Phil asked, following her and Bev inside and bracing herself for the descent.

"Straight off the farm. Marched right in and said she wanted to be a reporter. You gotta give her credit. I'm all for women taking a few of these jobs. Half the time the news you read is actually written by the women who typed up the scrawled half-sentences of the reporters and turned them into an intelligible story."

Phil and Bev exchanged looks. Martha Rive seemed a little bitter.

"But Harry." Marty shook her head. "She's sweet, enthusiastic, and types well. She makes eyes at Sydney and follows Tommy around like a puppy, but she'll never get any real assignments. She lacks brains and guts, if you'll excuse the expression. And the poor girl doesn't even have the pedigree to cover social events."

"Do you think she and Tommy were more than reporter and typewriter girl?" Phil asked.

"Were?"

"If she's crying over a breakup," Phil said, quickly covering her gaffe. "And he hasn't showed up for work. . . ."

Marty let out a guffaw. "Maybe, but not Tommy. He's a seasoned reporter, wedded to the news and probably an occasional something on the side. He's twice her age, overweight, losing his hair, and doesn't always remember to bathe. But damn he's good."

"Will she know where he is?" Phil asked.

"I sure as hell hope so. But I doubt it. Tommy's the best, but not even the best misses a deadline without a damn good reason. I wouldn't want to be in Tommy's shoes right now."

Nor would Phil. Every second was reinforcing what Phil had surmised upon first recognizing Harriet Wells. He was dead. Murdered in a nickelodeon while waiting to pass information to Phil. But what did Harriet Wells know? And what did she make of seeing Phil in the newsroom the next day?

The elevator jerked to a stop and spilled them out onto the first floor.

"That was really fast," Phil said.

"Three hundred and fifty feet per minute," Martha said. "You get used to it."

They headed toward the exit door on Forty-Second Street. They were halfway there when a group of men poured into the lobby from the street. Phil stopped dead, then grabbed Bev and Marty and turned them around to face the other way.

"What on earth?" Marty said, frowning as Phil began guiding them in the opposite direction.

"Don't look, Bev, but Detective Sergeant Atkins just came through the door. He shouldn't see us here."

"Why not? We're merely meeting a friend for lunch. And I haven't seen him once since I've been back." Bev turned to look. "He's absolutely delicious," she said to Marty, as she searched the lobby for the detective. "Just like a hero from the cover of a dime novel. Oh, there he is." She raised her hand and waved. "Yoo-hoo. Detective Sergeant Atkins. Over here!"

Phil cringed. She made a quick calculation on whether she could reach an open elevator before he noticed them. With the way things were going lately, he'd choose the same car to ride in.

He stopped, turned, looking for whoever had called his name. And Phil got a jolt of pure appreciation. Well over six feet, wearing a double-breasted overcoat with astrakhan collar, a felt homburg topping his chiseled features, he was a sight to behold.

Phil was fairly certain all three women sighed as he turned toward them.

He saw Bev, dipped his chin in hello, looked past her, and zeroed in on Phil.

She swore she could hear his sigh of resignation from across thirty feet of marble.

Bev didn't give him time to get away but bustled toward him. Marty was more than willing to follow, probably sensing an inside track—another term Phil had learned from horse racing—at the police department.

Phil smiled tightly and joined the other two.

"Imagine meeting you here," Bev trilled.

"But delightful," he said, taking Bev's proffered hand, and sliding a suspicious glance over her head to Phil.

Phil tried to look innocent.

"Oh, where are my manners," Bev said. "You do remember Lady Dunbridge, do you not?"

"But of course," he said without an ounce of irony. Fortunately, Bev had been out of the country during their last brush with crime. "Lady Dunbridge."

"Detective Sergeant."

Marty cleared her throat.

"And this is our friend Martha Rive. We're just on our way to luncheon. Would you care to join us?"

"Thank you, but I'm afraid I have business upstairs."

"At the *Times* offices? We just came from there."

His eyes narrowed.

"It's where Miss Rive works," Phil interjected, trying to signal Bev to say her adieus and leave.

"Oh yes," Bev said. "We went to Vassar together. Marty, this is Detective Sergeant John Atkins."

Marty nodded. Phil could see her mentally calculating which offices he might be visiting.

Phil wondered, too. "Fascinating place. And so busy," she said. Then reminded herself that sounding flighty might work for Bev, but the Detective Sergeant wouldn't buy it from Phil.

"Well, as lovely as it is to see you, I do have an appointment. Nice to meet you, Miss Rive. Ladies." He touched his hat and turned toward the blessedly open elevator.

Phil huffed out a sigh of relief.

"Oh, you old spoilsport. We're totally innocent . . . this time." Bev grinned.

Phil smiled back. Bev had no idea of what was happening. For that matter, neither did Phil. A reporter was dead, no one but Phil and Harriet Wells seemed to know about it, and the detective sergeant was going into the *New York Times* building. To inform them of Tommy Green's death?

And why was that? Neither Times Square nor Union Square were in his normal jurisdiction, which was the nineteenth precinct on the east side of Central Park. He was often called on to investigate society crimes, since he was obviously a cultured man. *Unlike some of his colleagues,* Phil thought as the image of Charles Becker going into the Theatre Unique shoved itself into her mind.

But journalism was hardly high society.

Some other situation that needed to be handled with sensitivity? That must be it.

But what?

"This sounds intriguing," Marty said. "But can we discuss it further over food? I'm a working girl these days and no longer have leisurely luncheons."

They stopped at the curb to wait for a break in traffic.

"I thought we'd go to the café at the Knickerbocker." Marty gestured across the street where a red-brick Beaux Arts building rose several stories before them. "The café has decent food, decent ambiance, and an accommodating attitude toward women dining without men."

Seeing a break, Marty hurried them between trolleys, carriages, automobiles, and other busy pedestrians attempting the same.

The Knickerbocker café was a large bright room with windows that looked onto the street. A row of tables for one faced the windows, and almost all of them were occupied. Other tables were spaced between the small columns of the café.

The maître d' welcomed Marty and showed them to a table near the windows. There were quite a few women dining alone or with other women, and Phil, who had not yet ventured by herself into an eating establishment, felt an enormous sense of possibility.

Not that she relished the idea of dining alone; she had spent many meals sitting at the foot of a vast empty table while the earl ignored his estates, his wife, and his responsibilities as a peer of the realm.

"It just opened last year and has been a blessing," Marty said. "One more sandwich from the corner lunchroom, and I might have committed a crime."

She zeroed in on Phil.

Obviously Phil's reputation had preceded her. Probably from Bev. Well, tit for tat. Phil had learned that game from some of the great society dames of Europe.

"It's delightful," she said. "Though I confess I've never been in a lunchroom."

"Believe me, you are not missing anything. Convenience and economy are the only two things going for them."

They ordered gin cocktails, which were delivered by a waiter whose expression said ladies enjoying cocktails at lunch was not all that common and might possibly encourage them to be dangerous.

Marty raised her eyebrows comically as he left. "I suppose he thinks we'll all get ripsnorting drunk if there's no man to restrain us. I, unlike most of the gentlemen you see here, work better after a good gin cocktail."

Bev laughed. "We really must see you more often, Marty. Mustn't we, Phil?"

"I couldn't agree more," Phil said. She was definitely looking forward to a long and hopefully productive relationship with Bev's old school chum.

"Wasn't that odd, seeing Detective Sergeant Atkins this morning?" Bev said. "Do you think he has business at the *Times*?"

"Possibly," Marty said. "But there are ten or so floors rented out to other businesses. Tell me, how did you come to know Atkins? Wait. Now I remember, Reggie's murder." She glanced at Bev—apologetically? "I hear the detective sergeant is not a man to be trifled with."

Bev laughed. "I've considered trying to trifle with him ever since he strode into my home like a Western cowboy and practically accused me of killing my husband."

Bev's last words got the attention of several nearby diners. She pulled a long face, but Phil could tell she was enjoying herself immensely.

As Bev continued to expound on the detective sergeant's qualities, Phil took a quick glance around the room, scrutinizing the waitstaff, the lone diners, the man in the bowler hat pulled low, the boisterous group in the corner, even the people who passed by on the sidewalk outside.

Any of them might be Mr. X. Or he might be loitering behind one of the topiary orange trees, tied with golden bows, that adorned the café's entrance, waiting for an opportunity to enlighten her about the situation. Why didn't he contact her? He couldn't expect her to read his mind.

Perhaps he would arrive along with her order of rarebit. He'd played a waiter before, unbeknownst to her at the time.

She would know more once she spoke privately with Harriet Wells. But how to maneuver it. She didn't dare ask Marty. She was too canny by half.

"You don't think it could do with your missing reporter?" Bev asked delightedly.

Phil had to stop herself from kicking her under the table. It might be exactly to do with Tommy Green, regardless of the ten floors of other businesses he might be visiting. And Phil didn't want Bev barging unawares into her nascent investigation.

Marty snorted, arousing several looks of censure from the surrounding diners. "A reporter missing a deadline? The police would hardly take it serious. Reporters are notorious for tying one on at their local pub. But not Tommy. And that's what worries me. If he wasn't so stubborn . . ."

"Stubborn? What *is* Mr. Green working on?" Phil asked the question nonchalantly, but Marty was a wily reporter for all her debutante-ball assignments. Her eyes flashed.

"La Mano Negra."

"The Black Hand?" Phil said.

"You've heard of them?"

"I've seen it mentioned in the papers," Phil said.

"They extort money from people by threatening to cut off their fingers and things like that," Bev said, and shuddered.

"Yes, things like that," Marty said. "There's been an uptick in activity in the Italian neighborhood east of Union Square; more recently it has spread into closer environs. That's Tommy's beat, so it was natural he was working on that. But he was like a starving dog on this one. I guess because he'd been foiled on his last big story."

"You should have asked John Atkins when we saw him," Bev said.

"I might have gotten a word in, except that you were too busy flirting." Marty took a healthy sip of her cocktail. "I know his reputation for playing fair, though in police jargon no one is certain what that means."

"Hmm," Bev said. "So Carr was waiting for Tommy to turn in copy about the Black Hand?"

Phil had forgotten that being Daniel Sloane's daughter, Bev must have picked up a certain amount of knowledge of journalism.

And Bev would invariably manage to insert herself into the investigation, whatever it was. Phil was glad of her enthusiastic, if somewhat flighty, help. They'd been fast friends since their Paris finishing-school days. It had given them outward polish and done nothing toward damping the evil genius that resided inside them both.

Bev might be able to lend a little inside knowledge, but to her it was just a game. Phil's catapulting into the investigative business had started from a desire to help her friend, but it had become much more than that. It had become a profession, one for which she was exceptionally well-suited. And this had more urgency than most.

Because . . . if Phil hadn't been a dowager countess whose sangfroid was impeccable, she'd have to admit that perhaps a little piece of her heart was involved.

"I get the feeling it's bigger than a few acts of arson and extortion," Marty said. "But neither Tommy nor Carr are talking."

"Too worried about another paper scooping them?" asked Bev.

"All I know is that rumor had it he was onto something big. But before you get excited, they're all on the trail of something big. Really big. Very few of them have the patience to actually follow it through. Tommy does. And that's why I'm worried. Maybe he's discovered something bigger than a bunch of thugs terrorizing a neighborhood. He's routed out big stories before.

"Just last spring, he exposed the real costs of the proposed new courthouse. The powers that wanted it moved to Union Square had estimated the cost at nine million dollars, when in actuality it would cost closer to twenty million—which the board would have missed if Tommy hadn't ferreted out the discrepancies. It was a beautiful investigation, but it didn't make him any friends, I can tell you."

"What happened?" Phil asked.

"The council nixed the plan, Union Square was saved from years of construction. But—" Marty bit her lip. "I don't guess it matters now, but somebody had been cooking the books, and somebody had been buying up real estate in anticipation of the new location. Tommy had them dead to rights on fraud, but when the police raided the offices, everything had been cleared out, the company disbanded. They'd been tipped off. Had to be."

"They were going to build near Union Square?" Phil asked.

"Along the east side."

"That's so far from City Hall and all the law offices," Bev said, astounding Phil, since Bev never showed much interest in current events outside racing.

"There's the subway. At least that was the argument. When

it fell through, all those real-estate speculators and property owners were a little miffed. But the neighborhood was saved."

"Did he ever get in trouble for his investigation?" asked Phil.

"He got called a lot of names, muckraker being a favorite, but I say, if there's muck then it should be raked. And Tommy was the one who could do it."

It was said with so much ardor that Phil knew Harriet Wells wasn't the only one who admired Tommy Green.

And Phil had no doubt that given the chance, Marty Rive would follow the trail and wrestle the information she found to its knees. As a journalist she could go places ordinary people didn't, poke about in people's personal lives because she was a woman.

It was frustrating, luncheoning on Welsh rarebit and green salad with a woman who might be able to give her a lead on who might have had a motive to kill Tommy Green. And being unable to confide in her.

Unfortunately, she would never be able to trust Marty with a secret. Phil got the distinct feeling that if it was ever put to the test, Martha Rive would be ruthless to get a story, even if it wrecked an investigation.

"Phil?" Bev said into her thoughts. "Is something wrong with your lunch?"

Phil looked up from the forkful of rarebit that had stopped two inches from her plate. Bev and Marty were watching her with concern.

"What? Oh no, my mind had just wandered to . . . Christmas presents. I haven't been able to find a book I wanted to give Preswick for Boxing Day. No, actually I mean Christmas Day. He and Lily and I will celebrate together."

"Lily is her lady's maid," Bev told Marty.

"That is modern of you," Marty said with a wry smile.

"Thoroughly," said Phil. Though she hadn't really broached

the subject with Preswick and Lily. Lily might welcome the change. Preswick would certainly balk. She would just have to convince him. Somehow.

"Shall we order coffee? I need to get back to the newsroom." Marty raised her hand to the waiter.

When cups of steaming coffee were placed before them, Phil asked, "Are you in the newsroom whenever you're not out on an assignment?"

"I make a point to be, because, you know, if I'm not describing dresses and canapés, I can always type someone else's real news."

And pick up on some leads of your own, Phil thought. "That must be extremely long hours."

"Yes, when the clock strikes five and the daytime typewriter girls bundle up in their department-store coats and scarves and head for the elevators, I work on my own stories."

"And then dresses in a screen behind her desk before going off to cover the social events of the evening," Bev added. "Isn't she amazing?"

"She is indeed," Phil said.

Marty pushed her chair back. "Well, amazing or not, this reporter must go back to work. I don't want to miss anything today."

"So that if Tommy Green gets the sack, you'll be ready to step into his shoes?" Bev asked archly.

Marty frowned. "If I had to. But he won't get fired. He's too valuable a reporter."

Not anymore, thought Phil, and felt a pang of sadness for the respected journalist.

"Ciao," Marty said. "Lunch is on me. I have an account."

And before they could protest, Marty Rive swept out of the café and out of sight. A minute later they saw her dodging traffic, barely slowing down as she made her way back to the *Times* building.

"Well, she is ambitious," Phil said.

"Always has been," Bev agreed. "And fun. But yes, now that I think about it, mainly ambitious."

Which meant at this point Phil would do better to try to confront Harriet Wells as she left after work. Find out what she knew, and why she was on the scene, before she talked to anyone else. Unless Harriet was already baring her soul to Detective Sergeant Atkins. He had a way of doing that, especially with young women.

"Shall I give you a lift?" Bev asked, once the Packard had been summoned.

"Thanks, but I think while I'm here . . . there's a bookstore on Forty-Third Street I want to visit. My usual store has already sold out of the book I wanted to get Preswick. Then I might look for a few things for Lily."

"Say no more. I'll leave you to it." The Packard pulled up, Bev climbed in, and was quickly swallowed up in traffic.

Phil waited for another minute while she perused the street for any possibly disguised mystery men, then went back into the hotel, where she telephoned her apartment.

At four o'clock, Phil was sitting in the Knickerbocker lobby, still empty-handed. A quick trip to the bookstore had yielded no book for Preswick. She would have to do something about that tomorrow. Christmas was rapidly approaching.

She was making a mental list of things she might have delivered and things she would have to shop for herself, when a rather odd-looking couple walked into the lobby. They were conservatively dressed in clothes of good quality but not quite in the height of fashion. The lady was much younger, perhaps not even out yet. Granddaughter and grandfather on an outing for tea?

He was tall and attenuated, slightly stooped but immaculately dressed in a dark brown overcoat and bowler hat. She was petite and had an exquisitely clear, porcelain complexion beneath a black felt hat. Her eyes and hair were dark, almost black. Much too exotic-looking for a lady's maid, and yet too demure for anyone to guess that beneath her sensible tweed overcoat she had a stiletto strapped to her ankle.

A habit that had appalled Phil on first seeing it, and which had now become an indispensable item in the household.

They stopped before Phil, obviously very pleased with their "mufti," as Preswick called it.

Phil gestured for them to sit down. And for the next few minutes, they sat on the plush couches of the Knickerbocker lobby while Phil told them about what had passed during her visit to the newspaper that morning.

"Her name is Harriet Wells. She's evidently Mr. Green's typewriter girl. I recognized her, she recognized me. She was frightened. We must be very discreet. Detective Sergeant Atkins was there today. I'm not certain he was going to the *Times* offices, but it pays to be circumspect until we know for certain.

"Unfortunately, there's more than one exit, and since I'm the only one who will recognize her, we can't watch separate doors. We'll have to risk waiting in the lobby for the change in shifts."

At a quarter to five, they crossed the street to the *Times* building, where they took up position across from the elevators to wait. When it came, a rush of people poured out of all four elevators. It was nearly impossible to find anyone, but Phil moved back and forth until everyone had pretty much departed.

Phil and Lily and Preswick reconvened just as a second load of workers were deposited at the lobby and made for the respective doors. Twenty minutes and several loads later, the rush had eased to a remnant of tired people, and no Harriet.

"We've missed her," Phil said.

"Or she's working late," suggested Lily.

"Well, we can't wait for her all night. I'll have to find another way of getting in touch with her. We might as well leave," Phil said, feeling inordinately disappointed. She could have been shopping, buying decorations. Or learning to make fruitcake, though she detested candied fruit. Nonetheless, it was Christmas in the New World, her new life. The possibilities seemed endless.

"This way, my lady," Preswick said. "There is a trolley stop right outside." Seeing Phil's expression he added, "And a taxi stand."

They headed toward the street but had to slow down as several pedestrians rushed past them and descended down the stairs of the ornamental kiosk that designated the entrance to the subway station.

"The subway! How stupid of me," Phil exclaimed. "I just assumed Harriet Wells would come out to the street to take the trolley home. But the subway would be much faster if she lived far from work. Hurry, maybe we can still catch her."

They joined the throng pressing down into the station. The platform was crowded, and she could hear the whistles of oncoming trains.

Preswick immediately strode through a set of iron railings to join the queue at the ticket booth. As Phil perused the crowd, a train came into the station and screeched to a stop. Its doors opened just as Phil spotted Harriet Wells at the back of a group, all cramming themselves into the already crowded train.

Phil ran to the gate just as Harriet pushed her way into the train; the doors closed behind her, leaving several passengers on the platform.

Preswick reached them, holding three tickets. He stopped to get his breath. "Sorry, my lady. I couldn't get them any faster."

"You did your best. I should have thought of the subway sooner. Oh well, since we have the tickets already . . ."

"But we have no way of knowing where she is getting off the train. We'll never find her now," groused Lily.

"Yes, we will, just not today, but since we have the tickets, and the train, I believe, stops at Union Square . . ."

"It does, my lady," Preswick said.

"We might as well talk to the theater manager. Then there are some lovely holiday things to see in the square."

6

Darkness had descended completely by the time Phil, Lily, and Preswick climbed up from the depths of the subway station and onto the sidewalk at Fourteenth Street. Phil's legs and teeth were still vibrating from riding the rails. It was truly amazing. They'd made the trip in fifteen minutes.

"Exhilarating," Phil exclaimed.

Lily didn't comment; Phil had noticed she'd gripped the strings of her purse so tightly the entire ride that her knuckles had turned white.

"Yes, my lady," Preswick said. "And much faster than the trolley or omnibus or taxicab when the traffic is heavy."

Phil nodded. "True." Though she didn't think she would make a habit of riding it as a way of transportation.

Phil led the way straight down Fourteenth Street to the Theatre Unique. She bypassed the ticket kiosk and told the ticket taker she wished to speak to the manager.

The ticket taker straightened slightly and just looked at her.

"Could you direct us to the manager's office, young man?" Preswick said at his most officious.

The man jerked his head to the right. "Down there."

Preswick led the way down a side hall to the manager's office and rapped on the door.

"Just a minute" was barked from inside, followed by sounds of hurried activity.

"Perhaps if you and Lily would wait at the entrance, I could ascertain—"

The door opened.

"Yeah?"

"Am I speaking with the manager?" Preswick asked.

"Who wants to know?"

Phil eased in front of Preswick and gave the man a good look. He was a large man, in height and girth, with a high, receding hairline and ears that stuck out to the sides.

"I do."

"Now listen, lady, if somebody picked your pocket while you were watching the show, we ain't responsible. The sign says so. Can't police people in the dark, now, can you?"

This was not the man who had ushered her out of the theater the day before.

"Were you here yesterday?"

"Sure. I'm here every day 'cept Sunday. And pretty soon I'll be here then, too, if they ever make up their minds about whether to let us open or not. We can, we can't, we do, and one of them groups complains. Bunch of baloney. If you don't want to come on Sunday nobody's makin' you."

"So you were here when the body was discovered."

The manager's eyes grew wary beneath beetled eyebrows. "Here now. What do you know about that? Some poor joker had a heart attack while watching the pictures. There are worse ways to go."

"Where did they take him?"

"Police took him. You a relative or something? We are not responsible for the man's bad ticker. You can't get nothing out of us, so don't even start."

"I was here yesterday," Phil told him, against her better judgment. She sniffed. "It was so upsetting. The man who introduced himself as the manager helped me out of the theater. I just wanted to thank him."

"Well, if you want to thank somebody . . ." He puffed out his barrel chest.

"But I'm quite certain he was a much smaller man."

The manager screwed up his face. "There ain't no other manager. Only got the boy that takes the tickets and the fella in the ticket kiosk, but he don't ever leave it till his replacement comes on. You musta misheard."

"That must be it. Did the police say where they were taking the poor man?"

"Nope. And the less you and I know about it, the better."

"Well, thank you for your time." She turned to leave just as he stuck out his hand. Preswick dropped a coin into it and hurried them away.

They walked quickly back to the street and didn't stop until they reached the square. Only then did Phil turn around, but if she expected to see the manager watching them from the doorway she was disappointed.

"Well, that answers one question," she said. "The man who hustled me out the back door was not the manager."

"No, my lady," Preswick said, attempting to keep their little trio moving.

"Well, we've done what we can do for today. And I see no reason to let this situation ruin our holidays. Shall we take in the novelties of the park on our way home?"

The air was filled with revelry, but not of the same kind as yesterday, which was beginning to seem like a bad dream. Vendors still lined the way, selling a variety of wares and Christmas greenery in the light of the lampposts. But the nurses with their perambulators were gone, the ladies and their shopping were now at home. The few women peopling the sidewalk were of a lower class than their earlier counterparts.

They passed a row of boys hawking the late editions, a knot of men laughing uproariously and emitting a distinct aroma of cheap whiskey.

Perhaps this hadn't been the best idea.

"Lily," Preswick ordered. And Phil realized they'd left Lily, who had stopped and was enthralled by a game of thimblerig being carried on under the light of one of the many lampposts that lit the way.

"He palmed the pea," Lily said as Preswick scuttled her away.

The girl was a constant surprise.

Farther along two young girls rattled tin cups and looked pitiful. Lily reached into her purse, but Preswick kept her moving. "Their handler is standing under that lamppost over there. They will see none of their alms. Use your money in a better way."

"How, Mr. Preswick?" Lily asked, returning her coin to her purse.

Phil glanced over to the other side of the walk and took in the girls' "handler," a lanky man wearing baggy pants and jacket and a porkpie cap pulled low over his face. She was tempted to walk right over to him . . . and do what? His kind were legion among the poor. As she'd lately begun to realize.

She was getting quite an education in America.

Ahead, the sharp scent of evergreens beckoned to them, and they stopped at a pile of pine boughs tied in bunches and overseen by a bent old woman, whose layers of skirts and capes of various lengths made her appear almost round. An old-fashioned poke bonnet covered her face except for the tip of a large nose.

All of Phil's senses came to the alert. She leaned in as if perusing the boughs but was really trying to get any whiff of exotic tobacco, because this was just the kind of disguise Mr. X would enjoy.

An unexpected anger seized her. If this was his idea of fun after how worried she'd been . . . but she could smell nothing beyond the pine boughs.

The old woman looked up. Her eyes were clouded over with cataracts. "A penny, lady. A penny for a nice thick bunch." She held out a hand, the fingers gnarled with arthritis.

Phil motioned to Preswick to buy something and turned

away, her emotions in turmoil—and bumped into another seller of holiday cheer.

"Mistletoe!" he warbled in a high voice, stumbling back slightly on the impact. He was underdressed for the weather with a misshapen suit jacket and a long muffler that wrapped around his neck in a way that reminded Phil of Scrooge's clerk in the story by Mr. Dickens.

"I do beg your pardon," Phil said.

But the man had wandered off, singing, "Mistletoe. Mistletoe for your sweetheart." She'd meant to buy something from him, too, but when she turned to tell Preswick to go after him, the mistletoe salesman was already weaving his way toward the street.

Another man seemed to be following him, a customer, perhaps. As Phil started to turn away, the customer reached out. But instead of giving the customer a sprig of mistletoe in return, the mistletoe seller doubled over, fell to one knee as if the customer was forcing him to the ground merely by holding his hand.

The mistletoe seller nodded spasmodically. The man let go and the mistletoe man hobbled across the street. When Phil looked back, the other man was gone.

For a full minute she could only stare at her surroundings, unable to feel relief, anger, or anything but confusion. What did it all mean? Why come in contact with her if he didn't have further instructions?

Though maybe he had.

While Preswick and Lily gathered their bundles of pine, Phil quickly unclasped her purse and peeked inside. No note. She checked the outer pockets of her overcoat: nothing in the first. But in the second, her fingers touched paper.

At last. Looking around to make sure she wasn't being watched, she slid the paper out of her pocket. It was one sheet folded over in haste. And rather dirty.

It didn't matter. She opened it there in the light of the lamp-post, and her breath caught.

"Anything else, my lady?" Preswick held a large display of boughs rolled up in newspaper.

Phil swallowed, opened her mouth, but no words came out. She turned the open paper for him to see. Printed in crude block letters: STAY OUT OF THIS OR YULL BE SORRY. It was signed with the picture of a black hand.

"Wher-r-re did this come from?" Lily blurted out.

Preswick quickly scanned the surrounding area.

"I believe from the mistletoe vendor who I bumped into—or perhaps it was he who bumped into me."

"I will find him and slit his thr-r-r-o—"

"I imagine he will be long away from here by now. I suggest we get into a taxi and go home, where we can analyze the situation." Phil folded the note and slipped it into her purse. Why would the Black Hand be after her? Had they killed Tommy Green? What could he possibly have discovered that would warrant such a fate?

And if the mistletoe man wasn't Mr. X, who was he, and who was the other man?

Her brain felt like a sieve. This wasn't following the pattern of her previous cases. In those, she was thrust into a family situation and from there was able to solve a murder as well as ascertain additional facts for the people who made subsequent arrests.

Between Mr. X and his—dare she say "their"—people, and Detective Sergeant Atkins—in spite of his—they had managed very well.

But tonight as the taxi rattled its way up Fifth Avenue, she felt more confused than she had since she'd watched her parents' carriage drive away from Dunbridge Castle, leaving her alone with her new husband, a cold, misogynistic man who had fancied her dowry and person in that order.

But she was no longer alone. She had Bev and the assortment of acquaintances and friends she'd made in the last few months. And most importantly, she had Lily and Preswick. Between the three of them, confusion would be put to rest.

Life was good, and Phil had no intention of letting something as ridiculous sounding as the Black Hand take it away from her.

Besides, hadn't Marty said they preyed on the communities of small-shop owners and immigrants in order to extort money from them? They wouldn't dare come after a countess— dowager or no—at the Plaza Hotel. Would they?

Later that evening, robed in one of her new Parisian kimonos, patterned in red, cream, and black for the holidays, Phil was lounging on the chaise in the parlor, having canceled her evening engagements in favor of a martini and an evening of scouring the newspapers for information about the Black Hand.

Preswick had collected all the available evening editions. They were lying in a pile at her feet.

She picked up the last remaining paper, snapped it open, and read:

Fourteen of Gang Caught in Pittsburgh.

Black Hand agents seeking to carry out repeated threats against Salvatore Scarito and his family, jeopardized the lives of sixteen other families early yesterday morning when they set fire to . . .

She wasn't as yet really concerned about being targeted by the Black Hand. But after reading several articles, she was beginning to worry about the safety of her servants.

Would the thugs attack them to get to her? She couldn't very well send them away until it all blew over, whatever *it* was. She had no country seat or hunting lodge. Just the Plaza. The whole idea was ludicrous.

She let the paper slide to her lap.

Why had they sent her to meet with Tommy Green? How was she supposed to investigate an unknown crime organization without an ounce of instruction to go on?

Why was the elusive Mr. X being more elusive than usual?

Did he even know what had happened? Had a simple exchange of information gone terribly awry?

Really, she could be so much more efficient if she was ever given a hint as to what her job was supposed to be.

She tossed the newspaper to the floor just as Preswick and Lily entered, carrying large vases trimmed with red ribbons and containing sprays of pine boughs that they deposited on each side of the fireplace.

"Oh, excellent," Phil said, sitting up and giving them her full attention. "Shall we go out tomorrow and get one of those trees they're selling on the corner? Is it too soon? I always thought it was silly to wait until Christmas Eve. And we'll buy some of those electric lights I saw in the store window yesterday."

Instead of causing a spark of excitement, at least from Lily, she was met with solemn faces.

"Now, look, you two, there is nothing to worry about. I've been reading the papers, and these people are not going to harm a countess living at the Plaza. They prey on the little man, those who don't have the means to fight back, those who are new to the country and don't speak the language."

She didn't seem to be making much of an impression.

"And besides, from what I've read, most of them seem singularly inept."

"Inept enough to kill a man in a crowded theater," Preswick reminded her.

"It wasn't that crowded. And besides it was dark, and thirdly, I'm not sure it was the Black Hand."

"But the note," Lily reminded them.

"Yes, the note," Phil said. "Considering the timing of the mistletoe man, I think the manager may have hired him to scare us away. He was probably threatened by Sergeant Becker not to talk.

"We dawdled in the square long enough for him to scribble a threat and draw a hand, because everyone knows that's how the Black Hand signs notes. He runs out or sends that man in the ticket kiosk to pay someone to do exactly what the mistletoe man did. Bump into me and slip the note in my pocket."

"But why would he do that, madam?"

Phil was trying to stay one step ahead of her servants. She didn't want to alarm them and she didn't want to spoil the holidays with needless fear. "Well . . . he wouldn't want anyone to know that the Hand or anyone else had murdered a man in his theater. People would be afraid to come. He'd lose business. He might have to close down. So far no one has talked. I imagine he just wanted to make sure I wouldn't, either."

Lily let out a slow breath.

Preswick's brow lightened minutely. "Nonetheless, my lady. We should all be at our highest alert whenever we leave the building."

"You're absolutely right, Preswick. And now I've suddenly acquired an appetite, I'll dine in tonight."

"Yes, my lady."

As soon as Preswick and Lily had left the room, Phil slipped off the chaise and carried her drink over to the windows that overlooked Central Park.

Below her, Just a Friend had left for the day, making his cold slow journey back to the Tenderloin, where he lived with a group of boys under the protection of a shadowy character named Clancy.

A line of horse-drawn carriages waited along the opposite sidewalk to carry patrons on a romantic ride through the park. Automobiles and carriages ran up and down the street, transporting people to plays or parties or Christmas celebrations. Men strode hurriedly down the sidewalk, coattails flying, hands holding their hats to their heads. A family dragged a Christmas tree along the pavement, taking it home.

It was Christmas in Manhattan. And she wasn't going to let the murder of a reporter, no matter how good he was, ruin her first Christmas in the New World.

It was obvious that she could not wait for instructions any longer. She would just have to find this killer herself.

7

Phil dined alone on a delectable cassoulet and then stretched out on the sofa, sipping an excellent cognac, something she would never have thought to do when she lived in England, where no one dared to put their feet on sofas. That ignominy was reserved for the chaise in her ladyship's boudoir.

She was startled out of this sleepy reverie by the telephone. Odd; it was after midnight. Who would be calling her now?

Preswick appeared in the doorway. "Mrs. Reynolds on the telephone, my lady."

"Ah." Bev was probably bored and wanted to talk.

"I won't take no for an answer," Bev said before Phil had even finished saying hello. "Marty just called. She has news. So get dressed. We're going to the Cavalier Club downtown. Very expensive, very exclusive, and very naughty. I'll pick you up in an hour."

Marty had news. About Tommy Green's murder? About why Detective Sergeant Atkins had been at the *Times* building? All feelings of fatigue evaporated.

"Preswick, send Lily to me. I'm going out after all."

True to her word, Bev arrived at the Plaza entrance exactly an hour later. She was in high spirits, wrapped in what looked like a new fur coat mostly hidden by a driving rug, which rather overshadowed Phil's fur-trimmed black velvet cape.

"Isn't it wonderful, Phil?" Bev said as they drove away. "To be out and about like the old days, when I didn't give a fig about what society thought."

"Do you now?"

Bev laughed. "Not in the least. But I will try a little for dear old dad's sake. Fortunately, the Elizabeth Abernathys of town will be in bed, and tonight we can enjoy ourselves as we used to do."

They drove downtown, and Phil was a little surprised to see Union Square. When they passed the Theatre Unique, its façade lit up in white lights, Phil couldn't prevent a shudder.

At the next corner they turned right and came to a stop halfway down the block. The Cavalier Club was a respectable-looking brownstone with an electric sign above the door. It was doing a lively business as couples bustled in and out of the wide double doors. Across the street a few lights still burned in the upper stories of apartment buildings, but the street-level stores were dark. One building was boarded over completely, its charred bricks illuminated like black flames from the lights of the after-hours club.

A fire? Phil couldn't prevent her mind from wondering if it had been an accident or the work of the Black Hand.

Bev barely waited for her driver to open the door before she jumped out of the Packard and bustled Phil inside.

They retired immediately to the ladies' lounge to divest themselves of their outerwear and repair any damage to their toilette that a drive downtown might have caused.

And Phil got her first good look at Bev's fur coat.

"Sable?" she asked.

"Yes. Isn't it divine?" Bev slipped the coat into the waiting hands of a uniformed attendant. "I had them send the bill to my father. That should give him a happy Christmas."

"It will certainly be a surprise," Phil said. "Shall we go find Marty?"

Marty was sitting at a table across the crowded dance floor from a horseshoe-shaped bar that was packed three deep. She looked very different than she had at lunch in her gored skirt and white tailored blouse. Tonight she was wearing a silver chemise made of one of the new metallic fabrics. Her hair was lifted and curled and kept in place by a bandeau of diamantés with a peacock feather that curled down past her ear.

Her notebook and pencil were tucked discreetly—but within easy reach—beneath a gold chain-mail evening purse that sat on the table to her right.

"Oh, how I've missed this," Bev exclaimed over the band as she sat in one of the four upholstered chairs at the table.

Marty blew smoke from her cigarette into an already smoky room. She nodded to Phil to sit on her other side, which gave all three of them a view of the room and the clientele.

"A crush tonight," Marty said, scanning the crowd and looking bored.

If she had news she was certainly not in any hurry to divulge it.

"Are you covering the club tonight?" Phil asked.

Marty blew out another long exhale of smoke. "In a manner of speaking. I plan to do a column on the nightlife of New Yorkers, if I can convince Carr that it isn't too lowbrow."

"He thinks it might not be 'fit to print'?" Phil quipped, quoting from the *Times*'s banner slogan.

"Sometimes I think I should be working for Hearst," Marty said. "Now there's a man who knows how to report a good scandal."

"Plus it would make your parents apoplectic," Bev added.

"That, too." Marty stubbed out her cigarette.

They ordered drinks, and as soon as the waiter walked away, Bev jumped up.

"Oh, there are some old friends of mine. I haven't seen them in donkey's years. I must say hello. Don't drink my cocktail while I'm gone." She rushed off across the room.

"If ever there was someone not made for mourning, it's Bev," Marty said.

"True," agreed Phil. "So Bev said you have news. Are you following a lead?"

"Actually, I'm following him." She turned her head and Phil followed her gaze across the room.

"Is that—?"

"Sydney Lord."

"Is this your news?"

"No, but I was covering the Buxton fête tonight. And Sydney was there. He sees himself as a player, but he's never even had a beat, just a desk, behind a partition. He's a news editor, one of several, I might add, under Carr, but he wouldn't recognize a lead if it bit him. He's invited everywhere, not to report, but to enjoy himself at other people's expense. I don't know how he manages to stay on every hostess's guest list."

"Probably because he's good-looking, charming—"

"And knows it and is willing to use it," Marty finished.

"Has he tried to use it on you, perhaps?"

Marty laughed. "Tried and failed. And consequently I get passed over for all the big stories in favor of one of his male friends in the newsroom."

"I'm sorry."

"Oh, I haven't given up. He'll have to accept me as an equal eventually."

Phil wondered. Men like Sydney rarely did. They rarely had to.

"But in the meantime, I won't take his officious attitude lying down. Where, in case you're wondering, he would like me to be. He's on to something. I overheard him tell someone to meet him here tonight. He sounded agitated. That alone was enough to pique my interest. He doesn't exert himself in anything but polo and . . . I can't think of anything else. Certainly not news gathering. Damn, he's seen us."

"We're not exactly hiding."

"Exactly," Marty said with an arch look, and lifted her chin in Sydney's direction, more of an acknowledgment than an invitation.

Sydney took it as an invitation, and he sauntered toward their table.

"I didn't know you were planning to be here tonight, Marty, we could have shared a taxi. Lady Dunbridge, a pleasure." He placed his drink on the table and, without waiting for an invitation, he sat down and pulled out a package of cigarettes.

"Bev Reynolds invited us," Marty lied. "She's over there somewhere."

"Ah," Sydney said, and patted his pockets for a light. Marty didn't offer hers.

Finally he came up with a box of matches, lit his cigarette, and tossed the matchbox on the table next to the cigarettes.

Phil stared at the matchbox. Black with a red rose on top.

"My, what a pretty box of matches," Phil said.

"Huh? Oh, couldn't find my lighter."

"Very distinctive," Phil added.

Sydney put them back in his pocket. "Not even sure how they ended up in my pocket. These things get passed around, you know."

Phil let it drop; she didn't want to appear too obvious and she didn't want to sidetrack Marty, who had an agenda.

"So what brings you here tonight?" Marty asked.

"Me?" Sydney shrugged. "Thought I might run into some fellows for a nightcap. You have to admit, the Buxtons' do was a dreadful bore."

"You know, Sydney, you're at every affair. You should be the one writing about them."

Sydney laughed and finished his drink.

Bev returned. "Oh hello, Sydney." She sat down.

"I've got to powder my nose," Marty said, and left the table.

Sydney watched her go, shook his head. "She'll come around eventually. If you ladies will excuse me?" He scooped up his cigarettes and took himself off.

"I doubt it," Bev said as soon as he was out of earshot.

"She doesn't seem to like him."

"A bit of a history there. But it was a long time ago. Back when we were girls."

"You old thing," Phil said just as Marty slipped into her chair. "I thought he'd never leave."

"You had news?" Phil reminded her, just as the waiter returned with their drinks. Really, at this rate it would be morning before Phil learned anything. Except Sydney Lord had the same matchbox as Tommy Green—and probably half the men in the club, though the Cavalier Club's boxes were red and embossed with a gold overlapping CC. There had been a bowl of them at the entrance.

Marty's attention had drifted away from the table.

Was she making Phil work for it? Delaying was a useful tactic in love, war, and sometimes investigation. It made the suspect nervous and more likely to spill the truth.

But Phil was not a suspect and she had no intention of playing that game. She leaned closer to be heard without shouting. "So why am I here, in addition to adding to my knowledge of Manhattan nightlife?"

"I found out what your police detective was after."

"Oh?" Phil didn't bother to correct her about whose policeman John Atkins really was.

"Charlie Miller and Carr asked him to come. It seems we have a leak in the newsroom."

So not because they feared Tommy Green was dead.

"Someone who is giving out information about what your reporters are investigating? To other newspapers? So they can get the—"

"So they can scoop us," Marty supplied for her. She tapped the rim of her glass with a manicured nail. "We do all the work, they get fed the results and come out with the headline before we do. And someone at our end gets a nice payoff. The worst of underhanded journalism."

Phil reached for her glass, put it down. She'd had wine with dinner, and a cognac. She needed to stay clearheaded. Marty was a clever woman, and determined. Phil hadn't been invited to the club for a ladies' night out on the town.

How much had Bev told Marty about her? She looked over to her friend, who seemed to be totally absorbed in the music, and probably longing to dance.

"Important stories have been killed lately because some other paper published them first. We don't just cover accidents and events and society teas. The *Times* does in-depth reporting. We should do more of it, but the times are slow to change at the *Times*." She shrugged.

"Do you think this snitch might be involved with why Tommy Green was—is late for his deadline? Did he ever show up?"

"No. Evidently Carr was worried enough to have Harriet talk to the detective. I don't think it went very well. Sydney managed to worm his way into the meeting. Word is she was barely there five minutes before she came out in tears and spent the rest of the day crying over her typewriter. Carr told her to take the rest of the day off."

Marty raised her eyebrows, inviting comment.

"Why on earth?" asked Phil. She already knew the answer, but she bet Marty didn't. Atkins must not have informed them of Tommy's murder. Then again, perhaps he didn't know of it, either.

"Who knows?"

The ball was back in Phil's court.

Phil could hold her own against almost any gossip in England. And her success in New York depended on her complete and unswerving discretion. She settled in to play this game of wills.

"Is he really worried?" Phil asked. He certainly should be; his reporter was dead. But Phil wasn't going to tell Marty that.

She might, however, have to have a little talk with John Atkins soon.

"Of course he is. We all are." Marty leaned closer. "It isn't like Tommy to be this late. At least he would have checked in. I'm afraid he might have come to some harm."

And here it was.

"Bev says that you're good friends with Detective Sergeant Atkins. I thought perhaps you might . . ." Marty trailed off. Took a sip of her cocktail. Smiled up at Phil, a coy, deadly expression that reminded Phil to never trust her. "You know, I can get you in to see the New Year's Eve ball drop up close." She raised an inviting eyebrow. "It will be the biggest event of the holidays."

Phil burst into spontaneous laughter. "Is that a bribe? I'm afraid Bev was overly enthusiastic about her claims on Detective Sergeant Atkins. I think we both annoy him and it's only his good manners that prevent him from giving us the cut direct."

She was actually dying to ask Atkins what he knew. But he would not be happy to see her involved in another one of his—evidently as yet unknown to him—cases. He would never believe her when she told him she'd just happened to have taken a whim to see the nickelodeon and sat down next to a dead man.

She'd love to dump the whole absurd situation in his lap and concentrate on the holidays. But without directions from the now missing—presumed to be the most annoying—specter in the night, she didn't feel comfortable telling the detective sergeant more than what was absolutely necessary.

"You know something, don't you?" Marty prodded.

"I know that Detective Sergeant Atkins is a tenacious man. That if Mr. Miller or Mr. Van Anda want him to find this snitch, or your missing reporter for that matter, he will."

"*You* certainly respect him, but no one will talk to him. Most of the police are in the pockets of some politician or other. At-kins will eventually sell out, or already has and is just putting on a good front. Either way, no one will grass out a colleague. You never know when it might come back to slit your throat."

Phil caught her breath.

Even Bev turned momentarily from the music and frowned at Marty. "Not John Atkins."

Phil didn't comment, merely studied Marty's face.

"Do I shock you?"

"Not really," Phil said. "I was just thinking about what a lovely throat the detective sergeant has."

"He does," Bev said, and sighed.

Marty laughed. "I noticed." Mentioning a handsome man would send Bev off on any tangent Phil desired, but Marty was more single-minded than her school chum. "But I'm more interested in what he knows."

"What are they saying in the newsroom?"

"Half are saying that Tommy just drank himself into a cel-ebratory stupor and forgot to turn in his copy. Others think whatever he was working on led him into trouble." Marty shook her head. "There's a lottery on whether he gets fired or not. It's got fifty dollars in it already."

Well, nobody would win that lottery, since Phil didn't think it was possible to fire a dead man. Why hadn't someone con-tacted them? She had been certain—well, almost certain—that Atkins had been on his way to inform the *Times* editors that the reporter's body had been delivered to the morgue.

But evidently not.

"So now, you." Marty leaned forward on her elbows. "What do you know about all this?"

"I beg your pardon?"

"Do you really think I believe you suddenly developed an interest in publishing at the charity-ball meeting yesterday?"

"Well, actually, yes, I did. Plus Bev talks so much about you and Roz, I thought it was the perfect opportunity to kill two birds with one stone, so to speak. Get to know you and have a private tour to the paper. But perhaps on a less tumultuous day."

"Lady Dunbridge, Phil, I'm not stupid. I saw how you looked at Harry when she stepped out of the elevator."

Phil tilted her head, trying to remember what her reaction had been.

"It was shock. And I wonder why."

"Well, perhaps because I had until that moment assumed Harry was a man. It took me a couple of seconds to readjust my expectations. That's all."

Marty lit a cigarette and watched Phil through a haze of smoke. "I don't trust you, Phil. If there's a story here, I want to be first at the trough. Get me out of society news."

"I have no desire to prevent you from doing that."

"Just as long as we understand each other."

Phil gave her a brief nod of agreement. "Now tell me, just what do you think the big story is?"

"Not a clue. But I'll bet you money Harry might. She typed all his notes. Tommy never really got past using two fingers."

"Then you should ask her."

"She'd never talk to me, too afraid I'll try to scoop her. Not that she'll ever have a story to scoop. The poor girl just doesn't have what it takes to make it in journalism."

"Moxie?" Phil said at her driest.

Marty laughed. "Money. Do you think I live on what the paper pays me? Harriet lives in a boardinghouse with the other typewriter girls where the closest telephone is downstairs and always in use. Good way to miss a story."

Marty's eyes drifted back across the room. She seemed almost as interested in watching the crowd as she was in getting Phil to help her.

"At last," she said with a sudden look of satisfaction. "Look what the cat dragged in."

Phil and Bev looked toward the entrance, where two men had just entered.

"It's Jarvis Chandler," Bev said. "But I don't see Roz any-where."

"That's because she isn't here. But look who is."

Bev craned her neck to see. It wasn't really necessary. The man with Mr. Chandler was well over six feet, big-boned, and barrel-chested.

"Oh, saints preserve us," Bev said primly. "No one with that much money should wear a toupee that bad. Does he do it on purpose?"

"Who is he?" Phil asked.

"Imogen Trout's husband," Bev said. "The man with his fingers in every pot, especially if the pot belongs to beautiful women or rich men. Samuel Trout."

Phil stared at her friend. "I guess you don't care for him, Bev?"

"Reggie had a few dealings with him. Could have lost a fortune but pulled out just in the nick of time."

"He's also bosom buddies with Roz's husband," Marty added. "We've been trying to get dirt on him for years."

The two men stopped briefly to speak to some acquaintances, then continued to the back of the room and through another door.

"Dare I ask what goes on back there?" asked Phil.

"At your peril. This is a favorite haunt of Tammany politicians. They sit at their offices discussing business, then come to the Cavalier Club, where the real deals are made in the back rooms. And if they're so inclined, they can finish up the evening with a trip to Sally Toscana's. It's right around the corner."

"Which I gather is a house of . . ."

"A high-class brothel. A favorite of our civic leaders. I've heard there's an underground passage between the two buildings, in case of inclement weather. Or a police raid."

"Were you expecting them?"

"I didn't know whom to expect, but I'm not surprised."

And suddenly Phil wondered if Marty might be subsidizing her own journalistic career with a spot of blackmail.

Moments later, Sydney Lord, who had been standing at the bar with a group of friends, quietly slipped away, wove through knots of patrons, and followed Jarvis and Samuel Trout through the back door.

"What is he doing?" Marty said. "So help me if he's onto something. He's already beaten me out of one story, I'll be damned if he does it again."

She looked at Phil, and Phil recognized that glint of anticipation she often felt herself at the beginning of a case. "Let's just take a look, shall we?" Marty stood and, without waiting for Phil or Bev, started across the floor.

After only a second's hesitation, they followed.

They were stopped at the closed door by a large man in a black uniform.

"Gents only," he said.

Marty looked like she might argue, but Phil had no intention of calling attention to herself.

"Sorry, we were looking for the ladies'."

"That way." He pointed across the room, and Phil dragged Marty away.

"What did you do that for?"

"Because the direct route is not always the best route," Phil said. She had no intention of causing a scene tonight.

"You have a better idea?" Bev asked.

"Actually, I'm going home to bed. It's been a long day."

Phil didn't think she could get much more information out of Marty. First thing tomorrow, she'd figure out a way to talk to Harriet Wells. Then she would lay it in the lap of John Atkins, and she and Lily and Preswick would go out to buy a Christmas tree.

"Let me know how it turns out." Phil collected her coat from the cloakroom and asked the doorman to summon her a taxi.

A remarkably short time later, a man in gray livery stepped into the entrance hall. "Lady Dunbridge?" he asked.

"Yes."

He bowed and ushered her outside.

She stepped out on the street to see not a taxi but a large enclosed limousine.

Phil hesitated, wondering if she was about to be kidnapped. The driver opened the door to the back, and an unmistakable aroma of that special tobacco wafted out.

Well, at last, she thought, and stepped into the limousine.

He was sitting at the far side, a wide-brimmed fedora pulled low so that she couldn't see his eyes. The rest of him was concealed by dark trousers and an even darker jacket.

She turned toward him as the auto pulled away from the curb, and her patience broke. "Where on earth have you been? What happened at the Theatre Unique? What did you do with the mistletoe man? Was that even you?"

"Chicago. You nag just like a wife."

Momentarily nonplused, she finally managed, "Do you have a wife?"

"Of course not. What would I do with one?"

Phil had a couple of ideas, but then men never were as attentive and creative toward their wives as they were to their mistresses.

"I wouldn't know. But things have been happening here and I had no way of contacting you or anyone else who might be involved. Why didn't you send me instructions? Especially if you're just going to lurk in the shadows and not tell me what's going on?"

She sucked in a breath. "When I sat down and realized the man was dead, I thought it was you. Do you know how that made me feel?"

"No, tell me."

"Ugh."

He laughed, then turned and looked her straight in the eye.

At least he seemed to, though the brim of his hat covered most of his face. "It's something we all face at one time or another, and if you stick with it, so will you."

Deflated, she asked, "So why was I there?"

"A reporter had information about a project I'm interested in. We were to meet, but I was, um, unavailable. It was decided that you would do in a pinch."

"In a pinch? Why, you low-down . . ." She turned on him, fists raised.

He grabbed her by her wrists. "Your Americanisms are charming, but would you really hit a defenseless man?"

"You are never defenseless. A machete couldn't get past your attitude."

"It wasn't supposed to be life-threatening. And you would have done admirably except for the assassin."

"Assassin?"

"Killer, if you will. It should have been a simple pass-off. Safe. Obviously a miscalculation on our part."

"Which brings us to who is 'our'? Are we even working on the same side?"

His slow smile made her mind and other parts of her wander into dangerous territory.

"Do you really have any doubt?"

She did, but so far he hadn't proven her fears.

"I'd rather be useful than safe."

Another of those smiles, which even the disguise he was no doubt wearing couldn't mute.

She looked him in the eye, or where his eyes would be if the brim of the hat wasn't hiding them. "Do you find that amusing?"

She longed to snatched the hat from his head. Make him understand that she was risking everything: her reputation, her livelihood, her future—but of course he understood already. Had understood from the beginning, even before she had.

"I find *you* fascinating."

She felt herself leaning toward him—she pulled back. "Nonetheless, this is a very inefficient way to do business."

"Perhaps, but of necessity at the moment."

"I didn't get home to see your note until it was too late to make the rendezvous on time. I might have saved the man's life if I had."

"Or gotten yourself killed along with him."

"I did think of that, too. So what was he going to pass on?"

"We don't know what he had. Either it died with him, it was stolen off him by the murderer, or it's locked up safe someplace."

"Someone got me out the back door of the theater. If it wasn't you, who was it?"

"We had a secondary man for backup. Obviously a total fiasco. Though he managed to get you away. That was something. Did you find anything?"

"I learned he was covering the Black Hand, but I learned that later," Phil told him. "And I got a letter with a black hand on it warning me to stay away."

He bit back an expletive. "It's probably nothing. Anyone with a pencil can claim to be a member of the Hand."

"Are you telling me not to worry?"

"No. You should always be alert. I'm saying that the note situation has been taken care of. Though perhaps you should stand down until I get back."

"Get back from where?"

"Can't say."

"Ugh. And how will I know when that is?"

"I'll contact you."

"That's not good enough. We need a better system. And I won't stand down. I sat next to a dead man, was dragged out of the theater by someone who said he was the manager, but you say was your security man. Just so you know, he had blood on his hands; it left stains on my winter coat."

"Buy yourself a new coat."

"I will. I have no intention of standing down. I've already made contacts at the *Times,* and I'm following a lead, albeit a thin one, into Tommy Green's murder."

"You are something else, Countess."

"So you've said before."

"Still, you should be careful," he said seriously, then breathed out a laugh. "Well, maybe not careful; just don't get yourself killed." He ran a finger down her jawline. "I have plans for you." He leaned forward to speak to the driver. "Let me off at the next corner.

"And as for you . . ."

Phil saw the glint—of a gold tooth?—before he pulled her against him and planted a memorable kiss on her all-too-willing lips.

The limousine stopped. He let go, and she felt the rush of cold air as the door opened. A quick touch to his fedora. "Don't forget me." And he shut the door.

Little chance of that. The auto took off, and though she turned in her seat to try to catch a glimpse of him, he had already disappeared into the night.

8

Instead of summoning Lily the next morning, Phil slipped into her robe de chambre and padded down the hall to the kitchen. It was only a week before Christmas, and she was feeling an uncharacteristic sense of excitement. There were plans to be made . . . and, alas, a murderer to be caught.

There was a new stack of newspapers on the table, and Preswick, in his shirtsleeves, was bent over ironing one of the sheets, a habit he refused to abandon even though at the rate they went through papers it seemed a waste of his time. Lily sat at the table sipping a cup of tea, forehead resting on her hand as she read one of the articles out loud.

"And listen to this." She read, "'The new ball is five feet in diameter, and the light for it will be supplied by one hundred electric lamps. And it will begin to descend exactly one minute before the new year begins.'" Lily looked up, her profile alight with excitement. "Imagine that. Do you think we could go see it?"

Preswick glanced up from his iron but bypassed Lily and saw his mistress. His mouth opened slightly with astonishment.

"Lily," he said sharply, then quickly put down the iron and shrugged into his jacket and gave it a sharp tug. "My lady."

Lily jumped out of her chair, ran her hand across her dress, and curtseyed at the same time, a habit she'd had no trouble abandoning when it suited her. But surprise had brought it all back.

"Madam—my lady. I didn't hear you call." She glanced toward the cupboard where the modern intercom system was housed.

"Most likely because I didn't call. I thought I'd come down and see what you two do when you're not waiting on me hand and foot."

To Phil's utter surprise, Lily's eyes filled with tears.

"Don't sack me, please, my lady." She shot a frightened look toward Preswick, who seemed to have been struck dumb.

Phil pulled out a chair and sat down. "No one is getting sacked. I just thought I would see what it was like to come 'downstairs,' as they say, without getting dressed. Quite liberating. Is that coffee? May I have a cup? And you can tell me all about this New Year's Eve ball descent I'm hearing so much about." She looked from Lily to Preswick. "Or must I return to my room?"

Both her servants stood stock-still, as if they couldn't believe what they were hearing.

"I'm sorry, I won't do it again," Phil said contritely. Evidently the age-old servant-mistress decorum was to be maintained in their new life. It was a venerated system, whose divisions were made so that everyone clearly knew their place. And, she supposed, which left guesswork and insecurity behind.

But it created quite a few needless barriers when you were running a household of one.

"Yes, my lady, and I'll call for breakfast immediately." Preswick poured her a cup of coffee, just as if the order of his world hadn't just been tested, and left the room.

Phil drank her coffee while Lily finished reading the article about the New Year's celebration, but in a much smaller, less excited voice. And Phil couldn't help but feel a pinch of disappointment, that she might be an unwelcome intrusion into their enthusiasms.

"Well, I think that is definitely an event not to be missed. But now . . ." Phil reached for another paper and began to peruse it for more recent news.

"Still no word of Tommy Green's demise," she said, when Preswick returned a few minutes later, rolling a cart of covered dishes.

She folded the paper and moved it to the side, only to see another headline about the Black Hand.

"Though there is more of this Black Hand business. What do you know about them, Preswick?"

"Only what I read in the papers, my lady. They're thugs who extort money from the Italian community, through threats and sometimes violence."

"Well, these Black Hands just bombed a grocery store not far away from the Theatre Unique. It says they didn't do much damage. In fact they seem peculiarly inept."

"I believe the point is to frighten people into paying so they won't do it again."

"Despicable," Phil said. "And is it really some widespread diabolical crime organization?"

"No one seems to know for certain, my lady."

"So why would they kill a journalist who was investigating them? You would think they'd welcome the publicity. A chance to further people's fear without them having to do anything at all."

"I suppose one might look at it that way."

"Well," she said, pushing the paper completely aside to make room for a plate of eggs, baked tomatoes, and toast, which, like all their food, appeared miraculously, and piping hot, via a dumbwaiter from the basement, where the Plaza engaged an exceptional chef in Monsieur Lapparraque.

"I think today we must attempt to talk to this Harriet Wells."

"Shall I telephone to the *Times* for you, my lady?"

"I think not, Preswick. I don't want to show my face at the *Times* offices. They will recognize me from yesterday and wonder what I want. And if I mention Harriet by name, I might be putting her in danger.

"You and Lily will accompany me there this morning, both of you dressed as you were yesterday, which I must say was an excellent disguise. Lily, you will go up to the seventeenth floor—the elevator is rather daunting, but my faith is in you.

"You'll go up to the news floor, and ask for her. If she is there, tell her you have some news to her advantage if she will accompany you downstairs or meet at an appointed time, but try to get her to go with you. She may not have returned to work. In which case you'll have to find out a way to get her direction."

Phil stopped for breath and a plan. "A relative. Say you're her . . . not a sister. She has red hair and freckles, so 'sister' wouldn't work."

"Cousin," Lily offered.

"Distant cousin," Preswick added.

"You're her distant cousin from out of town. And you were supposed to meet her at the paper. Insist that they give you her address. Take her a basket of homemade cakes or something that you promised to bring her. Don't take no for an answer.

"Preswick, do you think the Plaza kitchen can accommodate us with some homemade treats?"

"Yes, my lady, I'll call down. Monsieur Lapparraque would do anything for you."

"Well, that is gratifying to know. Lily, are you up for the task?"

"Of course . . . my lady." Lily dropped a well-rehearsed curtsey as an afterthought.

"Excellent. Then let us proceed to our toilettes and meet in the parlor in one half hour."

Lily didn't move but stood at the table biting her lip. "Shall I dress you first, my lady?"

"Oh yes, please. Something simple."

Phil, wearing a walking dress of russet merino wool, was waiting in the parlor for Preswick and Lily when they appeared in their day-off clothes. She'd spent the time thinking of ways to engage Harriet Wells without frightening her or making her defensive. Though that was something you really couldn't plan in advance. The interrogation of witnesses, she'd learned, hardly ever proceeded to plan.

Still, it was good to be prepared with several options.

They took a taxi to Times Square.

"I'm wondering if we wouldn't do well to buy an automobile," Phil said as they waited in traffic as it slowed around Columbus Circle.

"Whatever you think best, my lady," said Preswick, waving away a boy selling whistles who had taken advantage of the traffic jam to stick his wares in the window.

"Yes, I know, but what do you really think?"

"Well, that it is easier to get around the city with public transportation, but it would be nice for the country."

"And going to parties and the opera," Lily added.

"True, but then we would have to keep a driver. At least hire one when we needed one. Unless you want to learn to drive, Preswick."

"My lady." His voice and expression were pure disinterested butler. Which of course spoke volumes. He didn't know how to drive, wasn't interested in learning, the suggestion of which in England would be paramount to an insult that would require his immediate resignation.

But in this irrational new world, he would do whatever she wished him to do, because he was the family butler and he was totally loyal. Phil hadn't fully appreciated that relationship until she'd come to New York and he had insisted on accompanying her.

"Oh well, perhaps in the spring." They turned down Broadway; Lily craned her neck to see the shop windows. She sucked in her breath as they passed one store where a hundred different dolls were crammed into the display window. And kept looking until she was practically turned around in her seat.

At which point she realized what she was doing and quickly resumed her lady's-maid demeanor.

Would Lily like a doll for Christmas? Surely she was too old for that. Phil tried to remember playing with dolls, but the memory escaped her.

And she was suddenly worried about Lily. What if she was struck dumb with fear during the elevator ride? What if they ran her out of the newsroom, or worse, suspected a scam and called the police?

"Are you sure you want to do this?" Phil asked her as soon as they'd stopped in front of the *Times* building.

"Yes, madam."

Preswick and Phil stood at the door like anxious parents until she was inside. Then they crossed the street to wait.

It seemed an eternity before Phil caught sight of Lily's felt bonnet passing out of the doors of the *Times* building. She still had the basket of hotel treats.

She stopped on the sidewalk and looked around. She looked so small and young and innocent that Phil felt a momentary stab of guilt for using her for such an errand. Then Phil remembered Lily kicking and biting her way to freedom against four customs men, standing up to the meanest cop in Manhattan, the Fireplug, Charles Becker. The reassuring feeling knowing that she kept a sharp stiletto strapped to her ankle and was more than willing to use it.

Preswick had started across the street, and Lily met him halfway. Then they both ran across the street to Phil.

The first thing she said was "I'm glad we don't live that high up."

"We appreciate your bravery, don't we, Mr. Preswick?"

"Indeed we do, my lady."

"Well, she wasn't there. They wouldn't tell me when she would be back. I told them that I had come all the way from Pennsylvania and she'd promised to show me the town. And what was I going to do, I didn't have her address. Then this old beanpole told me they weren't allowed to give out addresses because of people wanting revenge." Lily paused at that. "Do you think that's why that newspaper man was killed, because of revenge?"

"It's possible, I suppose. Then what happened?"

"Then I begged and pleaded and resorted to tears, but he told me I should have better relatives, and walked away. Fortunately, one of the typewriter girls had overheard us, and she called me over. She said he was a heartless old miser and she lived right down the street from Harriet. I was afraid she was going to offer to take my cakes, but she didn't. She wrote the address down on a piece of paper."

Lily handed over a half sheet of paper. "'East Twenty-Ninth Street,'" Phil read. "Let us go see if Harriet Wells is receiving."

Harriet lived in a red-brick, ivy-covered boardinghouse a few doors down from the Martha Washington Hotel for women. The boardinghouse was modest-looking from the outside and guarded on the inside by a massive landlady, who asked a battalion of questions about their identities before agreeing to let Lily and Phil upstairs, though Mr. Preswick was invited to stay behind in the parlor.

"As I don't let any gentlemen up to my girls' rooms, no matter how gentlemanly they might appear." She finished this explanation with a smile and chuckle that made her face wobble and sent Preswick into his most stoic demeanor.

"Room twelve, up two flights and to the right." And Mrs. Mulvaney, as she introduced herself, trundled herself into the parlor to keep Mr. Preswick company.

Lily sputtered out a barely controlled laugh as soon as they were up one flight and had rounded the landing.

"We'll owe him a wonderful tea when we're finished," Phil told her.

They found room twelve at the end of a hall covered by

a shabby carpet runner. Phil knocked. At first there was no sound from inside.

"Drat the girl. I hope she hasn't absconded."

Phil knocked again. Listened. Heard nothing.

"Madam?" Lily said, and stepped in front of the door. She banged on the door. "Harriet, it's me, your cousin from Pennsylvania. Open up. Ma sent goodies."

At first Phil thought nothing was going to happen, then the door opened a crack. "I don't have any cousin from—" That's as far as she got before Lily thrust the basket of treats at her and forced her way through the door.

"Hey," said Harriet.

"Hay is for horses," Lily countered. "My mistress wants to talk to you, so no funny business."

Phil looked to heaven. *Too many dime novels.* But it worked. Harriet looked out the door to the only person left, recognized Phil, and gasped, "You!"

"And you," Phil said, and stepped through the doorway.

Harriet started shaking her head and backed away, just to stumble over Lily's outstretched foot.

While Lily was attempting to keep Harriet from falling, while at the same time trying to save the cakes, Phil closed the door.

Harriet had recovered by then, or nearly recovered. Phil couldn't tell if she was going to fight or flee. So they just stood facing each other for a few long seconds.

Away from the office, Harriet Wells looked even younger. Two braids, which had probably been coiled around her head, hung loose past her shoulders, and escaped tendrils wisped around her face. Her nose and eyes were red from crying, her freckles angry red spots across her cheeks.

Her mouth worked, and she began to cry again. "He's dead. I know he is."

"Yes, my dear, we both know he is."

Lily was quick to provide a hankie from her *valise dramatique,* the bag of necessaries she always traveled with.

Harriet snuffled. "Did you kill him? I won't say anything, I promise."

Phil stared at the girl. She felt Lily move and just managed to stop her with a quick shake of her head. "Don't be absurd. Of course I didn't kill him."

"Then why are you here? Just leave me alone. Nobody but us even knows he's dead. I won't say anything. I promise. Please."

"I'm not going to hurt you. I just want some information. Why don't we sit down and try to figure this out together."

"Why doesn't anyone say something?" Harriet whined from the other side of the handkerchief. "What are they waiting for? Where is he?"

Phil led her over to the sagging iron bed and motioned Lily to bring over the straight chair from the desk for herself. This was not the way any young girl should live. Clean enough, Phil supposed, a small desk and chair set beneath the one window that looked out onto another building, a table big enough for one, and a small boudoir chair that should have been put out in the trash years ago. And toilet down the hall that she probably shared with the rest of the floor.

The price one paid for freedom, Phil supposed. *The price some paid for freedom,* she amended. She had no intention of ever living in one room. The idea was barbaric.

"You were Tommy's typewriter girl," Phil began.

Harriet sniffed and looked over the balled-up handkerchief. "How do you know Tommy? What were you doing there?"

"I don't know Tommy," Phil said. "I was there taking in an afternoon picture show."

The girl looked incredulous, and really, who could blame her? It was a total fabrication.

"I was hoping to catch some scenes from home," Phil extemporized. "It's at Christmastime I miss England most." A total lie. She hadn't thought about merry old England in months. "The holly and the ivy; kissing a beau under a ball of mistletoe." Frankly she'd done more kissing—and what kisses they were—here and without the aid of mistletoe than she had her last year in England. "Sharing a bowl of wassail with friends." Actually she hated the stuff; give her a martini or a pink gin fizz over punch any day. "So I stepped in to catch a glimpse of home."

Lily was staring at her, horrified.

Harriet, dear thing, looked sympathetic. "I miss home, too . . . sometimes. But I came to the city to be a journalist. Not a fat chance. All they want me to do is type."

"But it must be so interesting to read the news first, so to speak. You see it before anyone else except the reporter."

"Do I? Oh, I guess I do."

Oh dear, surely one needed an inquiring mind to be a good journalist. Harriet wasn't proving to be thus equipped. Phil felt Lily growing impatient.

"Mr. Green must have really trusted you to let you see his unpublished notes."

"I guess. Actually it was Sydney who trusted me."

"Sydney?"

"He's one of the news editors. He recognized my worth, he said, and assigned me to Tommy full-time."

"Did he?" Sydney Lord certainly made his presence felt everywhere.

"He said Tommy was the best in the business, knew where to find news, and could get answers from a deaf-mute. And that I could learn a lot about reporting by watching and listening to Tommy work.

"And he was right. A couple of times when Tommy was covering the proceedings at the courthouse, he asked me to come along so I could take 'street notes,' he called them. Learning on the job, like, you know?"

Phil did know—all too well. She, herself, was learning on the job, but without the constant presence of a mentor. "So *you* were at the theater with Tommy?"

Harriet shook her head. "I don't understand. Is that why you came to the *Times*? You came after me? Sydney said not to say anything."

"Sydney knows that Tommy is dead?"

"No. I mean I didn't tell him. I was afraid to tell him. When he assigned me to Tommy, he said to never tell anybody anything but him and Mr. Van Anda. That there were snitches everywhere and that's what got Tommy's last typewriter girl fired."

This was news. "He had one before you?"

"Yes, Daphne. Someone must have leaked information, because Tommy was onto something big, but whoever he was investigating got tipped off and they got away with it. Daphne swore she wasn't the one who blabbed, but they fired her anyway. I can't get fired. I didn't do anything wrong."

"Do you still have Tommy's notes?"

"No. He always took them back as soon as I was finished, the notes and the typed pages." Her eyes narrowed, and she looked from Phil to Lily, who had drifted over to the window and was pretending to look out while sneaking a peak at the papers laid out on Harriet's desk.

"Wait a minute. How did you find me? They're not supposed to give out addresses. How did you even know Tommy was a reporter? Who sent you?"

Phil sighed, growing rapidly annoyed. Surely even a fledgling reporter would have learned to wait for an answer before asking another question. "My friend and I were meeting Marty Rive for lunch when you stepped off the elevator, and I recognized you. And you, I suspect, recognized me."

"What were you doing there?"

"I just told you." Really, if the girl didn't get better interviewing techniques, she'd do best to stick to typing.

"I mean, in the theater."

"I told you that, too. But you still haven't told me why *you* were there. If you didn't accompany him, how did you manage to be there?"

"I don't have to tell you anything."

"No, you don't, but you and I seem to be the only ones who know he's dead. And when the police get involved, we don't want to find ourselves accused of murdering him, do we?"

Harriet's eyes grew so round, Phil feared they might burst.

"I don't understand." Harriet's mouth began to twist again. Phil motioned to Lily for another handkerchief. Lily rolled her eyes and thrust another linen square at Harriet.

"So you were his typewriter girl, and then . . . ," Phil coaxed.

"Then a few weeks ago, he stopped giving me his notes to type. And Sydney said I must have screwed up. But I didn't. Tommy just—clammed up."

"Maybe he was trying to protect you?"

Harriet looked up at that.

"Do you know what he was investigating?" Phil asked.

"The Black Hand violence in the city."

"Do you think the Black Hand killed him?"

Harriet's eyes rounded. "I don't know."

"Did he mention any particular names in his reporting?"

Harriet shook her head. "I don't think so. I can't remember. And Sydney said—"

"Not to talk," Phil finished. "But you'll have to talk to the police and they won't be as nice as I am."

Harriet gasped. "Becker! They'll send Becker. He was there at the theater. I want to go home."

Phil didn't bother to point out she was home, unless she was considering returning to her parents.

"Let's start at the beginning. How did you end up at the theater?"

Harriet looked down at her hands, whose fingers were trying to tie themselves in knots. "I thought Sydney was going to fire me, but he said he'd give me another chance. That I should apologize for whatever I'd done and to show Tommy that I was serious about journalism.

"So I went to apologize, to explain I wasn't the leak, but Tommy was on the telephone. I stepped back behind the filing cabinet, to be polite you know, until he finished.

"I heard him agreeing to meet someone at the Theatre Unique. He was talking low in a real serious voice, so I just stayed still and waited for him to hang up. And I decided to follow him."

Phil was dying to ask her why, but she didn't want to interrupt the girl's narrative.

"So when he left, I said I was going to lunch and I left, too. I thought if I proved that I could follow a lead, he'd see I was serious about reporting and take me back.

"I waited until he got on the train, then I took the next train after his. I'd just arrived when I saw you sitting next to him. I thought he was there to meet you. I crept closer to see what you were up to. Then you touched his shoulder and he fell back and I saw his throat was slit. I think I screamed."

"You did."

"And I ran." She broke down completely. "I didn't know it would be like this," she sobbed through the second hankie.

She was shaking now, possibly from sobbing, possibly from fear, or possibly from putting on a good act.

"And you didn't stop to tell anyone?" Phil asked. "Alert the manager? Sound the alarm in any way?"

"No. Why are you asking me all these questions?"

"I'm just concerned for you. It was just happenstance that we ran into each other at the elevator. Nonetheless, I felt it was my duty to help."

"Why?"

"It isn't every day one sits down next to a dead man. Like Tommy, I was concerned for your safety."

"My safety?"

Phil somehow managed to hold onto her patience. "If I saw you, chances are someone else might have seen you." Phil felt a smidgeon of guilt frightening the girl this way, but really, someone should. She was ripe for the picking.

"The killer? You think he may come after me?"

"Possibly. Do you know who *he* is?"

Harriet shook her head so vehemently that her braids swung out like a whirligig.

"You saw nothing?"

"No. I ran across the street and hid just inside the door to the Academy of Music. But I couldn't just leave him there, but then I saw Becker arrive. He shouldn't be down here. His beat is the Tenderloin."

Phil nodded. She'd thought the same thing.

"Why doesn't anyone know? I thought that policeman who came yesterday was there to tell Mr. Van Anda that Tommy was dead. But he didn't. Or else Mr. Van Anda decided to keep it a secret. It doesn't make sense. Why would he do that?"

Phil had no idea, but she knew someone who might.

But did she dare call on the one honest policeman she'd met in her brief time in Manhattan? Would Atkins tell her why he'd been at the *Times* building? He, like Becker, had been out of his normal jurisdiction. Perhaps as a personal favor to the editor?

"Did you see anything, anyone who looked suspicious?"

"Just Sergeant Becker, and I knew I'd be in big trouble if he saw me. We all steer clear of him. He's horrible: he extorts money from everybody, does Tammany's dirty work. I hate him. I didn't know it would be like this."

Phil glanced at Lily, whose eyes had rolled so far back in her head that it would have been comical if Harriet hadn't been in such distress. Phil was loathe to admit it, but the best thing Harriet Wells could do was go back home. But Phil wasn't one to break another's spirit.

Phil patted her hand. "Perhaps you should consider taking some time off to visit your family."

"I can't. I won't."

"That's your decision to make, but if you need our assistance, you can find me at the Plaza Hotel." Phil stood.

Harriet fell across the bed sobbing.

Lily was already heading toward the door.

Phil followed but turned back. "Do you know where Tommy lives?"

Harriet sat up. "No. Why should I?"

"I just thought you might have had reason to go there, to drop off notes, to pick them up."

"I didn't. That would be fraternizing. The paper doesn't allow it."

Lily opened her mouth and Phil nudged her toward the door.

"We'll be going now. Good day."

"Stupid girl," Lily said as they climbed down the stairs to the first floor. "She acts like a child, a stupid child."

"Thank you for your opinion. She was rather silly, but I think she's also quite frightened. We should try to have a little understanding."

"Bah," Lily said, and put an end to the subject.

Preswick was sitting bolt upright in a straight-backed chair while Mrs. Mulvaney chattered away. He shot to his feet as Phil and Lily walked into the small parlor.

"Ah, thank you, Mrs. Mulvaney, for entertaining our friend while we were upstairs. Now, we really must be going."

Preswick nodded stiffly and bolted for the door.

"A singular waste of time," Phil said as the three of them walked toward the corner in search of the nearest taxi stand. "The poor girl doesn't seem capable of putting an intelligible sentence together."

But she had managed to learn how to lie.

9

"She's lying," Lily said as they walked down the sidewalk away from Harriet's boardinghouse.

"Most definitely," Phil said. "Lying and frightened. I think it would behoove us to find a nice spot out of the way, say, at the window of that luncheon place over there, from which to watch the street. Perhaps we've inspired Harriet to seek counsel with someone else. She seemed about to succumb to her fear."

They had just sat down at a table in the small restaurant when Lily looked up. "There she goes."

Apologizing to the waiter, they hurried out onto the street in time to see Harriet running toward the corner.

They stayed well behind, though Lily was impatient and ran ahead, moving in and out of shadows and trash receptacles and buildings in a way that ran a chill up Phil's spine.

Phil tried not to think too much about where her young protégée had learned those skills, but she was glad she had, because when Phil and Preswick reached the corner, Lily pointed to a taxi pulling away from the curb a half-block away.

"Rattled enough to take a taxi on her salary. Hurry," Phil said, and the three of them ran to the next taxi in line, edging out a businessman who cursed as they closed the taxi door in his face.

"Follow that taxi," Phil ordered.

The taxi driver turned around, surprised, but his expression turned to satisfaction when Preswick produced a bill and handed it to him. The taxi took off so fast that Phil fell backward against the seat.

They drove south, Phil, Preswick, and Lily all leaning forward, keeping Harriet's taxi in sight.

Phil was beginning to think the girl was leading them on a wild-goose chase when the taxi ahead of them passed Union Square and turned left on Fourteenth Street, past the Theatre Unique. It turned right, and Phil pointed out the Cavalier Club, looking very different in the daylight, and the boarded-over storefront across the street, looking much worse as the full extent of its damage was displayed.

Harriet's taxi slowed and turned left onto Thirteenth Street.

They turned after it. There was another boarded storefront on their right.

Farther down, Harriet's taxi came to a full stop, and Harriet jumped out and raced out of sight.

The taxi drove off, and Phil's taxi replaced it. While Preswick paid the fare, Phil and Lily looked for any sign of Harriet.

"Where did she go?" Lily asked, turning in a full circle on the sidewalk.

Phil shook her head. "I'm certain she got out here."

They were standing in front of a three-story red-brick row house.

Preswick climbed the steps.

"What are we looking for?" Lily asked, nearly treading on his heels.

"A clue, Lily, to whomever Harriet is visiting," Preswick said patiently.

They followed him into a dark vestibule. The light was broken, and he had to strike a sulfur match to read the names and apartment numbers.

Phil was hardly surprised to see T. GREEN printed on one of the tenant mailboxes. Harriet had definitely lied. She knew where Tommy lived and she'd hurried here. To do what?

Preswick blew out the match, took a moment to let the

match cool, then slipped it into his handkerchief. The three of them had studied Dr. Locard's theory that a person always left evidence to his identity wherever he went, including criminals . . . and investigators. They were always very careful not to leave anything obvious behind.

"Two B. It must be this one down the steps." Preswick took hold of the wrought-iron rail and started down into the stairwell just as the door opened and an old man stepped out.

"Whatcha want?"

Preswick stepped back. "I beg your pardon, sir, I was looking for Mr. Green's flat. I have something he wished to see and was told he lived here."

The old man peered from Preswick to Lily and Phil.

He let out a rusty cackle. "This is the first time I ever saw girls come his way. Keeps to himself, he does. Works long hours. I never heard tell of him bringing any women here. Get on now."

"I beg your pardon. These ladies are—"

"It's his birthday," Phil said. "You wouldn't want to spoil his birthday, would you?"

"His birthday, huh? Guess I wouldn't want to spoil that. His place is round back. You gotta go down to the alley to the back. It's the black door, Two B." He slammed the door closed, scurried past Preswick, and shuffled off down the street.

They turned in the opposite direction. Suddenly suspicious, Phil turned around: the old man was still making his way down the sidewalk.

Shaking off that all-too-familiar feeling that things weren't always what they appeared, Phil hurried after Lily and Preswick.

They ducked into the narrow gap between two houses, picking their way carefully over the broken pavement until they came to a cleared area in back that must have been used for storage and dirt closets during the last century.

As they approached 2B Preswick held out his arm, stopping Phil and Lily. He crept forward to a narrow door painted black with a small window secured by bars. *More like a jail than an apartment,* Phil thought in a moment of compassion for the lonely life Tommy Green must have lived.

There was a light on inside, which Phil had expected.

Preswick cupped his hands in an effort to see through the dingy window, then carefully tried the door. "Locked," he mouthed. Lily reached into her pocket and shooed him out of the way, then, lifting her skirts, knelt down to pick the lock.

But even after the click that meant the door was unlocked, Preswick held them back as he slowly opened the door.

Harriet Wells was standing with her back to them. She was surrounded by what had once been the tenant's possessions but was now just a jumbled mess of broken picture frames, torn papers, and cans and jars of food, some broken and spilling their contents onto the threadbare carpet.

Harriet started and whirled around. "You followed me."

Comment seemed superfluous, so Phil held her tongue.

Lily gave the girl her disgusted eye roll and began looking around.

Preswick closed the door.

"I take it you didn't do this," Phil said.

"Of course not. Someone has already been here. Those hyenas." Harriet began to pick up cans and books at random and put them on the rectangular table that appeared to serve as both desk and dining table.

"Wait!" Phil ordered.

"Why?"

"Do you know who did this?"

Harriet shook her head.

"Well, there might be clues that will tell us who did."

Harriet took a step back. "Oh."

"If you didn't tromp all over them already," Lily groused. "Go stand over there, out of the way."

"You can't tell me what to do."

"Ladies," Phil said. "This is not the time."

"I was just looking for his briefcase or . . . I thought maybe . . ."

"All in good time. How did you get in?"

"The door was unlocked."

"Did the mail boy, Eddie, have a key?"

"No," Harriet said indignantly. "Anyway, Eddie wouldn't do this. Besides . . ." She paused. "He said the door was locked."

"Then how did you get in?"

"It wasn't locked. I—I locked myself in."

So this could have been done anytime and there was no way to know. If Eddie was telling the truth.

Preswick had moved back to the door to look for signs of forcible entry. He stood up and shook his head. Lily systematically began peeling back the blankets and sheets and checking under the mattress of the narrow iron bed. Phil went to the table and began to riffle through a stack of paper, half of which had fallen to the floor.

Preswick perused the walls, three of which were unfinished red brick and the fourth plaster. Anything that had been hanging there before was now on the floor. Still, he checked for loose bricks that might be used as hiding places.

It was slow going, since their winter gloves were thicker than the butler's gloves they usually wore for just such circumstances. But gloves wouldn't leave prints and they kept their fingers warm. The only heat in Tommy's bedsit was a small radiator in the corner of the room.

Preswick peered behind it, reached beneath it, came up empty-handed.

Phil picked up a picture frame that had broken on the floor. She turned it over. Saw the grainy photograph of a young girl accepting a trophy from a bald dignitary wearing an old-fashioned three-piece suit. It seemed an oddly sentimental thing for a seasoned reporter to have.

Phil knew better than to remove evidence from a crime

scene, but as far as she knew, the only crime had been committed at the Theatre Unique.

She turned the frame over, opened up the cardboard backing, slipped the photo out, and slid it into her handbag. A quick look around the room revealed several other photos smashed on the floor.

Phil quickly picked them up and relieved the frames of their occupants. She would have to study them in better light and without Harriet looking on.

Preswick searched the drawers of the dresser, rummaged through the items on top, and slipped something small into his pocket. Lily had finished her search and turned back with empty open palms.

Phil looked around. No briefcase.

Harriet was still standing in the same place, picking up cans of food and putting them back in the cupboard.

Phil picked her way across the room to a small sink. Above it, a narrow wooden shelf held a mug with a toothbrush and powder and a safety razor and a jar of shaving cream.

Phil turned away, turned back, as a memory of catching a particularly nosy governess reading her diary rose in her mind. She'd consequently begun hiding her key in the one place that lady wouldn't think of looking: her freckles cream. The trick had carried over to Madame Floret's finishing *école,* where the *jeune filles* had hidden small contraband in their jars of cold cream.

What would prevent a journalist from using the same technique? She took the opaque jar off the shelf, twisted open the top, and peered inside. Almost full, smooth across the top, not like it would normally be after someone scooped out a shave's worth.

It was worth a try. Making sure that Harriet was occupied, Phil jabbed her finger into the cream and hit something that shouldn't be there.

She hooked her finger around it and pulled it out of the

jar. A quick wipe on a not-too-clean face towel draped on the side of the sink showed her exactly what she'd been expecting.

A key.

It was too small for a door but too large for a diary. She slid the key into her pocket.

"Harriet, you said Tommy had a briefcase."

"Yeah. An old beat-up one."

So where was the briefcase?

They'd looked under the bed, under the carpet for loose floorboards, checked the small closet, took a look into a small bathroom, evidently shared with the front apartment, and found nothing more.

"We should be leaving, my lady."

"You're absolutely right, Preswick." The key to investigation was to never take longer than you needed. Less time to leave your own evidence and less time to get caught.

Phil insisted on dropping Harriet off at her boardinghouse. There was nothing she could do to prevent the girl from acting irresponsibly once she was back at her lodgings, but they could at least see her home safely.

Harriet was eighteen, if she was telling the truth. At her age, Phil had been married for a year and had already learned that fate had no happy life in store for her and the earl.

As they reached Harriet's boardinghouse, Phil noticed a man huddled on the stoop. Phil grasped Harriet's arm. "Do you recognize him, or shall I have the taxi drive on?"

"I'm not afraid of them." The quiver in her voice said otherwise.

"Well, you should be."

Harriet peered out the side of the taxi. "Oh," she said with relief that quickly changed to annoyance. "What's *he* doing here?" She turned to Phil. "It's all right. It's Eddie from the mail room. He keeps asking me to go to tea. He just won't take no for an answer. He's such a boy."

"Well, don't confide in him—or anyone else," Phil said.

"In Eddie? He only works in the mail room."

"That we know of." Really, Phil couldn't think of a profession Harriet was more ill-equipped to pursue than journalism. "Just stay mum with everyone. Everyone. Understand?"

"Yes, everyone, but what do we do next?"

Phil just managed not to grit her teeth. "You will return to work, mind your own business, trust no one, and leave a message with the hotel concierge if you have news to tell. The less you are seen in my company, the safer you'll be."

"But—"

"We will find the murderer sooner if you just do your part. We . . . uh . . . need an inside man at the paper."

Harriet nodded. "Oh."

The taxi stopped.

"Is it safe to leave you alone with him?"

"Oh sure, he's harmless . . . and awkward and not terribly bright, but he's loyal, I guess that's something."

Phil could have told Harriet that loyalty was everything, but she just wanted to be rid of the girl.

Harriet got out of the taxi, and Eddie stood up. Tall and lanky, swimming in a heavy tweed coat, he snatched off his cap when Harriet got to the steps, and he followed her inside.

"She is such a ninny," Lily said.

"I'm afraid you're right," Phil said. "Now, if she can just stay out of trouble until we solve this case . . ."

10

When they returned to the Plaza, Phil took a moment to peruse the street, a habit she'd adopted while attempting to identify the illusive Mr. X.

There were a few of the usual shoeshine boys, most of whom were grown men, though the majority of them had found warmer places to ply their trade. Not even the most meticulous businessman wanted to stand in the biting cold to have his shoes shined.

Just a Friend was in his place at the entrance of the park. A Christmas-tree vendor had set up business along the sidewalk across the street from the hotel.

Phil and Lily both looked longingly at the trees and wreaths lit by a row of lanterns along the pavement, but Phil said, "First things first," and they went inside.

Egbert greeted them with a smile and a word of advice. "If you're planning on buying a tree for your apartment, I have a cousin who can get you a much better price than that guy on the sidewalk. They always run up the prices because of our clientele being rich and able to afford more. And he'll deliver it to your apartment, no extra charge."

"Excellent," Phil said.

When she and Lily stepped out of the elevator on the fifth floor, Preswick stayed behind to seal the deal.

* * *

Phil and Lily were in the study setting up at the table with note-books, notes, pencils, and the contents of Tommy Green's pockets spread out before them when they heard Preswick return.

A few minutes later, he took his place at the study table. "I took the liberty of ordering tea, and arranged for them to bring the tree day after tomorrow."

"Is it going to be a big one?" Lily asked, obviously unable to contain her enthusiasm.

He raised an eyebrow at her. "Very large," he intoned.

"Well, we'll have to shop for decorations and lights. Lots of lights," Phil said before Lily could risk Preswick's censure by suggesting the same. He had infinite patience with his protégée except when she began to "forget her place."

Actually, Phil was inclined to forget both their places, but she knew it would never do to ask Preswick not to be a butler. Thus far they had learned to live in a kind of no-man's-land where they crossed borders when necessary and returned to the established order when they could.

It wasn't easy, not knowing exactly where your place in the world was. Though easier for Phil, she supposed, than for her servants.

She planned to continue to maneuver her way through Manhattan society as best she could while she secretly investigated murder. If ever she had to choose between society and investigation, she thought she knew what her choice would be. But could she ask Preswick and Lily to make the same choice?

She rubbed her hands, rubbing away the thought. "Well. First order of business is to organize what we have so far."

She pulled over a side table where she'd arranged the several photographs she'd taken from Tommy Green's apartment and placed the key beside them.

Preswick reached in his trouser pocket and added a matchbox to the rest. A black matchbox with a red rose on the top.

"Ah," Phil said, eyeing the matchbox. "We know Tommy

was investigating the bombings and arsons allegedly perpetrated by the Black Hand. We know that Mr. X, for lack of a better sobriquet, sent me to meet him because he was supposed to have information."

"On the Black Hand?" Lily asked.

"Mr. X made a surprise appearance outside the club last night. Only long enough to say that Tommy didn't specify what the information was. Though it's obvious it was important enough to send someone—me, as it turned out—to make the exchange.

"We also know that Mr. X, as a rule, isn't very concerned with murder per se, which does give one pause, but I think he is after larger game. Which makes me think that whomever he—we—are working for is a large organization in itself. They may be more interested in bringing down the Black Hand than solving an individual murder. Though evidently they hadn't been expecting Tommy to be murdered.

"He told me to stand down. I, however, feel it's our duty to bring the man—or woman, I suppose—who murdered Tommy Green to justice. Do we agree?"

Lily nodded vigorously. "Yes, we do."

Preswick gave an assenting nod.

"Very well. Tommy Green. A journalist investigating the Black Hand's activities in the Union Square area, killed in a nickelodeon in the same area," Phil said as Lily wrote.

"And perhaps coincidently," said Preswick, "the area of Tammany Hall."

"Indeed," Phil said. "We have a murder scene, Black Hand activity, and Tammany Hall all in the same area. Coincidence or related?"

"I should point out, my lady, that though there has been an uptick in Black Hand activity, they have not targeted that area exclusively."

"True. But something had caught Tommy's reporter's zeal. Something that got him killed. And then led someone to search his lodgings."

Phil paused to rearrange the photos she'd taken from Tommy's apartment. "These had been thrown on the floor."

The three of them took a moment to study the photos.

"Possibly taken from events he covered?" Preswick conjectured.

"A children's award ceremony, a group of young women, some kind of ground-breaking ceremony. I think you're right." Phil gathered them up and moved them out of the way.

"And this key." Phil took it from the side table and placed it on the table. "Hidden in a jar of shaving cream."

Lily and Preswick both leaned in to study it.

The sight of them, heads together, Lily's dark coiled braids and the wisps of white over Preswick's shiny pate, made Phil feel of a sudden all . . . Christmassy.

"Too small for a door and too large for a diary," Phil said, trying to recollect her investigative thoughts.

Preswick picked it up, turned it over. "A trunk, perhaps."

"Or a briefcase," added Phil. "Harriet said he had a briefcase." She looked from Preswick to Lily. "There was no trunk or briefcase in his apartment."

"Perhaps he had a storage area somewhere else in the house," Preswick said.

"Or the police could have taken it away," Lily suggested.

"Possibly. I wonder if they were there before or after the break-in."

"Or if they were the ones who 'tossed' the place." Lily grinned. "I learned that word from a book I'm reading."

"I hope you're interspersing your dime-novel enthusiasm with some useful literature."

Lily nodded. "Mr. Preswick insists." And she smiled at him so devilishly innocent that Phil had to smother an answering grin.

"It certainly does look like the work of Sergeant Becker and his men," Preswick said. "As I have had occasion to know, they have no respect for a person's property."

"True. If he had no compunction about ransacking the Reynoldses' brownstone, he would certainly not draw the line at a hardworking journalist's apartment."

Lily frowned down at the key. "Why would the police want to search Mr. Green's rooms at all? He wasn't killed there. It doesn't make sense."

"No, it doesn't, especially since they hardly bothered securing the crime scene before they hauled the body away . . . unless they were looking for something else."

"Something they wanted," Preswick said. "Or wanted to suppress."

"Exactly," Phil agreed. "Something they didn't want found by anyone else. Something that Tommy Green knew or had found out. Why else send Becker to the crime scene?"

"And if they found the briefcase, we'll never know what he wanted to tell us," Lily said.

"Perhaps," said Preswick, "but would Mr. Green keep the briefcase and the key to it in the same place? His name was on the mailbox. His residence was no secret."

"You think he kept the briefcase at a different location?" Phil asked.

"Wouldn't you, my lady?"

"Yes, of course. So let us proceed with the possibility that finding the briefcase is still within our purview."

"And this," Preswick said, pushing the matchbox next to the key. "Black with a single red rose on the top. It was the only one of its kind that I found in the apartment. But it is the same as the one you found in his pocket."

"Sydney Lord, an editor at the *Times,* had one like it at the Cavalier Club," Phil said. "But they don't belong to the Cavalier Club; the club's matchboxes are initialed in gold. But some other establishment. Usually matchboxes have the name of the company or advertising of some sort, do they not?"

"Yes, my lady."

"But there's no name on these, like Rose Mechanics, or Flower's Pharmacy?"

"No, my lady. But I will endeavor to research the subject."

"Yes, please do that."

"And what shall I do?" Lily asked.

"You will help Mr. Preswick. It may lead to nothing, but we'll leave no . . . matchbox unturned."

The doorbell rang.

"Ah, dinner," Phil said as Preswick went to answer the door. He returned with Lorenzo, the fifth floor's resident waiter, pushing a trolley with several covered dishes.

"I thought something more substantial than sandwiches would be in order," Preswick informed her.

Lorenzo lifted the lid from a steaming dish.

"Roast beef," said Phil, inhaling deeply.

"And pudding," Preswick added.

"Heaven, so much better than sandwiches. Just put it here, Lorenzo." Phil gathered up their papers; there was nothing here that wouldn't wait. As she handed them to Preswick for removal, the matchbox slid to the floor.

Lorenzo bent down to retrieve it. He held it out for Preswick, but Preswick had turned away. Lorenzo looked at it, his eyes widened, and he closed his fingers over it.

"What is it, Lorenzo?"

"Nothing, Lady Dunbridge." He slid the matchbox behind his back.

"Well, it must be something."

"Is there a problem with the dinner, my lady?"

"No, but Lorenzo seems to be concerned about the matchbox we found. It slid to the floor when I handed you the rest of our papers."

She didn't miss the urgent look Lorenzo cast Preswick before he reluctantly handed it over.

Preswick considered the matchbox. "Do you happen to recognize this?"

Lorenzo's head ticked left. "I couldn't say, sir."

"No?" asked Phil. "We just found it and think it's lovely. I'm thinking about ordering some to put out for the husbands of my guests when they feel the need of a cigar."

"Oh no, you couldn't do that, madam."

"There's no rule against smoking at the Plaza . . . except the one forbidding ladies to smoke in the tearoom."

Slashes of color sprang to Lorenzo's cheeks. "Mr. Preswick?" Lorenzo's head ticked left again, this time ear to shoulder.

Preswick took the hint, bowed slightly to Phil, and accompanied the waiter out of the room.

"What's going on?" Lily asked.

"I have no idea, except there is some reason he doesn't want to identify the matchbox in front of me."

"Because you're a lady."

"Perhaps. But Preswick shall soon put him to rights."

They returned, Preswick practically herding Lorenzo, head bent, back into the room. They were both wearing faint color across their cheeks. "I've explained to Lorenzo that we found this matchbox while we were out and thought it interesting. It has a rather unusual provenance."

That earned a frown from Lorenzo.

"Where it came from," Preswick explained. "Could you please enlighten her ladyship? She is not so squeamish as you might think."

Lorenzo licked his lips. "I've never been there myself. But I've seen this same matchbox at my uncle Carlo's flat. My uncle Carlo is a bit of a black sheep."

"Yes?" Phil encouraged.

"He likes the ladies. He goes to a . . . How do you call . . . ? A . . . A . . ."

"House of ill repute?"

He coughed. "No, not that, but a very nice . . ."

"An exclusive brothel."

He let out his breath. "Yes, that is it. This is the sign of a certain establishment."

"Do you know its name?"

"No."

Phil permitted herself a sigh of disappointment. "Thank you very much, Lorenzo. Needless to say, I won't be ordering these for my parlor."

Lorenzo bowed. "Will there be anything else? Shall I serve?"

"That won't be necessary. It looks wonderful."

Lorenzo bowed himself out the door. Phil made a mental note to give him an extra generous Christmas tip.

"Well, that was like pulling teeth," Phil said as Preswick set food before them. "Preswick, are you blushing?"

"No, my lady."

"What is it then? Come now, fess up."

Preswick cleared his throat. "He thought it belonged to me."

Lily gasped.

Phil blinked, stared Lily into silence. If Lorenzo thought that her septuagenarian butler would frequent such places, well, good for him—and good for Preswick.

"Well, I suppose this will lead to another dead end, but do you think you could find out more about this place? I'm sure Mr. Holmes would not ignore it as a possible clue.

"Now, sit down and let's enjoy the lovely repast. It looks delicious."

They had photographs of an unknown woman, a key, and a brothel matchbox. *Not much to go on,* Phil thought as she bit into a succulent piece of beef.

There was one person she might finagle information from. He wouldn't like it, but needs must. . . .

As soon as dinner was over, Phil pushed her chair away and went to the telephone, gave the number for the nineteenth precinct, and asked for Detective Sergeant Atkins. It was a little late, but policemen didn't keep storekeeper's hours.

"I'm not sure he's still at the station, ma'am."

"Tell him that Lady Dunbridge would like to speak with him. Thank you, Sergeant. I'll wait."

It was a rather long wait, but at last, Atkins came on the line. "Lady Dunbridge."

"You sound rather wary, Detective Sergeant."

"Let's just say that though I always delight in hearing from you, you always manage to surprise me. What is it this time?"

"I thought you might join me in a carriage ride tomorrow morning."

A long silence, and she couldn't help but feel a soupçon of delight, because she knew he was trying to figure out what she was up to and how to beat her at her own game.

Really, men could be so amusing if they would only exert themselves.

When he continued to stay silent, she added, "The park is so enjoyable this—"

"Lady Dunbridge," he interrupted. "I'd be delighted."

"Excellent. Shall we say ten o'clock?"

"Yes, I'll see you then. Goodbye." And he hung up.

Interesting. He wasn't normally so abrupt. Perhaps she shouldn't have called him at the station, but really, how was anything to get done when there was no way to talk to people except the obvious?

She went back into the parlor, where Lily was listening openmouthed to Preswick read aloud from the *New York World,* a sensationalist newspaper whose facts weren't always correct and many times were not even facts.

"I have a rendezvous in the park with Detective Sergeant Atkins tomorrow morning. If anyone knows the dealings of an illegal operation, it will be he. I'll need something appropriate for a carriage ride through Central Park."

11

At five minutes to ten the next morning, Phil stepped out of the Plaza Hotel wearing a gored wool skirt of large red-and-black plaids and an emerald-green cashmere jumper in honor of the season. And with her fur-lined black carriage cape and matching muff, and a Russian sable hat to keep her ears warm, she was feeling quite up to facing the cold—and the detective sergeant.

Just a Friend stood in his normal place, a bundle of papers held safely under one arm while he hawked a single edition with the other. He was wearing a new scarf.

"Good morning, Just a Friend."

"'Morning, miss. He's over by that carriage waiting for you. I told him who was the best driver, and he takes good care of his horses, too. Not like some I could name."

"Why, thank you, Just a Friend. I can always depend on you for the best advice."

She handed him a penny; she had learned to always keep one handy for just this purpose. Even though she knew her largesse probably got stolen from him by larger boys or men or the shadowy Clancy, she wanted to do her part for him to have a little extra to eat.

"Don't you get too friendly with no copper, miss, can't trust them. Not even him. They'll lock you up for nothin' if they have a mind to."

She didn't doubt it, if you were poor or homeless or had no one to advocate for you.

"They'll do it." He nodded sharply. "You have any trouble with him, you yell and I'll come running."

"Thank you, Just a Friend, and if *you* have any trouble with the coppers, you yell to me, and *I'll* come running."

He grinned, crumpled his free paper under his arm with the others long enough to touch his cap to her—and then dropped the penny into it, before returning the hat to his head.

The detective sergeant was standing on the sidewalk close to a carriage drawn by an old but well-groomed chestnut, which formed a convenient barricade from curious eyes. Though he hadn't taken into account the sidewalk traffic; two ladies in full-length coats and enormous muffs tittered as they passed.

He looked up to find Phil grinning at him. Well, really the man was oblivious to his own charms, a rare and endearing quality.

"I'm so glad you could make it," she said, holding out her hand as she came to meet him.

"How could I resist?" He helped her into the carriage, arranged the blanket over them both, and signaled the driver to drive on.

They turned immediately into the open plaza that led to the drive through the park. The trees were bare and their branches captured the sky like filigree over aquamarine. They drove past the pond and the bench where Phil and Atkins had met several times to discuss information during other cases.

She shivered. She might never see this end of the park in the same way ever again.

"Too cold?"

"Not at all."

They were one of the few carriages in sight and had only gone a hundred feet into the park when the detective sergeant called out to the driver. "Hold up for one second, please."

The driver reined in his horse. "Anything wrong, sir?"

"No, we just seem to have picked up an extra passenger."

Atkins pushed the lap blanket away and leaned over the back of the carriage, reemerging a moment later with a twisting, struggling being.

Phil recognized the cap immediately, then the grinning visage of Just a Friend.

"I'll get rid of him, sir," the driver said, and put on the brake.

"That won't be necessary," Atkins said. "We're acquaintances of this inventive lad."

The driver tapped the brim of his top hat, which had a sprig of holly tucked in the band, and pulled his coat tighter to wait.

"Now, my young jackanapes," Atkins said, holding onto the boy's coat collar, "I don't believe we're in need of your chaperonage this morning."

"Gorn, what's that?"

"Something we don't need."

Just a Friend screwed up his face, showing his displeasure in lieu of his fists, which were busy keeping him attached to the side of the carriage.

"Where did you leave your papers? Somebody's bound to steal them while you're dallying your morning away on a carriage ride through the park, and then you'll catch hell."

"No, I won't, cuz I got 'em right here." He let go of the carriage to reach into his jacket.

Atkins just managed to save him from a nasty fall.

"Well, get along anyways. Or *I'm* going to give you what for."

"If I gotta. But don't think that means you can go and take advantage of the lady."

Atkins laughed, a sound that always gave Phil hope for the inner man. "I rather think that it will be the other way around, but I promise to return us both to the entrance unharmed."

Just a Friend glanced at Phil.

"I'll be fine," she said. "But thank you for your quick action for my safety."

"You sure? He ain't put the screws to you or anything?"

"I'm sure, and he's been a perfect gentleman," Phil assured him.

"Okay, then. But you—" He freed one hand from the carriage long enough to shake a finger at Atkins, and this time Atkins let him slide to the ground.

He landed on his rear end. Fortunately, the coat Preswick had purchased for him was very padded.

He scrambled to his feet, frowning fiercely at the detective sergeant.

Atkins reached in his trouser pocket and flipped the boy a coin. Just a Friend snatched it out of the air, and it disappeared into his cap to keep Phil's penny company.

"You mind your manners," he said, and scampered back toward the park entrance.

Atkins settled back in his seat. "Drive on."

The carriage jolted forward, and Phil burst out laughing.

All vestiges of the smile he'd been fighting disappeared. "You do realize that as insinuating as the little scamp might appear, you can't trust him."

That sobered her quickly enough. "Why can't I?"

"Do I really need to explain it to you?"

"No. But I think you're wrong about Just a Friend. He has a mission to protect me."

"Why?"

"You don't think I should be protected?"

"Not by a boy. And quite frankly I can't think of anyone less in need of protecting than you."

"Why, thank you, Detective Sergeant. You do say the kindest things."

"So, why have I been summoned to this 'delightful' outing?"

Phil sighed. "Because I fancied a drive in the park with a charming companion?"

"Spare me the sarcasm and tell me the real reason."

Phil glanced at the driver. The carriage made a turn, and

Phil moved closer to the detective sergeant. It was a calculated move both to prevent the driver from overhearing anything they might say and, she had to admit, to take advantage of the coziness beneath the carriage blanket. With their heads bent toward each other, they surely looked like lovers out for a morning rendezvous.

And it was tempting. Unfortunately, he was a gentleman in all ways.

Or perhaps there were other reasons for his reticence. Reasons she'd considered before but had never asked. She knew he had no wife, that his mother was dead, and absolutely nothing else about the man. He had to be in his thirties, the perfect age of maturity, that short span of life when boys changed to men and before the men began going to seed. A lover? A mistress? Kept in a little cottage . . .

"Lady Dunbridge."

"Sorry, I was taking a little flight of fancy. Isn't it lovely?"

"If you like bare trees in the freezing cold."

"Do you think it will snow? I think snow at Christmas is so lovely, don't you?"

"I think it's lovely in the country, inconvenient in the city, and I have cases piling up in my absence while we're discussing the weather."

"Then I will get to the point." She reached in her handbag, which now had two additional occupants to her compact, comb, and notebook: her warning from the Black Hand and her pearl-handled derringer.

She handed him the folded note.

He frowned at her but took it and read. It seemed to take forever while the carriage traveled out of the clearing and into the drive through the trees.

Finally he looked up. "Where did you get this?"

"I found it in my pocket after bumping into a man in Union Square."

"Rather far afield from the Plaza."

She didn't answer. She couldn't very well tell him the truth—even if she knew what the truth was—and jeopardize her mission—which she as yet didn't know the purpose of. Really, men could be so selfish.

"You think he bumped into you purposely in order to slip this into your pocket? I must say, Lady Dunbridge, usually it's the other way around."

She raised her eyebrows in question.

"As a rule, they lift things out, not put things in it."

"I know that."

"I'm sorry if he frightened you. But it's probably some practical joke, or possibly you were mistaken for someone else." He stopped, and the look he gave her sent a chill up her spine. "Unless perhaps there's something you want to tell me?"

The carriage slowed, letting another carriage cross in front of them. The horse snorted, shook his head, anxious to stay on the move.

They took the left fork and drove along the green, though today it was a stark blanket of brown grasses punctuated by patches of crusted snow.

"I'm not frightened," Phil said, and belied her statement by pulling the carriage blanket closer. Actually, she was petrified, but if she said that, she'd have to tell him the rest. Though it was becoming apparent, as they reached the inner paths of the park, that she would have to trust him with *some* information if she expected to get any back from him.

"There *is* something I feel I should tell you, but first I need to know why you were at the *Times* building the other day."

"On a personal visit as a favor to the editor."

"About the leak at the paper? Or the whereabouts of Tommy Green?"

He stilled, and for the longest time the only sound was the steady clip-clop of the horse's hooves on the path.

She had his full attention now. It was rather daunting.

Finally he said, "How do you know about either?"

"Well, Marty—Martha Rive, whom you met in the lobby—told Bev and me that Carr Van Anda, the managing editor, was very upset about information being leaked. That he thought that whoever it was might be in cahoots—is that the word?—with one of the rival papers."

She broke off, not quite certain how to proceed without betraying Harriet's trust. "I was wondering if your visit might have anything to do with the story Tommy Green was working on? According to Marty, Van Anda was in an uproar when Tommy didn't show in time for his deadline. Actually, we witnessed a bit of it when we went to pick up Marty. But—"

"Okay, that's it." He turned to her so abruptly that she couldn't evade the hands that grasped her shoulders, turning her to face him. "What do you know about Tommy Green?"

"Nothing, except he was evidently working on an investigation of the recent violence around Union Square."

"So *that's* why you were at the paper, not just to have lunch."

"I was having lunch. You can ask the maître d' at the Knickerbocker café if I need an alibi."

"So how did you end up at Union Square? What have you gotten yourself into?"

"Nothing that I know of." At least nothing that she could name.

"Then why did you say that Green *was* working on—twice."

Phil tried to repress a shudder but didn't quite succeed.

"What do you know?"

She watched a muscle twitch in that wonderfully masculine jaw. It was the kind of thing a woman found intriguing, but today was too cold for that kind of temptation. Besides, she needed answers now.

He dropped his hands. "Since you refuse to answer, I ask myself, How could you possibly go to lunch and end up involved in the machinations of the Black Hand?"

"So it was the Black Hand."

"What was?"

"Have you found Tommy Green?"

"We weren't looking for him." He hesitated. "But we did find him." Again, that hesitation. "Under the docks down at Clarkson Street Pier."

"Clarkson Street Pier? You're sure it was Tommy Green?"

"He was identified by Carr Van Anda. He had no next of kin. It wasn't pretty."

"Now, that's interesting."

"Why?"

Phil took a breath. *In for a penny . . .* "Tommy Green may have been found at the Clarkson docks, but he wasn't killed there. His throat was slashed at the Theatre Unique on Fourteenth Street."

His eyes narrowed and his complexion paled ever so slightly. Not from the cold but from incipient anger. It was another of his fascinating characteristics.

"And furthermore, his body was carried away by the police in a black van. Overseen, I might add, by Charles Becker."

The detective sergeant's sudden intake of breath told all she had feared. Someone was attempting to hide the real circumstances of the murder of Tommy Green. And it included members of the police force. No surprise, since after a short period of reform led by Mr. Roosevelt, the New York Police Department, for the most part, had rapidly and willingly slipped back in its habitual norms of bribes, graft, and corruption.

"Who told you this?"

His voice caught the attention of the driver. "Yes, sir?"

"The lady is cold. I think you can take us back now."

"Yes, sir." He slowed his horse and made the turn, and soon they were trotting back to the park entrance.

"But we're not—"

He leaned into her, his breath warm on her cheek. "Later."

"Why, Detective Sergeant, this sounds promising."

He was not amused.

Atkins had the driver drop them just inside the entrance of

the park, and once the carriage had driven away, he led Phil over the ice-crusted path to a bench by the pond. They had met there a handful of times to exchange information, and Phil only half-jokingly referred to it as "our place."

It was usually secluded by shade trees on three sides and the pond on the other, but today, with the branches bare and the pond frozen over, they seemed singularly exposed.

Though as Atkins was quick to point out, it also gave them the advantage of seeing anyone approach within hearing distance.

"Worried about my reputation . . . or yours?" Phil quipped.

"Both. If people know we meet under whatever guise—"

She barely caught the glint in his eye before it was gone.

"No one will trust us with any information," he finished.

Phil couldn't help but take a quick surreptitious look around. "I did think twice about telephoning you at the station. Perhaps I should have used an alias. Mrs. Dalrymple. I can be one of those terribly clingy clergy wives who always suspects someone is trying to steal her silver."

"You need to be serious for a minute."

"Oh, I assure you, Detective Sergeant, I'm serious. A man was killed because he was in search of the truth. I'm being threatened presumably because I was there, and the nastiest policeman I've ever had the bad fortune to encounter is involved. I'm deadly serious."

"What are you talking about? You were there? You need to tell me exactly what happened."

So she did, very careful to omit certain parts that would surely infuriate him and run her afoul of the police investigation, if there was one. "I went into the theater to watch the afternoon offerings, and sat down next to a man, who, as it turns out, was dead. It was dark, of course, but I managed to see all I needed to see. Someone screamed." She saw no reason to bring in Harriet's presence at this point. And not before consulting with Harriet first, if it couldn't be helped.

"Not you."

"Really, Detective Sergeant, I do my best to remain cool in all circumstances . . . though it was rather gory; the black stain across his chest flickering light and dark as if we were the picture show."

She shuddered, regained her composure when his hand touched her shoulder before quickly moving away. "Someone calling himself the manager whisked me outside through the back door, where I found myself in the alley." She plowed on.

"I made my way back to the street, where I arrived just in time to see Sergeant Becker step out of a black police auto and go inside. Moments later a black van stopped at the curb and took the body away. All in a matter of several minutes. Not enough time to do a creditable scene-of-the-crime investigation, if you ask me."

"What were you doing in the theater?"

"As I said, watching—"

"The moving pictures." He raised a disbelieving eyebrow. "What was your real reason?"

"Really, Detective Sergeant. It was a harmless pastime—or should have been."

"Was the theater crowded?"

"No. I had taken a seat in the back row and could see plenty of empty seats."

"Plenty of seats, and yet you chose to sit next to a stranger who happens to be dead."

"As you say."

"If you'll pardon me for saying so, I don't believe you for a moment."

She smiled at him.

"And what happened when this unknown person screamed?"

"The manager appeared at my elbow and hurried me out the back door."

"Just you? Not the entire house?"

"Just me." She frowned, remembering. "Odd. I thought so

at the time because everyone else was running for the front entrance. But as it turns out, it wasn't the manager at all."

He sat up at this news. "How do you know he wasn't?"

Now came the tricky part: telling him what happened but not saying too much. "Because I asked the manager and it wasn't he."

"Let me get this straight. You sit down next to a murdered man, the manager shows you the back exit, and instead of fleeing, you return to the front of the theater in time to see Becker take the body away, then went back inside to question the manager yourself? Lady Dunbridge, this seems a bit far-fetched, even for you."

Against her will, she winced. "Well, actually, I didn't question the manager until the next day."

"What? Do you have any idea of how dangerous that was?"

"Indeed, but I took Lily and Preswick with me."

"Saints preserve us all," he said. He swiveled to face her, looked her squarely in the face. "Please, for my sanity, if not for your own safety, stay very far away from this. These people are vicious, often incompetent, which only makes things worse. And they are, for some reason, lately emboldened."

"Are you referring to the Black Hand?"

"Exactly how much do you know about the Black Hand?"

"I read the papers, Detective Sergeant. Did they murder Tommy Green? Because he was investigating their increasing attacks in the Union Square area?"

"I don't know how you got yourself involved in this situation, but uninvolve yourself immediately. Don't think that because you're a member of the peerage or live at the Plaza that will protect you. These people are uneducated thugs. They're violent and remorseless."

He stood abruptly. "Now, I must get back to work, and you're going to go back home. Read a magazine, go Christmas shopping, but do not go to Union Square again. They've obviously marked you. Since the note doesn't demand money, we can hope they will let it drop. If. You. Stay. Away. Understand?"

She nodded. And she would take his advice if she could, though at this point, she didn't know how that would be possible.

Phil paused as they passed the carriage they had just ridden in, the chestnut standing placidly by the curb waiting for its next hire. She nodded a friendly thanks to the driver, who looked blankly past her from beneath a slouch hat. Phil looked again. The carriage and horse were the same, but the top hat and holly sprig were gone—and so was their driver.

"He wasn't very happy with me," Phil told Lily and Preswick as she sipped a cup of strong hot coffee. "He told me to stay out of it, for all our safety, and I left him buying a paper from Just a Friend and scowling at the entrance to the Plaza as I crossed the street. And it does seem a rather daunting enemy. A widespread crime organization that operates across the country."

"Yes, my lady," said Preswick. "Though according to Lorenzo, it isn't really an organization but a loosely associated bunch of petty crooks. So you never know who might be waiting for a chance to take advantage of the vulnerable, especially the new arrivals who don't speak the language."

"My goodness, you *are* a storehouse of information."

"Thank you, my lady."

"He warned me off," Phil said.

"And do you intend to be warned off, my lady?"

"How can you be warned off from something when you don't even know what it is you're being warned about? I hate that a man was killed for merely trying to shed light on wrongdoing.

"This seems like a rather broad investigation. Perhaps this is one instance where it's better left to the authorities." She sighed.

"But, madam, why would Mr. X ask you to meet that reporter if he didn't expect you to investigate?"

"I don't think he was planning for it to go that far, Lily."

And the reason she wasn't quite willing to wash her hands of the situation. Why had Mr. X made his presence known but refused to enlighten her on the case? Perhaps because he was just as in the dark as she.

"But now, I'm afraid social duty calls, and I don't dare be late to another meeting of the charity-ball committee. It's the last one. They'll think I'm not a serious philanthropist." Phil raised an eyebrow. "Was that a snort I heard from you, Lily?"

Lily bent into a curtsey so quickly that Phil was afraid the floor had developed a hole beneath her feet. "Oh no, my lady," she said primly. "A well-trained lady's maid doesn't snort."

"Good to know," Phil said, fighting not to laugh out loud. Preswick had turned away and was intently inspecting the mantel top. For dust? Or controlling a similar urge.

They'd certainly come a long way in the last few months, her little family. Certainly more of a family than she'd known in a long time.

"Besides, I'm hoping Marty Rive will be there with some news. And while I'm gone, you two will make a list of all the things we need to have the best Christmas we've ever had. And . . ." *How to put this?* "And we'll enjoy it together on Christmas Day." She hesitated. "Unless you've made other plans."

They both looked at her as if she'd sprouted horns.

She felt an unfamiliar lump tighten her throat. And realized that Lily and Preswick had long ago ceased to be her servants but meant so much more. If she were to lose them, she would be thoroughly undone.

But how did one treat people when they were no longer staff but had become family?

*   *   *

Dressed in a boxed-pleat skirt and matching bolero jacket, and a toque of green felt crowned by a stiff pheasant feather set over a newly coifed bouffant swirl of hair, Phil set forth to the last meeting of the charity-ball committee.

She met two of the members getting out of their carriage, and they all climbed the steps of the Sloane brownstone together. They deposited coats and muffs with a footman, and Tuttle showed them into the parlor, where Mrs. Abernathy, Roz Chandler, and the assistant mayor's wife were already sipping tea and helping themselves to savory sandwiches. But no Bev.

They'd barely stepped inside before Bev hurried into the room behind them. "Sorry not to be here to greet you. I was on the telephone with Marty. She's going to be late, some problem at the paper, but she promises to get here as soon as possible."

"Her father should really find her a husband before she gets herself into trouble," Mrs. Abernathy said.

Roz opened her mouth, then closed it again. It hadn't taken them all long to learn to ignore Mrs. Abernathy and her opinions, of which she had many. In addition to being committee chairwoman, she was one of the most influential wives in City Hall and Tammany politics.

And as Bev continued to remind them, she was also one of the richest. But not as rich as the last member who entered behind Bev in a rustle of blue silk velvet and taffeta. Imogen Trout swept in, the way she made all entrances, paused to get everyone's attention, drawled, "Am Ah la-a-ate?" Then condescended to make herself part of the group.

She sat down next to Roz on the sofa. Each committee head made their reports, just as they had at the last meeting, which for Phil was rather a wasted effort. She was on the committee mainly for show.

Amazing that Americans were so enamored of royalty, though it was only fit, since royalty was so enamored by the Americans' money.

Imogen began her report on the decorations of the Plaza ballroom where the ball was to be held. Convenient for Phil and certainly a feather in the committee's cap, as the ballroom had been rented for months in advance.

". . . tables will be positioned in a horseshoe facin' the front alcove where a twelve-foot tree will be ornamented with gold . . ."

Phil took a surreptitious look at the mantel clock, which was nearly hidden in an abundance of holly. Where was Marty? Maybe she would have news.

"And Lady Dunbridge will lead off the ball with Mayor McClellan," Mrs. Abernathy was saying, sending Phil a deferential look that Phil accepted with a civil smile. "We have subscriptions for four hundred and seventy patrons . . ." She paused to say, "Not even Mrs. Astor can boast such a number."

Everyone smiled or tittered at her little joke. It was old news that the four hundred most prominent families was based on the number of people who could be accommodated in the elder Mrs. Astor's ballroom.

"Poor Caroline," she continued with just the slightest hint of malice. After all, Mrs. Abernathy's family had been one of those first snubbed by the elite of New York, until their wealth bought them a place in the new-money society. A little tidbit Phil had learned from Bev before she'd agreed to be part of the ball. Next year she would put her clout, such that it was, toward an event that spent less and did more.

She was just about to beg a headache when the doorbell echoed.

Everyone looked toward the door. Bev popped up from her seat just as the door opened and Marty Rive burst in, unbuttoning her coat. She tossed it in Tuttle's direction as she rushed past him.

"Oh Roz, Tommy Green is dead."

Roz? thought Phil. How did she know the *Times* reporter?

"He was murdered."

Everyone turned to Roz, who had grown as pale as paper. Her hand pressed her cheek, her eyes round and unfocused. She pushed to her feet, reached out to Marty, and swayed.

"Good Lawd," Imogen drawled. "Somebody catch her, she's goin' to faint."

12

Imogen made ineffectual gestures while Marty rushed across the room to meet Phil, who had jumped from her chair. They shooed Imogen out of the way and eased Roz back onto the couch, Marty lifting Roz's feet and Phil placing a velvet throw pillow beneath her head.

"Tuttle, send for Elmira and my smelling salts," Bev ordered, and headed to the drinks table for the brandy.

"Really, Martha," Mrs. Abernathy said, "how could you rush in like a common newsboy and announce something so offensive?"

"Who is Tommy Green?" asked the deputy mayor's wife.

"Some reporter with the *Times*," Mrs. Abernathy said. "Always loitering around the Hall pestering men trying to go about their business."

"More than a pest to some," Marty said under her breath. "Nemesis is more like it." Her eyes blazed, and Roz slipped her hand into Marty's.

"Really," Mrs. Abernathy continued, "why they let this riff-raff run free among decent people is beyond me. *The press.* Good riddance, I say."

So even Mrs. Abernathy knew who Tommy Green was. And had an opinion, one that might push Marty into doing something extremely unladylike. Phil stepped in between the two women.

Roz began to rouse; at the same time Bev's maid, Elmira, arrived with the smelling salts, and Bev handed a glass of brandy to the prostrate woman.

Roz waved both away. "I do apologize. I haven't been my-self lately."

Mrs. Abernathy and Imogen Trout nodded knowingly to each other.

"There, there," said Mrs. Abernathy, trying to supplant Bev, Marty, and Phil from around the couch. "You shouldn't be push-ing yourself. I'll take you home. I think our business is finished for today."

Phil didn't miss the stricken look Roz cast Marty.

Bev came to the rescue. "Absolutely not. She can't go out into the cold in her weakened state. She'll stay right here and have some warm broth. I'll telephone to Jarvis and tell him he can pick her up here when he's finished for the day."

"It's no—"

Bev plowed on. "But you're absolutely right. I think we can adjourn for the afternoon. Thank you all so much for taking time from your busy schedules to volunteer for such a worthy cause. Tuttle will show you out. Elmira, ask Cook to send up some hot broth."

"It is getting late," said Mrs. Abernathy, who seemed al-most relieved at not having to cope with the swooning Roz. "I do have plans, but I hate to leave her here. Oh, not here in your parlor, Bev, but just what will Jarvis say?"

"You'll call Jarvis right away," Imogen drawled. "He does worry."

"He'll be glad she's being taken care of, I assure you," Bev said at her most condescending.

Imogen leaned over the couch and said in a low voice. "Roz, will you be okay if we leave you?"

She sounded sincere enough, but Roz involuntarily shrunk back. "Perfectly, dear Imogen. I'm better now."

Better, maybe, but not at ease—one might even think she was frightened.

"Ladies, " Bev said.

And Phil turned to watch in wonder as Bev—iconoclast,

fast-living modern woman who mercilessly flouted rules and decorum—usurped the meeting with the finesse of the dowager that Phil was and showed the women into the foyer, where Tuttle and a footman were waiting with coats and muffs.

When the door closed behind them, Phil turned to her friend. "I'm amazed."

"Oh hell, Phil, I did learn a thing or two in all those years at finishing school. Just because I don't choose to use them is a whole other thing."

"Thanks, Bev." Roz raised herself to a sitting position and finally took the brandy that Marty was still holding. She gulped a healthy swig down and shuddered. "I've made a fool of myself. Again. But oh, Marty, tell me it isn't true?"

Phil frowned and looked more closely at Roz as something niggled at the back of her mind.

"It's true," Marty said. "Tommy is dead. I didn't mean to blurt it out like that, but I was so beside myself. I couldn't get away from the paper because the police were there, because evidently there is some question as to how and where and why he died. Not that it matters, because they're not going to do one damn thing about it."

"Tell us what happened," Bev said.

"Charlie Miller came down to deliver a diatribe on what he would do if he found out anyone was leaking anything about what Tommy was working on. Then he and Carr went off, and when Carr came back, he yelled at Sydney for not running a tighter ship. I don't give two cents for Sydney, but I don't see how it could be his fault. Then Harriet Wells, who had just come back after a day off, tossed her lunch right there on the newsroom floor—sorry, a journalist's curse, too descriptive."

But very illuminating, Phil thought. Atkins must have corroborated her story and gone straight to the *Times* building. Had she put Harriet in danger? She'd been careful not to mention her.

Marty sank down next to Roz. "He always told me to watch my back, not take any time or place for granted. Why wasn't he careful?"

Phil was surprised to see tears in Marty's eyes. She motioned Bev to the far side of the room.

"I understand that Marty was Tommy Green's protégée," Phil said. "But how does Roz know him?"

"Not the foggiest," Bev said, looking worried. "But whatever it is, it can't be good. Tongues will wag starting with Mrs. Abernathy and Imogen Trout. They were already giving each other the look.

"I'm sorry I got you into this," Bev continued. "I let myself be dragged in and I dragged you in, too. Anyway, this is the last meeting, and when the ball is over, we'll wash our hands of it and do our own charity drive next year."

Marty and Roz sat close together on the settee, their heads together in low conversation.

Marty's voice rose stridently. "They killed him and I'm going to find out who did it."

"Oh dear," Bev said. "Let's see if we can help."

Phil and Bev pulled up chairs and sat down facing Roz and Marty.

"I'm so sorry about your friend," Phil said. "Did they say how he was killed?"

Marty bared her teeth in an absolutely feral expression of anger. "They refused to say. Only that there was some discrepancy and it was being investigated. But when I asked your detective sergeant what it was, he merely said it wasn't his jurisdiction and that the proper authorities were looking into the matter. So why did he bother to come at all? And why hasn't anyone else?"

She glared at Phil as if she expected her to know the answer, and although Phil did, she wasn't about to divulge it.

"I don't care if Sydney killed the story, I will continue Tommy's investigation and find his killer if it's the last thing I do."

Bev sighed. "In all your free time, between balls, soirées, the opera, and—"

"Sydney killed the story?" Phil asked.

"Yeah, because no one could find Tommy's notes and it would be old news before another reporter—not me but one of his drinking buddies—gets in gear."

"That's so unfair," Bev said.

"It doesn't matter. I'll do it somehow. Tommy was too smart to be taken unawares by some two-bit crook. It had to be something big." Marty jumped up and strode to the window. Turned back to the others.

And Phil saw the same investigative fever that she herself often felt.

But they didn't need two separate investigations working at cross-purposes. And she didn't need Marty Rive interfering in something that might get her killed, too.

"I have a better idea," Bev said.

Marty zeroed in on Bev. Bev zeroed in on Phil.

"Really, Bev, you think Lady Dunbridge could do better than I can?"

"Well, actually," Bev said. "Yes. And she has more time than you."

Phil cut a warning look to Bev, who ignored it. Phil would have to remind her to hold her tongue. If Phil intended to keep her reputation for discretion intact, she would have to make it perfectly clear to Bev she was not to be a subject of discussion with anyone, even good old school chums.

"Maybe we should leave it to the police," Roz ventured.

Marty turned on her full force. "They're all crooks. They'll either fail to investigate, grab some poor Italian off the street and arrest him, or if it turns out to be someone of importance or they lose interest, they'll turn a blind eye. Won't they, Lady Dunbridge?"

So now she was Lady Dunbridge again. "Some, but I have faith that there are a few good men left on the force."

"Then you're hopelessly naïve."

Hardly, thought Phil. But Marty Rive was a loose cannon. Phil had never really thought about what that term meant until now. It could wreck everything. Unless she somehow convinced Marty to let her handle the investigation, which seemed unlikely. Marty was out for vengeance.

"Lady Dunbridge, can you find Tommy's murderer?" Roz asked in such a small voice that it silenced them all.

"Roz. May I call you Roz?"

Roz nodded in short little jerks.

"Bev may have misled you somewhat. I'm no detective." Not admittedly anyway.

"Malarkey, Phil."

"Bev, please."

"Yes, Bev," added Marty. "Please."

"I'm afraid Bev has been a little overenthusiastic." Phil shot Bev a look that warned her not to say a word.

"Everyone knows you saved Bev from jail and discovered Reggie's real murderer," Roz said.

True, perhaps, but Phil was not about to acknowledge it. "I walked off the ship and into Bev standing over Reggie dead in the back seat of his Packard. I merely gave Bev what support I could."

Marty raised an eyebrow. "What about the Pratts?"

The Pratts? How did she know about that? Not even Bev knew the particulars of that situation, being conveniently abroad at the time. "I was merely a friend helping a friend in need."

"Well, then, you can be a friend in need to Roz and me," Marty said. "Tommy was no fool. He knew who to pay to get information and who to protect his back. They're trying to pass this off on the Black Hand, which as far as I'm concerned doesn't even exist."

"They do exist," Roz said. "Whether they're organized or not, people are getting hurt—and killed."

"Oh, Roz. Any hooligan who has to sign his threats with

pictures is not part of some widespread organization of crime. They'd do better going after the Sicilian Mafia; every indication is that they're consolidating their power with an idea of moving into the States."

This was news to Phil. Marty was a wealth of information, and would be an excellent source of the news. Unfortunately, Phil didn't think she would share without getting something in return.

"It seems to me," Phil said, "that the main thing here is to find out what really happened to Tommy Green."

"Why are you interested?" Marty asked. "You don't even know him."

"I don't." *Not in the classic sense of the word.* "And I have to wonder, Roz . . . how on earth do you know him?"

Roz shrugged slightly. "Everybody knows Tommy."

Phil looked to Bev, who looked clueless. "I don't."

"Sure you do," Roz said. "He photographed the ground-breaking ceremony for the new police headquarters. The mayor and Jarvis and Mr. Trout all wielding shovels while the wives stood looking on admiringly."

"After overspending several million dollars," Marty added.

"Why would I remember that?" Bev asked.

"Because you were there when he came up and asked if I would like him to send me a copy for my scrapbook, and you thought it was so odd that he would think to do that."

"Oh yes," Bev said. "It gave me hope you were becoming more democratic in your choice of friends." She cut a look toward Phil. "He was a bit of a lowlife."

"No, he wasn't," Roz said. "He just fit in with the people. Cared about them. That was what made him such a good reporter, isn't it, Marty?"

"Yes. He was, if you'll pardon the newsroom language, a damn good reporter. Damn good." Marty seemed to deflate. "Oh, Tommy. What did you get yourself into?"

A reminiscent smile flitted across Roz's lips. "I first met him when I won a citywide grammar-school poetry contest. I think I was in fifth grade. He must have been just starting out because he was covering the award ceremony. I just remembered that. They gave me a trophy that was so big I could barely carry it."

Alarm bells sounded in Phil's mind. *A young girl, a big trophy, a photograph in Tommy's apartment.*

"I kept that trophy until I married Jarvis. I can't explain it. Tommy was rough and uncouth, but he was always friendly in a not-always-friendly world. He always tipped his hat to me, smiled, not encroaching or anything. He never pushed for inside information. Not like the others. It can be pretty solitary being a politician's wife. When everyone is done asking favors, you're pretty much on your own."

Marty huffed out a breath. "He was a pain and a half, but he was a good reporter. And a good friend." She laughed, a dry sound that threatened to tumble into grief.

"Well, Phil?" Bev said. "You can't let Roz and Marty down."

Phil felt the frisson of chase fever rise in her blood. She had every intention of investigating. And Roz and Marty just gave her the excuse she needed to poke around at the newspaper for Tommy's notes.

"I always try to be supportive of my friends, and I hope you will consider me as one."

Roz nodded.

Marty gave a begrudging half-shrug. "I can pay."

"I can, too," Roz said doubtfully. "Perhaps not all at once. Jarvis is very frugal—and I wouldn't want it to come out that I was involved. They're planning to run Jarvis for mayor in the next election, and he can't have any scandal associated with his name."

"He's a tightfisted scoundrel, but you don't have to get involved," Marty spat out. "I'll pay whatever you need to retain your services."

"Phil would never charge to help a friend, would you, Phil?" Bev said.

"Certainly not."

"But you mustn't tell anyone." Roz templed her hands like a child's plea. "If it got out I'd hired a detective . . ."

"Of course not." Phil's reputation depended on it. "And I'm not a detective, just a friend. But if you're worried, the police . . ." *Will keep you out of my hair while I do investigate.*

"No!" Roz bleated.

"Forget the police," Marty said, giving her friend an odd look. "The lives of reporters are not worth much. They'll 'look into it,' find nothing, and then let it die. It happens all the time. Tommy Green deserves more than that. We all do."

A few minutes later, Bev closed the door on Roz and Marty and leaned back against it. "Sorry I got you into this mess."

"No, you're not. You volunteered me."

"True, and I'll reward you with another holiday cocktail I've invented." Bev breezed past her.

"What is it this time?"

"Schnapps and coffee liqueur and—"

"Say no more. It sounds like afternoon tea at the Hotel Sacher."

"Just what I was going for," Bev said blithely, and flounced over to the drinks cabinet where Tuttle was waiting to assist.

Once the drinks were poured into glasses, sprigs of mint gracing the edges and the aroma of peppermint filling the air, Tuttle left them, and Phil got down to business.

"Well?" she asked, regaining her breath from the potent mixture. "Just what have you gotten me into?"

"Me? I didn't, did I?"

"You know full well you did." And that it fit into Phil's own plans was a bonus, something she didn't need to tell Bev.

"I suppose you'll have to help them now."

"I'll see what I can do, but don't get your hopes up." Phil hated having to keep things from Bev. But Bev was too much of a free spirit, too enthusiastic and devil-may-care to trust with life-and-death information. Phil was all those things, but she had a finely honed sense of self-preservation. She'd had to in order to survive the shark-infested waters of London high society.

And her success had made her singularly qualified to deal with the plights of Manhattan's high society. And as for the Black Hand, it was nothing compared to the wrath of a spurned duchess, disappointed prince regent, or a Manhattan hostess.

Bev slipped off her shoes and sat down on the sofa, crossing her legs beneath the folds of her silk skirts. She took a sip of her drink, made a face. "Needs some fine adjustments, I think."

Phil put her glass down on the side table. "Bev, I'll need some information, but first, call Tuttle to get rid of this chewable cocktail. I need something dry so I can think."

Bev happily agreed. "Tuttle, my peppermint cocktail was a dismal failure. Would you mix us two dry—very dry—martinis?"

Tuttle nodded and, whisking the glasses away, strode to the drinks cabinet.

While they waited, Bev fell into silence, and Phil fell into rumination. She was either having a brilliant insight or else the fumes of her drink were impairing her thoughts.

A reporter investigating an organized crime ring; two women on a committee made up of the wives of the city's biggest politicians and businessmen asking her to investigate.

It appeared that she would have to expand her search beyond the Black Hand.

"Phil, have you thought of something?"

"I need to know more about Roz and Marty. I understand why Marty feels as she does about Tommy Green's murder, but Roz . . . You say her parents pulled her out of college."

"Yes, and the next we heard she was engaged to Jarvis Chandler."

"He's quite a bit older than she," Phil said. "Who exactly is he?"

"Building commissioner for the city, powerful both at City Hall and Tammany. Also very thick with Imogen's husband, Samuel Trout. Real-estate mogul who owns a good portion of lower Manhattan."

"A convenient friendship," Phil said.

Bev shrugged. "The only reason I know any of this is because Reggie, when he wasn't totally involved in his horses, tinkered with the idea of buying up property. A notion I'm glad to say evaporated when he won his first race.

"Horses are so much more interesting than land and buildings, don't you think? Oh, thank you, Tuttle," Bev said, taking a glass from the quietly appearing butler.

"You mean going to the races is more interesting," Phil said, and savored the dryness of her martini.

"Well, that, too. But I do love the horses. Strange, isn't it? I never cared that much before I owned them." She tittered. "And I love being at the stables, and even in that little house at Holly Farm. Who would have guessed?"

Certainly no one Phil had known.

"I know, why don't we all go out to Holly Farm for Boxing Day?"

"Bev. Tell me more about Jarvis Chandler."

Bev shrugged. "He's fifty if he's a day, rich, and just as unfaithful as most of the rich men in town. Unworthy of Roz."

"And Roz?"

"And Roz what?"

"Does she have a lover?"

"I rather doubt it. Why? What could that have to do with some reporter's murder?"

Blackmail came to mind, but Phil didn't say so. Right now, she was just trying to collect every odd bit of information that could be put into the pattern or discarded later. She certainly didn't want Bev going off half-cocked. Which was the only way Bev seemed to go.

"Maybe we could invite the delicious detective sergeant to join us."

"Bev, please concentrate. You promised your friends that I will find Tommy Green's killer, and now you keep changing the subject."

Bev sighed. "I wonder if that's what he was doing at the *Times* building the other day."

Phil gritted her teeth. "Roz has a typically boorish husband. What about Marty?"

Bev shook her head. "Sometimes I wonder about Marty."

"How so?"

"She just seems to have a one-track mind."

"Journalism."

Bev nodded, finished her martini, reached for Phil's glass, and took both over to the drinks tray to be replenished. "The whole time we were at school, she was fixated on becoming a journalist. Had several newspapers delivered to her digs every day. Went to every lecture, every conference they would allow her into, came down to the city to talk to professional journalists.

"She met Tommy Green at a suffragette rally. She came back singing his praises. After that, she was constantly meeting him in the city, and he became her mentor, and introduced her to his mentor, Jacob Riis. A really well-respected journalist.

"She's a really good reporter, but . . ."

"She's female," Phil finished.

"Exactly. She's stuck with society news. She should put her foot down, which she does, but it gets her nowhere. Carr will assign her a story, then Sydney reassigns it to one of the men."

"Sydney Lord? So that's why she doesn't like him."

"It's sort of a love or hate kind of thing. You saw him in action. Handsome enough, smart enough, but thinks much too highly of himself. Would definitely have his way with Marty if she'd let him. But she won't."

"Even if he promised her a good story?"

"Not even. She'll make it on her own terms, or die trying."

"What do you know about Tommy Green?"

"I guess I met him at that ribbon-cutting ceremony, but I don't really remember. I mean, why would Roz pass the time of day with a reporter, much less cultivate his friendship?"

Why, indeed?

There was a lot more she needed to learn about these people before she could begin piecing together a plan. But she wouldn't get it from Bev. She might learn more from Marty, but she'd have to be very subtle. If reporting was Marty's end-all, woe to anyone, including Phil, who got in the way.

No, this was a job for Preswick and his butler underground.

13

Phil let herself into her apartments. "Hello?"

Preswick and Lily stepped out of the kitchen.

"Sorry, my lady, we didn't expect you back this early."

"Because I have news. There's been an interesting turn of events. The editors of the *Times* have been apprised of Tommy Green's demise. Marty announced it rather abruptly at the committee meeting. When everyone else had left, Marty and Roz Chandler, who is also a college friend of Bev's, asked me to find the killer.

"Now, what do you think of that? Though I do think Roz was having second thoughts by the time she left. Which reminds me . . . Come with me."

She tossed her muff on the chair, strode past them and into the study, where she spread out the four photos she'd taken from Tommy's flat.

"Aha!" she said, jabbing her finger at the young girl receiving the trophy. She moved it to the far right, rearranged the other three chronologically across the table.

She turned to take in Preswick and Lily, who stood in the doorway.

"Come and see." Phil paused long enough to let Lily relieve her of her coat.

"When Roz Chandler, a member of the committee, heard the news, she fainted. I thought it odd that she would even be acquainted with Tommy, and said so. She said that she'd met him when she won a poetry contest when she was a schoolgirl and Tommy photographed her for the newspaper.

"She mentioned a big trophy." Phil pulled the award photo closer. "Now look at this."

Preswick and Lily leaned over to peruse the photograph. The bald master of ceremonies, the dark-haired little girl, the trophy that seemed to dwarf its recipient.

"You think this is a young Roz Chandler," Preswick said.

"I think there's a good chance that it is. And it wouldn't be all that unusual on its own, but . . ." She pulled over the other three. "I believe these are all of Roz Chandler at different stages of her life, and they were all framed and presumably hanging on the wall or set upon a dresser. There were no other photos that I found."

"It appears," Preswick said, "that Mr. Green took an inordinate interest in Mrs. Chandler."

"It may have nothing to do with his murder. But it does cast a new light on his character. I just wonder if his motives were spurious or benign. Though perhaps we'd rather not know. It does, however, open up another line of investigation."

She caught sight of a stack of newspapers on the sideboard. "Ah, are these the evening editions?"

"Yes, my lady. They arrived just before you did."

She picked up the top paper.

ANOTHER OUTRAGE BY THE BLACK HAND.
Appalling Arson.

Another deplorable act of arson swept through the lower floor of a three-story tenement on East Thirteenth Street . . .

Phil looked up. "Tommy Green's?"

"Yes, my lady."

. . . wrecking the lower hall and two street-level apartments, ripping through the walls, and breaking all the windows. All tenants, many of who were scratched and bruised, were removed from the premises as the stability of the building was in question.

An elderly gentleman who lived in the front first-floor apartment was overcome by smoke while he slept and was taken to the hospital. The building is expected to be condemned and all residents will have to look elsewhere for lodgings immediately.

Phil dropped the paper to the table. "A journalist murdered. His lodgings set on fire. An innocent old man nearly killed. And at Christmas. I am not amused." In fact she was angry and . . . stymied.

"Something isn't making sense. Why kill a man and *then* burn down his apartment? . . . Rather defeats the purpose of extortion. And there is no mention of Tommy Green living there, or that he'd been found dead. Does it seem reasonable that the Black Hand just coincidentally decided to burn down Tommy Green's lodgings after someone else killed him?"

"That does stretch the boundaries of logic, my lady."

Phil dropped the paper back on the stack as a sense of injustice swept over her. "Think of all those people suddenly without homes, and at such a time. Something should be done about them. Perhaps the *Times* would sponsor a resettlement venture in Tommy Green's name. I'll have to suggest it to Marty.

"And something else. How is Sergeant Becker involved?"

"Maybe he's a member of the Black Hand," Lily said.

"Why? He already has the Tammany and City Hall officials in his pocket. Surely they keep him busy and rich enough for any man."

"Because someone in the government is in league with that illegal organization?"

That gave them all pause.

"A ringleader," Lily said.

"But for what purpose?" Phil frowned and looked over the

stacks of notes and books they'd already accumulated in their investigation. "Preswick, where is that map of the city?"

"Here, my lady." He unfolded the map and spread it out on the table.

She took a pencil and ran it over the city grid until she found Union Square. "So, here is where it all started. For us anyway." She drew an "X" where the Theatre Unique stood on Fourteenth Street. Two more Xs across the street for Tammany Hall and the Academy of Music.

She traced Fourth Avenue to Thirteenth Street, where she drew an "X" for Tommy's apartment.

"We saw another burned-out building on our way to Mr. Green's building." She added another "X" in the approximate location of the boarded-over storefront.

"And one across the street from the Cavalier Club." She added another "X" to the map.

"Preswick, do you remember the others we read about?"

"Yes, my lady, I took the liberty of cutting out the articles and putting them in a folder." He went to the desk, picked up a cardboard folder, riffled through the contents until he brought out a clipped news article.

"A tenement on East Eleventh, one on East Twelfth. Both with similar addresses to Mr. Green's, which would put them in the same vicinity."

"So five recent acts of vandalism. It does seem that someone is targeting this neighborhood in particular." Phil studied her cluster of Xs. There was something there, a half-revealed picture, like the pieces of a jigsaw puzzle all offering a glimpse of what wouldn't be made clear until all the pieces were in place.

"May I point out," Preswick said, "that the Italian neighborhood the Hand usually targets is somewhat farther east than these?"

"So their activities are spreading out?"

"It would appear so."

"Why here? And why Tommy Green?" Phil tapped her pencil on the paper. "This is an established neighborhood, not a tenement district for recent immigrants. Why the Theatre Unique? That seems to be taking a lot of unnecessary chances. Why not just kill him while he slept? Or in an alley somewhere?"

"As a warning to others?" Preswick ventured.

"What others?"

"The other journalists into not reporting about them," Lily said.

"Or because he was about to hand over important information to me."

"Have we become too enamored by the reprehensibility of these Hand people? I really don't think 'our people,' whoever they are"—and she intended to find out at her next meeting with Mr. X—"would expect us to take on a national crime organization.

"What if it isn't the Black Hand at all?"

"A copycat crime to throw the investigation off the real perpetrator?" said Preswick.

"Exactly, a red herring to keep us from finding out what Tommy really had to tell. His investigation of the Hand must have led him to someone important. Why else risk his life to divulge it to some organization that even I don't know about?"

Lily bit her lip. "But didn't Mr. X say it was about the Black Hand?"

"No. He didn't know what it was about. Tommy would only tell them in person. I assumed it was about the Black Hand because of the note in my pocket and because Tommy was investigating them. Something I'm sure Sherlock Holmes would not condone."

Which reminded her that she had still to find a copy of Sir Arthur Conan Doyle's latest book.

"But he left a key, and close at hand so he could retrieve his notes once the deal was done."

"But that means it would all be ashes," Lily said.

"Perhaps, but would a secretive man, worried about leaks, hide his information in his lodgings and where it would be easy to break into? No, whatever this is about, it wasn't solved by burning down his apartment. And unless they had time to cut his throat and risk discovery by searching his pockets before I arrived, whatever he knew is still out there.

"Someone is very determined, or very frightened. And we must be careful.

"Tomorrow morning, the two of you will attempt to discover what this type of key might fit. I'm sure you know exactly where to look and whom to ask. Once we know that, we'll have a better idea of how to proceed.

"We'll meet back here in time for our tree delivery, and then we will all go shopping for decorations."

"But where are you going?" Lily asked.

Preswick cleared his throat.

"My lady," she added.

"I'm going to make a morning call on Rosalind Chandler. Confront her with the photos we found. Tommy obviously had an interest in her that went beyond being nice to her and not trying to curry political favors from a powerful city official's wife. There has to be more to it than that, at least on his part. Now, if I can just get her to tell me exactly what *her* relationship was to Tommy Green, and if it could possibly have anything to do with his murder."

The next morning, dressed in a visiting dress of turquoise wool, Lady Dunbridge stepped into the foyer of the Chandlers' East Side mansion and gave her card to the butler.

He flicked his fingers at a footman, who relieved her of her outer cape and muff. She kept the rather large handbag she'd brought for the occasion and followed the butler to a small secondary parlor, where he announced her in stentorian tones.

Roz was completely alone, her feet tucked under her as she sat comfortably reading a book. She'd barely had time to jump to her feet before Phil came forward, holding out her hand.

"I'm so glad to find you home."

Roz slid her feet into her shoes and met Phil halfway. "Lady Dunbridge—Phil. What a . . . delightful surprise."

A surprise, to be sure, Phil thought, though perhaps not delightful.

Roz looked quickly toward the closed door and led Phil to the far side of the room to a love seat by the bow window. "Have you found out anything yet?" she asked, thus alleviating the need of the story about seating arrangements for the ball Phil had carefully constructed on her ride over.

"Would you like tea? I hope you don't mind me receiving you in my parlor rather than the salon. It's so much cozier here, and private. I'll ring."

It was a lady's parlor, furnished in comfortable pastels that complemented Roz's long-sleeved yellow tea gown. A cheery fire was blazing in the grate, and colorful Christmas postcards were lined up along the white marble mantel. Phil could imagine Roz passing her free hours here. Entertaining her select friends, reading, snatching some peace away from her hurried life as Jarvis Chandler's wife. Phil wondered if Jarvis ever joined her here.

Tea was ordered, and after one attempt at inquiring whether Lady Dunbridge thought there would be snow for Christmas, and Phil's reminder to call her Phil, they lapsed into silence. There was only one thing on each of their minds, though perhaps not the same thing.

The butler returned, followed by two maids in black uniforms and crisp white aprons rolling a tea trolley filled with pots and cups and several tiered plates of edibles.

"Will there be anything else, madam?"

"No, Willis, that will be all." Roz smiled at them; the maids quickly curtseyed and hurried away.

While Phil was congratulating herself for not having to

employ and manage a household full of servants, Jarvis Chandler strode in.

He'd been frowning as he entered but, seeing Phil, he smiled. "Lady Dunbridge, isn't it? What a delightful surprise." The exact same phrase uttered by his wife a few minutes earlier.

"Yes," Roz said. "Lady Dunbridge was so kind to bring over the last decisions on the flower arrangements for the charity ball."

Evidently, Phil and Bev weren't the sole proprietors of fabrications in this group. And Roz had lied without a falter. "We were just about to have tea. Will you join us?"

She seemed eager for him to stay, but a little apprehensive.

And Phil got a mental picture of another young girl, fresh out of finishing school, waiting for the Earl of Dunbridge to call for the first time. Had she worn that same eager, innocent, slightly fearful smile that Roz showed toward her husband?

If she had, she'd lost it soon enough.

"Then I'll leave you ladies to it. I won't be home to lunch. Some more ruckus over building the new courthouse. It never ends. You'd think it was the only building on the agenda for demolition. How men can be so shortsighted." He shook his head. "And don't forget, we're due at the McCaffertys for dinner. So come straight home from mass. I don't want to be late."

Recalling they had a visitor, he turned to Phil. "I think Roz is responsible for keeping Friday-night mass going. She doesn't miss a one." He smiled down at his wife, kissed her cheek, nodded to Phil, and strode out the door, leaving the butler who had been waiting just outside to close it after him.

"I must apologize for his gruffness," Roz said as she poured tea. "Cream? Sugar?"

"Please," said Phil.

"Politicians seem unable to agree on anything. It was worse last spring and during the social season. All we heard about was the new courthouse . . . I'm surprised it didn't lead to fisticuffs in someone's drawing room." Her eyes rolled back. "It's led me to a few too many gin fizzes, I can tell you."

She handed Phil her cup. Phil just caught sight of a dark shadow around her wrist. A bruise?

Phil looked up, questioning. But Roz had turned to take her own cup and sat down on the love seat next to Phil.

"Now that he's out of the way, tell me everything you've learned."

"I don't suppose you've seen the morning papers?" Phil asked.

"No. I used to have my maid smuggle them in with my tea tray, but I've been so busy lately I haven't had much time for reading."

Interesting, Phil thought, casting a look over to the open book on the sofa cushions.

"Last night, a fire was set in the building where Tommy Green lived. An old man was seriously injured; tenants are now homeless."

"Oh no, that's terrible."

"It was deliberate, I think, to destroy any material he might have been working on. Did he ever discuss his work with you?"

"Me? Of course not. I hardly knew him, much less talked to him other than a friendly hello." Her face melted into sadness. "Tommy was always polite when I saw him. Treated me kindly. Not like other reporters, who are always prodding and poking and trying to get you to tell them something you shouldn't. Most of the time I don't even know what they're talking about. I hate politics."

Her pale and delicate fingers came to her throat. There was a definite bruise around her wrist as if someone—her husband?—had gripped her too tightly. "I shouldn't have said that."

"I take it this wasn't the life you would have chosen."

"Oh, I didn't mean—Jarvis is wonderful and I never lack for

anything, except . . . just sometimes I would give just about anything to live the life Bev and Marty . . . and you live."

Phil didn't think that Roz would be more fit for a life of freedom than that of a politician's wife. There was something about the woman that was singularly helpless. She was about the same age as Phil, Bev, and Marty, but her air of naïveté and innocence made her seem younger.

For a second Harriet Wells flashed into Phil's mind. Another one whose appearance and actions were younger than her years and who was as equally temperamentally unfit for her chosen profession.

But perhaps neither of them were quite as innocent as they seemed?

"Perhaps I should get to the reason for my call," Phil said. She reached for her bag and brought out the photos from Tommy Green's apartment.

"Yesterday before the fire, we went to Tommy's lodgings. It had been searched, possibly by the police; they seem to have a blatant disrespect for other people's property."

Most do, anyway, Phil thought. To give Detective Sergeant Atkins his due, he would never "toss" a place in a way that would leave it in that kind of disarray.

"Did they find anything?"

"I don't know. I'm not in their confidence. But they overlooked these." Phil handed Roz the first one of a young Rosalind accepting a medal for her poem. "Is this the occasion of your poetry award?"

"Yes, yes," Roz said, taking the photo with trembling fingers.

She peered at it, while Phil watched for her reaction and remained alert in case Roz tried to consign it to the fire.

She needn't have worried. "How sweet. He asked my mother if she'd like a copy. She was so grateful."

"Mrs. Hastings?" Phil said.

"Yes." Roz frowned. "Marty told you I was adopted."

Phil nodded.

"It was when I was a baby. The Hastingses were the only family I ever knew." Tears sprang to Roz's eyes. "I miss them so much."

Phil steeled her sangfroid. "There are three more photographs. They all had been framed and were the only photographs we found."

Phil handed Roz the next one, a picture of a group of girls in their graduation dresses standing on the stairs of what must have been their high school.

Roz dabbed at her eyes with a dainty initialed handkerchief. "I don't recognize this."

"Your high-school graduation?"

"My—Oh yes, the newspaper did take a photo."

"Why do you think Tommy had it framed in his apartment?"

"I have no idea." Roz handed it back to Phil. "Why would he keep either of these?"

"I was hoping you could tell me."

"No."

"What about this one?" Phil handed Roz the third photograph.

"This was a ground-breaking ceremony. The one I told you about, when Bev was there."

"And this." A wedding photograph that had to be Roz Chandler's.

"I don't understand. These were all in his rooms?"

Roz shoved the photograph back at Phil. She seemed genuinely surprised and frightened. Was she playing a deep game, or was she really this unaware of his attentions?

"Well, it's academic now. He won't be bothering you again."

"But he didn't bother me. I mean, I didn't know."

Unrequited love? It could eat at a person, Phil supposed. Especially if it went unexpressed. Had these been merely the product of a lonely man's obsession? A lovely young girl met on his first assignment and . . .

"He never said or did anything to make you think he was interested in you in a more—"

"Licentious way?" Roz finished for her.

"Well, perhaps it was more platonic than lurid."

Roz got up and walked to the window, where the bare branches of the trees turned the panes into broken shards of glass.

Roz turned suddenly. "I hope that you'll keep this to yourself. It's all so sordid."

"It may have been innocent admiration."

"Men never have innocent admiration." Roz's words were so sharp and bitter that they took Phil aback. "Unfortunately, I'm rather busy, I have a—"

"I completely understand," Phil said, sliding the photographs and newspaper article back into her bag, and standing up. "I'll leave you now. But are you certain that Tommy never confided anything to you that might put him—or you—in danger?"

"Or course not. Like I told you, I hardly knew him. But I'll light a candle for his soul at mass tonight."

"Then I'll wish you good day. Though you realize that I will continue to investigate his death. Someone . . ." She paused long enough to give Roz a pointed look. ". . . should care about what happened to him."

She picked up her purse and started for the door.

She heard the rustle of Roz's skirts, then Roz caught up to her and closed the door again.

"Please don't tell. I do want you to find out. I don't know why he had these pictures, but he was always kind. Always the perfect gentleman. Always."

Her hand was pressed to the door, leaving no doubt about the bruise on her wrist. Phil noticed, and Roz saw her. Their eyes met and, like all well-bred upper-class women, they pretended that nothing was wrong.

"I'm always discreet." Phil left her then. She didn't even

wait for the butler to call a taxi but went down the steps and turned into the wind. A brisk walk in the fresh air would do her good. She felt like maybe she had stumbled into something private that she should probably leave alone.

But that wasn't the way investigations worked. You collected all the pieces first; you only dismissed that which was known to be impossible.

And as Mr. Sherlock Holmes would say, "When you have eliminated the impossible, whatever remains, however improbable, must be the truth."

And Phil intended to get to the truth. She tucked her hat into the wind and strode down the sidewalk, her determination rising. She just hoped it would be solved by Christmas.

14

Phil returned to the Plaza trying to fit the pieces of her investigation into some kind of picture. And ended up with more questions than answers, a situation that she didn't enjoy in the least.

A series of bombs and arsons. A shadowy criminal organization. A leak at the newspaper. A dead reporter, his protégée, his typewriter girl, and a politician's wife in whom he had taken an inordinate interest. A key, a matchbox, and a few measly pages of a notebook that were illegible.

How to make sense of it all.

It was in this state of fierce ratiocination that she arrived at her apartments to the sound of rough voices and the smell of forest pine.

Preswick hurried to take her cape and muff. "The tree has arrived, my lady."

"So I perceive. What is the commotion about?"

"There seems to be a difference of opinion on where it should stand."

"Indeed?"

"Yes. I'm afraid Lily and one of the men, a self-proclaimed expert in the proper placement of trees, though nothing but a rough hauler, if one were to ask my opinion. I'm afraid I was rather ineffectual in the standoff."

"Oh well, let us see." Phil strode into the parlor to find the petite Lily on her tiptoes, better to yell at the burly workman, who towered over her, face nearly as red as his bushy beard or the poinsettias on the mantel.

Oh, but the tree.

Phil was so amazed that she halted on her way to intercede in the altercation just to stare.

It almost reached the ceiling. It filled the center of the room, where two other workers had untied it and were holding it upright while Lily and their cohort argued.

"What seems to be the problem?" she asked, skirting around the behemoth of a tree.

"Oh." Lily made a hasty curtsey. "My lady."

Phil swore the workman snorted out a laugh.

She beaded her eyes at him.

"And what do you say, Lily?"

"That it should go in the round window, so at night when it's lit up, they can see it on the moon."

"Then it shall go in the window." Phil nodded to the man to move it.

He grumbled, displaying missing teeth, then went to help carry the tree to the alcove. It took a while to set it upright, and Phil sent Lily and Preswick off to get water to pour into the stand that the men had brought.

As she directed them on the proper angle in which to secure the tree, the burly man brushed past her.

"Where have you been?" he said under his breath. "I've had a hell of a time keeping Lily at bay." He turned his head back to the men. "Naw, over to the left more." He watched his fellow workers adjust the tree. "We need to talk. Send Lily and Preswick to bed early. Unless you'd rather go on another carriage ride, but surely once was enough in this weather."

"How did you know I—"

"Naw, it's too far right!" he bellowed, and strode over to adjust the tree until it was perfect.

Of course, Phil thought testily. He could even put up a proper

Christmas tree. Which gave her pause. Had he had a lot of experience with Christmas trees? Cozy Christmas Eves by the fire with kiddies around his knee?

She dismissed the idea. Not the elusive Mr. X. Unless he was like Madame Orczy's Scarlet Pimpernel. No, she couldn't imagine it.

When he was at last satisfied, he turned back to her. "How about this way?"

"Perfect," she said, and didn't miss the twinkle in his eye. Fortunately, the other two men were collecting their twine and didn't see the interchange.

He touched the brim of his cloth cap and followed them out, letting his fingers brush hers as he passed.

Heavens, the man was brazen.

He stopped at Preswick long enough to collect the tip that Preswick begrudgingly handed him, and winked at Lily before shuffling out the door.

Lily stared after him, then whirled around. "He winked at me, that man who had the stupid idea about the tree. How dare he—" Her face went slack, her mouth opened, and she slowly looked at Phil. "Oh, madam, he wasn't . . . was that . . . ? It was!" She bolted for the front door.

"Don't bother, Lily," Phil said, hurrying after her. "You know he's like a cat—or a rat—and can disappear into the most impossible places. I don't know why he goes to all this trouble when he could just telephone . . . Ears," she reminded herself. Telephone operators, policemen, and people on the street willing to sell overheard information to anyone who would pay.

The three of them went to the door anyway, and Preswick swung it open. Unsurprisingly, the corridor was empty.

After several minutes of admiration of the tree—Preswick and Phil both agreed with Lily that the alcove window had been

by far the best place to put the gigantic piece of greenery—
Phil gave a quick précis of what happened with Roz Chandler
that morning.

"She says she has no idea of why Tommy Green had these
photos of her, and was rather unsettled that he might have
held a certain infatuation with her.

"Now, I would like to go out to purchase decorations immediately," Phil said. "Because I'm expecting a visit from our
elusive friend this evening and I don't want to chance being
late."

Unfortunately, it turned into a rather longer process, beginning with a stern look from Preswick.

"Don't scold, my dear Preswick. You will never be able to
turn me back into that innocent young girl who first stepped
over the threshold of Dunbridge Castle."

"No, my lady, nor would I want to, if I may say so."

"You may."

"But I am concerned with your safety."

"She will have my stiletto to pr-r-r-rotect her," Lily said,
and reached for her ankle.

"All situations cannot be solved by violence," said Preswick. "But do give her your stiletto."

"And I will sit—"

"No, you won't, Lily," Phil said. "Tonight is a strategy meeting. You know his own safety depends on his identity not being
known. Even to me. We must trust him to do what's best." But
she would make use of Lily's stiletto if the occasion arose, not
to mention the pearl-handled derringer she'd taken to carrying
in her handbag. She trusted him as far as it went. But she was
never absolutely certain of his loyalties.

"I intend to question him on exactly who we're working
for and to insist that we get a better means of communication.
Tommy Green might still be alive and we would be enjoying a
carefree holiday if they had just contacted me at once instead
of slipping a note under the door to be found who knew when.

"I will be perfectly safe with you down the hall. Though you might have some champagne sent up. No reason I should go thirsty while we strategize."

Preswick's lips pursed slightly, but he merely said, "Yes, my lady."

"I'm past praying for, Preswick."

"Yes, my lady. And I will never forgive his lordship for driving you away."

"Thank you, my dear man, but it was doomed from the beginning. It's my parents who should be horsewhipped and . . . perhaps Rosalind Chandler's. I'll have to ask Bev for more particulars of that marriage . . . but in the meantime, we are putting on our coats and going out to the shops to buy decorations for this most gigantic tree.

"Hurry up now! Shall it be Bloomingdale's or Macy's?"

"Macy's," Lily said without hesitation. "They say they have the most wonderfully decorated windows."

"Macy's it is. Come along."

A few minutes later the three of them were rounding Columbus Circle on their way to Thirty-Fourth Street.

Macy's windows were indeed a delight. People were pressed three deep, and men carried their children on their shoulders to get a peek at the marvels displayed.

Even Preswick unbent long enough to laugh at a mechanical clown that popped out of a box, swayed and threw up his hands, and laughed back at them.

Inside was a fairy world of invention. Glass balls in bright colors, crystal icicles that hung from gold threads, pinwheels and angels, handblown cars, boats, and Yule logs made in Germany and Poland. Bunches of miniature paper flowers and holly sprigs, tatted snowflakes. Boxes of silver strips of tinsel and garlands to wind around the tree.

A veritable wonderland of shiny excess.

They joined the excitement and very quickly gained their own personal salesclerk as they added ornament after ornament to their purchases. Truly, sometimes doing things for one's self was so exhilarating.

But when they came to the display of electric lights, Phil paused.

Lily pointed to the sign above the display and shot a horrified look to Phil. "A string of sixteen lights costs twelve dollars. That's more than most people make in a week."

"It does seem rather overly conspicuous when you consider the number of poor people in need at this time of year," Phil agreed.

Lily reluctantly put the box back.

"Not to mention, my lady," Preswick said, "I'm not certain that we are equipped to run this much electricity."

Not to mention a possible fire hazard, though they had lived all their lives with candlelit trees. Of course trees were only lit on Christmas Eve and Christmas morning, then taken out, never to be seen again.

"Perhaps just a few lights here and there," Phil suggested, feeling a little disappointed. God forbid they burned down the Plaza when it had just reopened.

"And we could use these, my lady." Lily reached into the next display and held up an apple-sized ball covered with little mirrored squares.

Preswick took it from her and held it up; it sparkled and danced in the department-store lights. "Perhaps some reflection would be in order."

"How true," Phil said, smiling at his play on words. "Lots of those." She motioned to the clerk to add them to their growing stack of purchases.

"And chains of shiny ribbon," Lily added. "We used—" She clamped her mouth down on what she was about to say. Phil's hand tightened on the accordioned paper bell she was holding. Preswick acted oblivious, but Phil knew he had also heard.

It was the first time Lily had slipped—at least had almost slipped—a morsel about her past. She'd caught herself, and Phil's heart broke a little knowing that she still didn't trust them enough to talk about her life before they had found her on the Southampton docks.

"How about these?" Phil asked over-brightly to make up for the terrible silence. She held up the crumpled bell. "Oh dear."

Preswick took it from her and restored it to its original shape. "I think these will do nicely. A dozen, my lady?"

The moment passed. When they left the store, they had all regained their holiday enthusiasm. But there had been a slight shift in their relationship that they wouldn't admit and yet couldn't ignore.

One thing about their life in America, it was never dull.

Phil gave the address for their decorations to be delivered, and they squeezed through oncoming customers until they were back on the sidewalk.

They stopped for hot chocolate and pastries at a crowded patisserie. Purchased mistletoe from a street seller, whom Phil did not recognize either as her elusive confederate or the villain who had slipped the Black Hand note in her pocket in Union Square.

They bought hot chestnuts folded into paper coronets, adding an extra one for Egbert, then three more for the other elevator operators who might be on duty, before climbing wearily into a taxi.

While they waited in traffic, Phil took a notebook from her purse and, with Preswick's help, made a list of everyone who would be expecting a tip for the holidays. It was rather extensive and, for the first time in a while, Phil worried whether her allowance and bonuses would actually cover her expenses.

By the time they reached Fifty-Ninth Street and were headed back toward the Plaza, Phil decided not to worry about the expenses. If it came to it, it wouldn't be the first time she'd lived on tick, though she devoutly hoped it might be the last.

Miraculously, their packages arrived a few minutes after they did.

"I wonder if the kitchen makes eggnog," Phil said. "Lily, help me get out of this dress and into something more comfortable."

They spent the rest of the evening unpacking and decorating, which consisted mostly of Preswick and Lily debating where to put things. And Phil dictating the results from where she lounged on the sofa in one of Poiret's flowing and exquisitely comfortable new kimono gowns. After several hours and eggnogs, and having joined the looping of garland over the branches, Phil declared a moratorium until the following day and sent Preswick and Lily off to bed.

Fortified with eggnog, Lily's stiletto, and her pistol, Phil retired to her room to await her enticingly mysterious visitor.

It was a long wait.

Phil wasn't totally surprised when she awoke to the hint of exotic tobacco in the dark, followed by the sense that she wasn't alone. She wasn't alarmed. The Plaza was perfectly secure to everyone, except perhaps to one man.

And she was expecting him.

She didn't bother reaching for a light; he could move like a phantom in the dark and would be there before her, which was rather galling.

At least she could try. She stretched her arm out; a hand clamped over her wrist.

She sat up, stifled a yawn, and he let go.

"I was beginning to wonder whether I would be seeing— and I use that word in a completely metaphorical sense—you tonight."

"You doubted me?" said a disembodied voice in the dark. A rich American accent that spread chills up her spine and heat to everywhere else.

"Not really," she said, trying to get an idea of where he was exactly.

"You knew I would come. Or are you expecting someone else to share that bottle of Moët chilling in the ice bucket? I doubt the good detective sergeant would stoop to sneaking into your boudoir in the dead of night."

"Unlike you." Now she really sat up. "How long have you been here, pawing around in my room?"

"My dear, I do not paw around. What inspection I do, I do with finesse. Which I will give evidence of after we open the champagne."

"Some people would call that attitude arrogant."

"Is that what you call it?"

"I'm tempted, but I must admit you haven't exaggerated thus far."

"I try never to exaggerate." The opposite side of the bed from where she was looking dipped, and his lips touched hers. It surprised her, and she laughed before she succumbed.

"You've lost considerable weight since this afternoon, and the beard is gone."

And so was he. One moment she was in his arms, the next he'd slipped away like smoke.

"Now what are you doing?" She could see his shadow moving across the room.

He stepped back into darkness. A pop. The fizzing sound of champagne being poured.

"Before we get any further," she said, focusing on the one thing she could actually see, which happened to be the nacre inserts of the wardrobe, "I have a few questions."

A laugh in the dark. Not where she expected it. Then a champagne glass appeared before her, and she tried to memorize the long tapered fingers before she was holding the glass and his fingers were gone.

Like "The Blind Men and the Elephant," the poem by John Godfrey Saxe, she might only get to know him by piecing the parts together. Only in the utter darkness was he himself. And that, Phil told herself, might be the metaphor of her place in this partnership.

"Since you left so abruptly the other night, I am still waiting for a plan. We need to be able to communicate more efficiently. I could have saved Tommy Green's life."

"We've already been through that."

"Surely you must agree that better communication is needed. The exchange of information would be most efficacious."

He ran a finger up her forearm to her shoulder. "It would, perhaps, but a division of labor can also be efficient."

"I don't understand. Investigation isn't like Mr. Olds's assembly line. It involves crossovers and intersections and things that may or may not be a part of the evidence."

"Hmm" was all he said.

"I'm quite serious," she said, removing his hand from a particularly sensitive area of her person. "Combining information could speed the investigation up. Actually, I'm not sure what you expect I can do against the Black Hand."

"Nothing. That's not what you're needed for."

"Then for what? Or did Tommy Green's information relate to something else entirely?"

"Countess, watching your mind at work is an exhilarating experience."

"Not about the Black Hand." She sat up. "I knew it."

He pushed her back down again. "Peripherally."

"How so? What is it about?"

"Tommy Green was going to tell us."

"Us? You and me? Or 'us' as in you, me, and the others whom I've never met and whom I assume I'm working for."

"You are."

"And will you tell me who they are?"

"Not at liberty. The champagne is getting warm. Now *that* would be a crime."

He poured more champagne, and they both sipped without talking.

Phil had meant to wait him out until he gave her a better answer, but she didn't have the finally honed patience he had. "Where have you been? What have you been doing?"

"I've been out of town."

"Where?"

"On a different matter. Well, not entirely, coinciding but potentially unrelated, except in a tangential way, I believe."

If she hadn't been confused before, she was now. She changed tack. "Do you want to know what I found at Tommy Green's apartment?"

"Yes," he said, toying with the tassel at the point of her nightgown. He didn't even seem surprised at her question.

"It may have nothing to do with the Black Hand."

He flashed her a quick smile. One that she might have seen, or possibly just imagined.

She tried to ignore the feeling it set off in her. "Did you know it had been ransacked before we arrived?"

"We?"

"Preswick, Lily, and I. We had to outwit his typewriter girl and follow her to his rooms. It was completely destroyed. I don't know what they might have taken, but we found several photographs of Rosalind Chandler, she's—"

"I know who she is. What else?"

"A matchbox and a key hidden in his shaving cream."

"Have you ascertained what it's for?"

"Not yet. A briefcase, safety deposit box, a locker perhaps."

"I wonder why they left that."

"Maybe they didn't think to look in his shaving cream. The surface was smooth."

"Amateurs."

"So what is next?" she asked.

"Tommy Green's wake is tomorrow. I need you to go there."

"I would have gone anyway. Should I be looking for something in particular?"

He sighed, and his hand resumed its journey. "You said yourself: crossroads and interjections and superfluous details."

"I said no such thing."

"Hmm." He ran his finger down her collarbone, dipped it beneath the lace of her gown.

And she said no more.

"I do have one question," Phil said some time later.

"You've already had quite a few."

"I don't even know your name."

He turned to his side to give her his full attention. "I fail to hear the question in that statement."

She propped herself up on her elbow until they were face-to-face. "What is your name? Your real name."

"What do you call me?"

She pursed her lips. "I'm afraid some of the things are not befitting a lady."

"And you are, above all, quite a lady, Countess."

"I'll take that as a compliment."

"As well you should." His eyes flashed in the dark. She didn't even know their real color. She'd seen them brown, black, gray, blue—glass lenses, Preswick had told her. Sherlock Holmes had often used them in his many disguises. And people thought fiction was stranger than life.

Not *her* life, Phil was happy to say.

"What else do you call me?"

Phil's breath caught. "Mr. X."

He laughed. It was melodious and carefree, and Phil marveled, because she knew he could be ruthless.

"You don't really? It sounds like a character from a dime novel."

"Well, what do you expect, with you coming and going

through windows, appearing and disappearing in the fog, handing out pistols like cocktails."

"Hmm. I like it." And that put an end to further conversation.

It was almost light when Phil roused enough to find herself alone again. She still didn't know his name—but she felt his presence.

And not in a mystical way. He was still on the premises.

She slipped out of bed, snatched her robe from the chair, and fastened it together as she hurried down the hallway.

He was standing before the tree, his back to her.

"It's not a bad-looking tree," he said as she reached the door. She slipped inside and came to stand beside him.

He turned his head ever so slightly away, just enough to blur his features. But she at the moment was more taken with the feeling that standing side by side evoked. Imagining a life much different. But not for her. And she didn't mind.

Bringing villains to justice was much more interesting.

"Just keep doing what you're doing. I have to go." With one last—dare she say, longing—look at the tree, and a quick but deep kiss, he turned on his heel and strode out of the room.

She caught up to him at the front door.

"You're using the door?"

"Yes. Really, it's much too cold to ask me to scale five floors of hotel walls tonight."

"Could you have?"

"For you? What do you think?" He smiled, and for a second, she thought she actually caught a glimpse of the real him. But she knew better than to congratulate herself. He would be different next time they met.

"And could you go back down that way as well?"

"Of course, but tonight I'll take your elevator. Good night, Countess." And he closed the door in her face.

Oh, how she wanted to open that door and see him in the glow of the corridor sconces. But she didn't. It was almost as if she'd taken a code of honor. One day they would meet face-to-face in the light.

15

Thomas Green's wake was held on the twenty-second-floor reception hall of the *Times* building.

Phil rode the elevator with several other attendees, four of whom had the familiar slouch-fitting, cigarette odor–saturated clothing of beat reporters. The other two were a man and woman, both midheight, darkly clad, and suitably somber.

Phil gritted her teeth and counted the floors as they passed, sometimes stopping at various levels to let on passengers and finally coming to a stop at the reception hall.

She stepped into the vestibule on rather shaky legs, but feeling considerably more comfortable than she had in her first trip up.

She stopped to check her coat with the check girl and slipped her ticket into her handbag. Phil had to resist the temptation to touch Tommy's key, which was safely sequestered beneath her bolero jacket. She'd had Lily sew special pockets into several of her outfits for items such as this.

She'd worn this particular ensemble for that purpose, on the outside chance she might stumble onto a lock it actually opened. Preswick's search had identified the key as most likely fitting a briefcase or small strongbox. She didn't have much hope of finding either, since she knew from Marty that Sydney had already had Tommy's desk cleared out and his work turned over to someone else—not Marty.

But there might be other places, if she could just get to them.

She went inside, where she stopped to peruse the high-ceilinged room, which took up most of the floor and was already filled with a large crowd. Colleagues in rumpled suits crowded around one of the bars. Printers and compositors, editors and office workers mingled with people from all walks of life and nationalities. The well-dressed rubbed elbows with the not-so-well-dressed at the buffet table.

All had come to pay their respects to Tommy Green.

The first person she saw was Detective Sergeant Atkins, standing across the room with Charlie Miller, Carr Van Anda, and Sydney Lord, and looking very distinguished in a gray wool suit.

Standing several yards away was a not-so-distinguished-looking policeman, just as tall but heavier, and not so handsome or honest as Detective Sergeant Atkins.

Sergeant Charles Becker. The Fireplug.

He was talking to a group of men who hovered over the food table and looked as if they wished him elsewhere. The Fireplug was not liked at the best of times. He was unforgiving, ruthless, and the hatchet man for many a crooked politician.

And any newsman who got too close to any of his dealings would pay.

Is that what had really happened to Tommy Green? He'd discovered something about Becker and his associates, something provable and damnable? Heaven knew Becker had so far escaped every suspicion that fell on him. He had powerful friends and ruthless henchmen.

Was Tommy's murder as simple as that? Becker had him removed from a trail that led to him, or that led through him to someone more important?

Had one of his thugs done the deed while he waited nearby

to whisk the body away in an official-looking van to be dumped where it might not be discovered until days or weeks later, and across town from where he had actually been killed?

Becker had threatened Phil once. He would not hesitate to use bodily harm to her person if he thought she was poking her nose into something he was involved in. She would keep a wide berth from him if she could.

She saw Marty and Bev standing at the edge of the room and made her way toward them.

"Phil!" Bev said. "I didn't know you were coming today. I only came myself to support Marty."

Marty didn't look like she needed support—she looked ready for battle.

Bev shrugged. "Besides, when you're still considered to be in mourning, receptions and wakes are the only events where you can have fun without censure."

"Not that you give a hoot about censure," Marty reminded her.

"No, but dear Papa has to live in this town, and without Reggie leading me down the path to hell as an excuse, I have to somewhat toe the line. Try the punch, it's not bad. I saw Ernie Galloway pour a bottle of rum into it. Oh good, the divinely rugged Detective Sergeant Atkins is on his way over."

Phil cut a sideways look across the room. He was definitely heading in their direction, taking his time, stopping to talk, as if he didn't have a destination, but headed inexorably toward them. And she had no doubt Charles Becker would notice.

"Detective Sergeant," Bev said. "So delightful to see you." She frowned suitably. "Even at such a solemn occasion. You know Lady Dunbridge. And you remember my friend, Martha Rive?"

"Ladies," he said, and settled back to his usual unflappable demeanor.

Small talk ensued while Phil merely observed, thinking how well Atkins fit into any situation. She'd never seen him ruffled, whether in high society or "under cover" as a bum at the docks where she'd first come into contact with him.

When several other people joined them, Atkins took the opportunity to move closer to her. "Why am I not surprised to see you here?"

"Because," Phil said, looking straight ahead, "you know I have a respect for investigative reporting."

"Investigative being the real reason?"

"I would think respect would be the reason."

"Touché. Just steer clear of Becker. He smells blood, figuratively, at the moment. I wouldn't want him to spill yours." He nodded to her.

She nodded to him. "Are you trying to frighten me?"

"Yes. Is it working?"

"A bit."

"Ladies." He nodded to Bev and Marty and took his leave.

Bev sighed as she watched him walk away. "Those shoulders."

"Would clap you in jail so fast your head would spin," Marty said.

Bev chuckled. "He almost did, didn't he, Phil?"

"Pardon? I'm sorry, I wasn't listening." She'd just noticed Harriet Wells, red-eyed and morose. Atkins was headed straight toward her.

Now, if Harriet could manage to not blurt out the whole story of their visit to Tommy Green's apartment. . . . Phil had every intention of telling Atkins about the episode, but not here, where so many curious eyes and ears might overhear.

Just as he reached her, she was joined by Eddie, the mailroom boy, who took a protective stance. Atkins didn't even look their way, but walked past and joined a group of reporters.

Eddie handed Harriet his handkerchief, but she seemed not to notice. Sydney Lord had just walked by, and her eyes followed him, until Eddie shook the handkerchief at her.

"I wondered where she'd gotten to," Marty said. "She hasn't

stopped crying since Tommy didn't show up for his deadline. At least she has a real reason now. Though I guess I feel a little sorry for her. So did Tommy, I think.

"But he soon lost patience with her. There are things a journalist is born with, some things you can learn, hone, but not if there isn't a germ of them to begin with.

"Tommy had it." Marty took a shaky breath. "When I first landed a job here, they put me on society news, but Tommy told me not to resent being there. That there was where the real dirt was to be found. And digging it out sometimes led to major news.

"Tommy Green taught me about good reporting." She breathed out a laugh that managed to sound sad. "That was four whole years ago. And I'm still covering birthday balls and opera openings.

"But he was right. There is plenty of dirt just below the façade of polite society. And I have more of the tools I need to learn the truth than most other journalists."

"Let me guess," Phil said. "Polish, money, and a brain."

"Exactly. One day he took me to meet Jacob Riis. He's one of the most important social journalists we have. His wife had just died, and he seemed like a broken man until he started talking. Then you could feel the power of his insight. And his photos, a whole world unseen by most. I would have taken up that work if given a beat of my own."

"But you didn't?"

"No. I did get a promotion. Now I'm the assistant editor of society news, but I've learned something about paying attention to the normal and deducing a story from what isn't said. And I learned that from the best."

This was a different side of Marty than she had shown before.

"Tommy took you on as his protégée?" Phil asked.

"Not really a protégée. Tommy was about the news. I didn't expect more from him."

"But it sounds like Harriet did. Perhaps she was just looking for a father figure."

"In Tommy? Unlikely." She physically shook herself. "I don't know why I'm blathering on like this."

Phil thought she did. It was a way of saying thank you to a man she admired and respected.

Somewhere in the room a glass tinkled. Followed by another, silencing the room. Charlie Miller, editor in chief of the *Times*, climbed to a dais that had been placed at the front of the room, and everyone turned to listen.

He looked over the crowd, maybe looking for the Tommy he'd never see again. Cleared his throat.

"Tommy Green's first assignment for the New York *Sun* was back in seventy-eight. He was barely out of high school, and they sent him to Pennsylvania to cover the Molly Maguire trial. He was called back to New York right after the hangings. But when he came over to the *Times,* he told me that he was never totally convinced of the identity of the Molly Maguires or whether those miners were really guilty. He always said that being called back before he finished his investigation to his own satisfaction made him the man and the journalist he was. Pushed him to have the tenacity to get to the truth, no matter where that truth led."

Hmm, thought Phil. So covering Roz's award ceremony was not his first assignment. And unless something had happened to make him fall from grace, it wasn't the kind of assignment he would have been given once he joined the *Times*.

"It's only fitting that he end his work on assignment investigating the Black Hand. I only wish he'd lived to tell his story.

"We'll tell your story, Tommy." Charlie Miller lifted his glass. "To you, Tommy, give 'em what for in heaven."

"To Tommy," added Carr Van Anda, whose voice sounded a bit wobbly.

Everyone lifted their glasses; noses were blown; hard-hitting journalists broke down in tears. Tommy Green had been respected and well loved. And he'd been cut down at the height of his career.

From the tail of her eye, Phil saw Marty wipe a tear from one eye.

So, not so hardened as she put on.

Phil waited an appropriate moment, then turned to her. "You were saying Tommy was a bachelor."

"Do you never let up? We're at a wake." Marty laughed. "I completely understand. Very well, here's your last piece of gossip, and do not spread it around; the man is dead. Do you see that woman over there talking to Sydney?" Phil followed Marty's gaze across the room to a woman whose deep black dress did nothing to hide her voluptuous figure any more than the fur-trimmed shoulder cape around her shoulders hid the deep V of her décolleté.

Her hat, one of the smaller silhouettes advanced for the coming season, set off thick black hair; a half-veil covered her eyes but left the rest of her face strangely vulnerable. Perhaps fifty years of age, she had the air of someone just outside the acceptable.

"Who is she?"

"Mrs. Toscana. She owns one of the most exclusive brothels in the city. On Thirteenth Street, a hop, skip, and scurry away from Tammany Hall. They say her girls are favorites of some of our most respected politicians."

A brothel, thought Phil. "Her name wouldn't be Rose, by any chance?"

"Sally, I believe."

"Is there any particular reason for her being here?"

"Paying her condolences?"

"Is she acquainted with Tommy? Or sold him information, perhaps?"

Marty shrugged in a very noncommittal way.

"Are you saying Tommy Green frequented her house?"

"There were rumors he'd been seen there, but there are always rumors about everything."

"You didn't believe them?"

"Not exactly. Mrs. Toscana's is above Tommy's touch. There are many cheaper places adequate to relieve a man's itch, if I may be so crude."

"And it's near Tammany Hall? By any chance the brothel attached to the Cavalier Club by the underground passage?"

"The same."

Mrs. Toscana slipped a black-edged handkerchief beneath her veil. Crocodile tears, or real emotion?

"So if not a mistress, perhaps an informant?" Phil guessed.

"You do have a vocabulary, Phil. But I don't know. No one has ever said for certain."

"But do *you* think he was using visits to Mrs. Toscana's as an opportunity to uncover political secrets?"

"Can you think of any other reasons beside the obvious?" said Marty. "I'm sure you'll agree with me, that men tend to talk more than they should when they've sated themselves."

"It can be a lucrative business, selling secrets."

"Yes," Marty said slowly. "It can. But Mrs. Toscana would never jeopardize her very singular connection to Tammany Hall and other men in power."

Not unless it was for a very important reason or person, Phil thought. She would have to look into that relationship.

"Do you think it could be important?" Marty asked.

"Probably not. I'm sure you're right about Mrs. Toscana— she would know the value of discretion."

But it might be. Tommy was working on a story about the Black Hand; lived in the Union Square area; befriended Roz Chandler, a politician's wife; and had some relationship with Mrs. Toscana, a brothel owner.

Disparate pieces of information. But like Marty, Phil had insight, patience, and grit. How else had she navigated the treacherous society of the London peerage and survived? And survived rather well, if she did say so.

But she also recognized her limitations. Whatever Mr. X was interested in, it was larger than her expertise.

It was time to make a new plan of attack, leave the Black Hand to those better equipped to deal with them, and concentrate on what she did well, and better than any man. Insinuate herself with the individuals involved.

"What are you thinking, Phil?" Marty's eyes were intense, her voice low but insistent.

"Yes, Phil," Bev said. "Have you learned something?"

"Maybe."

"Was it something that John Atkins told you while you were monopolizing his attentions a few minutes ago?"

"Yes, that's it," Phil lied.

Did she dare trust Marty not to speculate and publish prematurely, or Bev to keep quiet about it?

"It isn't much, Marty. And you must not tell a soul, not even your boss."

"And if I promise?"

"Then . . . whatever I learn, I'll tell you first."

"Before the other papers get wind of it?"

"Yes." *If she could.*

"Okay, I swear."

Phil chose her words carefully. "Atkins thinks that Tommy was meeting someone when he was killed." She paused long enough to look around to make sure they weren't being overheard.

And caught sight of Harriet glaring at them across the floor. Eddie was no longer with her. But Sydney Lord was, and next to him stood Charles Becker.

"Marty, don't look now, but what relationship does Sydney have with the police? Charles Becker in particular."

Marty managed not to look, but Bev couldn't help herself. "Euww. He's fraternizing."

"Ingratiating himself is more like it," Marty said with a quick glance in Sydney's direction.

"Marty," Phil said. "Do you think you can stifle your disdain and use your feminine wiles long enough to get Sydney and Becker away from Harriet? No telling what she'll say."

"Why?"

"Do you want the story, or not?"

"I'm on my way."

"And be careful."

Marty crossed the floor and wedged herself between Harriet and Sydney, and slipped her arm into Sydney's, effectively cutting out Harriet with the finesse born of years of etiquette training.

After a hard glare at the back of Marty's head, Harriet stalked away.

Becker wandered off toward the bar.

And Phil went in search of Harriet Wells. Really, the girl was courting trouble. Someone had to impress upon her the need to not talk to Becker, or Sydney, for that matter. Phil wouldn't trust him not to blurt something out just to make himself seem more important. Perhaps Phil could convince her to pay her parents a visit for the holidays.

She made the rounds, speaking to people and looking for Harriet. Perhaps she'd chosen the wise thing to do and gone home.

Phil went out into the hallway, where several people were waiting to take the elevator down. Harriet wasn't among them.

Phil started to go back inside and heard someone sniffling nearby. She followed the sound around a corner to the stairs that connected all the floors of the building.

And there was Harriet, sitting on the stairs, clutching a handkerchief to her nose.

Phil sat down beside her. Harriet's reddened eyes appeared above the white fabric. "What do you want?"

"I just thought you might want some company. And to

warn you not to talk to Sergeant Becker. Stay as far away from him as you can."

"I'm trying, but I needed to talk to Sydney and Becker was there."

"So did you talk to Sydney?"

Harriet's shoulders hiccupped. "No. I meant to ask him something, but then Becker came up. And then Marty butted in. I'm so unhappy."

"Maybe you're missing your family," Phil said, hoping to give the girl a nudge about leaving town, but Harriet was not one to be inspired by deep thinking.

"No, I want to be here for New Year's and see the new ball drop."

"You can come back for New Year's Eve." Surely they would have solved Tommy Green's murder by then. "I just thought a little change of scenery would help. Where it's safer," Phil added in a solicitous voice meant to instill fear.

Loud voices broke into their conversation, and Harriet cowered back against the steps. "It's him," she mouthed.

Becker. Phil didn't need to be warned. She'd recognize that voice anywhere.

Harriet eased to her feet. Phil put out a hand to stop her, but the girl bolted up the stairs. It only took a second for Phil to follow.

They stopped on the next floor.

"In here," said Harriet, and ran across the small lobby to a door that opened onto a similar room as the reception area, except it was lit from above and appeared to be unfinished.

"What is this?" Phil whispered as Harriet closed the door behind them.

"The storage room. Do you think he followed us?"

"I don't know," Phil said distractedly.

The walls were lined with steel lockers with preinstalled locks. Several rows of shelves held stacks of papers, boxes, and old typewriters and other small equipment. On the far side was another row of what must be temporary lockers. Some were closed by padlocks, others had no locks at all.

Phil touched the key in her inner pocket. Was it possible . . .

"Harriet, what is stored up here?"

"Junk," she said uninformatively. "They're going to fix it up, but everything else seems more important. So anyone who doesn't know what to do with something they don't need, they toss it up here. And stuff waiting to be archived in the library downstairs. Eddie's forever having to cart junk up here."

"Eddie, the mail boy?"

"Yeah, he delivers the mail and picks up stuff that needs to be stored. Oh, and they're storing the New Year's Eve ball in here before they take it up to the flagpole for its test run."

"Really?" Phil said, only half listening; she was interested in the electrically lit ball that would be the centerpiece of this year's New Year's celebrations, who wouldn't be? But at the moment, she was more interested in the possibility of her key fitting one of these lockers.

Unfortunately, she couldn't very well test it in Harriet's presence, which meant at some point, she would have to confide in Marty.

"So, what's above us?"

"The observatory. You can see all of New York and Long Island and New Jersey from there, but it kind of makes you feel queasy. Above that's the Lantern, a little room where they attach the ball before hoisting it up the flagpole. You want to see the ball?"

"Sure," Phil said, wondering at Harriet's sudden enthusiasm.

Harriet ducked under a rope that separated the ball from the rest of the room, to a corner where a tarp covered what had to be the ball. It was at least five feet in diameter. Harriet used both hands to lift the cover a few inches, and Phil caught a glimpse of curving wooden and metal lathes all fitted with round light bulbs that would turn it into a giant glowing globe when lit.

"How on earth will they get it onto the flagpole?" Phil asked.

"How should I know?" Harriet dropped the tarp and went back to the door.

Evidently her fit of the dismals was over, and the sullens were fully back in place.

Phil stopped her at the stairs.

"Remember, no talking to anyone about anything. And think about spending Christmas at home. I'm sure the paper won't mind."

Harriet nodded, then climbed down the stairs to the wake.

They reached the vestibule to find Mrs. Toscana being helped into her coat.

Drat. Phil had meant to make her acquaintance during the wake.

Oh well, it couldn't be helped. Phil quickly handed her ticket to the coat-check girl, who seemed to take an inordinate time finding her coat.

When the girl finally returned, Phil practically snatched her coat from her hand and raced out the door to the elevators with it in her arms.

Mrs. Toscana was just stepping into the elevator. Phil stepped in beside her.

As the operator started to close the gate, a hand reached out and stopped him. Sergeant Becker stepped in.

Phil kept looking straight ahead. She imagined Mrs. Toscana did the same, though she didn't dare look.

It was the longest elevator ride Phil could imagine.

At last they reached the ground floor. She was afraid Mrs. Toscana would continue down to the subway.

But Becker gestured to the open door. "Ladies."

Phil stepped out of the elevator behind Mrs. Toscana. She

didn't dare look up; his voice had been enough to chill her blood.

Mrs. Toscana kept walking toward the Forty-Third Street exit, but Phil paused to put on her coat and adjust her hat, acutely aware of Becker, who headed for the Forty-Second Street exit. As soon as he was out the door, Phil took off after Mrs. Toscana.

She was just getting into a waiting automobile.

Phil didn't hesitate but ran after her. "Mrs. Toscana. I'm Lady Dunbridge. I'd like to come see you tomorrow, if I may. It's about Tommy Green."

Mrs. Toscana's face, what Phil could see of it, had been a sepulchral mask, but at the mention of Tommy's name, her lip twitched violently.

"Truly, I only wish—"

"Shh—" She hissed so violently that Phil shushed.

Mrs. Toscana's lips formed into a semblance of a smile, and her focus moved from Phil to someone who was passing by. Phil didn't have to look to know that she'd been outsmarted by the crookedest cop in Manhattan.

She could kick herself.

With the same smile rigid on her face, Mrs. Toscana said, "Do not come. You do not want to get involved in this." With that she climbed in. Her chauffeur shut the door and ran around to the front of the car.

Mrs. Toscana stared straight ahead as they drove away.

Phil hurried toward the taxi stand, not to follow Mrs. Toscana but to get home. And to get away from Becker, who was probably still lurking nearby. It hadn't been coincidence that put him in the same elevator. She didn't relax until she had given the driver her direction and leaned back against the seat.

Traffic had become more and more congested as the season progressed. Taxis were parked two deep along the Plaza curb. Another Christmas celebration being held at the hotel, Phil supposed. She had the driver let her off on the opposite side of the street

She waited for him to drive away and waved to Just a Friend at the park entrance before stepping out into the street to cross to the hotel.

She never made it.

A heavy black town car swerved toward her, barely grazing her side. She stumbled back as a door opened and a man jumped out. He grabbed her around the waist and pushed her inside the car.

The last thing she saw was Just a Friend dropping his papers and running toward her. Then a cloth was pushed to her face, a sickening sweet smell clogged her nose, and she saw no more.

16

There was a rattling in Phil's head and a grinding noise that hurt her ears. *Someone should close the window. The noise woke her. Lily, close the window.*

She felt sick, all this swaying and the noise and her stomach heaving with every move.

Then it stopped. Just like that.

A door opened, a nasty smell, brackish like Brighton at low tide, trash in summer . . . She bolted upright, started to flail, before her senses caught up to her instincts.

Someone dragged her out of the . . taxi? *No, she had gotten out of the taxi . . . was about to cross the street to the Plaza. . . . A big black auto . . .*

She swung out her arms; hit something hard; heard an "oof."

Open your eyes, fight for your life. They were going to kill her.

Her eyes snapped open, though they didn't want to stay that way, they wanted to close, she wanted to sleep like before the carriage woke—

"There is no carriage!" she screamed, though no words came out. They were just in her head. *A taxi. A big black automobile. Just a Friend running. You've been kidnapped.*

She was being dragged down a street or an alley. Why did no one stop them? *Think. Use your faculties.*

Her faculties seemed to be sleeping.

Her eyes had closed again against the jarring of her teeth

as her feet bounced over . . . cobblestones. No . . . bricks, the street. Narrow, buildings on each side. An alley?

Don't close your eyes. The sound of a foghorn. London. No. New York. Freezing salt air. The docks. *Tommy Green's body.*

They stopped. Two men held her up. Another one bent over a door. *Three men.*

The door creaked inward. Inward. *Remember that; it could be important.*

Dragged across the floor and thrown onto a long . . . cot. *At least not the floor.* She'd just bought this coat.

Think.

"Now what do we do?"

"Wait. He'll be here soon."

He. So, the leader was coming.

That would be important. She tried to straighten. She couldn't move her hands.

"Where is he? She's coming round."

"You better give her another dose."

Play dead. Childhood games. *Nanny can't find us.*

This was not a game. But Phil didn't flinch at the realization. She didn't move; she couldn't afford not to stay alert, and who knew what they'd given her or how long it had lasted.

And was there anyone who had missed her yet?

Just a Friend running toward the car. She'd seen him through the passenger window. Surely he'd run to the hotel for help. But would they believe him? Preswick would, but by that time it would be too late. How could they find her in this huge city?

She carefully slid her hands under the fold of her coat, tried to separate them. They had tied her hands.

And her feet?

She rolled her ankles, felt no constraints. Her feet were free; now, if only her legs would work when the time came. She tightened her muscles; they seemed to respond, but it was hard to tell how much in her state of fog.

Two hard knocks at the door.

The three men jumped so violently that they didn't see Phil do the same.

She watched the door through half-closed eyes, and saw the shape of the man who entered before she recognized the man himself.

Fireplug.

She'd wandered into something way over her head. And where the hell was Mr. X when she needed him?

Waves of panic tumbled through her thoughts. *Stop it.* She would either die or get herself out of this unacceptable situation. And it would be up to her.

Becker didn't say anything, just took a step toward the cot. He moved, then his shadow moved.

That wasn't right. Phil squinted into the darkness. The only light in the room seemed to be above her, making it impossible for her to identify any of them.

Clever, but not so clever. She'd recognized Becker. Then she understood what that meant. It didn't matter if she saw him, because they weren't planning to let her live.

He stopped about four feet away. His shadow moved to the side. Not a shadow, a second man. Who was he?

Now there were five of them. Not very good odds, as her racing friends would say. But not the worst, either. Not that she thought she had any chance against them physically. Where was her purse? Surely they'd relieved her of it, and of her pistol. She didn't dare look.

But she'd be damned if she'd die lying down.

She sat up. Brushed at her skirts and saw her purse tucked under them. How thoughtful. Now, if she could only reach it . . . and do what? Shoot an officer of the law?

He didn't bother to take off his overcoat or that stupid hat. Honestly, she was developing an outright antipathy toward bowlers, even though Preswick still wore one in keeping with his status as butler.

She took a breath. There. *Remember, you are a countess,* and this ghoul is . . . well, better not to think about that.

"I'm sorry I can't offer you tea, Sergeant." Her voice almost sounded countess-like.

"Don't mess with me. I don't care if you're the Queen of Sheba, if you get in my way, I'll be inclined to remove you. Lucky for you, you're needed for the charity ball."

Was he being sarcastic?

"You mean, there are certain wives who would make their husbands' lives hell if I wasn't available to lead off the dance . . . and after all this publicity."

He cast what she knew must be a reactive glance over his shoulder. His shadow shifted. Who was standing there in the dark? Why didn't he show himself?

Becker snarled, actually snarled, his mouth moving like a ventriloquist's dummy. "But there's nothing to prevent you from having an accident on your way home from the ball."

She wouldn't remind him that the ball was being held at the Plaza and her home was upstairs.

"So back off or face the consequences."

He'd seen her talking to Mrs. Toscana. Had that been the catalyst? But what did the brothel owner have to do with the Black Hand—or Tommy Green?

What had she stumbled into?

"I'm trying to decide if even that's worth the delay."

Phil sighed. "And I've had a sensational gown shipped from Paris just for the occasion."

"Don't get smart with me. You may be full of pomp, but that lovely little maid and that old stick of a butler won't be spared, either." Becker turned his back, and she strained against the ropes that bound her hands. She had the most overwhelming desire to break his neck with her bare fingers. If they would even fit about that bloated sausage of muscle.

He turned back. "And don't bother buying a Christmas present for that sniveling little newsboy—he will be taken care of, too." A villainous sneer right out of one of Lily's dime novels. Phil couldn't think of anyone she despised more at the moment.

"I don't put up with uppity women who poke their noses into where they ain't wanted. Do I make myself clear? Your highness?"

Really, why was it so hard for Americans to get titles right?

She nodded. She knew what Becker did with people who crossed him. *Fireplug,* she reminded herself. *He's just a fireplug. A vicious, murderous fireplug.*

"Do you plan to make this look like another Black Hand murder?"

He lunged so swiftly, Phil was sure he had read her thoughts. His bulk shut out the light from the one lamp burning ominously above her, turning everything to shadow but him, his arms spread like the harbinger of death.

He grabbed her arms, lifting her off the cot, held her trapped in the air. Then he shoved her away. She dropped back to the cot, banging her head on the brick wall. For a moment she was afraid she was going to pass out as tiny black dots filled her vision. But Phil was a Hathaway and the Hathaway women were made of sterner stuff.

"Do you understand?"

"Perfectly," she managed.

"And don't bother to go whining to your friend Atkins. His days are already numbered." He was so close, she could have scratched his eyes out, if her arms would only move.

He stepped back for his final coup de grâce. "This is my town—you'd do best not to forget that. Stay out of my way or else."

The sound of a door opening and closing. Becker was gone. But his shadow was still there. She could hear his footsteps on the floor. She could sense him. A second of mumbling. Then, "Kill her," and he, too, was gone.

The second lantern was relit, and Phil could see the three

men, two standing facing her, one leaning against the door, not to keep her in, she realized, but as if he could keep whatever had just left out.

The three men looked from one to the other, then to Phil.

"I ain't killing no woman," one said.

"Then kiss your arse goodbye," said the other.

The third said nothing at all.

"Okay. Let's just dump her in the river. Nobody could survive in those clothes in this temperature."

Phil was shaking violently. She was the Countess of Dunbridge. It simply wouldn't do.

Somewhere deep inside her, pinned beneath a trash heap of fear, a spark of something flashed. *Don't be bullied. Find a way out. Don't stop. Don't be cowed.*

When her father force-marched her down the aisle, she'd withstood her fear. When the earl came to her bed, she'd bit her lip until it bled, but she didn't succumb to the fear. When he raised his fists, called her names, paraded his mistresses for the world to see, she'd lifted her chin, faced the world, and took her own lovers.

She'd be damned if she'd let some bent cop in a bowler hat be her downfall. She knew how to survive, and she'd make certain that those she cared about would be safe. If she could just get out of here.

She ran her tongue over dry lips.

"How long are you keeping me here?"

The men jumped as if they'd been goosed.

She eased her wrists apart, but it only made the knots tighter. If they would just leave her, she could use her teeth, but all three just stood at the far side of the room and stared.

Probably working up the courage to dump her in the river.

She had to get out. She glanced toward the one window, so grimy no one could possibly see through it, if they were even looking.

Was that a face she saw?

No. It was nothing. Fear was slipping ghosts of false hope into her mind. It was up to her. Thank God none of them had been willing to tie her feet. Modesty among thieves.

If she survived this, she would never scoff at old-fashioned prudery again. No, better not to make bargains she knew she could never keep.

Three of them, one of her—with tied hands. She needed a plan, but she couldn't seem to think past the first step. Her thirst was distracting, as was the tumult in her stomach, caused, no doubt, by whatever drug they'd used to subdue her.

One of the men turned over a bucket; liquid splashed on his feet, and he swore an oath before moving it aside, placing it on the floor, and sitting down on it.

Perhaps she wasn't the first prisoner they'd brought here. She tried not to wonder about the others.

The room was larger than she'd thought at first, the size of her parlor at the Plaza, but worlds away in décor. Brick walls. A virtual prison. A high window, a basement? She didn't remember bouncing down steps, just straight down an alley.

Not that that helped.

She strained to hear any sounds from outside. Faint knocks, footsteps? She couldn't tell what was real and what she imagined.

She might yell, but even if someone outside did hear her, which she doubted considering the walls, her captors would have subdued her, possibly killed her, before help could be summoned.

She fingered the ropes at her wrists, careful not to struggle, which would only tighten the knots. She managed to find a free end and used her finger and thumb to push the end toward the knot.

But even if she managed to free her hands, how could she possibly outmaneuver three crime-hardened thugs?

If she did survive, lessons in self-defense would be put into practice immediately for all three of them.

Two loud knocks sounded on the door.

Once again, all three men jumped, and so did Phil.

"He's back," one blurted, his fear palpable.

This was going to be her end, and she'd just gotten to America.

The one closest to the door pulled back the bolt.

To hell with subterfuge. Phil lifted her wrists to her mouth and took the knot between her teeth. Just as the knot gave way, the door slammed open, driving the first thug up against the wall. The other two were overrun by a score of young boys.

Just a Friend stood in the doorway. "Lady, hurry!"

Phil grabbed her bag and hobbled over to the door. Her legs were slow to respond. But she was buoyed up by Just a Friend and an older, larger boy. They fairly dragged her down the alley toward the street.

Phil couldn't help but look over her shoulder, waiting for shouts, running footsteps, gunshots, but when the thugs finally appeared, two newsies who had been hiding on either side of the door bent down in a game of leapfrog, upending the assailants, who were then jumped on by the others.

Phil and her escorts stumbled along the last few feet of bricks until they reached the street, now dark but for the lampposts that spread cones of light on the ground. They skidded around the corner and ran straight into a large man coming their way.

The boys fell back. The man grabbed Phil, holding her so tight she couldn't even struggle.

"Let me go," she said, without much hope. She hoped the boys had run away, saved themselves.

"If I do, you'll probably fall down."

Her ears buzzed. She recognized that voice: not the Fireplug's. Felt a familiar chest, though she'd never actually been this close to it before.

"Detective Sergeant," she said superfluously. "How—?"

"All in good time, but you can thank your news friend for sounding the alarm."

"But how—?"

"As I said, all in good time. Right now, let's get you home."

She realized she was still balanced against his chest. She moved away.

"Pardon me for a second." She hurried over to the curb and proceeded to expel several glasses worth of the *New York Times*'s excellent punch.

A white handkerchief appeared before her downturned face. She took it gratefully, wiped her face, and stood up.

"Thank you. I've been wanting to do that for the last several hours."

"Okay now?"

"I think so," she said, letting him help her into a waiting police auto. "Nothing a nice cup of tea and a gin martini won't cure."

He shook his head.

"But what about the boys?"

"They are being handsomely recompensed."

"By the police department?"

"By me. Now get in."

She waved to the young men, close to a dozen, who were happily counting their largesse, and sat back to the comfort of the padded seat.

"You, too, Jimmy." Atkins motioned Just a Friend over.

"Jimmy? His name is Jimmy?" Phil asked as Just a Friend reluctantly came to the automobile.

"Aw, 'Tective Atkins, you blew my cover."

"Sorry, what is your code name?"

Just a Friend looked shyly at Phil. Shuffled his feet. "Just a Friend."

The detective sergeant's lips twitched. "Well, Just a Friend, how would you like to ride back to the Plaza in an automobile?"

"Would I?" He clambered onto the seat between them. "Making sure you mind your manners," he told Atkins with a cheeky grin.

Atkins threw the traveling blanket over the three of them, and the auto headed uptown, followed by an entourage of cheering, cavorting newsboys.

They dispersed when they reached the corner, back to their lives on the streets, maybe with enough in their pockets to buy something extra for the holidays.

"Where will they spend Christmas?" Phil asked.

"The boys? The ones who don't have homes will be provided for. A warm meal, a little entertainment. New Yorkers can be generous on the odd holiday."

For an embarrassing moment, a knot twisted in Phil's throat. She'd showed some concern for Just a Friend, but it had been Preswick who had actually seen that he'd received a new coat, hat, and gloves.

Phil would have to do more. Those children—though she imagined they considered themselves men, and they'd proven they were today—had saved her bacon. She didn't know how, but Just a Friend had managed it.

"I have a million questions," she said over Just a Friend's head.

"I'm sure you do, and I'll answer as many as I can once you're safe at home."

"Then just one," she said. And of the millions of questions—like How did he find her? How did Just a Friend find her? Were they going after the ruffians who kidnapped her?—the one she asked was:

"Detective Sergeant, do you have children?"

17

He stared at her. Phil was rather surprised herself. She couldn't begin to guess why it had come to her mind, much less had gotten past her mouth. "It's just . . . that you handled those boys so well, I thought maybe . . ." She'd just been kidnapped, thought she was surely going to be killed. Her coat was smeared with offal, and she'd thrown up at his feet. Surely there was something more important to discuss than his fatherhood.

Though at the moment, she couldn't think of anything.

"No, I don't."

"By choice?" She could kick herself. What was wrong with her?

"I think you must be in shock. Or still a bit tipsy from the wake."

"Neither, I assure you. But I thought he was going to kill me and that shifts the things that are important to you." As soon as the words were out of her mouth, she wished she could put them back in. He might ask what she meant, and she wasn't quite sure herself.

But he wasn't interested in her feelings.

"He? One of the men that held you?"

"Yes," Phil said, sitting upright. Good heavens, maybe she *was* in shock. "Becker. He was there. He threatened me. Actually, he told me to keep my nose out of whatever this is. Made it clear he wouldn't stop at just me if I didn't."

"I see that you paid him absolutely no mind."

"I did for a minute. But once you let someone bully you,

there is no escape. I learned that the hard way, Detective Sergeant. Fortune helped me the first time. I don't plan to trespass on her goodwill more than necessary."

Atkins rubbed his face with both hands, which didn't stop the muffled "Almighty God" that exploded from his covered lips.

"Detective Sergeant!" She looked down on Just a Friend's head. She'd totally forgotten about him, he stayed so still.

Atkins nudged the boy's shoulder. "You know the importance of tight lips."

"Don't need to warn me," he said, fingering the coins in his coat pocket.

"Just so we understand each other."

"Right."

The auto pulled to the curb, Atkins opened the door, and Just a Friend crawled over him and jumped out to the street.

"Tarnation, someone took off with my papers."

With a resigned sigh, Atkins reached in his pocket. "Here's something to cover your lost papers."

Just a Friend's eyes glinted.

"Pay up first, understand? You can keep what's left."

"Yes, sir."

"Thank you for saving my life," Phil called after him.

He pulled the wool cap from his head and made a comical bow. "My pleasure," he said, and scampered away.

"I'm worried about him out on the streets," Phil said.

"So am I."

"Maybe I should call Bobby Mullins and ask him to put the boy to work at Holly Farm. He said he might be willing earlier this year." Bobby Mullins, ex–welterweight boxer, lover of women, formerly engaged in marginally legal occupations, right-hand man to Bev's deceased husband, Reggie Reynolds, and now the stable manager at Holly Farm, and Bev's right-hand man. He could keep Just a Friend safe. At least for a while. He also might know more about what was going on than any of them. Just because he was managing Bev's horse farm didn't mean he didn't still keep his finger on the pulse of Manhattan's underworld.

"In fact," she continued, "I should have thought about asking him sooner."

Atkins smiled. "I think you will have a hard time prying the boy from his post. It's very lucrative, and it gives him a sense of doing something important."

"Selling papers?"

"And saving you."

"Not if it gets him killed."

Atkins looked out to the park, suddenly distant. "It's like an avalanche that you can't stop; just watch it take everything in its wake."

"What is?" Phil asked.

"Crime, poverty, you."

Phil blinked. "I thought I might die."

He huffed out a long sigh and leaned back against the seat, his eyes closed.

She risked a glance at him. "There was someone else there. I think there was. I thought it was just Becker's shadow, but it moved separately from him."

"The aftereffects of being drugged," Atkins said.

"I—perhaps. But . . . no. It was someone real. He stayed just out of the light so I couldn't see him, but I heard him. He told them to kill me."

"Are you sure you didn't just confuse Becker's voice in the heightened emotion of the situation?"

"No. I'm certain."

She had his attention.

"Who was it?"

"I don't know. But I won't forget it. And when I hear it again . . ."

"You will come straight to me. Not act on your own."

"And you'll do what? Arrest him because I said it sounded like him? I don't know that much about courtroom proceedings, but I don't think that piece of evidence will wash."

"And what do you think you can do? Confront Becker? If that's all it would take, we would have brought him to book years ago. Do you think it's easy watching him, year after year, run roughshod over the justice system? Systematically crippling the city with bribery, extortion, murder, and God knows what else, and not being able to do a thing about it?

"He'll get his own one day. But not from you—nor me, most likely. God, haven't you been listening to me at all these last few months?"

"Yes, I have," Phil said, taken aback at his uncharacteristic outburst.

"But you don't take my advice."

"I do, but I also have responsibilities. And I would do it all again. I had to do what I did . . . I just didn't anticipate the . . . helplessness."

Phil thought his eyes softened for a moment, but she might have been mistaken, for his voice was just as demanding as ever. "Will you stop doing this now?"

"I can't."

"You won't."

"I can't and I won't. I was taken by surprise, unprepared, so, yes, I was frightened, but I'll recover from it, and be prepared to do what needs to be done. I must."

"Because of the excitement? The challenge?"

"In part." Plus she needed the money, the best way she knew of staying independent. Though, she had to admit, she craved the challenge. She would not let fear or insecurity rule her life. Because you couldn't rule your own life without the courage to do so, and if you didn't, someone else would. And she would not subject herself to that ever again.

"I'm afraid I still need some answers about today."

"Then will you deign to come upstairs? I really feel the need to change out of these clothes. Look at them. And I loved this coat. I've ruined two new coats already this season. I have a good mind to send Becker my cleaning bill."

He coughed out a dry laugh. "Redoubtable, a pain in the . . . neck, but . . ." Another short laugh. "The first time I ever saw you, sprinting across the Reynolds's foyer in that purple gown—"

"Eggplant, chosen for just that purpose."

"To appear . . . ?" He finished the phrase on a question.

"*Formidable*. Though I must admit, it was not one of my more formidable appearances."

"You bowled me over."

"I did?" she asked, a spark coming back to her senses.

"Yes, but fortunately I recovered."

She smiled. The dirty warehouse—for warehouse it must have been—the dirty coat, the dank walls, they all receded from her mind, like a bad dream that disperses to the fringes once the lights are on.

"But yes, I will accompany you to your apartment. I don't want to question you more here." He glanced toward the driver, another policeman, and Phil understood.

What Just a Friend called "ears."

Phil had already learned to trust only one detective. She nodded her understanding.

He dipped his chin. "This one time only, because I need to question you in private."

Bless him, so upright and serious: his statement actually brought the sense of adventure back to her sorely tried psyche.

"In private. That sounds absolutely scintillating, Detective Sergeant."

For the first time ever, Atkins laughed at one of her little witticisms; either she was making progress or he was more rattled than he let on. She certainly was.

"I will tell the Plaza staff that you were grazed by a passing carriage and that I promised Preswick to see you to your door."

"If you say that, they will know you are lying, because Preswick would be waiting for us at the curb."

"True." He frowned. "Perhaps . . ."

"Perhaps you should just let me handle the situation."

A slight nod was the only acknowledgment she got.

As it turned out, the well-trained staff of the Plaza lobby merely nodded greetings, and Egbert took them to the fifth floor without comment. Which meant even heftier tips for the holidays. And what was that doing to her ready cash for Christmas shopping? To be sure, it was leaving even less toward her good intentions to help the unfortunate.

She would have Preswick consult the state of their bank account.

Too rattled still to search for her key in her purse—organization of travel equipment would have to be dealt with as soon as the holidays were over—she knocked. Preswick answered the door so quickly she wondered if he'd been waiting there all day.

With one quick, assessing look, he stepped aside for them to enter and shut the door behind them.

Lily came running. "What has happened? Ar-r-r-r you hur-r-r-rt?" she demanded, glaring at Atkins.

"I'm fine. I was kidnapped, and I need—"

"To get out of these dir-r-r-rty clothes." Lily hustled her down the hall with a last scowl back at Atkins.

"And a—" Phil added over her shoulder.

"A martini, yes, my lady."

"And a glass of water."

A few minutes later, cleaner but still in need of a soak, wearing a soft, moss-green tea gown, Phil returned to the parlor. She had convinced Lily to ask no questions until they joined Preswick and the detective sergeant.

Atkins was sitting in a club chair with a glass of what Phil recognized as double malt whiskey that Preswick insisted on keeping for gentlemen who eschewed the notion of "cocktails." Evidently the detective sergeant was one of them.

He was perfectly framed by the swags of pine and ribbon that festooned the window behind him. A candelabra of red-tapered candles sat on the table at his elbow, presenting a magazine-perfect picture of a gentleman at home for the holidays.

He stood as Phil and Lily entered. Sat when Phil sat and Preswick handed her a glass of water, which she guzzled down. Followed by a very dry martini, which she sipped appreciatively.

Atkins put his glass down and reached in his pocket for his notebook, dispelling Phil's momentary flight of fancy.

Lily reached in her apron pocket and brought out her own notebook, glaring at Atkins, daring him to say anything. She sat on a stool nearby Phil, one side of her skirt lifted to reveal her ankle stiletto within easy reach.

Phil gave her a quelling look.

Lily lifted her chin and gave Phil her full attention.

Phil told them of being snatched outside the Plaza and Just a Friend's having the wherewithal to summon the detective sergeant.

And then something struck her. "But how did he find you? And how did he know where they had taken me?"

Atkins smiled, and for a second Phil forgot her near escape with death.

"He saw them force you into the town car. He managed to run and grab hold of the back. He rode the whole way to the docks clinging to the back of the automobile."

"Good heavens, he's clever. You must never scold him again for such feats of boyhood."

"I don't intend to."

"But I do worry about his safety. The safety of all of you. He threatened Preswick and Lily and whomever was close to me."

"Who, madam, I mean, my lady?"

"Sergeant Becker, Lily. You remember him."

"Yes. I should have cut his hear-r-rt out the fir-r-rst time he came to the door."

"Lily, *pas devant le*—"

"I'm afraid my French is quite adequate," Atkins said. "You will not cut out anyone's heart, slit anyone's throat, or do bodily harm in any way. Or you will go to prison."

Phil sucked in her breath. "That was rather harsh, Detective Sergeant."

"It is a reality. Do you understand, Lily?"

"I will protect my mistress."

"Please do, but do not use that stiletto."

Lily sniffed. Bent her head over her notebook.

Atkins lifted his eyebrows toward Phil.

She nodded. She would talk to Lily. They would protect themselves as the need arose but would not "throw the first punch," as Bobby Mullins would say.

It took nearly an hour of Phil piecing together what had actually happened, especially when she was still under the influence of the drug that Atkins pronounced was probably chloroform.

Preswick had poured her another martini, which was beginning to make her feel light-headed.

Atkins refused another drink, even though he had sent his driver back to the station.

They were surrounded by an excess of holiday decorations; the clove, orange, and pine scents of Christmas filled the air. They were drinking fine spirits and should be celebrating the coming of a new year instead of discussing Phil's near miss with murder. But the detective sergeant was all business, all the time, and yet . . . he'd known how to treat the newsies.

Which reminded her . . .

"I think I owe you money for the largesse you spread among the boys."

He waved her off. "We're allotted a certain amount for . . . emergencies."

Like bribes and payoffs and other small bits of everyday police business, she thought.

"Well, I appreciate it."

He stood. "Do I need to remind all of you that this is no light matter? It seems to me that you've stumbled into more than just a Black Hand operation. And if that is the case, you must all be doubly aware, all of the time.

"I can't put a man to watch you without causing undue publicity. But please, please, be careful. And stay out of anymore investigating. There's nothing you can possibly do about the death of Tommy Green. The police will look for a motive and a suspect. Please stay away from it."

He made a small bow, and Phil stood. "What do you know? What aren't you telling me? Why would Becker come after me now? It's been months since our last encounter. And no one knows I'm involved in these purported Hand attacks but you and a few others . . . unless . . ."

Phil took a fortifying breath. "I had just left the wake—but there were many people there." She hesitated. "Of course. I stopped to talk to Mrs. Toscana as we were leaving. That must have been what set him off. But what does she have to do with this? She runs a brothel."

The detective sergeant's eyes rose to the ceiling, threatened to disappear behind his very thick eyelashes.

"I don't know. But you are not to go snooping around brothels. Do you understand?"

"Is that a police order?"

"Yes."

"Very well."

"Then good day."

"And merry Christmas," Phil added.

He turned back to the room, taking in the tree, the poinsettias, the swags of pine, and the cluster of angels that had appeared on the windowsill as if seeing it all for the first time.

"Merry Christmas. It looks very nice," he returned in a voice that seemed surprised at what he saw.

As soon as Preswick closed the door behind him, Lily said, "Are you going to obey him?"

"Of course," Phil said. "We are not going to snoop around a brothel. I will go on a formal visit to Mrs. Toscana. Perhaps tomorrow, when most of her clients, I suppose, will be at church and Sunday dinner with their wives and families.

"But for now, I would like a hot bath and my dinner."

18

Sunday morning was clear and cold but not uncomfortably so. A perfect day for an outing, though Phil was tempted just to stay in bed with the covers over her head. Her sleep had been haunted by dreams of kidnappings and murders and, strangely, her mother.

She couldn't hide even in sleep. She got up.

Lily appeared immediately from the dressing room. "I will bring your breakfast, my lady."

Phil sighed. She could feel Lily's fear. And determined to swallow her own. "I'll have coffee in the kitchen as usual. You may bring me the houndstooth walking dress."

"No. I mean—"

"Lily. We cannot let fear rule us. Especially not three days before Christmas. We have much to do."

"I know, but . . ."

"No buts, bring me my dress." Phil pushed away the covers and sat up. She felt awful, but nothing coffee and a little determination wouldn't fix.

She dressed in silence and accompanied Lily to the kitchen, where Preswick was waiting to take up the cudgels.

"She wants to go to that woman," Lily informed him, ignoring Phil's presence.

Preswick poured her coffee. "Do you think that wise, my lady?"

Probably not, and she would happily cede her obligations and stay inside; after all, she'd been kidnapped yesterday. But

she knew her duty—more or less. She knew she had to warn
Mrs. Toscana and reestablish order in her own household.

Phil drank her coffee, while Preswick set a plate of eggs
and toast before her. She forced herself to eat.

"I shall make the trip downtown," Preswick announced.

"Then I'm going, too," Lily said.

"Thank you," Phil said. "But this is something I must do."

Lily said, "They might be waiting outside for you."

"I will be careful. But Mrs. Toscana needs to know what
happened and be doubly cautious for her own safety."

"You could telephone her," Lily pleaded.

"Lily," Phil said.

"I know, 'ears.' But you shouldn't go."

Phil felt an unusual tightening in her throat. What had she
done to deserve such loyal servants? And was she right to put
them in danger because she, for the first time in her life, felt
she was doing something important?

She'd spent her whole life taking servants for granted. Not
seeing them as people with their own dreams and fears and
feelings. What dreams did Preswick have after a lifetime in
service? And what about Lily?

In the end, Lily and Preswick insisted on coming, and
truth be told, Phil was glad of their company. She sat squeezed
between them in the taxi as they headed downtown to Mrs.
Toscana's brothel. But not before participating in some subterfuge of their own. Preswick and Lily went out the main
entrance and took a taxi around to the back entrance of the
hotel, where Phil—heavily veiled, at Lily's insistence—was
waiting.

They sat upright, prepared to defend her in case someone
considered making a second move on her person.

She had to admit she was a little nervous. Just coming outside had set off an anxiety that kept her looking around to see
if they were being followed.

She still didn't have a plan of attack for questioning Mrs.

Toscana. She'd never had to actually confront a madam of this sort before. She'd been in company with several in London at various parties and entertainments. She had probably rubbed elbows with a few more since she'd arrived in New York.

To look at Mrs. Toscana, she would have never guessed that she was a prosperous seller of women's favors, and most likely the collector of men's secrets. She'd appeared respectably dressed. Not ostentatious, not tawdry. A perfect balance of quality and decorum.

Phil reminded herself not to always judge a book by its cover.

She sat back, overly conscious of the erect, alert postures of her two servants, and she tried to curb her own fluttery nerves. She'd done so many, many times before. From chasing a murderer to audience with the queen. Just because a woman appeared self-assured and in command didn't mean there weren't times she was quaking on the inside.

It would pass; it always did. The queen turned out to be perfectly lovely, and if Phil didn't care to be kidnapped again, she imagined she would be more successful in that endeavor also.

Thank heavens for Just a Friend and his quick wits and newsboy contacts. They'd saved her life. And now she must keep him safe, too.

Mrs. Toscana's turned out to be a respectable brownstone right around the corner from the Cavalier Club. There were no markings, no sign to advertise to anyone who might be strolling down the street. This was a high-end pleasure palace, and most likely by invitation or recommendation only. *What secrets these walls could tell.*

Curtains covered the windows, and Phil could see no lights on inside.

"Maybe they're still asleep," Lily said. "They stay up late enough."

"Perhaps, and all the better. They won't be on their mettle. Besides, I imagine that Mrs. Toscana will be on the alert. Now, you two make yourselves scarce. I saw a little coffee shop on the corner. I'll meet you there when I'm done."

Neither of them moved.

"That is an order. We don't want her to think she is under attack."

Reluctantly, they walked away.

Phil waited until they had reached the corner before walking up to the front door and ringing the bell.

She was surprised when in less than a minute, the door opened, and a young woman—pretty and blond, wearing a gray skirt and blouse—opened the door.

"Oh," the young woman said. "I thought . . ." She narrowed her eyes, lifted a pair of glasses that hung around her neck, and peered at Phil. "Can I help you? If you're collecting, we've already given."

"I came to see Mrs. Toscana."

"She isn't here. I'm her secretary, if you would like to leave your card?"

"Where is she?"

"She's gone to church."

"Ah. When do you expect her back?"

"I can't say. Why don't you leave your card?"

"I don't mind waiting. Please, I'm no irate wife or sister. I'm here on a personal matter that involves a mutual friend. Possibly a matter of life and death."

As they stood facing each other, a van came to a stop at the curb. Phil tensed, but a delivery boy jumped out and muscled past Phil, carrying a large box.

"Package for Mrs. Toscana." He thrust the box into the secretary's hands and trotted back into the van, which rattled off down the street.

The young woman wrestled the box through the door, but when Phil started to follow, she found the door shut in her face.

"What a singularly unsatisfying visit," Phil said to the

crisp air, and started back toward Third Avenue in search of Lily and Preswick.

She'd barely gotten down the steps when she saw Mrs. Toscana coming her way. She was dressed in a well-fitted wool coat and dark stole falling almost to her knees, and she was carrying a small black prayer book.

She saw Phil and hesitated, just as an explosion sent a shower of splintering glass onto the sidewalk behind Phil. The pavement shuddered beneath her.

Mrs. Toscana screamed and ran clumsily toward the brothel.

"No!" Phil reached for her, but she was too late. Mrs. Toscana stumbled up the steps to the stoop.

Glass and debris littered the ground like so much rubbish. Only a ragged gaping hole was left where the window had been. Phil tried not to think about what had become of the secretary.

Mrs. Toscana was attempting to fit her key to the lock with shaking hands.

"Wait." Phil took the key and opened the door. Mrs. Toscana rushed inside as black, acrid smoke poured out.

Phil followed Mrs. Toscana into the house, into the cloud of choking smoke. She could barely see the forms of several women huddled on the stairs above. They were in dishabille, wrapped in blankets and quilts or shivering in their bare arms in the cold morning air.

"Stay back," Mrs. Toscana ordered. "It may be unsafe."

The girls moved closer to each other. No one spoke.

Mrs. Toscana stepped into a room to the left, crying, "Nellie, Nellie, are you there?" What had been an office—was now the remnant of the office.

The explosion had toppled lamps, overturned tables, breaking glass and leaving black matchboxes everywhere. Scattered papers littered the floor or were trapped against the broken glass of the windows. The shreds of the delivered box had burned into the wood of a kneehole desk that was placed near the window. But at the back of the room, a settee, easy chair, and bookcases had come through the explosion unscathed except for smoke.

A package bomb. Diabolical and deadly, and Phil recoiled.

The desk chair lay on the floor, and beneath it . . .

Phil heard a low moan. As she looked for the source, Preswick and Lily ran into the room.

Preswick took in the situation in one look. He moved Phil aside and gently lifted the toppled desk chair from the fallen secretary.

Mrs. Toscana let out an unearthly wail and tried to reach the girl, but Phil held her back.

Preswick and Lily were already on their knees. Lily automatically lifted her skirt and tore off the bottom ruffle of her petticoats. Preswick began tying it around the woman's arm trying to staunch the flowing blood. Lily dabbed at the cuts on her face.

"Is she—is she—"

Preswick stood. "Telephone for an ambulance." He turned away. "Lily, help me move her to the settee."

Mrs. Toscana looked toward the door, where several girls had ventured and were staring at the destruction.

"Angelina, call for the ambulance. And for Dr. Battista." One of the girls disappeared from the doorway. "Triana, help them with Nellie."

Mrs. Toscana turned back to Phil. "What?" It was all she could get out.

"A package came," Phil said softly. "There must have been a bomb inside. A malicious, cowardly act."

Mrs. Toscana saw the bomb's trappings and reached toward it.

Phil grabbed her arm and stopped her. "Don't. This is a crime scene."

Mrs. Toscana spun around. Phil braced herself for tears and hysterics. What she got was sheer cold fury.

"Will she survive?"

Phil looked toward Preswick. He looked grim but said, "Fortunately, the bomb seems to have detonated facing toward the
window, not back toward the room. She was protected by the
desk somewhat. Her wounds are numerous but don't appear to
be deep. With proper medical attention, she should survive."

"I will kill them for this," Mrs. Toscana hissed, her prayer
book clutched to her chest.

"The Black Hand?" Phil managed.

Mrs. Toscana spat over her shoulder. "The Hand." She
laughed, low and horrible.

"I will kill *him*."

"Who?" asked Phil.

"This has nothing to do with you."

"Becker?"

Mrs. Toscana spun around. "You all must leave! The police
are arriving and I must appear to be afraid of the Hand."

Phil heard the sound of sirens, then automobiles stopping
outside.

"Please, I'm looking into the death of Tommy Green." Phil
reached into her bag for her card case and extracted a card,
which she shoved into Mrs. Toscana's hand.

"This way! Quickly. You must not be found here." Mrs. Toscana pushed Phil, Preswick, and Lily into the foyer.

"Carly, take them out the back."

One of the women dropped the quilt that had been covering her and ran down the stairs. "This way!"

She was wearing a flannel nightgown, which seemed an
odd choice in a brothel, but everything was odd to Phil at the
moment.

Carly motioned them past the stairs and into an unlit
room. Phil could just make out dark paneling and bookcases
filled with books. One of the bookcases suddenly swung open
to reveal steps leading downward.

Carly pushed them onto the steps and followed them in.
The bookcase closed behind them.

And they ran, herded from behind by a young woman in a flannel nightgown. A scene from a gothic horror story.

For several long moments, Phil was only aware of the cold and the uneven bricks beneath her feet. The only light was a lantern that Carly had picked up somewhere near the beginning of their subterranean flight.

At last, Carly eased ahead of them and knocked at a heavy door. She knocked again, louder. The door opened.

A big, dark, muscular man looked in at them. "What's happening?"

"A bomb, at Mrs. Toscana's. Nellie's hurt. These people tried to help."

"This way." His voice was very deep, and it reverberated behind them down the passage.

Preswick hurried Lily and Phil up the steps and into what must be the back hall of the Cavalier Club.

The man led them to a room that was equipped with several mirrors and sinks. And Phil saw for the first time how ghastly they looked.

Preswick and Lily were disheveled and blood-splattered. A length of Lily's petticoat had been dragged over the bricks and hung filthily from the hem of her coat.

Phil hysterically wondered how many coats they would ruin before they captured Tommy Green's murderer. Because it must be the same villain, or group of villains. The murder, the injuries, the people left homeless. She'd been kidnapped, her servants had been threatened, and there seemed to be no end in sight.

Mrs. Toscana wanted her revenge?

Well, now Phil wanted hers.

They cleaned up the best they could, and when they agreed they could pass on the streets without causing alarm, they made the slow, silent walk back to Union Square and the taxi stand.

Phil stopped at the statue of George Washington at the southeast corner of the square. "Show me where they were going to build the new courthouse."

"The courthouse, my lady? Along the east side, just there." Preswick pointed out the row of buildings that ran along the avenue.

"Is that important?" Lily asked.

"I'm not sure. It just seems so much of our investigation centers around this area of town: the bombings, Tommy's courthouse investigation that had been leaked, Tommy and Mrs. Toscana . . . I wondered if they're all somehow connected."

As soon as they were home and changed into clean clothes, Preswick rang for tea, and Phil and Lily went directly to the study.

"Where is that map?" Phil asked, rummaging through the papers on the study table.

"Mr. Preswick mounted it on cardboard so it would be easier to study." Lily reached beside the table and pulled out the map.

Phil added another "X" for Mrs. Toscana's and stepped back to regard her handiwork.

Preswick brought in tea and sandwiches and placed them on the sideboard. The tea was welcomed, but no one could eat just yet.

Phil tapped the map with her pencil. "Why so many in such a small neighborhood in such a short time period? And not their normal haunt.

"And why Mrs. Toscana's? What do they expect to gain, unless it was to pay her back for talking to me?"

"It isn't your fault, my lady. If they went after Mrs. Toscana, it was because she knows something they are afraid of."

"Thank you, Preswick. But why now?"

"Because Mr. Green's investigation must have frightened them."

"But why?" Phil asked, pacing, trying to keep control of her temper.

"The crooks want to take over," Lily said.

"Perhaps it's not all the same miscreants," Preswick suggested.

Phil nodded. "Someone could be taking advantage of the Hand bombings to commit one or two crimes of their own."

"Using similar actions as a cover for their own," Preswick said.

"But why would they do that?" Lily asked.

"For the insurance?" Phil said.

"Or to buy up property cheaply," Preswick said. "I believe there was a similar incident in London a few years back. As I recall, there was a railway station involved."

"Land speculation over the relocation of the courthouse, before it was voted down. That's what Tommy had been investigating last spring before his article was killed," Phil said triumphantly. The triumph didn't last. "But this isn't where they planned to build the courthouse." She stabbed the pencil at the place on the map where the new courthouse would have been.

"Maybe they're planning on building something else," Lily said.

Phil and Preswick both looked at her in astonishment.

"Or somewhere else. Brilliant, Lily," Phil said. "Perhaps they plan to try again. Just a block or two away." She sat down and frowned at the map.

"Is that what Tommy Green discovered during his Black Hand investigation? That it wasn't just the Black Hand doing the damage? Is his evidence hidden in whatever this key in my pocket unlocks?"

Phil jumped up and began to pace again. Were his papers in

one of those lockers in the *Times* storage room? Could Tommy have possibly hidden them there among the hundreds, possibly thousands, of other papers stored there? And if they were, how was she ever going to find them?

She turned suddenly. "Preswick, do you think Detective Sergeant Atkins is working today?"

"I couldn't say, my lady. Shall I call the station?"

"Yes, please. Tell him Mrs. Dalrymple would like to speak to him."

19

Detective Sergeant Atkins was not at the station, and when he hadn't returned her call by ten o'clock the next morning, Phil made a decision. She didn't want to, but she knew the value of climbing back onto the horse after a fall.

Between being kidnapped one day and barely missing a bombing the next, she was feeling a little desperate to get to the bottom of things.

And to top it off, she had to host the charity ball this evening. So she did what any successful lady of society would do. She announced that she would be staying in bed for the rest of the day in order to look her best at the ball, and sent her servants on an errand to the jewelers on the pretext of having one of the facets of her tiara tightened.

As soon as she was certain they were gone, she got out of bed, dressed in her most nondescript traveling suit, covered it with a coat she'd been about to give to the ladies' guild, and headed downtown.

She didn't take a taxi from the Plaza but walked three blocks down to the St. Regis and took a taxi from there.

The front window of Mrs. Toscana's brownstone had been boarded up, and there was debris piled at the curb: a broken lamp, a pile of books, a cushion, and an upholstered chair, the stuffing spewing out of the jagged rip in its fabric.

Phil looked away.

She was surprised to find the front door open. She knocked, purely for form's sake, and stepped into the house.

The foyer was cold, but at least the fresh air was beginning to carry away the acrid smell of smoke. Three women were cleaning the stairs; two more scrubbed the soot-covered paisley wallpaper.

They looked up as she entered but returned to their work without speaking.

Phil looked into the office where the package bomb had done the most damage. A new desk chair sat behind the desk. The carpet had been removed, to be beaten clean in the back alley or thrown out completely. Phil rather suspected the latter. The rest of the room had been cleaned out.

What an evil way to harm someone. An innocent person. Opening a Christmas package. It was beyond dastardly.

One of the young women who was on her hands and knees picking up pieces of indistinguishable material looked up at her.

"You again," she said.

"I came to see how you're all doing."

The woman sniffed. "How do you think? Poor Nellie almost got killed. And she ain't even a whore. It ain't fair to do that to somebody."

"No, it isn't. Do the police have any idea of who did this?"

"That's a laugh. Mrs. Toscana is in the back parlor, if you're looking for her. She's pretty ticked. You better just go on back yourself. Nellie always took care of the—of Mrs. Toscana's guests." She sniffed and ran an arm across her face, leaving a smudge of ash on her cheek.

"Thank you," Phil said, and went down the hall to where the parlor must be.

She knocked on the door, received an "Enter," and let herself in.

Mrs. Toscana sat in a high-backed chair. Her dark hair was pulled back in a bun and covered by a black mantilla. She wore a black, unadorned bombazine dress. The only relief from unrelenting mourning was the white streak of hair that ran from her hairline to her low bun like a bird's wing.

For Tommy Green? Surely not Nellie. "I came to see how you all are."

"Nellie's in hospital. For the rest . . . as you see." Mrs. Toscana didn't invite Phil to sit.

"I only came yesterday to warn you. I was too late. I wondered if there's anything I can do?"

"We take care of ourselves."

"I can see that."

"We'll be expected to be open tonight."

"Are you afraid of more attacks?" Phil asked.

"Of course, but this is their home as well as their place of business," Mrs. Toscana said, unbending a little. "It's important for me to keep the girls healthy, and it is harder to do when they are not under my wing."

Her hand tightened on a black-edged handkerchief. "These hyenas will not intimidate me. Please thank your servants for helping Nellie; the doctor says it saved her life. But you might as well leave. I have nothing to tell you."

"Please, Mrs. Toscana. Do you think this was the work of the Black Hand or someone else?" Not getting an answer, Phil shrugged out of her coat and sat down.

"If you think that getup will protect you," Mrs. Toscana said, sweeping her hand toward Phil's dress, "you're a fool."

"I may be a fool, but two days ago I was kidnapped by Sergeant Becker and another man, whom I didn't see. Yesterday I came to warn you, and a bomb exploded. Now I'm here to say that I will help in any way I can."

"You can't help. Best you go back uptown where you belong."

"This wasn't the work of the Black Hand, was it?"

"I pay the Black Hand to stay away. I pay the other groups— the Camorra, the Mafia—to stay away. I pay the police to stay away. I pay and pay and pay. Now I will make them pay."

"Who, Mrs. Toscana? Do you know who it was?"

"I know. That is all you need to know."

Phil deliberated. She was probably wandering into territory she had no business entering. But since she hadn't been given any instructions and her own investigation into Tommy Green's murder had led her here independently, she refused to budge.

Mrs. Toscana narrowed her eyes. "Why are you here? Why were you at Tommy's wake? Are you a newspaper woman, like the Rive girl?"

"No, I'm here because I want to bring Tommy Green's killer to justice."

"Why?"

"Because it's what I do, very discreetly, usually, and because Martha Rive and her friend Roz Chandler asked me to."

Mrs. Toscana's fingers grasped each other where they lay in her lap. "You would do best to leave this alone. You don't know what you are getting into."

"Then tell me."

Mrs. Toscana's eyes didn't move from Phil's face, but they seemed to be looking through her rather than at her. All the while her fingers worked as if saying her rosary on imaginary prayer beads.

What could Phil say to convince this woman to help her? "I was supposed to meet with Tommy the day he was killed."

Mrs. Toscana's gaze returned to Phil's. "Why? Why would a countess want to meet Tommy? I don't believe you."

"He was supposed to have information for me."

Mrs. Toscana's fingers became completely still. Only her eyes flicked with some inner fire. And Phil got the distinct impression that she was sizing Phil up.

"What information could a beat reporter have that would be of interest to you?"

What could Phil say? That she had no idea? That she'd gone to meet him because she was following orders? "He didn't say. I thought it was about the Black Hand. He was supposed to be investigating them." Though Phil had to admit it was looking less and less likely.

"And what would you know of the Hand?"

Phil deliberated quickly. Could she trust this woman? *Should* she trust this woman? "Only what I've read, but since I began looking for Tommy's murderer, I've been threatened, followed, and kidnapped. I want to know who is behind this."

"*Furfante.*"

"To be sure, a villain," Phil agreed. "Perhaps more than one. But right now, I'm only interested in who killed Tommy Green and why. Can you help me?"

"And did you meet him? Did you get your information?"

"I met him, after a fashion. We were to meet at the Theatre Unique. I went, he was there, but he was already dead."

Mrs. Toscana sucked in a searing breath and crossed herself. "He was found at the docks."

"His body was moved by the police, by Sergeant Becker himself."

Mrs. Toscana made a hacking noise as if to spit. "That devil."

"I can only surmise he had Tommy's body dumped at the docks because for some reason he didn't want him found at the theater. Do you know that reason, Mrs. Toscana?"

"Why should I? Why are you asking me? I know nothing. I don't—" She looked up suddenly, as if she had heard something. But there was nothing. Then her face crumpled. She moaned, a soft, ungodly sound that chilled Phil's bones.

"I knew it would get him killed. I told him so many times, but you couldn't get Tommy to change. Reporting was in his blood, and now he is dead."

Her eyes were black pools of grief.

It was obvious that Tommy Green was more than one of her customers. Was she his informer? friend? confidant? lover? Beneath her severe mourning, Mrs. Toscana was not an old woman.

"How did they kill him?"

Phil didn't want to answer. She didn't want to remember. "His throat was slit."

"*Assassino,*" Mrs. Toscana hissed, and broke down completely. Phil could do nothing but watch. There was more here than Phil had first conjectured.

"Let me help," Phil said. "Let me help find his killer."

But Mrs. Toscana, her head lowered, seemed to have forgotten Phil was there. Phil took the moment to look around the room. Saw three framed photographs arranged on a round mahogany table at her elbow. She turned on the table lamp—Tiffany, she noticed—to examine them more closely.

They were all old and sepia-toned. One of a young man in knickers and short jacket. A family portrait of the same young man and a mother, father, several other children, and . . . a young girl with dark hair and pale complexion. Surely this was Mrs. Toscana as a child.

"That was when we first came to Queens," Mrs. Toscana said out of the silence.

"You have a very large family." Phil smiled. "You must have lovely Christmases."

"Yes, two large tables, the dinner of the twelve fishes. Everyone comes, everyone feasts."

"And this one. What a lovely photograph."

A young woman in her late teens, wearing a simple white gown. For a debutante dance, perhaps. Surely the same little girl.

It looked just as she imagined Mrs. Toscana would have looked at that age. And yet so familiar in the present. Phil thought of her own Lily, pale with dark hair, but not the round face and pointed chin of the girl in the photo. Familiar, but not Lily.

"I was sixteen and that was my coming-out dress, such that it was."

"And this is you, also?" Phil asked, picking up the third

photograph of the same young woman and three young men taken out of doors. "Your brothers?"

"The one standing on the right. Giuseppe. That one sitting on my left is Tommy."

Tommy Green. Phil wasn't even sure of what he looked like except in death. And even then, every time she'd tried to conjure his face, it blinked in and out like the circling carousel of light and dark in the theater.

But this young Tommy Green broke her heart. The serious expression necessary in those days to get a proper photograph. Stretched out on a lawn with Mrs. Toscana—Sally—sitting upright with her skirts spread out around her in the grass.

"You were childhood friends," Phil said.

"We were still friends."

"And who is this?" Phil pointed to the third young man: a little older, stocky, and big, with a square, determined jaw.

"That one . . ." Mrs. Toscana said. "That one was Giuseppe's friend, Samuel Trout."

Phil stared at the images, caught in time. "You all grew up together?"

"No, Tommy and I grew up together. Samuel was Giuseppe's friend." Mrs. Toscana's head snapped toward Phil, as if her mind had been drawn into the past. "How did you find me? Why did you come here? Who sent you?"

"No one sent me," Phil said, taken aback. "I found this in Tommy's pocket, and another in his lodgings." She reached in her purse and brought out the matchbox. *The Rose*. She placed it on the coffee table in front of Mrs. Toscana.

Mrs. Toscana took the box from the table, held it in her open palm, then closed her fingers gently around it.

Not the gesture of some paid occasional congress. She had cared for Tommy Green deeply.

"And this," Phil continued. She reached into her inside pocket and brought out the key she'd found in the shaving-cream jar. "Do you know what this opens?"

Mrs. Toscana reached for it, but Phil's fingers closed over it.

Mrs. Toscana gave Phil an appraising half-smile. "Open your fingers so I can see. I will not attempt to take it from you."

Slowly, Phil opened her fingers.

Mrs. Toscana scrutinized the key. Shook her head. "He left a few things here . . . but nothing that locked."

A simple sentence fraught with meaning.

"You're certain?"

"I am, but please don't ask me to show you."

"I understand. There's just one other thing, and then I'll stop bothering you; I know you must have many things to do. I noticed yesterday that after the explosion, all the girls came downstairs, but there were no men. Are you closed on Sundays?"

Mrs. Toscana laughed. "As the moralists wish? No. They can close the movie houses, but not Mrs. Toscana's. I told you, I pay. And I pay handsomely. Besides, men's desires know no schedule."

"So there were men here yesterday morning."

"Of course, but they rarely use the front entrance." She murmured a laugh. "Like you, they use the underground tunnel, only whereas you were fully clothed, they sometimes flee wearing nothing but their drawers and carrying their shoes in their hands."

"I saw Jarvis Chandler and Samuel Trout leave by the back door of the club. Did they come here?"

Mrs. Toscana raised her peremptory hand. "I do not give any information about my clients. I am known for my total discretion. That is how I stay in business. I hear you are also completely discreet. That is the only reason I am talking to you now."

Phil nodded her understanding. Mrs. Toscana must have been doing her own bit of investigation since yesterday.

"I assumed there was a back room at the club where men either conducted business or gambled."

"So convenient, wouldn't you say?"

Phil nodded. "Because they can also enter your establishment the same way."

"Consider. They make deals in the club's back room and celebrate by coming here to use my girls. And consequently tell them anything they want to know."

Phil smiled at that. "A man talks after he's been satisfied."

"Exactly so."

"And the girls tell you, you engage in a spot of blackmail. Then I imagine you give the girls a cut, and pay the rest back to the men for their protection."

"You are very astute, Lady Dunbridge."

"But it is a very dangerous game."

"No one has ever accused me of such a deed."

"But someone might have found out. Could they have killed Tommy to punish you?"

Mrs. Toscana shrugged that off. "Everyone knows Tommy comes here; they think he is here to see one of my girls."

"But he isn't," Phil said. "Are you Mrs. Green as well as Mrs. Toscana, by any chance?"

"No, and you should stop asking questions. He is gone, and I will make whoever did it pay. You do not have to worry about justice. I will see to it."

"But I must," Phil said. And here she did something that she was certain broke every crime-investigation rule ever made. "I'm after bigger game."

For a moment, Mrs. Toscana just looked at her, then said, matter-of-factly, "I hope we're not going to be competitors."

To Phil, it sounded more like a threat than a hope. "Absolutely not. I'm not after money or power or dictating people's morals."

"What are you after?"

"Justice."

"That's a good thing to reach for. I wish you luck."

Phil rose to leave and retrieved one of her calling cards.

"I imagine you might have lost the one I gave you yesterday. Please contact me if you learn anything that would help my investigation. And please don't exact your vengeance until I exact mine."

Mrs. Toscana took the card. "Are you sure you want to leave this with me?"

"As evidence of my visit? Mrs. Toscana, my reputation has been in shreds more than once, but I, like the phoenix, always rise from my ashes. Do your worst."

Mrs. Toscana placed it on the table next to the matchbox. She didn't even look at it. Phil turned to leave, then an idea struck her.

She turned back to Mrs. Toscana. "Does Sydney Lord visit your house?"

"Sydney? He's too tightfisted. And I don't give my girls for free."

"I see. Well, thank you."

Phil left to the quiet sobbing of Manhattan's most exclusive madam.

So, Sydney Lord didn't frequent The Rose, Phil thought as she went back to the corner in search of a taxi. But he had a box of their matches. And he had followed Jarvis and Trout out the back door of the club. So, not to enjoy a night of wanton lust, but to stop at the club's back room and do business?

Now, that would open up a whole new avenue of investigation. A politician, a real-estate mogul, and a newspaper editor. What business could they have together? One idea leaped to mind.

It was time to enlist Martha Rive's help.

The Plaza was abuzz with activity when Phil returned. The entrance that led to the ballroom was open, and trolleys and men carrying boxes passed each other on the stairs as they prepared for the evening's charity ball.

The main lobby had added a new layer of sparkle during the night. And rumor abounded about the number of trees that would appear on Christmas Eve for the Plaza residents. But for tonight, swags of pine and holly adorned the walls, and baskets of Christmas greenery stood on the registry desk and every reading table.

Even Egbert had a sprig of holly in his buttonhole and hummed a well-known carol under his breath all the way to the fifth floor.

And Phil could think of nothing but how to find Tommy Green's killer.

Her own apartments had gone through another transformation. An arrangement of Christmas flowers had arrived from the chairwoman of the charity-ball committee, another from *The New York Times*.

The scent of oranges, cloves, cinnamon, and pine suffused every room. Every surface had something that celebrated the holiday. It was certainly festive, and had to be Lily's work. Phil didn't begrudge her enthusiasm in the least; she was, however, rather amazed that Preswick had countenanced it.

Preswick came out, putting on his jacket. He'd obviously been doing something unusual: there was a sprinkling of glitter across his nose.

"My lady. We didn't hear you." He took her coat. "You shouldn't run off like that. We were worried."

"I'm sorry, Preswick. But needs must. What have you been doing?"

"I've taken the liberty of moving all of our investigatory tools into the small study, as you will no doubt want to invite guests in for the holidays."

Actually, that was the furthest thing from her mind at the moment.

"Excellent idea, Preswick. We might even have a few people in to dine, though perhaps we should take advantage of the excellent private restaurant downstairs."

Though his expression didn't change, she could tell immediately that dining out would not pass muster. She had rarely
eaten in their own dining room, since she preferred to take her
breakfast in the small kitchen with Preswick and Lily, her
other meals at the round table at the parlor window, or even
sharing sandwiches with her servants around their study table as they discussed murder and mayhem over egg salad
and watercress.

"How many do you think our dining table will fit comfortably?"

"A small party, my lady. Ten or twelve at the most. Not
ideal, I realize . . ."

"More than enough. For we must think of our new lives.
We can't have our investigative materials glanced at by curious eyes, or have wine spilled on our texts and notes. Ten
seems more than enough for me. Perhaps after the new year,
when this investigation hopefully will be resolved, we'll start
entertaining.

"But that's not what I meant. Why do you have glitter on
your nose?"

Her well-trained butler didn't flinch. "I'm afraid we were
making Moravian stars. To pass the time. Lily was concerned,
and I thought it would take her mind off your absence."

"Shall I order some luncheon, or shall I send Lily to you? It
may be a minute or two. I don't remember the making of the
stars as quite so . . . untidy."

"Perhaps I'll join you," Phil said brightly. "I'd like to see
these Moravian stars. If you have an extra apron, I may try my
hand at making them, too. And there are a few things I want
to consult you on."

So while Phil folded and plaited the strips of white paper under Preswick's guiding fingers, she told them about her morning with Mrs. Toscana. "She's very reticent. If I were in her

business I would be, too." Which raised an eyebrow from Preswick.

"I showed her the key we found. I didn't have much choice. But she didn't recognize it. So . . ." Phil paused to get a particularly obstinate edge of paper to slide beneath the others.

Finally achieving success, she started on the next. "I'm thinking that the next step is to ask Martha Rive for her help. What is your opinion?"

"She is a journalist, my lady."

"Exactly, Preswick. Can we trust her not to divulge what she learns before we're ready?"

"She could ruin the whole investigation," said Lily. "Those muckrakers will do anything for a story."

"Lily, your vocabulary never ceases to amaze me."

"And it is quite inappropriate to a lady's maid," Preswick agreed. "Nevertheless, I agree. Can she be trusted not to—I hesitate to say it—blow our cover prematurely?"

This earned a smothered grin from Lily.

"I don't see any other way. Marty knew Tommy better than anyone." *Other than perhaps Sally Toscana.* "And yet I hesitate . . ."

"Make her sign in blood," Lily suggested.

"Perhaps we could conceive of a less gruesome way of ensuring her silence."

"An exclusive, my lady."

Phil stopped stirring. "You mean promise to let her be the one to break the story, before any other paper knows about it—on the condition that she remains silent until our investigation is completed, the whole story is known, and the appropriate actions are taken."

"Yes, my lady."

"I think we must," Phil said. "In fact, I think I will invite her over for a pre–charity ball cocktail."

"What if she won't come?" Lily asked.

"I will make it clear that it is something to her benefit, but that I can only tell her here." Phil smiled. "How can she possibly say no?"

20

Marty Rive did say no to Phil's invitation . . . at first.

Phil had managed to get put through to Marty's desk at the *Times* office. But from the sounds of the background noise, even the society news was in a state of bedlam.

"Normally I would be delighted to, Phil. But I have twice the work, twice the number of events because of the holidays. I've taken to carrying several evening kits to work and changing from here."

"There's something I want you to see."

There was silence at the other end of the line.

Finally, a suspicious "What is it?"

Phil could practically hear Just a Friend saying, "I don't use the telephone 'cause of 'ears.'" "I can't say now. Only here, before the ball. And unfortunately I have to be downstairs at eight to receive the guests. A ridiculously early time to begin a ball, though I suppose with all the others being held, someone must go first."

Phil thought she heard a snort over the line, then another long pause while Marty deliberated whether it would be to her advantage or not. Phil didn't add any prodding. She had no doubt that Marty's silence was an attempt to trick her into telling her more.

"All right," Marty said at last. "I'll try to make it."

"Come through the main lobby on Fifty-Ninth. I'll advise the concierge of your visit. And be discreet. I don't want any of your ambitious colleagues to be on the alert."

"I think I can manage that," Marty said.

"Good. Until then." Phil rang off and went back to the kitchen. The table was now spread with newspaper that was the home of a dozen stars that had been dipped in melted paraffin and sprinkled with glitter.

"They're beautiful," Phil said. Even her rather lopsided one rose to the occasion with its adornments of silver and gold. Something she could use herself. A little glitter, a little gold, but perhaps first a lie-down.

Investigating could be an arduous occupation; she could do with a short respite from being jostled by mistletoe salesmen, being kidnapped, narrowly escaping a bombing, and trying to piece this puzzle together with the noted absence of Mr. X.

Not to mention the tight lips of Detective Sergeant Atkins. Was he or was he not looking into this matter?

He didn't seem particularly interested in pursuing Tommy's killer or whoever had kidnapped Phil. And to her discredit, she had her first doubt about the good detective sergeant. He was one of the last holdouts against the return to corruption after Mr. Roosevelt's period of reform.

How long would he, like that poor Dutch boy with his finger in the dyke, be able to hold out against the pressure, the sabotage, the temptation? Would he gradually give up, be dragged back into the morass?

No, she wouldn't believe it.

And just where was Mr. X in all of this? On another case? Doing a parallel investigation?

"Did she agree to come?" Lily asked.

"What? Oh yes, she agreed to come. But she doesn't trust me any more than I trust her. I just hope she can help us get a break in this case," said Phil. "Tomorrow is Christmas Eve and I still have shopping to do."

She had packages galore waiting down in the Plaza storage rooms. She'd rather overdone it, but she still hadn't been able to find the new Sherlock Holmes.

"I want us to have the best Christmas ever." *Their* best Christmas ever. One not mired in dissolute husbands, opinionated society—or murder.

"Yes, my lady."

"So, after tonight, I'm declaring a two-day, no three-day—to include Boxing Day—moratorium on investigation. Hopefully, Marty Rive can identify this key and is willing to work with us."

"And if she isn't?" asked Lily in a small voice.

Never let servants see you falter, Phil thought. Even though she had long ceased thinking of Lily and Preswick solely as servants, they hadn't quite managed to make the reverse leap themselves. "If she isn't, we'll just have to attack the problem from another direction.

"And in the meantime, I've arranged it with Mr. Sterry for you to have a seat in the balcony to listen to the children's choir and to enjoy the ball." The managing director of the Plaza, dear soul that he was, was happy to do Phil that favor. "So enjoy yourselves. The guests are bound to be as glittering as our Moravian stars. But not as beautiful."

"But what if you need us?" Lily protested.

"Then I know where to look for you," Phil said with a smile.

"And Mr. Preswick and I will keep an eye out for possible suspects," Lily added.

"By all means," Phil said. She, herself, would be on the lookout for a general, an ambassador, a wealthy businessman, or a busboy who smoked an exotic blend of tobacco. She needed to confer with someone about the investigation, and since the good detective sergeant hadn't seen fit to return her call, she would have to depend on Mr. X to make an appearance. And if she was truthful, she wouldn't mind waltzing with someone who waltzed as well as he did everything else.

*   *   *

Lily was just putting the finishing touches on Phil's hair when Preswick announced the arrival of Marty Rive.

Phil stood and, feeling suddenly optimistic, did a little twirl for them to see her new gown—just arrived from Paris a week earlier. Monsieur Poiret had outdone himself. Not the festive, bright colors of holidays but a watered silk of pastel blue, edged in a crenulated band of sequins, with a girdle of silver blue sequins that fell into points to either side and ending in tessellated crystal ornaments.

It rather took her breath away. Structured enough to forego any but the lightest corset, though the train would be an impediment to chasing a suspect. Or running for one's life.

Never mind. She had no intention of doing either tonight. And the swirl of the silk, which she would hold for dancing, would be a dazzling waterfall of color.

Yes. She was definitely pleased with the effect.

"Lily, your hairdressing skills surpass everything tonight. Thank you."

In her embarrassment, Lily dropped a curtsey so well rehearsed that Phil knew Mr. Preswick was still putting her through her training.

Phil swept down the hall to find a determined Marty Rive standing in the parlor, still wearing her coat. Phil could just see a wide band of burnished-copper braid at the hem of a Roman ochre skirt.

Marty lifted her chin when Phil entered but immediately dropped the pretense.

"Wow," she exclaimed. "You look like the Ice Queen."

"Heartless?" Phil asked.

"Still to be decided. Shall we forego the small talk? What do you want to show me?"

"I was rather hoping you could identify this." Phil went to the escritoire and brought back the key.

She held it out. Marty reached for it, but Phil snatched it back. She'd seen the spark of recognition in Marty's eyes.

"Where did you find this?"

"All in good time. First, we need to establish some ground rules," Phil said. "Preswick."

Preswick appeared in the doorway.

"Please take Miss Rive's coat before she perspires through her ball gown."

Marty begrudgingly let Preswick have her coat, revealing a lovely bronze chiffon gown, crossed in pleats over the front and gathered in a key-patterned brocade across the high waist.

"I see you haven't given up your dress code for journalism," Phil said, and gestured for Marty to sit.

She sat. "You know, I would have never guessed from talking with you at Bev's and the Cavalier Club that you were actually a snob."

"Whatever it takes to get the job done," Phil said.

"And what is that job? You live in this posh palace, with a view of the park, and servants, and I know for a fact the earl left you penniless."

It was Phil's turn to betray herself by a look.

"And you know this how?"

"Phil, or should I call you Lady Dunbridge now?"

"Phil will do."

"Phil, then. I'm a journalist. I'm paid to search out the facts, even if it's for the society pages. The earl was a wastrel and you were notorious. I'm impressed. Really. I just don't understand. Either your family capitulated and gives you an allowance, like my mother, who slips me the odd dress money. Or you're being kept by someone . . ."

"Or?" encouraged Phil.

Marty shrugged. "Why are you investigating Tommy's murder?"

"Because you and Roz asked me to."

"I guess we did. So you should be more forthcoming with us, at least me. I don't know why Roz is so upset about this, she hardly knew the man. But I did know the man—"

Her voice cracked, and for a moment she hovered on the edge of tears. She forced them back. "He was my mentor, my friend." She looked up, eyes blazing, defying Phil to scoff at the notion that an unkempt, middle-aged reporter could have been her friend.

"I understand," Phil said. "But time is passing. Do you know what this key goes to? I'm hoping that it will lead us to where Tommy kept his notes, and no one has found whatever box, case, or trunk that key fits."

Marty tightened her lips.

"Perhaps one of the lockers in the *Times* storage room on the twenty-third floor?" Phil asked, but she already knew the answer, and Marty's expression of surprise, though quickly subdued, confirmed it.

"Well, it's possible. . . . How do you know about the lockers?"

"I saw them when I was at the wake."

"When?"

"While you were distracting Sydney, and I went in search of Harriet. She was blubbering in the stairwell. She heard Becker's voice and ran up the stairs to hide in the storeroom."

"What do I get in return?"

"An exclusive, once the murderer is apprehended and possibly other arrests are made."

Marty sat up at that. "Other arrests?"

Phil warned herself to go very carefully. She couldn't really promise that—she wasn't even sure about the other arrests—but she would try.

"Something's going on beyond you helping Roz and me. Tommy was on to something big, wasn't he? Something bigger than random extortion threats and bombs. What is it?"

"I don't know," Phil said. "Not yet, not entirely."

"But you have an idea?"

"A theory. Tommy's notes would shed light on whether I'm going in the right direction or not."

"A way that will lead us to his murderer?"

"Possibly."

"Why are you so interested? It's one thing to help out friends but—"

"Marty, if Tommy really was onto something big, and he was killed, this is bigger than both of us."

"Oh no, not the police? They are totally corrupt."

"Not the police," Phil said.

"Then who? Who do you know? Are you working for them?"

"My dear Marty. I'm a countess. I know everyone. And I'm working for you and Roz. But you must agree to certain terms. The notes, if we find them, will remain in my possession—"

"Not a chance."

"I'd like you to help me decipher them. I suspect you may be the only person besides Harriet who can read his scribbles, but . . ."

"Don't you trust me, Phil?"

"Not one jot. I believe you would do whatever you needed to do to get your story. I will do whatever I need to do to find Tommy's murderer. What do you say?"

"What's to stop me from breaking into the lockers myself?"

"How? With a crowbar? There must be a hundred of them. Do you even know which one is Tommy's? How will you explain that to your bosses?"

Marty huffed a breath. "Fine. I agree. But if you double-cross me, I will make you pay. I know the ins and outs of society. I will find a way to destroy your reputation."

Phil laughed. "Oh, my dear Marty. My reputation was destroyed years ago and several times since. So this is what I suggest . . ."

* * *

A few minutes later, Phil left to take over her hostess duties, with instruction to Lily to have her winter coat at the ready downstairs at midnight. Marty agreed to remain behind for another fifteen minutes, enjoying one of Preswick's excellent martinis, then leave the hotel from the main lobby and return by the ballroom's separate entrance.

They would meet at one o'clock outside the Oak Room restaurant and take a taxi to the newspaper, hopefully to find it fairly empty of journalists trying to make a late-night deadline.

The grand ballroom had been transformed. The coffered ceiling rose like a celestial dome over arches lit by fairy lights and ionic columns surrounded by sprays of holiday flowers. The balcony that ran the circumference of the room was festooned with swags of pine floating in clouds of light pink tulle and pinned with red ribbons.

Very effective, Phil thought, and very beautiful. But she couldn't help but wonder if all the money spent on decorations and orchestra and dining and champagne would have been better spent if it was given directly to those who needed it.

But, of course, no one, especially the rich, wanted to give something for nothing. Phil had learned long ago that the more they paid for their own enjoyment, the more they gave to the charitable cause that was entertaining them.

The orchestra was playing softly on the balcony. The children's choir was lined up along risers placed at the far end of the ballroom. They were dressed in their school uniforms, red sashes tied crosswise over white blouses. Tinfoil crowns sat upon each head, reminding Phil of rows of little monarchs.

At the end of their singing, the children would leave the stage, and the platform would be raised to become a part of the balcony to make more room for dancing.

The choirmaster took his place at the podium, and Phil made her way toward Mrs. Abernathy, who stood in the receiving line with her husband and Mayor McClellan, who would lead off the dance with Phil.

As the choir began to sing, the doors were opened, and the first arrivals entered to the cherubic sounds of "Good King Wenceslas."

For the next hour, Phil greeted an endless stream of revelers. Strangers, people she knew, people she had only heard of, people she had no idea of, several more whom she'd like to know better.

Some bypassed the line altogether, but Bev, who had deliberated until the last minute as to whether she would attend or not, stopped to say hello and, if Phil knew Bev, to flaunt it before Mrs. Abernathy.

She was wearing an exquisite lavender—she *was* still officially in mourning—taffeta gown that rustled as she moved down the receiving line and smiled at a speechless Elizabeth Abernathy. Marty followed a few minutes later, dodged the receiving line, and took her place with the other reporters in one of the alcoves behind the columns.

That hardly seemed fair. She was better dressed and had a better pedigree than most of the guests, but she'd made her choice, much as Phil had made hers. At least Marty's was settled. Phil was still juggling her future in both worlds.

The choir ended "O Holy Night," their innocent young voices rising to the great coffered ceiling. As the last note reverberated above the listeners, the orchestra broke into "We Wish You a Merry Christmas," and the children filed off the risers and out of the room.

Mrs. Abernathy stepped onto the podium, welcomed everyone, gushed over the children, and thanked the attendees for their generosity. "And now Mayor McClellan and Lady Dunbridge, who has graciously lent her name and presence as our hostess, will lead off the dancing."

The orchestra struck up a waltz, and Phil crossed her fingers that the mayor was adept enough to get her around the floor before the others joined in.

He made it exactly halfway around the room before some-one cut in, and he thankfully went back to his wife.

As Phil spun around the room with her next partner, she caught a glimpse of Marty looking on from the alcove, her notebook and pencil in hand, and thought, *What a waste of a lovely gown.*

The first chance she got, Phil made her way over to the journalists. There were ten or twelve of them, mostly women, and mostly dressed simply to denote their station, writing and talking and watching the antics of the guests.

"Got it," Marty said drily, as Phil came up to her. "Tulle, chiffon, the most god-awful conglomeration of ball gowns you can imagine. Is it time?"

"I'm afraid not," Phil said. "Another two hours or so. Nothing interesting?"

"I've already seen Carr and Charlie Miller, and guess who? Sydney. He gets to come as a guest. I bet you money he didn't pay for a ticket. It's infuriating."

"Oh gawd, look who just made her entrance. As fashion-ably late as the unfashionable can be. My mother always said money can't buy taste. But damn, that's an amazing gown."

Phil looked toward the entrance, where Imogen Trout and her husband stood framed by greenery and tulle.

And the gown was indeed amazing: black velvet scrolls on a background of ivory satin, a low-cut, rounded décolleté, and puff sleeves with inserts of black velvet. Her hair was swept back and up into curls. A tiara of . . . rubies? . . . sparkled under the lights.

"Worth," Phil said, recognizing the famous designer's hand.

"Definitely a Worth," Marty said, starting to write. "But neither he, nor anyone in his studio, put that red sash across her waist. She had to have added that in the spirit of the season."

"Sad, but true," agreed Phil. "Your mother was right."

"She generally is."

Next to her, Mr. Trout, fully kitted out in tails, looked like a hulking dockworker.

Heads had turned, and a murmur went through the crowd.

Imogen moved, not to enter the ballroom but to strike another pose.

"The Queen of Tarts, she broke some hearts," Marty murmured. "She might as well be on the runway. Or a museum wall."

Imogen continued to pose for whomever was still watching, until her husband took her by the arm and led her into the ballroom, leaving a view of the couple behind them, Jarvis and Roz Chandler.

"Dammit," Marty muttered under her breath.

The Chandlers didn't pause to be noticed, though Roz's dark hair and pale complexion above a long-sleeved high-neck ecru gown of overlaid gold lace was striking enough that she could have made an entrance on her own account.

As Phil and Marty watched, the couple drifted into the sea of guests.

"Poor Roz," Marty said. "I don't see why she seems determined to stay in the shadows of Imogen's illuminating presence."

"No," Phil agreed, frowning. Roz was striking much the same way Lily would be if she ever wore a ball gown. Lily and . . .

"Isn't that the policeman Bev introduced us to in the lobby?"

"John Atkins?" Phil followed Marty's gaze to a tall, elegantly dressed man standing several feet from the dance floor, talking to Carr Van Anda.

"It is, and I wonder . . . Excuse me." Phil moved away, skirting the couples coming off the dance floor and weaving through pockets of guests well on their way to good cheer. It took her a considerable amount of time to reach the other side.

The *Times* editor was just walking away. "Good evening, Detecti— Are you here in an official capacity?"

"Security," he said, smiling affably at her. "Though I would appreciate it if you didn't announce it to the world."

"Jewel thieves and the like?"

He tipped his head. "Christmas isn't just a time for giving."

"Do you ever stop working?"

"Not lately."

"Well, if you are supposed to blend in, perhaps you might ask me to dance. Are you allowed to dance?"

"Certainly." He took her hand, but looked around, caught someone's eye before leading her to the floor.

"How many of you are here?"

"A handful in the ballroom," he said, as she lifted her train. "Mostly as waiters. Another squad outside, ready to give chase."

And, Phil thought, Preswick and Lily sitting erect and formal in their freshly cleaned uniforms, keeping watch from above. But the detective sergeant didn't need to know that.

They joined the other swirling couples. "Are you expecting a heist?"

He actually smiled. "Hopefully not, but the Plaza requested extra help." He smiled ruefully. "I seem to be the only officer in the nineteenth who owns a tail suit."

"I can believe that, and you wear it well. Have you—" Phil began.

"Do you think that for once, we could not discuss murder?"

"I'm duly chastised, Detective Sergeant."

"You are not chastened one whit."

"I am known for being incorrigible."

He laughed, and they whirled around the floor. They passed Bev dancing with Max Rosarian, a delightful man Phil had met just this past fall, and, oddly enough, Marty and Sydney Lord, who must have managed to coax her out of her banishment in the journalists' alcove, but hopefully not into blabbing about their plans for later that evening.

It was something she hadn't considered . . . that Marty might be the leak.

"Is there something wrong?" Atkins asked as the room spun around them.

"No, just a clumsy moment. I do apologize."

"I can't imagine you being clumsy. Well, not often." He grinned, and she knew they were both remembering their first meeting and the dreaded eggplant gown.

When the music came to an end, he led her from the floor.

"Wait, when will I see you again? You didn't return my phone call."

"I didn't receive it."

"That's not promising."

"I'll remedy it immediately. Ah, there is Mrs. Reynolds. I'll leave you to her. Unfortunately, I can't neglect my duties any longer." He bowed to her before heading in the opposite direction.

Phil spent the next two hours conversing, dancing, and wondering if Mr. X was here and had managed to elude her again. Though she carefully scrutinized every partner, she couldn't distinguish him in their faces or their dancing, though she did manage to spot a couple of policemen acting as waiters.

Atkins didn't dance again, and she had to admit she felt gratified that his one dance had been with her. Though perhaps she shouldn't be, since she had asked him.

As midnight came and went, Phil became less interested in the ball and more impatient to carry out the evening's real assignment. She hadn't seen Preswick or Lily, though she imagined they had come down to view the proceedings, and she knew they would be prepared and waiting for her when she went for her coat.

Just before one, Phil noticed that Marty was nowhere to be seen, and hoped she wasn't going to be late because she had stopped to powder her nose. Then she saw her waiting near the door, notebook returned to her bag.

Their eyes met, and Marty left the room.

It was time at last.

But as she moved toward the exit, she was stopped by some-one. At first she didn't recognize him, since he was a mere sil-houette from the lights behind him. A chill skittered through her as she relived, for a second, Becker in the dark warehouse and the shadow looming behind him.

"Leaving so soon?"

Samuel Trout stood before her. "Surely you can spare a few more minutes for a last dance. I would not think myself a man of culture if I missed such an opportunity."

Phil didn't think dancing would help that, but she said, "I can't think of anything I'd enjoy more." She took his arm.

He wasn't as bad as she'd feared. For his size, he was amaz-ingly agile. He even managed a little conversation as they made their way around the floor.

"Are you spending the holidays in the city?" Phil asked, not really caring. He was potentially involved in a real-estate scheme that Tommy may have uncovered, and probably wasn't Trout's first. And having him out of the way would give her one less thing to worry about.

"I'll drive Imogen over to Schuylkill to visit some friends."

Phil didn't hear the rest. What she heard was *Kill her, kill her, kill her* echoing in her mind. She looked up to find him smiling down at her, and it sent a chill through her.

She smiled back, tried to swallow, but her mouth was sud-denly dry.

"And you?" he added.

"I . . . I haven't completely decided," Phil heard herself say, but didn't know how she managed it, or how she was able to keep up her steps, because she was no longer hearing the music, but *Kill her, kill her, kill her,* echoing in Samuel Trout's voice.

Phil never knew how she made it to the end of the dance.

"That was delightful, Lady Dunbridge. I hear Newport is

lovely this time of year, though a little sparse. Or you might try Saratoga. Wherever you decide, I hope you have a wonderful and safe holiday. Ah, there's my wife and Roz Chandler, shall I leave you with them?"

21

"Ready?" Marty asked as soon as they met outside the Oak Room.

"Of course." Phil had been having second thoughts about trusting Marty, but after her dance with Samuel Trout, she knew she had no other choice. She needed an ally, one she knew wouldn't kowtow to Trout or his money and power.

Marty could get her into the *Times* storeroom. Without her, the notes might as well be in Egypt, and Phil would be looking over her shoulder until someone else brought Trout to his knees.

"Is something wrong? Are you thinking about going back on the plan?"

"No," Phil said. "However, do not try to pull a double-cross and attempt to keep them if we do find them. You can't print whatever is there, or Tommy would have done it already. But you can screw up a very important investigation and ruin Tommy's legacy."

And get me killed, she added to herself.

"I don't get you. Who are you? Some kind of secret agent?"

"Just a countess with friends in, shall we say, high places?" Phil couldn't very well say that she had no clue as to who her employer was, except they wrote on official-looking stationery and made major arrests that seemed to coincide with the end of her murder investigations.

"Are you saying that if I try to take the notes, you'll have me arrested?"

"Are you willing to take that chance?"

"That didn't answer my question."

"Then you'll have to search your own motives for what you're willing to risk."

"And if I let you keep them?"

"As I said, you can study them at my apartments in the Plaza. You could even help me discover who killed Tommy."

"I could do that myself."

"Perhaps. But would anyone listen to you?"

"I would make them."

"Certainly, and have Sydney turn the story over to someone else, or kill it completely, and Tommy's murder will go unpunished." Phil leaned forward and spoke to the driver. "Pull over here."

"Wait, what are you doing?"

"Letting you out."

"You think you can get into the building without me?"

"Needs must . . ."

The driver pulled to the curb.

"Okay. It's a deal."

Phil would have shaken hands, but she was afraid her hand might be too unsteady.

Fortunately, a lifetime of her mother's training had made her understand the importance of outward show. Four years of marriage to the earl had taught her to win at all costs.

"Drive on," Phil said at her most imperious. The driver grumbled, but the taxi continued on its route.

Times Square was quite empty, though the surrounding hotels seemed busy with holiday celebrations. The taxi stand had waiting taxis, Phil was glad to note. In case they needed to make a precipitous exit.

Marty let Phil pay, which she was equipped to do, because of the coin purse Lily had put in her coat pocket. Along with something else. Not Lily's stiletto, but Phil's pearl-handled pistol.

The night watchman was sleeping at his desk but woke long enough to nod and say, "Another late night, Miss Rive?" before closing his eyes again.

They got into the elevator, Marty nodded at the attendant. "Going up to the twenty-third, Henry."

"The storeroom is locked after midnight on account of the ball being stored up there. If you have your key, you can get there from the library, if you don't mind the stairs."

"Not at all. Stop at editorial and let me get my key, then take us up to the library."

"Yes, ma'am."

The elevator doors closed and the car ascended. When the doors opened, Marty stepped out. "I'll be right—"

"I'll come, too," said Phil, and followed her out.

Marty walked straight to a desk on the far side of the room, sat down, and opened the top drawer. She rummaged through a variety of noisy objects and took out a key ring.

Without glancing at Phil, she walked back to the elevator.

"Remember," Phil said, catching up to her, "I have the key that counts."

Marty was getting surlier by the second. She obviously was resenting Phil's conditions, and Phil wondered if she had too easily trusted the newspaperwoman to do what was right.

They were let off on the library floor and climbed the stairs to the storeroom side by side, each wary of the other.

The building was designed to furnish daylight into every office. Being the highest full story, the storage room was lit from overhead, but in the dark of night, the lobby was filled with shadows and the echoing of their own footsteps.

Marty unlocked the storage-room door, and it swung open. It was pitch-black inside. Then Marty turned on the light, and the New Year's Eve ball rose out of the darkness like a giant medieval cannonball.

"Key?" Marty said.

Phil unbuttoned her coat, slid her hand into the décolleté

of her bodice, and pinched the key out of the special pocket that Lily had installed in the ball gown.

Marty shook her head, her smile leering out of the partial light. "You've been dancing around the ballroom with that key in your bosom?"

Phil shrugged and followed her around the room until she came to one locker. "This is Tommy's personal locker."

They both stared at the locker: there was no lock on the door.

"This isn't right," Marty said. "Tommy had a lock. I know he did, because after his courthouse story leaked, he went out and bought one."

She grabbed the door and yanked it open. Papers slid to the floor; others were piled haphazardly, crammed into the space without any concern for organization.

"How did Tommy ever find anything?" Phil asked, but she was already getting a sinking feeling. "Tommy wasn't this messy, was he?"

Marty shook her head. "Not with his notes. Someone has been here before us. Someone broke in and stole his notes."

Phil moved closer to inspect the latch. "There is no sign of the locker being forcibly opened. So the lock was already off the door, or someone had a key."

"I didn't even have a key." Marty turned a stricken face to Phil.

And Phil knew what she was thinking: that Tommy hadn't trusted her.

Phil couldn't worry about Marty now. She'd been certain they were close to getting a break. She didn't want to admit they had come too late.

"This doesn't make sense. If Tommy took the lock off himself, he would have transferred the notes, not left them in the locker for anyone to find and take or sell."

Marty didn't answer. Distraught and balancing on that

point where grief and rage and disappointment commingled, she sagged against the wall of lockers.

"Marty!"

"What?"

"Do you have a locker?"

"Yes, but this isn't the key." She fiddled through the ring and held up her own locker key.

"Pull yourself together and open it."

Marty moved several lockers away and unlocked a padlock, slipped it off the security ring.

Her locker was completely organized except for a tottering stack of boxes wrapped in the bright greens, reds, and white paper of Christmas.

"I haven't had a chance to send these around. What with all the social events to cover, and then Tommy."

"It's Christmas Eve. Maybe you should take them home tonight."

"I'll do it—"

"Just take them out."

Marty scowled but looked around and, finding a cardboard box in the corner, she dumped out the detritus at the bottom and began filling it with the Christmas presents.

"Voilà!" Phil said as Marty dragged a rather large box out and dropped it on the floor.

Behind it was a battered briefcase, a wire cable coiled around it and through the handles, and locked with a padlock similar to the one Marty had on her locker door.

Phil pulled the briefcase out. Inserted the key and turned it. A beautiful click followed, and the lock popped open.

Phil half expected Marty to grab it and run, but her hand flew to her mouth. "He trusted me to keep it safe."

"He did. Now, let us get it out of here before any industrious reporters come to make their deadline and catch us." Phil locked the padlock and slid the key back into her bodice.

They emptied the box that Marty had just filled, put the briefcase in the bottom, and filled it up again.

"Now, on the outside chance we run into anyone, you can say we came to get your presents, it being Christmas Eve."

They had to leave a few of the gifts behind, but soon they were going down the stairs to where they could call for the elevator to take them to the ground floor.

Henry opened the door, and Marty and Phil stepped in.

"Boy, you sure are waiting until the last minute," he said.

"I know," Marty said contritely. "But I've been so busy at the paper."

"No call to miss the holidays," Henry said, and for the first time Phil noticed the THANK AN ELEVATOR OPERATOR can tied to the rail.

Phil was reaching into her pocket for some spare change when the button pinged and Henry brought the elevator to a stop. Phil looked up. The seventeenth floor.

She and Marty exchanged looks. Marty grasped the box tighter.

"Someone else is working late, " Henry said, and opened the door to Sydney Lord.

"Sydney," Marty chirped. "What are you doing here? I thought you were at the ball."

"I was, but like you, I wanted to catch up on some work." He stepped inside.

The doors closed and they descended.

"Hey, what's in the box?" Sydney peered at the presents. "Something for me?"

"Maybe, but if you look, I'm giving it to Eddie the mailroom boy."

"Oh, c'mon," Sydney cajoled. Phil noticed that he, unlike Marty, had been drinking rather heavily. "Just a little peek." He reached for the box.

Phil slapped his hand, a little harder than she meant, and

said. "Naughty, naughty. You don't want coal in your stocking."

Marty giggled. It sounded so forced that Phil couldn't believe Sydney fell for it.

"I've been a good little boy."

Phil cringed and prayed that if they would just reach ground level without having to bring out her pistol, she'd never complain about fast elevators again.

Then blessedly they were in the lobby.

Phil dropped some coins into Henry's can, said "Happy Christmas," and followed Marty and Sydney out to the street.

"How about a drink to the season?" Sydney suggested. "The Knickerbocker is still open."

"Some other time," Phil said, and hustled Marty toward the taxi stand, where now only one lone taxi waited for a fare.

"But I'm leaving for Connecticut later today. I won't be back till right before New Year's."

They kept moving toward the taxi.

"Well, at least share a taxi with me," Sydney said.

A man who had been leaning against the building stepped forward.

"Got a match, buddy?"

Sydney rummaged in his pockets, and Phil dragged Marty and her box toward the waiting taxi, getting a whiff of unmistakable exotic tobacco as they passed.

Sydney pushed a matchbox into the man's hand.

"I'm kinda lost. Can you tell me how to get to Columbus Circle from here?"

Phil and Marty tumbled into the taxi, and Phil shut the door. "Plaza Hotel." The taxi started up and drove away just as Sydney turned from the man and tried to hail them down.

"How fortuitous that that man just happened to need a light," Marty said.

"Yes, how." Phil hadn't recognized him at the ball. He'd

managed to avoid her for the entire evening. But he must have been there and noticed her premature departure. She knew it was him. Though he'd covered his evening kit with a bulky overcoat and muffler, he was still wearing his patent evening shoes.

Phil sat back and smiled. She didn't even bother turning around. She knew that Sydney would be standing in the street waving after them, and that Mr. X would have vanished into the night.

"You can drop me off at my place," Marty said once they were traveling north and Phil had ascertained that they weren't being followed.

"Certainly, but I'll be taking the briefcase with me," said Phil.

Marty clutched her box of packages. "Tommy obviously wanted me to have it."

"I'm sure he did. But what are you planning to do with it? How are you going to protect it? Put it back in your locker? Carry it around with you while you report on all the balls and soirées over the next few days? Take it to work so the leaker can nab it when you aren't looking? While you're typing up your articles? Carry it with you to the ladies' room? Think, Marty."

Marty just hugged the box tighter.

Phil sympathized, but she wasn't letting that briefcase out of her possession.

"People are looking for it. They torched Tommy's apartment. He gave his life for what is in those notes. How would you protect that?"

Marty's grasp loosened. "What will you do with it?"

"Put it in my safe in my fifth-floor apartment in a very secure hotel. We can go through them together. We can even take a quick look tonight to see if it even makes sense, then I'll put it in the safe until after Christmas. It's Christmas Eve and I still have shopping to do."

"What's to keep you from double-crossing me?"

"My integrity."

"Forgive me if I don't trust that. I'll get out here." Marty knocked on the glass window. "Driver."

"If you do, you'll get out without the briefcase."

"How are you going to stop me?"

Phil pulled the pearl-handled revolver from her pocket. "With this?"

"Yipes! You'd really shoot me?"

"Let's not test the hypothesis, all right?"

Marty slumped back in her seat. "You win. For now."

"Drive on," Phil called to the driver.

"I don't get it," Marty said after a long silence. "Who are you, really?"

"Philomena Amesbury, Countess of Dunbridge."

"Dowager countess," Marty said sourly. "I've done my research."

"A mere happenstance." Phil still saw red every time she heard that word. No woman her age should be saddled with the odious burden of "dowager."

"Are you some kind of detective?"

"Just a friend who's trying to help a friend."

"What friend?"

"You and Roz Chandler. You asked for my help, remember? And Bev insisted. What could I do but do what I could?"

"A friend who just happens to discover bodies all the time?"

"Not totally true. I did solve a murder once back in England, but it was merely by chance. And really, anyone could have done it. A particularly inept metropolitan police inspector was in charge of the case. And then when Bev asked for my help to keep her out of jail, I couldn't desert her."

"And the others?"

"What others?"

"I think you're full of bull, Phil, but I won't press you. Bev says you're okay, so I guess I'll have to take her word for it."

"She says the same about you," Phil said. "Truce?"

"Truce."

As soon as they were safely upstairs and Preswick had been dispatched for coffee and sandwiches, they took the briefcase to the dining room.

Marty eased the papers onto the table, the largest clear surface in the apartment. A letter addressed to Marty was taped to the top.

And Phil was hit by an unsettling déjà vu. It would be just like *him* to be there before her.

But this letter was not written in the neat, classic script of the ones she received from her elusive colleague. "Gee," she said, looking over Marty's shoulder. "It looks like hen's scratching."

Marty began to read: "'My dear Marty . . .'"

She took a breath, and when she began again, her voice was steadier.

If you've found this case and the key—rather clever hiding place, huh?—I'm either dead or missing. It's your turn to take up where I left off. The data is collected. Meeting with someone this afternoon who is authorized to start proceedings. In case of my absence, they may contact you.

Insist that you get an exclusive—or if you're frightened, I understand, just

Marty swallowed and, in a lower voice, continued,

just give them the information and walk away. But I don't think you will. This investigation has turned into much more than about the Black Hand. Just as the new courthouse story would have if it hadn't been leaked. I have total faith in you, but be very careful. There is still a leak at the Times. I thought it might be Harriet. Can't be sure.

You're the brightest journalist I've met in years. You can make it. Just watch your back and stay alive.

Tommy

P.S. Look after your friend Roz. She should have never married Jarvis Chandler and soon she will need your help.

When Marty looked up there were tears in her eyes.

"I'll see what Preswick's doing about that coffee." Phil stepped away to give Marty time to compose herself. Though she only moved as far as the hall, where she could keep one eye on Marty. She still didn't trust the journalist not to grab the notes and make a run for it.

So, Tommy was expecting to meet with those "authorized to start proceedings." That was her, but what proceedings? More than the Black Hand.

Phil returned to find Marty arranging papers. And when Phil sat down at the table, Preswick and Lily, looking as freshly starched as they had that morning, took their normal places.

"Them, too?" Marty asked.

Phil nodded. She felt a little guilty about having kept Marty in the dark. That she, herself, was also in the dark didn't help matters. But she had the upper hand, at least for a while, and she would not cede that position unless absolutely necessary.

"Now will you tell me where you found the key?" Marty asked.

"In Tommy's jar of shaving cream."

"You went to his apartment? When? It was set fire to the night we learned he was dead."

"It was set after I was there and found the key. The apartment had already been searched. I don't know by whom. But by someone who perhaps hadn't found what they were after and decided to make sure no one else found it."

"You knew he was dead?"

Phil nodded.

Her eyes widened, then flashed. "How? What do you have to do with it?"

"*I* was to meet Tommy the day he wrote that note. I was delayed, and when I got there he—he'd been killed."

"At the docks? You, a countess, were meeting him at the docks? I don't believe you."

Phil deliberated. They were wasting valuable time. "He wasn't killed at the docks. He was killed at the Theatre Unique on Fourteenth Street. He was dead when I sat down next to him. I barely got out before someone screamed and alerted the whole theater. A young woman was standing at the end of the aisle. I saw her clearly in the light of the moving pictures."

"And?"

Phil hesitated again. Could she trust Marty in her anger and grief not to mistakenly alert the malefactors, and in turn jeopardize Harriet's life as well?

"First you have to give me your word that you will not go off on some vendetta. This is bigger than either of us."

"Did you recognize her? Who was it?"

Phil waited.

"Oh, hell. Fine. You have my word."

"You have to swear to secrecy—forever," Phil added for good measure.

"You sound like a child. Are we going to have to prick our fingers and exchange blood?"

"Be sarcastic if you must, but I mean forever." Phil couldn't have rumors flying about town that she was part of some secret crime-solving organization. It would kill her social life, not to mention her ability to investigate.

Lily and Preswick had sat stock-still during this exchange, eyes lowered to the table, becoming furniture in the usual *pas devant les domestiques* way.

"Okay, I swear. Who was it?"

"Harriet Wells."

"Harriet? She's a typewriter girl. Wait. She was with Tommy?"

"According to Harriet, she heard him make the arrangements to meet someone over the telephone and decided to follow him."

"So when you and Bev met me for lunch . . . That's why you were shocked at seeing Harry. Not because she was female, but because you both knew Tommy was dead. And she didn't tell? I swear to heaven. I'll—" Marty jumped up.

"You'll sit down and think calmly."

"You sit calmly. Where's my coat?"

Phil glanced at Marty. "Preswick, fetch Miss Rive's coat, and don't forget her box of packages. It wouldn't do for her to arrive at her family's Christmas dinner empty-handed."

Marty turned on her. "There's a name for women like you."

"And I'm sure I've been called it, and many others. So run off in a snit if you must, but be aware that if you tip off Tommy's killer, we may never bring them to justice."

"Them? Then you do think it's the Hand?"

"Or someone attempting to appear to be the Hand."

Marty blew out a breath, glanced toward the hallway, but finally sat back down. "Fine," she said through her teeth, then ruined it all with a sheepish grin. "But just because I remembered Harriet left for home this evening. She won't be back until the day after Christmas."

"Only three days," Phil said. "But it is now Christmas Eve, so if you want to take a look at these notes until they go into the safe until after Christmas, I suggest you have another cup of coffee and we get on with it."

"Do you already know what's in the notes, too?" Marty asked testily.

"No." Phil chose her next words carefully. "We know what he was working on, but he didn't divulge the nature of the information he was willing to share. . . . He was concerned about . . . security."

She caught Marty's expression. "And he was concerned for your safety."

"I'm not afraid."

"Tommy didn't think you would be, but he wanted you to stay alive to carry on if he couldn't."

22

They spent the next hour trying to decipher Tommy's hand-writing and reorganizing his notes, which consisted of scraps of typing paper, brown wrapping paper, the margins of news-papers, and smaller pages from a pocket notebook. It wasn't easy.

Even Marty had trouble deciphering some of them. But by the time the sun appeared in the east window, they were bleary-eyed from trying.

"I suggest we take a break," Phil said.

Marty glanced at the clock. "Lord. It's only four hours before I have to be at the Children's Aid luncheon." She pushed up from her chair, braced her hands on the table, and looked over the stacks of paper.

"Both the Black Hand, and the courthouse fiasco. Tommy was really steamed about that leak. But why would he put it in with his Black Hand notes? And what about these others?" She moved several miscellaneous pages so they were aligned in a row. "Notes to Harriet. They don't seem to mean any-thing. Just instructions about typing."

"And where are the notes she typed?" Phil asked.

"She'd return them to Tommy for final okay."

"So no one else would see them before he wrote the arti-cle?"

"Absolutely not."

"Then where are they?"

Marty looked around the table like they might magically appear. Flipped through several sheets. "They're not here."

"So either he hid them somewhere else?"

"Where? There is no other place."

"Or the miscreant found them and destroyed them and thinks he's safe."

"Or," Marty said, "Tommy destroyed them himself to prevent them from falling into the wrong hands."

"Then what was he going to pass on to me?"

Marty shrugged. "His notes. These go back several months. Of course, I'm probably the only one who can decipher them and actually understand what they mean."

"I wouldn't count on that," Phil said. Surely her people had experts trained in deciphering codes and bad handwriting.

Phil picked up a sheet of paper. "What do you think these are? A whole list of numbers. Could they be a code for finding the missing pages?"

"It doesn't sound like Tommy." Marty frowned at the paper. "They seemed to fall in patterns of twos, ones, and threes separated by a dash mark."

"You know Tommy's work," Phil said. "What do they look like to you? A combination to a safe? A date? No, that doesn't make sense, unless . . . could it be a kind of shorthand for date and time? Day and month? What else?"

Marty huffed out a sigh. "I don't know. My brain seems to have shut down. And I barely have time to get to the paper to get in my copy for the charity ball, which I still have to write—wearing my evening dress; it won't be the first time—then get home to dress and make the luncheon by noon."

"You forgot about sleep."

"Tomorrow."

"Tomorrow is Christmas," Phil pointed out.

"If I don't show for the family dinner, even my mother will disown me." She looked at the papers, then to Phil.

"Don't worry," Phil said. "I won't do anything without you.

I am going shopping, then spending a lovely Christmas Eve at home." Probably sleeping. "This information isn't going anywhere, and I doubt that we will discover the name of the killer in these sheets of paper. There is research to be done. And we need to find out what these numbers are before we go any further."

"I suppose you're right."

"I am." The only thing Phil worried about was what Harriet knew or didn't know, and that would have to keep until she returned—if she returned.

Marty's eyes had closed. If it was possible to sleep standing up, Marty Rive had reached that point.

"Preswick, please fetch Miss Rive's coat and Christmas box and see that she gets into a taxi."

Marty waved her away, but her hand was limp.

"You're not going out onto the street, alone, especially not in that gown."

"Not a taxi. I'm a—"

"Pain in my derriere," Phil finished. "You can pay me back later."

Preswick had already gone for her things.

"The notes."

"Will be safely secured in my safe."

"Don't dare try to pull a fast one."

"I wouldn't dream of it. I can't read his writing," Phil said. "Now, go home."

"Huh." Marty allowed Preswick to help her into her coat. Lily returned with the box of presents, sans the briefcase, which lay on the floor by Phil's chair.

They both accompanied Marty downstairs.

"I'll be back," she said as the door closed behind them.

"Merry Christmas," Phil called, somewhat belatedly, and went back to studying the forest of papers before her. She stared at the one sheet of numbers until they swam before her eyes and coalesced into an undifferentiated blur.

"Madam. Time for bed."

Phil stirred, blinked, and Lily's drawn face came into focus.

"Time for all three of us to see our beds. Did she get off safely?"

"Yes, though she is very stubborn."

"Yes. I hope she doesn't go off on her own quest for vengeance."

"What if she only told us half of what she was reading?" Lily asked as she led Phil down the hall to bed, though who was leading whom was unclear. "Maybe she's holding out on us."

"Possibly," Phil agreed. "But she'll be busy through Christmas Day, then I think I'll have Bev invite her to join us at Holly Farm for Boxing Day."

The clock was striking two and sunlight was streaming through the window when Phil roused from a deep and much needed sleep. She sat bolt upright. Had they remembered to lock away the notes before going to bed?

She could hear Lily rummaging about in the dressing room. "Lily!"

Lily appeared in the doorway. "Did I waken you?"

"No. But the notes."

"Mr. Preswick locked them in the safe before we went to bed." Lily stifled a yawn.

"How long have you been up?" Phil asked.

"A while . . ."

"Well, you and Preswick are both to take the rest of the day off."

"But we're taking tomorrow and Boxing Day off."

"I insist. But after you bring me something to wear."

Lily ducked back into the dressing room.

By the time Phil appeared at the table, breakfast had arrived and Preswick was pouring coffee for her. A half hour later, she took the elevator downstairs for her final search for the latest Sherlock Holmes novel.

Mr. Norris, the concierge, was at his desk, and she stopped for his advice.

"Have you tried Brentano's?"

"No. Do you think they might have a copy?"

"It is getting rather late for something so popular, but you never know." Mr. Norris wrote the address down on a hotel card and walked her outside and to the taxi stand.

"Brentano's," Mr. Norris told the driver. "Thirty-one Union Square at Sixteenth Street."

Phil started to put away the card, then looked at it: 31 UNION SQUARE, BET. 15–16.

The numbers on Tommy's pages floated to her brain. Was it possible the numbers were not dates, not combinations, but addresses? She tried to recall the numbers. Was tempted to turn back to make sure, but priorities overcame impatience and she continued on her way.

She was still pondering this possibility when the driver stopped in front of a corner building with striped awnings protecting the display of books in the windows. The address was printed large across the front—31 BRENTANO'S—and to her right a street sign read 16TH. Was there a correlation between Tommy's numbers and the addresses of vandalized buildings? Or was she just grasping at straws?

"Please wait," Phil said, and got out.

"The meter's running, just so you know."

"Excellent. I won't be long."

And she wasn't. She returned a minute later, empty-handed. They'd sold out of the book weeks before. Fortunately, her taxi was still there, and she climbed into the back. "The Plaza, please."

No Sherlock Holmes for Preswick. He'd have to make do with the muffler, the handkerchiefs, and the bottle of Old Angus that she knew he enjoyed when he was off duty.

* * *

"The numbers aren't bank accounts or dates or lock combinations. They're addresses!" Phil announced when Preswick opened the door to her apartment. She strode down the hall, shedding outer garments, until she got to the study.

"They're addresses!" she said to Preswick and Lily, who had crowded into the doorway. The map of Union Square with its series of little Xs was sitting on an easel, and Phil walked right up to it, hands on her hips.

"At least I think they are. Preswick, where are those news articles you clipped out?"

Preswick crossed to the bookshelf and sorted through the stack of folders. He handed her a folder, and she opened it on the study table.

"And I'll need that list of numbers from the safe."

Preswick bowed and left, returning a minute later with a single sheet of paper, which he placed on the desk next to the folder of articles.

"Now. Let's see if I'm right." Phil picked up the first newspaper article.

"Here it is. Three thirty-two East Eleventh. So a combination of three and three and two and eleven." Phil ran her finger down Tommy's list of numbers. "Nothing that fits Tommy's list. And there are too many numbers in each of his entries. Maybe I was wrong."

"Keep trying, madam." Lily looked as expectant as a child at Christmas, which, Phil noted, they should be celebrating instead of investigating.

"Three thirty-two. Where would that be on East Eleventh? Preswick, do you know?"

"Well, addresses run from Fifth Avenue in each direction, my lady, so I would surmise it to be between Second and First Avenues."

Phil frowned. "Too far away from the ones we're interested in. Let's mark it with an H for 'Black Hand.'"

Lily snared a pencil from the pencil case and made an "H" where Preswick pointed on the map.

"Three forty-five East Twelfth." Again she searched through the list of numbers.

"Also not on Tommy's list," she said. "And also too far east."

"Yes, my lady. Nearer the Italian neighborhood, where the Black Hand generally operates."

"And I was certain I had a new line of inquiry."

"Try again with one of the places we saw." Lily was standing on tiptoe to see over her shoulder.

"Okay, that place right across the street from the Cavalier Club. Preswick?"

"The avenues are more difficult, my lady."

"Then we'll just have to go down there and see for ourselves," Phil said. "And on Christmas Eve."

"If I might suggest . . ."

"Please do, Preswick. I seem to have gotten ahead of myself."

"Lorenzo is on duty today. Perhaps he knows the address of the Cavalier Club. We might be able to figure out the others from there without making the trip."

"Excellent idea. And Mrs. Toscana's, if you don't think that would be untoward. Actually, I think I wrote down her address somewhere. No, that won't help. That occurred after Tommy's death. It wouldn't be on his list. Nor would his apartment building."

"I'll return shortly," Preswick said, and took himself off.

While he was gone, Phil drew in Tommy's apartment building and Mrs. Toscana's, the store along Tommy's block with the missing glass, and the vegetable stand across from the club.

"It certainly looks like, of late, the Hand is narrowing their destruction to these two blocks—if it is the Hand.

"What do the ones around Fourteenth Street have in common? A vegetable stand, a florist, a tenement building, an exclusive brothel, and a brownstone. And those are just the ones we know about."

Phil glanced at the desk clock. It was coming on late afternoon. She still had packages to be sent up from the storeroom. She couldn't wait until Preswick and Lily were asleep, as her mother and father had done when she and her sisters and brother were children. They would waken at the commotion.

"They're all close together," Lily said into Phil's thoughts.

"What?"

"Not the ones in the newspaper. But the ones that we know about are all closer together than the ones in the paper."

"They are indeed," said Phil, drawing her thoughts back to the investigation. "For what purpose? And what, if anything, do they have to do with Tommy's list of numbers?"

Phil crossed her arms and stood back to study the map. Tommy dead in the Theatre Unique, across the street from Tammany Hall. The Cavalier Club, where Tammany Hall politicians congregated, and Mrs. Toscana's house, The Rose, where they went for more intimate entertainment.

Was Tammany Hall the key? They controlled much of the city's operations. Didn't Marty say that Jarvis was influential with the Tammany crowd? Tommy definitely took an interest in Roz. Was that the connection?

At that point, she hit a brick wall. Fortunately, Preswick returned with the address of the Cavalier Club.

"One eleven Third Avenue."

"But it wasn't blown up," Lily pointed out.

"No, but we can deduce that the store across the street would be an even number somewhere around one hundred eleven."

Phil perused Tommy's list. "One-one-two-three. One twelve Third Avenue," she said triumphantly and somewhat prematurely. "But there's a dash and three more numbers after those." She felt an indescribable stab of disappointment. She'd been certain. . . .

"Try another one," Lily said. "There are more articles in the folder."

Phil read the next address out loud. Preswick drew boxes in the approximate location. There were numbers that didn't correspond with some of the boxes, and some boxes for which they didn't have the address. But a pattern was emerging.

"Maybe we *are* on to something. Marty will know more about how Tommy made his notes. I'm surprised she hasn't managed to stick in a visit between the events she's covering.

"At least there's enough here to warrant further investigation. I suppose we'll have to find out the addresses of these other buildings and see if they correspond with the remaining numbers on Tommy's list. And try to figure out what these additional numbers mean."

"If your ladyship is amenable, Lily and I thought we'd go down to help serve food for the newsboys tomorrow afternoon. Each year, a Mr. Filess serves Christmas dinner to over two hundred boys.

"Mr. Tuttle and Mrs. Reynolds's cook, Mrs. O'Mallon, will be serving. Mr. Sloane is one of the sponsors. It's for the newsboys and, well, I want to make sure that Just a Friend has a good hot meal at Christmas."

"By all means, a good cause. We'll all go. Now, I think we have done enough work for a Christmas Eve. I wonder if Monsieur Lapparraque knows how to make a good English punch?"

"I'm sure he will do all he can to accommodate you, my lady."

"And would you also call down to the concierge and ask him to send up the packages I left with him?"

"Yes, my lady."

Phil stretched out on the parlor sofa. The tree rose almost to the ceiling. The mirrored balls sparkled in the glow of the electric lights and cast hues of color over the Moravian stars they'd made themselves. Popcorn and cranberry garlands had magically appeared, and Phil marveled that her two servants were so creative and still managed to run their residence—and investigate—with ease.

She'd made the right decision leaving England. And if she occasionally was hit with a longing of waking up on Christmas morning to find the fields outside her family's country estate covered in mounds of soft white snow, there was Central Park just outside.

At the moment, it was wearing a two-week-old coating of smoke and soot. But just after a snowfall, it was as beautiful as any English countryside. And besides, there was Broadway, and Holly Farm, and Bloomingdale's, and—murder investigations.

Yes, she was definitely where she wanted to be.

Lorenzo and the punch arrived along with five bellmen dressed in hotel uniforms and carrying more packages than Phil remembered buying. They marched through the front door, and Phil suddenly remembered the list of numbers she'd left on the study table. One couldn't be too careful, even with the security of the Plaza.

She ran down the hall to make certain no one came that way.

Lorenzo set up the punch bowl while the bellmen arranged the packages around the tree, then they lined up to accept the tip Preswick had at the ready and filed out of the apartment with wishes of "Merry Christmas."

Preswick turned from the door. "They seemed to have left some of the packages in the entryway."

"They're for you and me, Mr. Preswick," Lily said, peering around the edges of a very large, strangely shaped package. "They say 'Do not open until Christmas morning.' Are they from you, madam?"

"No. I don't recognize them. *Those* are from me." Phil

pointed into the parlor, where packages overflowed from beneath the tree to litter the table and floor nearby.

"All of those?"

"There are two for Mrs. Reynolds, but I admit I got carried away," Phil said. "Well, never mind. Put them with the other packages."

Lily reached for the package.

"Stop!" Phil yelled.

Lily froze. "What is it, madam?"

"Don't touch either one. Just don't touch them."

"You suspect another bomb, my lady," Preswick said more than asked.

"Possibly. I don't recognize either of those packages."

The three of them stood staring at the packages.

"There's an envelope with them," Lily said.

Preswick moved her aside, leaned over to study the packages and envelope. Very carefully, he slid the envelope off the packages and let it fall to the floor. Then he picked it up and looked at it. "It is addressed to you, my lady." He handed it to Phil. "I believe it is safe to open."

Phil turned the envelope over, dismissed the idea of retrieving her letter opener, and tore it open.

Countess. "'Countess,'" she read aloud. "'I had to borrow Green's notes. No time to spare, and I knew you would argue. I'll return them. Enjoy Christmas and Boxing Day. You'll hear from me.'

"Heavens!" Phil rushed toward the safe, nearly oversetting her servants, who were quick to follow. She knelt down and quickly ran through the numbers of the combination, yanked the door open.

Tommy Green's notes were gone.

The only things left were a few personal papers, her jewelry, the tell-all diary that she had as yet not had to use—and empty space.

Preswick and Lily bent over her to peer into the safe.

"He did it again!" Phil said, exasperated beyond belief. "He could have just asked. And he didn't even take the list of addresses—if they are addresses—because I hadn't returned them to the safe as yet. I believe they may be the key to it all or at least the proof of something—someone—besides the Black Hand at work.

"You might as well put his packages with the others." Phil paced across the floor, then turned back to her surprised servants.

"This is why women—and butlers, of course—run households. We'd all starve to death and never have clean linen if it was left up to the man of the house.

"Now what do we do? Oh Lord, and Marty will show up any minute to continue investigating and we've lost the materials."

Phil strode back to the study, followed by Preswick and Lily close on her heels. She picked up the list from the study table. Drummed her fingers on the tabletop.

"He must have come in with the bellmen carrying the packages. While they were depositing the gifts in the parlor, he was cracking our safe. The nerve of the man. I—we—do all the legwork, and he comes in and reaps the benefits."

"He is rather remarkable," Preswick said. "He managed to avail himself of a uniform, deposit his packages, break into the safe, steal the documents, and then stood in line to accept a tip for his trouble."

"You gave him a tip—again?"

"I beg your pardon, my lady. In my defense, I didn't know it was he."

"Neither did I. I panicked, and instead of paying attention, I ran to protect the list. Which I might have been persuaded to loan to him, if he wasn't so sneaky and conniving. It's not the first time he's left me—us—high and dry.

"But, so help me, this will be his last."

23

A little later, Phil sent Preswick and Lily downstairs to enjoy the Plaza staff party. When at eleven o'clock, Marty still hadn't appeared, Phil wandered back into the study to peruse her map.

She didn't think that Mr. X would return with the notes tonight; probably not until the day after tomorrow, when they were scheduled to go out to Holly Farm.

Still, he'd left without the list of properties that had to be key to whatever he was investigating.

She would return the list to the safe so that when he returned the notes, he could see the errors of improper communication lines. But first she copied the numbers onto a separate sheet.

Then she put the original list into the safe with a short note from herself.

You forgot these. Really, you only need ask.

Now when he used whatever unconventional way he chose to break into her apartment in order to return the notes, he would find hers.

She hoped he didn't take too long. Marty would be furious if she discovered the notes gone. And Phil wouldn't blame her.

She looked back at the map. Tommy dead in the theater. A leak at the newspaper. Harriet present at Tommy's murder. Was she the leaker? Or conduit to the leak? She was friends with the mail boy, Eddie, who obviously wanted more from her. But Phil remembered the way she'd looked at Sydney the day of the wake. And she'd gone to Sydney before going to Carr Van Anda's office, even though Marty had warned her not to. Had she inadvertently blabbed to one of those two?

Then there was Mrs. Toscana at the wake, and her meeting with Phil downstairs, witnessed by Charles Becker. Phil kidnapped before she could visit the lady. Kidnapped by Becker, and frightened by his companion. The chilling "kill her." And Samuel Trout saying, "I'll drive Imogen over to Schuylkill to visit some friends." She shuddered just remembering. What was Trout's part in all this? Tommy and Mrs. Toscana. Samuel Trout and . . .

Trout was a wealthy real-estate mogul whose name had been linked to some shady dealings. A normal state of affairs in the city, everyone assured her. He had also known Mrs. Toscana in childhood, and known Tommy, too.

The day after the kidnapping, a bomb had ripped through the first floor of Mrs. Toscana's brownstone just as Phil had left the building. A warning to Mrs. Toscana—or had it been meant for Phil as well?

It couldn't be just coincidental.

She went back to the map. The new neighborhood where the Hand was increasingly active was only three blocks away from the planned location to build the new courthouse.

Maybe they were going to try again nearby. Once the new courthouse was built, other buildings, other businesses, would grow up around it. Union Square over time might become the new center of municipal government.

And real estate would be at a premium.

Was this the plan? Terrorize the neighborhood and buy them out cheap? And who could expedite the sale better than Jarvis Chandler, building commissioner and devoted friend of Samuel Trout. With Trout rich enough to back such a scheme, and Jarvis to expedite the sales, all they needed was a snitch to keep them one step ahead of Tommy's investigation. . . .

The different threads of her thoughts that had been floating around in her brain like seaweed in a Brighton tide pool

suddenly began to connect into a reasonable scenario. Not the
Black Hand, but real-estate fraudsters taking advantage of the
increasing violence to mimic them and throw the blame off
themselves.

Tommy must have discovered the subterfuge during his
investigation. Or suspected. He hadn't named names in his
notes either because he didn't know or because he was being
extremely careful. And his words to Marty to take care of Roz
were because he knew that her husband would soon be arrested for fraud.

That's why he was meeting Phil. To set up his testimony
to some federal group to which she must be unofficially connected.

But where did Mrs. Toscana fit into all of this?

The telephone rang. Phil started. It took a few seconds for
her to realize that Preswick was still downstairs at the party
and she would have to answer it herself.

She hurried down the hall. Hopefully, it was Marty saying
she was too busy to make it until after Christmas.

Fingers crossed, Phil thought, and picked up the receiver,
realizing that she had never actually answered her own phone.

"Uh, Dunbridge residence. Lady Dunbridge speaking."

"Phil? Oh, thank God. I was afraid you'd gone out for the
evening."

"Bev? Is something wrong? You sound upset."

"I just got home from the hospital."

"Hospital? Are you hurt? What happened?"

"Not me. Marty was mugged. She wouldn't give them her
real name, because you know, her parents, and refused to stay
at the hospital. She told them to call me, but it took me hours
to convince them to let me take her. She's here now. Dr. Endicott is coming over, bless him, on a Christmas Eve. But he's a
good friend of Father's, and he's right down the street."

"Bev, stop talking. Is Marty badly injured?"

"Bruised, nothing broken but her head. She has a big bump

on her forehead and, oh Phil, a black eye. It's just awful. She won't be able to be seen in public for I don't know how long.

"She keeps saying she needs to talk to you. She's tried to get out of bed twice. So I finally promised I'd call you and ask you to come over."

"She should rest."

"That's what I told her, but she's angry, and I think a little frightened, but don't say I told you that. Can you please come? Oh, and she said to bring the notes, whatever that means."

"Of course I'll come. I'll be right there."

Phil dressed in a comfortable skirt and blouse; chose a heavy tweed cape and cloche hat that didn't require pins; remembered to stop by the study to retrieve the copied list of numbers, which she folded and stuck inside her corset; and went downstairs.

The concierge came to greet her when she reached the lobby. "Good evening, Lady Dunbridge. Going to a party?"

"Yes, just a little get-together. A last-minute affair. Could you please tell Mr. Preswick that I've gone to Mrs. Reynolds's?"

"Of course," he said, and personally saw her into a taxi.

This was not her idea of how to spend a Christmas Eve. And certainly not the way Marty Rive had intended to spend hers. Phil couldn't imagine what had happened, but she had a niggling suspicion that it had to do with finding the notes.

Sydney Lord came to mind, though perhaps that wasn't fair. Anyone could have had them watched. Becker also came to mind.

Tuttle met her at the door, looking graver than usual. "Mrs. Reynolds is with Miss Rive upstairs. The doctor just left."

Phil handed him her cape and pulled off her hat. "Thank you, Tuttle, I'll see myself up."

*   *   *

"My ball gown is ruined," Marty announced when Phil stepped into the guest bedroom. She was lying on a chaise, wearing one of Bev's dressing gowns.

Excellent, Phil thought. *She can't be seriously hurt if she's complaining about her wardrobe.* Then she thought again. If Marty was still wearing her ball gown . . .

"When did this happen? I take it, not leaving the children's hospital luncheon?"

"No." Marty started to shake her head, thought the better of it. "I never made it to the luncheon. I never even made it home from your place. I was jumped as I was going up the steps to my front door. They stole all my Christmas presents. The thugs."

She shuddered. "Not that it matters. I can't really show up at the old homestead with a shiner and without presents. They might lock me in my bedroom and never let me out."

"At least they didn't steal your sense of humor," Phil said.

"I'm not joking. Alva Vanderbilt has nothing over my mother. Those old stories about her locking Consuelo in her room so she couldn't escape marrying the duke? They were true. Fortunately, I didn't have to get married to escape. I got a job. I guess times haven't changed that much.

"It turns out you were right about taking a taxi. Unfortunately, you were wrong about getting from the taxi to your door."

"So I'm beginning to realize," Phil said. "If you feel up to it, could you tell me what happened?"

"Oh, I feel up to it. I got out of the taxi, reached back in to get the box of presents, and was just going up the steps when someone grabbed me from behind, pushed me down into the stairwell below, and took off with my box of presents."

"The idea of those thugs stealing people's Christmas presents," Bev said. "It's un—un-Christmas-like. I told her she should call Detective Sergeant Atkins, but she refused."

Marty and Phil exchanged looks. They were obviously thinking the same thing. These were no ordinary thieves. They had to have been after the notes.

Bev looked from Phil to Marty and crossed her arms. "Okay, you two. I saw those looks. What's going on? I want to help."

Phil didn't see how they could keep Bev out of it any longer. "Those weren't just any thugs," Phil said, and explained the barest bones of what she and Marty had been up to, and why.

"So they were after the notes you got at the *Times*?" Bev asked when Phil had finished.

"They had to be," Marty said. "And the only person who knew we had been at the *Times* building was Sydney. I'm going to kill him."

"But not before we find out who killed Tommy, please," Phil said.

"True. Though I can't imagine Sydney rousing himself to commit murder, especially if it involved blood." Marty frowned, winced.

Bev called for Tuttle and asked for two pink gin fizzes—"I still haven't perfected my Christmas cocktail"—and a pot of tea for Marty.

"I'll have a cocktail, too," Marty said.

"The doctor said you shouldn't drink until tomorrow." Bev turned to Phil. "Though I don't see why not. She refused to take any of the pain powders that he left."

"I told you; I need to think." Marty lay back against the chaise and closed her eyes.

"You need to rest," Phil said. "Besides it's almost Christmas and I've declared an investigation moratorium until after Boxing Day."

"But—"

"But Christmas comes but once a year—murder happens all the time. Besides, all the obvious suspects are celebrating. We have time, and besides, we made a little headway after you left."

"You kept going without me?"

"Not exactly, but we did try a little later. We think the numbers are addresses and, if we're right, they coincide with the addresses of the buildings bombed or torched recently in the neighborhood of Union Square.

"We had to estimate some of them because we didn't have the exact addresses for all of them, but we're fairly certain. And we plan to confirm the others on Tommy's list tomorrow after we finish at the newsboys' charity dinner."

"Tuttle and Mrs. O'Mallon and several of the servants are going to help serve," Bev said.

"Yes, Preswick suggested we join them."

"Did you bring the notes?" Marty asked.

"No," Phil said. "They are not leaving my safe." *Once she got them back.* "But I did bring a copy of the list. I was hoping you were up to looking at it. Each address has additional numbers after it that we couldn't decipher. I hope you might have an idea, but not if—"

"Let me see." Marty sat up. Pressed her hand to her forehead.

"Perhaps you should wait," Bev said.

Marty wiggled her fingers. The knuckles were scraped. "Let me see."

"Be patient." Phil unbuttoned the top buttons of her blouse and slipped her hand in to retrieve the folded paper.

When she looked up again, Bev was grinning; Marty grimaced.

"I figured it was the safest place."

"Or one sure to get you violated," Bev said.

"I suppose, but . . . what do you make of these?" Phil handed Marty the paper and sat down beside her. Bev moved behind the chaise so she could see over their shoulders.

"These are the addresses," Phil continued. "See. 'Three, three, two, one, one.' Three thirty-two Eleventh Street. The others fit a similar pattern, but they each have these additional numbers at the end that don't seem to have any kind of pattern. Sometimes there is one number or two. Neither Preswick nor Lily nor I had any idea what it could mean."

Marty looked at the paper for so long that Phil began to worry.

"Marty, are you still with us?"

"Shhh. I'm thinking."

Tuttle brought in drinks, and Phil and Bev both tiptoed across the room to fortify themselves while Marty thought.

"He did this before," Marty said finally. "Can I have some tea now?"

Bev poured her a cup and took it to her.

"Tommy?" Phil asked as she sat back down next to Marty.

"Yes. While he was covering the ins and outs of the court-house relocation, he discovered that several parcels had been bought by investors. These extra numbers might be lot numbers."

"Did he discover who was buying up the property?"

"I don't know. The news of the buried costs broke in *The Sun* before he finished, and Tommy's reporting was left high and dry. With the proposition dead, Carr decided just to print the outcome, which was not to build the courthouse at Union Square, and the whole thing became academic."

"Do you think he could be following a similar pattern here?" Phil asked.

"It sure looks like it," Marty said. "But we can find out at City Hall. The building department keeps track of all that."

"It will have to wait. Tomorrow's Christmas," Bev reminded her. "Then we all go to Holly Farm for Boxing Day. The servants are off, but Tuttle will go out earlier with a couple of house-maids to set up, then return to the city, and we'll be on our own. Like the pioneers."

"Bev," Marty snapped. "We're following a lead. We can't go on an excursion. There are Tommy's notes to be studied. And we should get down to the records department first thing and see if these properties have been sold."

"The Department of Records is already closed for today," Phil said. "Preswick said all of City Hall will be closed for two days since Christmas was in the middle of the week. So we won't be able to get in until Friday. If then."

"Ugh. First thing Friday, then. I'll go down there."

"*You* are not going down there."

"Why the hell not? Where do you get off being so bossy? We're the same age and you don't even have a college degree, do you?"

"True," Phil said.

"But she graduated from Madame Floret's École de Jeunes Filles," Bev said, in Phil's defense.

"Sometimes attitude is everything," Phil said.

"I suppose," Marty said. "Still maybe I should stay behind—"

"Absolutely not," Bev said. "I just lied to your mother about you being out on assignment covering a breaking story and being stuck at the paper. Though what could possibly happen on Christmas I can't imagine. You're off the hook, but I still have to make the rounds of Papa's charities on Christmas Day, so you have to humor me and celebrate the next day at Holly Farm.

"Besides you've never been to the farm, and even though most of the horses are wintering in Virginia, we have a few lovely ones left behind for riding. I should buy a sleigh."

"Bev!" Phil and Marty cried together.

"Very well. But you have to admit, some time away might clear the palate and make us see things more clearly."

Phil nodded. She was more inclined to agree with Marty, but with a kidnapping, a bombing, and a mugging, Phil must be making someone uncomfortable, and perhaps it was time to regroup. Besides, going to Holly Farm would give Mr. X an extra day to return the notes, and give her a chance to consult with Bobby Mullins. So she merely said, "I've been so looking forward to it."

"I'm not," groused Marty.

"It will be good for you," Bev said. "The doctor said for you to take it easy. Which means a quiet Christmas dinner here and a trip to the country for the benefits of fresh air."

"It's December."

"Fresh and invigorating."

"Oh, all right," Marty said. "But first thing Friday we go to City Hall."

"Not *we*," Phil said. "We'd be bound to run into Jarvis or Trout or someone else who will recognize us. We'll send Preswick. And he'll report back to us."

Marty crossed her arms. "I want to be out there, doing something."

"So do I, but doing what? Here's the major problem . . ." *Besides the missing notes.* "If this were about leaking news to another newspaper, that would be a matter for you and the paper. If it's leaking to crooks so they can cover their tracks, that's another situation. Everything we've learned so far has been perpetrated by nameless thugs.

"We need to look for a specific someone. Someone who killed Tommy for some reason, find out the reason, and work out from there."

"But the notes," Marty insisted, but sounding decidedly sleepy.

"We read through them last night. He doesn't mention anything that will lead us to his killer."

"Because he was being careful. He might have left hints throughout, but I wasn't looking that closely last night. *I* need to look at them again. I know him better than anyone. And I might be able to pick out hints."

Phil suspected they could get more out of Mrs. Toscana than from Tommy's scribbles, if she would only talk. But Phil didn't want to drag the brothel owner into this more than she already had. Besides, she bet Bobby Mullins would be a storehouse of information. He might be living in the country, but that didn't mean he didn't keep in the know about what was going on in the city. Another good reason for visiting the farm.

"And you will," Phil assured her. "But it's my first Christmas in America. Preswick and Lily are looking forward to celebrating. You're banged up and can barely keep your eyes open. We're all going out to Holly Farm on Boxing Day and then we'll take up the investigation again."

Marty didn't argue. She'd fallen asleep.

"She must be done in," Phil said.

"She is now," Bev said. "I slipped one of Dr. Endicott's sleeping powders into her tea."

It was late when Phil returned home. There were a few Christmas Eve revelers still on the streets, but mainly everyone was nestled in their beds waiting for the arrival of the St. Nick of Mr. Clement Moore's poem.

Still no sign of snow.

And still no notes.

With any luck, it wouldn't be St. Nick visiting her boudoir on Christmas Eve.

24

Christmas dawned on a sunny, snowless morning and Lily sitting in a chair near Phil's bed, patiently waiting for Phil to rouse herself.

Which she did, with a start, then realized she was alone and had been for the entirety of the night, alas.

Lily popped out of her chair. Her uniform had been starched so stiffly that it might be capable of standing up without her. Phil had meant to tell her and Preswick to be comfortable on Christmas. Though Preswick was probably more comfortable in his livery than in a cardigan and corduroys.

"Happy Christmas, madam."

"Happy Christmas, Lily."

"Shall I have Mr. Preswick order breakfast?"

"Yes, indeed. Though I took the liberty of requesting a special meal for three, you and Mr. Preswick and me, to be served in front of the tree."

"But Mr.—"

"Yes, I know, but we have a busy day and you want to have plenty of time to open your presents, don't you?"

"Oh yes—I mean, if you wish, my lady." Lily bobbed a curtsey and nearly ran from the room.

Phil lay back in satisfaction. She had gone a bit overboard, and she couldn't prevent one of the many words of advice her mother had drummed into her innocent head from asserting itself now. "Do not be too friendly with your servants. They will take advantage of your leniency."

Phil drove the thought from her head. She had broken down finally and sent her family Christmas wishes in the form of a card, but that was all she was willing to endure from that corner of the world. From now on her familial feelings would not be reserved for those who were related by blood, but for those whose loyalties and caring had earned hers in return.

Shaking off her moment of retrospection, she climbed out of bed and donned the robe de chambre Lily had draped carefully over the dressing screen.

By the time she'd done up the buttons, Lily had returned to unbutton them again and dress her mistress in a tea gown of large red roses. It had been one of her rather spontaneous purchases and not altogether successful, but if Lily wanted red roses on their first Christmas together, then Phil would wear it festively.

Lily and Phil arrived at the parlor just as two waiters rolling laden trolleys came through the front door.

It was a mistake, of course. Lily and Preswick had already breakfasted. And Phil, for one, and she suspected Lily, was too excited about opening the presents to be hungry. As soon as coffee had been poured and the waiters departed, Phil gave up the notion of eating and said, "Presents first."

And she got up to pass out her largesse.

There were ice skates, much to Lily's dismay. And Preswick's exclamation of "I haven't skated in years," said in such a way that Phil knew he would be out on the rink at the soonest available occasion. And she wondered if she had been wise to give a man of his years something so fated to result in injury.

There were scarves and mittens and handkerchiefs; chocolate-covered cherries and marzipan in the shape of fruit. Lily had monogrammed Phil a set of lace handkerchiefs; Preswick had found a copy of *A Pocket Book of Poisons and Their Antidotes*.

Soon the gifts were spread around, and only the two from their elusive Father Christmas remained to be open.

Preswick lifted the heavy, oddly shaped package and placed it before Lily.

She just stared.

"It says, 'To Lily.'" He showed her the note card attached to the ribbon.

"But what is it?"

"Open it and let us see," Phil said.

Lily tore into the paper covering. A huge metal tulip emerged.

"It's a phonograph," Lily said, in awe.

A round black disc was already positioned on the rotating table. Preswick gave the crank several impressive turns until sounds rose from the tulip, indistinguishable at first, then finally blossoming into a triumphant "Hark! The Herald Angels Sing."

Lily and Phil both clapped their hands in appreciation.

"Now yours, Mr. Preswick," Lily said, and handed him the one rectangular package left.

Phil knew before he opened it what it would be, and she marveled at how her elusive, infuriating mystery man had known the perfect gift for each of them.

The paper fell away to reveal *The Return of Sherlock Holmes.*

She had looked everywhere, and Mr. X had done the impossible. Maybe he wasn't so infuriating after all.

"But what about you, madam?"

"Oh, I expect he'll think of something," Phil said. And if he couldn't, she certainly would.

At noon they traveled down to Chambers Street and the Newsboys' Lodging House, where the dining hall was filled with tables and one long serving table with more turkeys than Phil had ever seen.

At first the other volunteers were flummoxed to have a countess in their midst, which Phil had never intended to divulge if it hadn't been for one enthusiastic reporter who recognized her and insisted on taking a photograph for the *New York World* Christmas edition.

All afternoon they fed hungry newsboys: tall ones, short ones, thin, and thinner ones. Boys who were almost men; boys who were hardly old enough to count their change. They all came empty-handed and left with plates piled high with turkey, ham, potatoes, yams, turnips, peas. All topped by a thick slice of bread that, more often than not, went directly into pockets to be savored later.

After an hour or so, Phil was surprised by a familiar face.

"Ah, Just a Friend, I was hoping to see you today to say happy Christmas."

Just a Friend nodded brusquely, and said, "Best if you act like you don't know me. 'Cause you don't know who's listening."

"Of course, very smart idea." She handed him a plate with a solemn expression. He took it and went off to join his compatriots.

But when Phil, Lily, and Preswick were leaving after the dinner had been opened to others in need, they were stopped by a hiss from the end of the street. Just a Friend motioned them to join him, then ducked into a narrow walkway between the buildings.

"I'd better go first," Preswick said, and cut in front of Phil and Lily.

Lily reached for her ankle and hurried to catch up. Phil brought up the rear.

Just a Friend was waiting with another, taller boy. They were alone, so Phil muscled her way past her protective staff, frowning at Lily to put away her stiletto as she passed.

"What's afoot?" she asked.

"This here's Big Nose Mike."

"How do you do?" Phil said.

Big Nose Mike scrunched up his face, which accentuated his namesake.

"He sells papers over round the docks where those guys took ya. He's got somethin' to say."

Big Nose Mike didn't look like he was about to say anything. Just a Friend gave him a jab in the ribs.

"I seen him. The man what with the big car."

"A very large man?" Phil coaxed.

"Yeah, in a big silver car."

"Would you recognize him if you saw him again?" Phil asked.

"Ain't gonna squeal. They'd do me for sure."

"Who?"

"Them." He turned to Just a Friend. "Now gimme my nickel."

Just a Friend reluctantly shoved his hand into his pants pocket.

"Wait a minute, my good man." Preswick held out a dime. "Do you know what kind of car it was?"

"Gorn. It was one of them new ones everybody's talking about. I seen pictures of it. The Silver Ghost."

"A Rolls-Royce?"

Big Nose Mike nodded sagely. "Ain't ever seen one in person before."

"And you're certain it was a Rolls?"

"Not likely to mistake it for a horse buggy. I'm gonna have me one of those one day."

Just a Friend snorted. Big Nose Mike cuffed him. Preswick flipped them each a dime.

"Thank you very much," Phil called over her shoulder as Preswick herded her and Lily out of the alley.

But the boys had already disappeared into the shadows. Phil couldn't help but think of Mr. X and wonder if he'd learned his similar skill of vanishing on the streets of New York.

*   *   *

By eight o'clock the next morning, their bags were packed, Bev was scheduled to arrive soon, and Phil called Preswick and Lily in to receive their Boxing Day envelopes.

Lily took her envelope, looking confused. "But you gave us presents yesterday."

"Mr. Preswick will explain," Phil said, adding this tidbit of information to the little she knew of Lily's past. Lily didn't know about Boxing Day envelopes, so she'd not been a servant in England; well, that had been obvious from the start. And not a resident of any house in England that gave its servants a little something extra on the day after Christmas.

It didn't matter.

The Lily of the present was her own person, so much so that Phil had stopped being concerned about her past. And had stopped prying. Until she'd visited Mrs. Toscana and had seen the picture of that lady as a young girl, and for a stabbing second, thought it looked like Lily.

It wasn't, but still, the familiarity of the image lingered in her mind. And she had a fairly good notion as to whom it resembled. And why.

As soon as Preswick and Lily left to prepare for their day off—there had been mention of teaching Lily to ice skate in Central Park—Phil sat down to wait for Bev.

She checked the safe once more, but like the proverbial watched pot that would not boil, the notes had still not been returned. Hopefully, her mysterious comrade knew they would be gone today and would take their absence as an invitation to let himself in and return the notes before Marty discovered them gone.

Bev arrived an hour later, a Christmas miracle, since in the old days Bev would just now be getting home from a night on the town. Marty was bundled up under blankets and pillows in the back seat of Bev's yellow Packard.

"She's treating me like I'm an invalid," Marty groused as

Phil climbed into the front next to Bev, adjusted her goggles, and tied her motoring hat tightly around her chin.

"Enjoy it," Phil called back.

"And they're off," Bev yelled delightedly, and swerved into the line of traffic.

Phil held her hat to her head and leaned back to enjoy the ride.

Bev drove east, then turned down Second Avenue, steering the Packard in and out of traffic with ease. Soon soon they were speeding over the bridge and through the other communities that had built up on the far side of the river.

The day was cold but sunny when they first started out, but grew cloudy the farther they got from the city. The houses and businesses gave way to trees and farmland, the fields brown and brittle as the earth hunkered down for the winter.

"You may get your snow yet," Bev yelled over the roar of the engine and the wind whizzing past Phil's ears—her frozen ears. She looked back to see how Marty was faring, but she was fast asleep.

Less than an hour later they were turning into the lane to Holly Farm.

"Is this it?" Marty asked, sitting up to look around.

"Holly Farm!" Bev announced, taking one hand off the wheel to flourish it in the crisp air.

Bev was in her element, Phil thought, as she took a moment to revel in the unexpected paths their lives had taken. Her flirtatious, trouble-loving, scandal-creating friend was now a savvy racehorse breeder and businesswoman.

And Phil? She wasn't certain what she would call herself, but she was committed to doing it with all her energy.

Bev stopped in front of the cottage, and Tuttle came out to greet them just as Bev shut off the engine and the first snow-flake fell.

"Wonderful," Phil said.

"We better not get snowed in," groused Marty, and let Tuttle help her out of the auto.

"It's wonderful to be back," Bev said, throwing off her goggles and hat and taking several deep exaggerated breaths. "I feel like I've been gone for ages."

The stablemen must have heard the Packard's engine, because a score of them came out of the barn and headed down the hill toward the house.

Bobby Mullins arrived ahead of the others. He'd lost several pounds since last spring. Farm living seemed to agree with him, though Phil knew for a fact he was still enjoying himself with the ladies of the theater and frequenting those watering holes that kept him in the know about the underground goings-on of Manhattan.

And Phil planned to have a lengthy discussion with him before the day was out.

He pulled the wool cap from his head, releasing untamable orange hair now showing just a few strands of gray. "Mrs. Reynolds; your lady-ness." He nodded to Marty.

For the next few minutes, Bev flitted about, handing out envelopes of Christmas bonuses, ending with Bobby, whom she invited to come down for a drink once they got settled.

With many thanks in many accents, the staff hurried back to the stable and no doubt back to work.

Phil, Bev, and Marty followed Tuttle into the cottage.

It was warm and toasty inside, and someone, probably Tuttle and Mrs. O'Mallon, had filled the doorways with greenery. The sofa and chairs had been rearranged around a roaring fire, while crystal vases of winterberries sparkled in the light of the flames.

"Ah," said Bev. "I feel like I'm home."

Tuttle immediately appeared.

"Now, Tuttle. Just see that we have food and drink and be on your way. Have a nice day off. We'll serve ourselves, and make do."

"Thank you, madam. Luncheon has been set up on the dining table. Dinner is in the refrigerator. Mr. Mullins will send down his cook to heat it for you."

"Thank you, Tuttle. Now go home and have fun."

"Yes, madam." Tuttle bowed and took himself off.

"Now, let's get cozy."

Bev insisted on Marty lying down on the sofa, and covered her with a knitted afghan.

"Bev, I appreciate your solicitation, but you're going to drive me crazy. I'm perfectly fine."

"You were mugged, for heaven's sake, and half your face is black-and-blue. Less well-trained servants than mine would have gasped in shock to see you."

Marty fought with her frown and gave up, laughing and holding her head in reaction. "Those so-and-so's. What a way to go into the new year. Speaking of which . . ."

"I wondered how long it would take you to get back to your investigative reporting," Bev said. "But first, you have to try my new and improved Christmas cocktail."

Marty groaned.

"No, really, this one is quite good."

"Okay, let's get it over with."

"Phil?" Bev said. "What are you doing?"

"Enjoying the view." Phil had walked over to the window that overlooked the little pond that in summer was home to a family of ducks. The snow was floating down like fairy wings, and dusted the ground like powdered sugar. And Phil was surprised by the memory of skating on the lake at her father's country seat. Racing her siblings to be the first on the ice. Falling and pulling each other over in the soft snow.

But that was in the past. Like Lily, Phil was a new person with a new future. Her past seemed like a dream in comparison.

She turned back to the room to see Bev holding a pitcher of red liquid. Phil steeled herself for Bev's latest concoction.

Bev handed her a glass. Phil looked at it skeptically and took a small sip. Took another.

"Bev . . ." she began.

"Oh Lord, it's good," Marty said.

"Whew!" Bev took a healthy swallow, shook her shoulders, and said, "Now, that's what I call a Christmas cocktail."

They ate, drank, sang carols, and watched the snow come down.

"I just hope we don't get snowed in. I have deadlines to catch up on," Marty said, and snuggled beneath the blanket.

Phil had just been thinking how peaceful it was, but she had to admit she was a little impatient to find Tommy's killer and enter the new year with a clean slate.

So, when they heard a knock on the door, followed by Bobby Mullins in the flesh, it didn't take long for the conversation to turn from the snow and horses to the demise of Tommy Green.

As soon as he'd sat down with his tumbler of whiskey, Phil apprised him of Tommy Green's murder.

"Lord, you're at it again, your . . . lady . . . countess-ship."

Marty's mouth opened. Bev rolled her eyes.

Bobby had never managed to arrive at the proper form of address when talking to Phil. Bev said it was because he'd been hit in the head a few too many times, but Phil thought it gave him a certain charm, so she never corrected him.

"That reporter fella. Yeah, I heard. Thought he was mugged."

"I was mugged," Marty said. "Tommy was murdered." She was sitting up now, and alert. Her newsman's nose practically twitching for all of them to see.

"Murdered? You mean like on account of who he was, not on account of what was in his wallet?"

"He was found at the docks, but he was killed at the Theatre Unique on Fourteenth Street," Phil said.

"Oh, tarnation, your lady-ness. How do you know that? No, don't tell me. You have your ways, but I'll be damned to know how." He scratched his head, unleashing his freshly po-maded hair. "Does Becker know you know?"

"He might. I'm not sure. But he did see me talking to Mrs. Toscana at Tommy's wake."

Bobby slapped his forehead. "Sally Toscana? What are you doing talking to somebody like her? She's connected in so many ways that even I can't keep track."

"Connected?"

"You know, like to Tammany and that crowd. And Becker and his thugs." He stopped to rub his fingers and thumb to-gether. "And some others I rather not name."

"Like the Black Hand?"

Bobby drank off the rest of his whiskey. "Bunch of thugs. Best to stay away from Sally. She's a fine one, but all the same, she's got some powerful gentlemen making sure she don't get out of line. 'Course, being a smart woman, Sally keeps their reins pretty tight in return."

Bev refilled his glass.

"She might pay them protection money," Phil said. "Not that it did her any good. Did you know her place was just bombed?"

"Naw, don't tell me."

"And since someone had kidnapped me the day before on my way home from the wake after meeting her . . ."

Bobby slapped his forehead.

Bev gasped.

Marty reached for something, probably her notebook, but it was out of reach.

"You were kidnapped?" Bev said. "Why didn't you tell us?"

"With everything else, I haven't had time. And I didn't want to alarm you. They were told to kill me, but I was rescued by some quick thinking on the part of Just a Friend."

"Who?" Bev, Marty, and Bobby exclaimed in chorus.

"The newsboy on the corner."

"That's what he calls himself?" Bobby chuckled. "That kid is gonna go far in this world."

"Wait? What about the kidnapping?" Bev said.

Phil held up a finger. Marty had found her bag and her notebook and was searching for a pen.

"No reporting," Phil ordered, and turned back to Bobby. "I'm worried that there will be reprisals."

"On the kid?" Bobby asked.

Phil nodded, and quickly told him how Just a Friend had clung to the back of the automobile, then gathered his troop of newsies to rescue her. "Maybe he could come be a stable boy?"

"He's gonna go far, I tell ya. If he stays alive long enough. But I already offered him a place here for the winter. He won't leave you, your . . . He's got a mission, saving your—uh, ladi-ness. He's . . ."

"True blue," Phil finished.

"Like I said."

"But who kidnapped you?" Bev demanded.

Phil told them about waking up in the warehouse, the Fire-plug threatening her. "But he wasn't alone, there was another man, he was the one who told his thugs to kill me."

"Do you know who it was?" Bev asked, wide-eyed.

"I have an idea. Bobby, who drives a Rolls-Royce Silver Ghost?"

This time Bobby's hand covered his entire face.

Finally, he looked up. Chewed on his lip. Took another swallow of whiskey. "Don't have too many of them in town."

"I didn't think there would be."

"You sure it was a Silver Ghost?"

"I didn't see it. They chloroformed me. But that's what Big Nose Mike said, that's his paper beat, but it's best that we leave him out of this."

"You sure do get around," Bobby said, shaking his head. More hair sprang out from his head.

"Who is Big Nose Mike?" Bev interjected.

"You gotta watch yerself, your—ness. You really gotta watch yerself. In fact, maybe you oughta go on vacation for a while."

"I have a hunch who it is already," Phil told him. "I just need your confirmation."

"Well, there's only one I know in town. They ain't even come out yet. It belongs to Samuel Trout. And you don't want to cross him." Bobby smacked his forehead. Phil was beginning to worry he might knock himself out. "You ought'na get involved with any of those folks. It ain't like Trout to make a personal appearance when he's having somebody iced. And I never known him to give nobody a second chance."

25

Marty and Bev stared incredulously at Phil.

"Samuel Trout? Imogen's husband?" Bev asked, her disbelief palpable.

"Yes. I wasn't positive until yesterday. But one of the newsboys saw a man in a Rolls-Royce Silver Ghost, a car that I'm told isn't even on the market yet, come and go from the warehouse where they were keeping me. And now with Bobby confirming that Trout owns the only one he knows of . . ."

"Are you sure?" Bobby said. "Men like that, they have muscle do their dirty work. Other people," he elucidated. "What's he up to this time?"

"That's what we want to know."

"I guess you want me to ask around."

"That would be helpful."

He chewed his lip, scratched his head.

"Of course he'll help," Bev said. "Won't you, Bobby?"

"'Course I will. I'm just trying to figure out where to start."

"We should have talked to this guy sooner," Marty said under her breath.

Phil was inclined to agree with her. "So, where does Mrs. Toscana fit into all this?"

Bobby looked from one face to the other, then he turned red. "Aw, your countess, I don't go down there so much anymore. I mean, not to The Rose, Miz T. is way above my wallet. But to Tammany Hall. Now, those politicians love her place.

Word is she owns a few of them, lock, stock, and, um, well, never mind."

"I get the point. And her and Mr. Trout?"

"They're both from Queens. Same neighborhood. That's all I know. He's got a wife that's a real looker. Don't know nothin' about what he has—" He glanced at Bev, probably remembering what a philanderer Reggie Reynolds had been, and added, "You know, what he has on the side."

Phil nodded. Was there a husband in Manhattan—or London, for that matter—who didn't cheat on his wife?

Bobby stood up to leave. "I'll ask around, but I ain't promising nuthin'."

"We think it's about real estate," Phil said.

Bobby sat down again. "First of all. Everything is about real estate with Sam Trout. He owns a good portion of the city, and he didn't get it all by paying a fair price, if you get what I mean."

"Like extortion?"

"It's Manhattan."

"Arson?"

"Wouldn't put that past him."

"Maybe even a well-placed bomb or two, pretending to be the Black Hand?"

"Oh Lord, how do you get yourself into these messes? I never knew a woman—lady—countess like you in all my life for getting into trouble. Reggie and Mrs. Reynolds here had their fun. But nothin' like you."

"Bobby, we need to know the word on the street."

"If I hear, I'll let Ji—Just a Friend know. Now I gotta get back to the boys and make sure they don't enjoy themselves too much. Tomorrow's still a workday." He stood, shook his head, and started for the door, weaving slightly on his way.

"Phil," Bev said as soon as he was gone, "you were supposed to help find out who killed Tommy Green, not bring down the whole kit and caboodle. Tammany Hall? The Fire-plug? The Black Hand? Are you crazy?"

Phil looked over to Marty for a response, but she was furiously writing. "Remember, no reporting until I say."

"Well, you better hurry up. This is too good to let anybody else scoop me on it."

"Once we get Tommy's killer, but not before then. If you print anything prematurely, we could lose everything."

Marty looked up at that. "What do you know, Phil?"

"Nothing provable, but we're getting closer. And I think it's time we started thinking about forcing the killer to show his hand."

They went through the list of players . . . again.

Bev wandered over to the table and filled her plate with food.

Marty paced from one end of the room and back again. "What about Eddie?"

"Who is he?" Bev asked, contemplating a salmon sandwich.

"The mail boy. He's a friend of Harriet's. Maybe more than a friend, well, maybe not, but he'd like to be. It would be just like that stupid girl to let something slip to him."

"But does the mail boy have access—"

Marty cut Phil off. "To the storage room? Of course he does. He carries up all the material to be archived. Most of it is placed in the storage room until it can be filed in the archive library. He would have a perfect opportunity to rifle people's lockers. Pick up some dirt and make a nice bit of cash on the side. He might have even seen Tommy hiding the notes in my locker."

"Then why were they still there when we found them?"

"Maybe he couldn't get to them."

"Maybe he was blackmailing somebody with the information and he figured they were safe there," Bev suggested, and finished her sandwich.

Phil and Marty both just looked at her.

"Who?" Phil asked.

"I don't know, but anybody can be a blackmailer if they are privy to damaging information."

"And can prove it," Marty added.

Bev shrugged. "Not necessarily. Maybe the threat was enough."

"Possibly," Phil said. "As a mail boy, he might pick up tidbits around the newsroom. Harriet might have even made him privy to some of the news she typed. But what kind of contacts did he have time or the clout to make on the outside? If Eddie was involved, it's likely that he was a dupe of someone else."

"Well, we won't know if we don't get back to town." Marty strode to the window. "And if we don't leave now, there's a good chance of that."

Bev joined her. "Isn't it beautiful? I could spend weeks and weeks here."

"Well, I couldn't," Marty said, and grabbed her shawl off the sofa.

"Where are you going?"

"We're all going back to town."

"Marty, calm down," Phil said. "It will be too late to do anything by the time we get back, even if we left now. We can leave early tomorrow morning. Preswick is going to City Hall as soon as it opens tomorrow, but I'm sure it will take several hours for him to find what he's looking for. Sit down and concentrate on getting your strength back."

"There's nothing wrong with my strength," Marty said, and promptly tripped on the carpet.

"In that case, I think we would all enjoy a nice walk in the fresh air." Phil set action to her words and went to the porch, where three sets of wellies sat by the back door.

Phil needed time to think and wanted to stay away from the city long enough to devise a plan, and to keep Marty from running off half-cocked. She was beginning to wish she had never confided in her. She was a dedicated newswoman, but she had as yet to develop the patient investigation skills of her mentor.

Marty looked out the window. "Not me. I don't really feel up to tromping through the snow. I'll keep the fire fed and maybe have another glass of Bev's Christmas punch."

"Well, I'm game," said Bev. "Don't get sloshed while we're gone."

The two of them bundled up and stepped outside. The snow was falling in heavy, wet flakes as they started walking up the hill toward the barn. Everything around them, including the air, was white. They would have never made it home in this weather; even walking required intense concentration as the wind sent drifts across their feet and piled up against fence posts.

They stopped by the barn where the horses were bedded down, then started off toward the open fields. Ahead of them, the sun was lowering in the sky, creating a dark pink frame above the distant woods.

"It's beautiful," Bev said. "No automobile fumes, coal smoke, or even footsteps but our own. And it's so quiet. Maybe it was a mistake to bring Marty, but I was afraid to leave her alone."

"No, you did the right thing. She would only get herself and the investigation into trouble in her current state of mind."

Phil's toes and nose were numb by the time they turned to retrace their steps to the house. The snow was coming down in a heavy curtain of white and accumulating on the ground at an alarming rate.

But it was the sound of a motor starting that had both Phil and Bev racing back to the cottage. They reached it just in time to see the back of Bev's yellow Packard disappear into the snow.

"Ugh. Drat you, Marty." Bev stamped her wellie-clad foot. "You'd better not wreck my car."

Or strand them at the farm while Marty wreaked havoc on the potential suspects and wrecked any chance of bringing Tommy's killer to justice.

They met Bobby coming out of his office, shrugging into his farm coat.

"Gawd, I was afraid that was you. No way can you get out tonight."

"It's Marty, driving the Packard. Ten to one, we'll find her at the bottom of the drive. That turn is a mean one even on a good day."

Bobby strode over to the barn door, rang the bell that would summon the farmhands, who wouldn't appreciate being pulled from the warm comfort of the bunkhouse to dig an auto and its driver out of the snow.

Phil just hoped Marty wouldn't seriously injure herself. Then they would be in a fix.

They found the Packard at the end of the drive, its front end stuck in a ditch and covered in snow.

Marty was standing ankle-deep in the snow, arms akimbo, and staring at the Packard.

Bev gave her a look as she walked past to inspect the damage.

Bobby moved the women back from the car, gave orders to his men, then jumped into the driver's seat. After much grunting from the men and groaning from the engine, the Packard was back on the drive proper and facing toward the farm.

"Ladies." Bobby gestured them into the car.

"Thanks, Bobby." Bev edged past him.

"If you don't mind, Miz Reynolds, I have more experience in the snow than you do."

Bobby stopped Phil as she started to climb in. "He wants to see you up at my office."

She was surprised but managed not to blurt out "Who?" There were only two people she could imagine who would waylay her out of town on an isolated farm. She refused to consider the first, and thought, *It's about time,* when she considered the second.

As soon as they were back inside, Bev put Marty to bed with hot soup and a glass of wine.

And with a brief explanation, and the order to stay mum, Phil once again climbed the hill to the barn. And Bobby's office.

He was sitting in Bobby's desk chair; Bobby was nowhere to be seen. The aroma of exotic tobacco swirled around the room, a nice change from Bobby's cigars.

"Well, it's about time," Phil said, stamping on the bolt of thrill that coursed through her.

"I rather thought you'd be surprised to see me." He was fully bearded, dressed as a common laborer in a rough flannel shirt and thick shepherd's sweater. His hair was dark and long, almost to his shoulders.

"I was. I am." Even if he was unrecognizable in his disguise.

"And maybe just a little glad?"

"I am, but things are reaching a climax."

His mouth lifted in a slow smile that ordinarily would have made her forget everything else—even with the beard. But they were too close to the killer to stop for fun. Well, maybe just a little bit of fun.

"Did you put back the notes?"

"All in good time."

"When we return home, Marty will demand to see them. If she thinks I've betrayed her, she'll go rogue. And that will unravel everything. Bev and I can hardly keep her constrained as it is."

"Well, you have until New Year's, then we're going to start rounding up people. If you want your murderer, you'll have to get him—or her—before then."

"What? What people? The killer? What am I supposed to be doing?"

He put his pipe down, stood, and walked around the desk.

"What you always do."

"Care to elaborate?"

"Don't you understand yet?"

"I know I've been able to help catch the odd murderer."

He laughed. "My dear, you are the linchpin."

A statement that left her as confused as ever. And his closeness, that heady scent of determined male and pipe tobacco, was making it hard for her to be rational.

She stepped away from him. "I'm working on a plan, but I'll need the notes back to make it work."

"Those notes are essential."

"I know, but I don't see any other way."

He nodded. "You're going to use them as bait."

"Do *you* see any other way?"

"Not my specialty."

She smiled at that. His specialty was dressing up in outrageous costumes and disappearing into thin air. She wasn't certain what his actual position was, but whatever it was, it got results.

"Preswick is going to City Hall tomorrow to determine if the vandalized buildings were sold."

"Good man. I'll need the results. When you're finished with them," he added with a lightning quicksilver smile that was unsettling.

"But how—"

"If you need me, slip a note to your newsboy. Bobby will make sure I get it."

"You trust Bobby more than—"

"It doesn't work that way. Now I have to go."

"How does it work? How did you even get here in the snow?"

"The same way I'll leave. Now remember what I said." He

reached for a heavy, fur-lined coat that had been hanging on the coatrack behind the door. "I'd kiss you goodbye, but I know how you hate hairy kisses."

"I'll make an exception this time."

And she was glad she did. She had her orders, as much explanation as she'd come to expect from the other part of her team. And she knew he wouldn't let her down if it came to that.

So she gave into the kiss and to him, and all his ridiculous, secretive, life-saving habits.

And when she'd recovered, she was alone.

26

Fortunately for everyone, the next morning dawned clear and warmer, and with the help of Bobby's snowplows, they were able to get to the road and head for home.

Phil almost hated to leave. The country visit had been relaxing and revitalizing, except for Marty, who was driving both Phil and Bev to distraction with her desire to get back.

By the time they reached the Plaza, it was almost noon. Phil was longing for a proper breakfast or lunch and copious cups of coffee.

Marty insisted on coming upstairs with Phil, and Bev wasn't about to be left behind, so she left the Packard with Mr. Fitzroy while the staff unpacked Phil's belongings.

The elevator ride went far too quickly, and even though Phil managed to drop her keys twice, the front door opened, and Marty pushed them inside.

"Where are they?" Marty demanded, rushing past a startled Lily.

"In the safe where we left them," Phil said, praying that they would actually be there.

"Where?"

"In here." She went to the safe with Marty practically stepping on her heels and Bev following close behind. Lily hurried after them, attempting to take hats and gloves and coats as they went.

Phil was careful to shoulder Marty out of the way while

she worked the lock. She didn't trust Marty any more than she trusted Mr. X. But at least he had other virtues.

The lock clicked, the safe opened, and Phil breathed a thanks to her mystery colleague.

The packet of notes was there.

He'd left an additional note on top. *Thanks, I'll need these back.*

Phil slipped that note into her pocket. The original list of addresses lay on top, which meant whoever needed to see them had seen them and had made a copy. She imagined someone whose job it was to decipher codes and bad handwriting sitting in an airless office surrounded by ceiling-high stacks of illegible scribblings.

They would need the originals back. It was a huge responsibility, but Phil didn't see any other way to ferret out the murderer than to dangle the bait before him.

Phil pulled the now neatly arranged stack of notes out of the safe and carried them to the dining room. While Bev consulted Lily about food and drink, Phil and Marty spread out the papers on the table.

"I don't remember us arranging them so neatly," Marty said. "Did you do this after I left?"

"Uh-huh," Phil said noncommittally, and reached for several sheets.

For half an hour they pored over Tommy's handwriting, looking for any tidbit they might have missed the first time around.

Lunch arrived, and they ate while they worked.

"What exactly are we looking for?" Bev asked.

"Anything pertaining to real estate and/or Samuel Trout or Jarvis Chandler," Phil said.

"Or anything that sounds like code or shorthand for those," Marty added, and handed Bev another stack of papers.

They spent another hour poring over the notes.

"This is mainly just what happened when," Bev said, clearly disappointed not to have discovered the key to it all.

"Then write it down in chronological order," Marty said.

Bev sighed but picked up her pencil.

Phil wasn't having much luck herself. She was actually looking for something outside Tommy's original investigation of the Black Hand.

It had been niggling at her ever since she'd visited Mrs. Toscana. Her childhood in Queens, Sam Trout, and Tommy Green, all from the same neighborhood. The other photo of Mrs. Toscana in her white coming-out dress.

Roz Chandler standing in the doorway of the Plaza ballroom in a long white-and-gold gown, not the simple dress of an eighteen-year-old, but the resemblance was uncanny.

The truth may have gone with Tommy to his grave, for after having taken measure of the brothel madam, Phil was certain she would never divulge if she was indeed linked to Roz. Or if Tommy was in ways Roz had never suspected.

"Eureka!" Marty shouted, interrupting Phil's train of thought.

"Maybe." She handed a sheet of paper to Phil. "Look at this, the fourth line two-thirds across the page." She got up and came to stand over Phil's shoulder, while Bev leaned over the other, and Lily's head appeared in the doorway.

Marty pointed to a scribbled word in the sentence. Phil squinted at the writing and read aloud as she deciphered each word. "'M. Elliott, 68, prop of Elliott Flor. 1 5 yrs in bus. lives 3rd flr. ld noise 11–2 pm 11–22–07, Bmb. Entire store, damgd 2nd flr. 5–12–09–07.'"

"Look again at the last set of numbers," Marty said.

"Five. Twelve. Not 'five' but capital 'S,'" said Phil. "Sold? He sold his property three weeks later."

"At last a break," Marty said. "Look for more sales."

They pored over their respective piles, but though there

were close to ten properties on the list, they only discovered three more Ss.

Marty walked away, came back. "Oh, where is your butler? Why is he taking so long?"

"Mr. Preswick is very thorough. He'll return when he's obtained what he's looking for."

What Phil really wanted was for Bev to take Marty home and leave Phil to make some plans. But she knew it would be futile to argue, so she gritted her teeth and hoped Preswick would return soon.

If she only had until the new year to catch her killer, she needed to act. Four days. With the possible suspects all celebrating the holidays, most out of town, there would be only one chance to ferret out the killer.

Mr. X had said she was the linchpin. Did he meant that she was holding their investigation together the way a linchpin kept the wheel from falling off a wagon?

Would solving Tommy's murder make it possible for them to begin arrests for what she could only assume was fraud? The link between a killer and the rest of the culprits?

She could spend the next four days running around and trying to get someone to confess. Or . . . set a trap and hoped to heaven it worked.

But she would need the cooperation of others, and she would have to play her hand very carefully.

By the time Preswick returned, Lily had gone back to her household duties, Marty was pacing a path across the Aubusson, Bev was curled up with a short story in the latest issue of *Collier's* magazine, and Phil had a list of things to do to put her plan into action.

"We're in here," Phil called, and after a few moments of low voices, and the rustling of coat and hat being shed, Preswick appeared in the door to the dining room. He was wearing a black suit and starched collar and carried a briefcase, not

Tommy's. The epitome of a businessman with business with the city.

"My lady."

"Oh, do come in, Preswick, and sit down. We're overcome with anticipation."

Bev and Marty had already returned to their places at the table as soon as they'd heard the front door open and sat like eager schoolgirls waiting for his news.

He sat and opened the briefcase, methodically taking out several sheets of precise, neatly written notes, which he spread out before him.

Lily appeared discreetly in the doorway and slipped in to sit beside him.

"These are the properties that coincide with the ones we knew about or estimated the addresses of. Here is a list of other vandalized properties in somewhat the same vicinity that we were not aware of."

There were at least fifteen listed on the second page.

"Could you tell if any of them had been sold since the vandalism?" Marty asked.

Preswick slid another sheet next to the first one. It neatly aligned with the first paper, only to this one was added an additional column of SOLD and the dates.

Phil looked for their own notes and found the same numbers corresponding to the three they had found. But Preswick's list was much more extensive.

"All damaged and all sold," Phil said. "And I bet for considerably less than they were worth."

"Much less," Preswick said.

"Excellent work, Preswick," Phil said. "Now, if we only knew whom they sold to."

"That took a little longer. The actual transactions are kept on a different floor." He took out a third sheet, similar to the first two. Only this sheet held the name of several buyers. Two companies and the rest individuals.

"There goes your theory about Trout trying to corner the market," Bev said.

Preswick pulled out a fourth sheet of paper with only six lines of writing.

"And these are the resales. Six out of twelve resold within two weeks."

There was silence around the table.

"Someone was destroying property and convincing the owners to sell cheap," Phil said.

"But all the separate buyers?" Marty said, frowning at the last sheet.

"That is what took the bulk of my time. As to the individuals. They appear to be who they are, though possibly hired by someone in order to use an entity untraceable to the actual buyer. I believe they're called 'straw owners.' They're hired for a percentage or a flat fee to buy the property, then turn it over to the person who hired them. Each time, the price is inflated and resold.

"And this is where it becomes quite interesting." Preswick turned the sheet for them all to see. "Within weeks, they were all resold to the City of New York."

He had everyone's full attention.

"It took some digging; these dummy companies can be very well shielded. That is what kept me, but eventually I discovered every one of those companies and possibly the individuals were controlled by one man. Samuel Trout."

"And expedited through by someone in the building department?" Phil asked, already suspecting the answer. "Commissioner Chandler comes to mind."

Bev's eyes grew wide. "Roz's husband? Oh no. Poor Roz."

Poor Roz indeed. With Jarvis as building commissioner, they would have an inside track when the government decided to build on or nearby the property.

"Anything else, Preswick?"

"Just one, my lady. It may just be an outlier, having nothing to do with the others. Actually, I couldn't make sense of it at first, my mind naturally going to ships."

"Ships?"

"Yes." Preswick pulled out a final sheet of paper, and Phil couldn't help thinking how much he must be enjoying this in pure Holmesian fashion. He placed the paper on top of the others and tapped his finger to one address. "Sold to an 'SS Lord.' The 'SS' fooled me for a second."

"Sydney!" Marty exclaimed, "Sydney Steiling Lord. That no-good, double-crossing—"

"Easy, Marty," Bev said. "Think of your poor head."

"Sydney will be the one with a poor head when I'm finished with him."

"It might not mean he's involved," Phil said, though she thought he might be. "We can't prove anything as yet."

"You've done excellent work, Preswick. Now, go have your tea, but first add your papers to the others and return them to the safe."

Preswick nodded, began to gather up the papers.

Marty jumped up. "No! We should run with this."

"Not yet," Phil said.

"We have the facts."

"But not evidence of criminality."

"But—"

"Evidence," Phil shouted over her tirade. "If you go off half-cocked before there's a case—"

"What case?"

"I thought you wanted to find Tommy Green's killer? Have you forgotten about Tommy in your news lust?"

The expression drained from Marty's face. She jerked her head no, followed by "No. This is about finding who killed Tommy and bringing them to justice. I just . . . for a moment . . ."

"I quite understand. We are getting closer, but this will require great discipline on all our parts, and Marty, if you can't control your need for vengeance, you'll have to bow out, and you, too, Bev."

"Me?" Bev asked, indignant. "What did I do?"

"Nothing yet, but you're a loyal friend, as I know all too well, and I know if it came to it, you would come to Marty's aid, and to Roz's."

And then it hit Phil, why she was the linchpin.

"We need to smoke out a snitch."

Marty sank into her chair.

"Think, Marty. Somehow Tommy was closing in on them, and they had to keep him from exposing them. And they knew he was closing in because someone in the *Times* office was tipping them off."

"But that could be anyone with a desk near Tommy's," Marty said. "One of the printers, the switchboard operator, Eddie the mail boy. Mr. Carr himself, though I really doubt that. Maybe someone who overheard a conversation at the bar."

"You're not thinking, because you're frustrated. Are you telling me Tommy would be that sloppy with a lead? That Tommy was his own leaker?"

Marty looked up, horrified. "Of course not."

"Then help me figure out who it was." Phil reached for a notebook. "Who did Tommy think was leaking his leads?"

"Harriet Wells," Marty said. "She was his typewriter girl, until Tommy became suspicious."

"And she was at the crime scene," Phil said.

"That young thing?" Bev asked. "Could she actually slit a man's throat?"

"She could have had an accomplice," Marty said. "Sorry, I was jumping ahead. I know better."

"Perhaps she just let something slip unawares. Like chatting to Eddie the mail boy, perhaps. He was waiting for her when we took her home from questioning her one day."

"You questioned Harriet?"

"Well, yes. And I noticed when we came to pick you up for

lunch that Eddie was very friendly, and he was very attentive to her at the wake."

"Except that Harriet worships Sydney." Marty grimaced. "From afar, anyway, stupid girl."

"I did notice the way she looked at him at the wake," Phil said. "But would Sydney play both sides of the news game?"

"Sydney?"

Phil lifted both eyebrows. "We did see him with Jarvis and Trout at the Cavalier Club."

"But we all hang out there. It's where all the real news is. Someone gets drunk and . . . Oh, wait, you think Sydney might have mistakenly dropped something about Tommy?"

"Mistakenly, or for a price?" Phil asked. "Would he jeopardize his career for money?"

"That would mean he might have been instrumental in Tommy's death."

"Possibly."

"No. He'd never actually get his hands that dirty. He doesn't even like to touch ink."

"And what about you?" Phil asked.

"Me? What about me?"

"Are you sure you didn't share Tommy's investigation with anyone, even accidentally?"

Marty didn't answer, just stared back at Phil, eyes afire. "How can you even ask me that?"

"It's necessary to question everyone involved. You are no exception."

"I didn't. I would never. I'm a journalist, first and foremost. I might steal someone else's story by beating them to the facts, but I would never undercut someone like you're suggesting."

"You're certain you spoke to no one about it?"

"I told you—"

"Marty," Bev said. "You asked Phil to help, and she is. She has to ask uncomfortable questions." She paused long enough to give Phil an understanding look. "She even asked me a few when they were investigating poor Reggie's death. So don't get all huffy. It doesn't become you."

Marty glared back at Bev, then her rancor seemed to melt. "You're right. Journalists—good ones—do the same thing. They don't let it get personal. I apologize, Phil. To my recollection, I never talked to anyone about it except Tommy himself.

"And then not even to him."

"He was just trying to protect you," Bev reminded her. "He wanted you to take over for him when he retired. He just retired sooner than he thought."

"Fine, so what am I supposed to do? Since Phil seems to be the boss," Marty asked.

"You asked me to do this," Phil reminded her.

"Yeah, okay. What's my job?"

Phil deliberated. She didn't trust Marty, who seemed to get more volatile by the minute. But she had no choice.

"Do what you do. Return to the paper, keep your eyes and ears open. There must be some parties during this week before the new year. Listen, but do not engage anyone out of the ordinary. Report fashion and gossip, but listen for any slip or insinuation about real estate or anything else."

"And what about Sydney?"

"That's just what I mean. We don't know if Sydney is actually involved with this. It could be coincidental; maybe he was acting as one of those 'straw owners' and Trout used him to buy property for him.

"But if he *is* involved," Phil continued, "and he becomes suspicious that you're on to him—"

"They might kill you, too," Bev finished.

Phil didn't even try to soften Bev's reaction. Hopefully, she would drive the point home, before Marty did something reckless.

"Don't let Tommy or Mr. Riis down, Marty. They saw your potential. Live up to it. Be patient and follow the lead to its natural conclusion."

"Okay, I'll back off. Keep my eyes and ears open, and won't move until we have proof."

"Thank you. Bev, I need you to stop by the Chandlers' residence this evening. Arrive a little after five; wait if you have to."

"It's Friday. Roz will be at mass," Bev pointed out.

"Exactly. You've come to consult Jarvis on the state of your finances, since your father is on the Continent."

"Me? My finances are just fine. Oh." Bev's shoulders slumped comically. "I feel so in need of guidance. Poor Reggie." She paused to sniff. "His finances were . . ."

"Okay, don't overdo it. Everyone must know that you're making a fortune off your horses."

"I was going to say, so complicated that I don't understand a thing."

Phil and Marty laughed.

"I'm not sure he would believe that, either."

"Fine. I'll just play it as it goes, and bat my eyelashes a lot."

"Good," Phil said. "Keep him occupied until after six."

"What have you got up your sleeve, Phil?"

"Nothing, but it's time to start making some people uncomfortable. I want to go into the new year free of crime." *Actually, she had to.*

Marty stood up, resigned but not happy. "And what are *you* going to be doing?"

"Me?" Phil said. "I'm going to mass."

27

Phil stepped out of the taxi across the street from St. Patrick's Cathedral just as Christmas bells filled the air, calling the faithful to mass.

St. Pat's, as the locals called it, was an aspirant construction to hope and faith. Phil didn't have that kind of faith; hers had been sorely tested in the last few years. But she could appreciate the beauty of the deeply recessed neo-Gothic façade, the spires that rose upward, piercing the night as the streetlights gave way to darkness. It was moving in ways she hadn't felt for a long time.

But this evening she was on a more worldly mission.

Phil joined the last-minute worshippers hurrying up wide marble steps, and stopped just inside the bronze doors. While others genuflected and found a seat, Phil searched the pews for Roz.

She was sitting by herself near the back. Her head was bowed, just as Tommy's had been in the Theatre Unique, and for a second Phil was stopped by that horrible image. The top portion of Roz's face was hidden beneath a heavy veil, but Phil could just see her lips moving as she prayed.

Phil sat down in a nearby pew. She wouldn't interrupt.

Organ music wove quietly through the narthex. Soft, soothing, perfect for calming away the worries of the day. The priest lifted his arms in welcome, his white-and-gold embroidered robes a beacon for the lost.

And Phil's mind drifted to England and the Dunbridge parish church in the village where the Amesburys had had their own pew for centuries. The earl had never graced it with his presence while she had been his wife. Phil had been too miserable to go alone at first, and later, when she did venture to a service, the stares and whispers were so pointed that she never returned.

A hymn rose up around her, and she quickly glanced to make sure Roz was still there.

Do not get distracted now, Phil warned herself. Everything would soon come to a head, and once they arrested the killer, for surely they must be successful, she would sleep for a week.

The mass ended. The priest and acolytes recessed into other parts of the cathedral. A few people stayed to light candles, the others headed for home or other engagements.

But Roz Chandler didn't move, leaning slightly toward the side chapel that Phil could see between two massive columns. Phil slipped out of her own pew and went to join her.

Roz didn't look up when Phil sat down beside her. She showed no surprise at all. "Why did you come here?" she whispered without lifting her head.

"I wanted to talk to you where we could be alone," Phil returned, checking her surroundings to make sure they *were* alone.

"Well, I've changed my mind. I don't want you to investigate anymore."

"Why?" asked Phil, though she was afraid she knew the answer. "I thought you cared about Tommy."

"I did. I do. But . . . you don't understand."

"I think perhaps I do," Phil said softly.

Roz shook her head.

"Roz, lift off your veil."

"I can't."

So Phil lifted it for her, to reveal the shadow on Roz's cheekbone in spite of the heavy powdering she'd used in an attempt to hide the bruise.

Phil took her hand. She didn't have to ask who had done this.

"I'm so ashamed," Roz hiccupped, swallowing back a cry.

Phil didn't answer. She knew better than to try to convince Roz it wasn't her fault. No one ever believed that until they'd gotten fed up and angry enough to fight back.

"Jarvis is worried. I don't know why, but it's gotten worse since you started investigating Tommy's death. He acts like it's my fault. I didn't kill Tommy. I barely knew him. He was just a nice man who sometimes said hello. I shouldn't have asked you to find his killer."

Unless Phil missed her guess, Tommy might be more than just a nice man. But to know that for certain required another visit to Mrs. Toscana, whom Phil was certain was either the mother of or some other close relative to Roz Chandler. And who at least might know the truth.

"Is that what you told Jarvis? That I was investigating Tommy's murder?"

"Of course not. He doesn't like me to involve myself in business. He says my job is to make friends with the wives. And if he knew I hired you to investigate—"

"I think you mistook me, Roz. I know a lot of people and I hear things. I said I'd help, but I'm not a private investigator. Just a—" Phil gritted her teeth. "—dowager countess trying to help my friends."

"Then you'll stop?"

Really, for a friend of Marty and Bev's, Roz seemed particularly clueless. Though perhaps it was panic that clouded her ability to think.

"I don't know what you think I'm doing."

Roz grabbed her hand. "Jarvis said—" She broke, let go. "I mean—"

"What did Jarvis say?"

"I wasn't supposed to tell."

"Roz, please."

"Nothing. He didn't say anything."

"Look up, Roz. Look at the stained-glass windows. The stories of good and evil. You're in church . . ." It was a cheap shot, in a way, but if you could lie in church, there wasn't much hope for you.

"He's afraid he'll be associated with the investigation. He's going to run for mayor in the next election. I guess Mayor McClellan hasn't turned out to be the man Tammany wanted, though he seems nice to me and he does a lot of things to help the city. They're grooming Jarvis already. Tommy's investigation could ruin it all."

"But Tommy's dead."

A sob broke from Roz, and she buried her face, veil and all, in her hands. Phil quickly looked around to see if they had attracted attention. The church seemed to be empty but for an old lady in black lighting a candle at the rail and several individuals whose heads were bent in prayer.

"Jarvis hasn't done anything wrong. He's friends with Samuel Trout, but that's all. Sometimes he expedites things for him, but nothing illegal. He promised."

Maybe not illegal, Phil thought, though she doubted it.

"Please stop."

"Roz. Don't let him mistreat you."

"I have no choice."

"Of course you do. Bev will take you in. She has plenty of room and a big heart."

"No. I can't." Roz grabbed the pew in front of her, pulled herself to her feet with an effort.

"Did your parents die of influenza?"

Roz turned spasmodically toward Phil. "Yes, of course they did."

Phil cast her eyes to the vaulted ceiling.

Roz collapsed back on the pew. "Please don't ask."

"I have to." Phil reached into her handbag for the photograph of Roz's graduation that she'd found in Tommy's apartment.

Roz glanced at it. "What does that have to do with any-thing?"

"I saw one very similar to it in Mrs. Toscana's private par-lor. Do you know Mrs. Toscana?"

"No. I've never heard of her. Why should I—" The sound of heels on stone drew nearer. A man dressed in dark robes, a crucifix on a chain around his middle, walked past them, nodded, slowed to give them time to call him over and request confession.

They did neither, and he walked on toward the front to the altar.

"I have to go." Roz started to get up.

Phil grasped her by the wrist to stop her.

Roz let out a gasp, and Phil remembered the bruise she'd seen at the edge of Roz's sleeve.

"I'm sorry, I didn't realize."

Roz touched the veil where it covered her bruised cheek.

This was going nowhere. Time for a little more force. "Did you know that your mother was a Toscana?"

Roz didn't answer at first. Phil waited.

"No."

"But Jarvis did?"

"Yes." Roz hung her head. "He said our marriage was based on a lie. He accused me of marrying him under false pretenses. I didn't even want to marry him."

Phil could sympathize. "How long has he known?"

"I don't know. He's been under a lot of pressure all year, even before that. For a while, I just thought he was busy with his work in City Hall and then with the plan to run for mayor. He's always gone a lot, and stays out late. He says most real business is done after-hours. But I'm no fool. Well, maybe I am. But I know what men do at night when they leave their wives at home.

"Then this started." She gestured toward her eye. "Like his bad mood was my fault. Like he hated me, and I've tried to be a good wife. He said I was going to ruin his life. I begged him to tell me what I had done.

"I thought it was because I hadn't given him children, but now I know it's because of who I am, really am—the daughter of a brothel owner. If it comes out, his career will be in shambles, his favorite-son status with Tammany Hall, his social life, destroyed, all because of me. It's so humiliating."

From the bruises Roz was attempting to hide, it had the potential for being a lot worse than humiliating.

"Roz, Jarvis's problems go a lot deeper than your birth. And none of that is your fault. Please promise me, you'll go to Bev if things get worse."

"How could I ever face her or Marty? They've done something with their lives, I've thrown mine away by agreeing to marry Jarvis. He was only interested in my inheritance, and I was easy for the taking. My mom and dad, the Hastingses, only wanted to ensure my future. Almost like they knew they were going to die, though I know that's impossible. It was an accident."

Phil let that one pass.

"So, I agreed. They'd been so good to me; they were my parents. I'm sure he's spent every penny of my inheritance by now. I wish I were dead."

"Absolutely not," Phil snapped. "Then he will have won. And he doesn't deserve that. He's a scoundrel." She leaned closer. "I'll tell you a secret. The earl took my fortune, most of it, anyway. I have risen from the ashes." She was beginning to wax a bit too theatrically; she pulled back. "You can recover from this. You must."

"I'll be shunned by society. He'll make me pay, somehow, I know he will."

Phil had a pretty clear idea that Jarvis himself would be paying for his misdeeds behind bars, if they could link him to the real-estate fraud. And Tommy's notes were pretty clear about that. She'd leave it to Mr. X and his "team" to be able to prove it.

But that wouldn't help Roz.

And Phil wasn't quite sure what to do. She had survived because the earl had had the good taste to die. So, even though society knew what a cad he was, they could all pretend it didn't happen. It helped that Phil had had time to hone her survival skills. She wasn't sure how Roz would weather the storm.

"Do not tell Jarvis we met. Just hold on."

"And make my New Year's resolutions to . . . what? Be stronger? Be a better wife? I don't know if I can face much more of this." Roz gulped back a sob.

"Just hold on." Phil stood and let Roz pass out of the pew first, then followed her to the door.

Phil had work to do. So far they had been untangling a web of real-estate fraud from Black Hand activity and newspaper leaks. Add a scandal of birth . . .

But which of these roads led to the murder of Tommy Green? For his notes might or might not implicate Jarvis in real-estate fraud. Or Black Hand activity. Or was it simply because Jarvis had found out about Roz's real mother? Or because someone else had, and decided to staunch the rumors before they started? Someone who depended on Jarvis for success. Or someone who might have found out from Tommy, and instead of leaking the news, decided to try on a spot of blackmail.

Murder was often, as Phil had learned, done for the shabbiest of reasons. And blackmail was the lowest of all.

She would have to be very careful. This murder was just a piece of a larger operation, and if she failed, it could jeopardize the entire investigation.

It was time to solidify her plan, then act on it. She had no intention of carrying all these loose ends into the new year with her. Like Kipling, she always made one New Year's resolution, begin the first day of the year with a clean slate.

And this year would be no different.

Phil waited to give Roz time to get down the steps and into her waiting carriage or automobile, then she took a final look around. She felt small in the expanse of all this glory; small, and not the best believer, and yet, not powerless.

She pushed open the heavy bronze doors and stepped into the night.

As soon as she was home, Phil did what she'd been waiting to do since they returned from Holly Farm. She called the nineteenth precinct and left a message for Detective Sergeant Atkins to call Mrs. Dalrymple.

He called back an hour later.

"I'm getting a reputation for being a scoundrel," he said without preamble. "The desk sergeant even asked if there was a Mr. Dalrymple."

"Well, you said I shouldn't call you."

"Now that you have, and sound as if you're not in imminent danger, what can I do for you?"

"Meet me, the usual place."

"Now?"

"Yes, it's important."

"And so is your safety. Will tomorrow be too late? I don't want you to take any chances."

He was right, but she couldn't help but be impatient. "I suppose not," she said. "But early."

"As early as you wish."

She hung up and made another call, explained what she had in mind. When she hung up, she knew there would be no going back. Everything hinged on one chance. Now, to convince John Atkins.

* * *

"I know who ordered Becker to kidnap me," Phil said, once she and the detective sergeant were walking down the path of Central Park the next morning. As she hoped, it got his attention.

He stopped. "Who?"

"Samuel Trout."

He tucked her hand through his arm. She'd conveniently left her muff at home for just such a situation.

"Why would Samuel Trout involve himself with your kidnapping?" His eyes narrowed beneath the brim of his trilby. He was so terribly handsome; it was a shame he was so straight-laced. She would have much preferred to discuss the situation over a couple of brandies in her apartment. But needs must . . . "Because Tommy Green was investigating the bombings of the Union Square neighborhood."

"I'm afraid that is a leap that my poor policeman's mind can't make."

"We've—well, Preswick, actually—has identified at least ten buildings that have been the victims of the 'Black Hand' bombings and arsons, whose owners sold within a few weeks of these deeds, to people we think were straw buyers, and who in turned resold them to two dummy companies owned by Samuel Trout."

"And just how did Preswick uncover this?"

"City Hall records."

He pulled her to the side to make way for a nurse and pram coming in the opposite direction. "I don't know what to do with you," he said in pure exasperation.

She could think of a few things, but kept them to herself.

"It was a matter of public record."

"And dare I even ask how you arrived at this harebrained scheme?"

"Well, I happened to stumble across some notes Tommy left behind. Actually, they were in Martha Rive's locker."

"She's in on this, too?"

"She's aware of the situation. Actually, she and Roz Chandler asked me to help them find Tommy's killer. Since your hands are tied."

"There are separate jurisdictions and separate precincts for a reason," he said patiently.

"That didn't prevent you from saving me from those villains."

"My curiosity got the better of me."

Phil laughed.

"This still doesn't tell me how you leaped from Tommy Green's notes to Samuel Trout. No, let me guess. Real estate."

"Eventually, but the thing that alerted me to my kidnapper was actually at the charity ball."

"I'm listening."

She told him about the shadow person at the warehouse telling the men to kill her, and Trout's "Schuylkill" at the ball.

"That's hardly evidence."

"Perhaps not, but when we were at the newsboys' home serving luncheon—"

He flicked a look of surprise at her. "You did that?"

"Yes. I'm not without charitable feelings."

He nodded solemnly. "I beg your pardon."

"Anyway, a newsboy named Big Nose Mike, whose paper corner is across from the docks, saw a Rolls-Royce Silver Ghost stop at the same docks. A man got out and went in. His description fit with that of Samuel Trout, and he saw that man come out with Becker a few minutes later, then drive away, minutes before you arrived."

"Circumstantial at best."

"But he can identify him."

They had reached a curve in the walk, and he stopped her. "Do you really think any court will take the word of a newsboy? Hired thugs are more likely to kill him and dump his body in the river before he sets foot in the courthouse."

Phil sighed. "I hadn't thought of that. Do you think Trout had Tommy Green killed?"

"Very likely."

"You don't sound surprised."

"I'm not. We've been trying to get him for years. Or at least, we were, before things returned to the status quo. We could never pin anything on him. Men like that are always very well insulated; they have others to do their dirty work for them."

"That's just what Bobby Mullins said."

"He's in on this, too?"

"No. I just saw him out at Holly Farm." She looked out to the trees. A few evergreens were the only spots of color among the bare branches. It all seemed so lifeless. "So he'll never be brought to justice."

"One day, but not under the current conditions."

"How do you stand it? Being fettered like that?"

"My only other choice is to turn my back on justice and walk away."

"And you would never do that."

"Not yet, anyway."

They stood looking past each other. Phil at the somewhat bedraggled wreath someone had dropped over one of the concrete signposts. The detective sergeant, who knew where, perhaps into his future.

"It's so lowering," she said at last.

"Yes, it is."

"So I brought you out for nothing?"

"I wouldn't say that. Your company is certainly more appealing than the stack of paperwork on my desk."

"You do know how to make a lady feel special."

"Tell me about these buildings and sales."

She told him about Preswick's trip downtown, about the correlation between vandalized buildings and sales to the dummy corporations. And how several of them had already been sold to the city for big profits.

"And you found this all out from Martha Rive, who had Green's notes in her locker at the *Times*. Why am I having a hard time thinking this is the whole story?"

"Well, it isn't *exactly* the whole story. Did you just groan?"

He shook his head.

"You did. I clearly heard you."

"Just tell me the truth."

"Always, Detective Sergeant."

He scowled at her.

"When I can."

"The story?"

"We—Preswick, Lily, and I—followed Harriet Wells to Tommy's apartment." She held up her hand; she didn't have time to explain how they'd gotten to Harriet Wells or why. "It had been 'tossed,' I believe is the word. So, in tidying up— Now I know that was a groan."

"You do realize that you were obstructing a police inquiry?"

"Not at all. The police hadn't bothered to come. Not even the Fireplug would leave such a mess. Someone was looking for something. They didn't find it."

"And just what makes you think they didn't?"

"Because I believe I did."

"You are cutting years off my life."

Phil sucked in her breath. "Is your life in danger?"

"No. My sanity."

"Oh, that. Well, try to calm yourself, because there's more. And this involves Mrs. Toscana."

"Toscana? The—the—?"

"Madam. Yes. I met her at Tommy Green's wake. We had found a matchbox from her, um, establishment. So I introduced myself and asked to meet with her. Becker overheard.

"That's when he kidnapped me, I think to prevent me from talking with her. Because I went there the next day. I barely missed being killed by a package bomb that was delivered while I was there."

"You were there?"

Phil nodded. "I don't think it was meant for me. I mean, how could they know what I intended?"

"I don't know. I certainly never know what you're going to do next."

"Don't get huffy with me, Detective Sergeant."

One eyebrow quirked up, probably because he was too exasperated or angry to speak.

She wouldn't tell him about Roz and Mrs. Toscana. Whether it was related or not, it was information she wouldn't divulge until absolutely necessary, not if she wanted people to continue to trust her with their worst secrets.

"But I did return, just a compassion call, you understand. Her secretary had been badly injured. Mrs. Toscana seems to know more about who might have killed Tommy than the rest of us. And she is privy to information that even the police might not be able to get."

Both his eyebrows lifted at that.

"Men do tend to—"

"Yes, I get your meaning."

"I realize that she may just be speculating; she wouldn't confide in me. It may have no bearing on Tommy Green's murder. Or it might be everything."

"It could be. But there isn't much I can do about it but turn your information over—"

"So Becker can bury it, after killing me? Absolutely not."

He looked shocked, then smiled. "So you're not going to let it rest?"

"Good heavens, no. I have a plan."

"I'm not going to like it, am I?"

"I don't expect you to like it, Detective Sergeant. Though I do expect you to participate, unless you have a better idea?" She inclined her head. "Or are you afraid you might get in trouble?"

He gave her the look that her question deserved.

"In that case, just listen. The *Times* is having a celebratory reception before the inaugural ball drop on New Year's Eve. All the staff and quite a few dignitaries will be there. Including a few that I've had my eye on.

"A word or two in the appropriate suspects' ears, and I think I—we—can at least snare the leak who is responsible for setting this off, and possibly lure Tommy Green's murderer to give himself away. You just have to be on hand to catch anyone who takes the bait."

"No. I can't and I won't be responsible for you getting yourself killed."

"Do you think it will really come to that?"

"In a word, yes. This person has already killed once, is possibly responsible for more in the guise of bombings and arson. And even if you do find the leak, it doesn't mean that the actual man or men who ordered Tommy's murder will be arrested. This is probably not a spur-of-the-moment crime of passion but a carefully decided murder."

"Perhaps, but regardless, whoever did this or ordered this needs to be caught. And I will do my best to do just that."

"You frighten me when you talk like that."

She smiled. "And *you* make me feel all toasty when you talk like *that*."

"I'm serious. I don't like it."

"Come now, Detective Sergeant, you don't want to miss all the fun, do you?"

"I can call Mr. Miller and tell him just what you're up to and have him cancel the reception altogether."

"You're a bit late: he's just become one of my coconspirators. And Mr. Van Anda has approved the scheme. So, you see, you might as well agree to attend and be on hand to make an arrest."

"On what grounds? You don't expect to startle a confession out of a hardened criminal?"

"No, but perhaps one who is realizing he's in over his head."

Atkins narrowed his eyes. "Do you know who it is?"

"I have my suspicions. But it will take a bit of organizing and perfect timing to pull it off."

"And if no one shows up to your little trap, what then?"

"Then I will have wasted a perfectly good New Year's Eve."

28

It took several days of clandestine meetings, fraught with impatience and much argument, but at last a plan to catch the leaker and hopefully have him or her confess enough to lead to Tommy Green's murderer was agreed on. Bringing him to trial would be another matter, and outside of Phil's ability.

Phil continued to wrack her brain for any detail she might have missed, and any hitch she hadn't foreseen.

And when she couldn't put it off any longer, she made another trip downtown to visit Mrs. Toscana.

There was new glass in the windows, the street had been cleared, and only the faintest acrid odor served as a reminder of the bomb that had exploded a few short days before.

She wasn't welcomed. The woman who answered the door tried to shut it in her face, but Phil managed to get her booted foot inside. After a brief tussle and the appearance of Mrs. Toscana herself, Phil managed to slip into the foyer.

"I'm not here about Tommy's murder," Phil said without preamble. "Shall we go into the parlor?"

She didn't proceed, but waited for Mrs. Toscana to demur and lead the way. She didn't want to spar with the woman today, or any day, for that matter. But she did want some answers.

Once inside the parlor, Mrs. Toscana didn't offer Phil a seat. That was fine with Phil. The sooner she could leave, the better.

She crossed to the table of family photos and picked up the one of Mrs. Toscana in her white coming-out party gown.

"Strange," Phil said, and turned the photograph to face Mrs. Toscana. "When I was at the charity ball Monday night, I was struck by another white gown. White can be so becoming on someone with dark hair, don't you think?"

"If you say so." Mrs. Toscana made no move to sit down; she wanted Phil gone.

"Yes, so becoming. I thought so at the time, when Rosalind Chandler entered the ballroom. And I remember thinking, the resemblance was uncanny. Almost as if you were from the same family."

Mrs. Toscana's expression didn't change; only her fingers tightened on the handkerchief she'd been holding. "What do you want?" Her voice was low, venomous.

"Nothing at all. Nothing, at least, that I intend to share. Is Roz Chandler a relative of yours, your daughter, perhaps?" Not getting an answer, Phil plowed on. "Is Tommy her father?"

"No!"

"Good God, not Sam—"

"Never. It was some boy visiting for the summer. He left. The Hastingses wanted to adopt; my father came to an agreement with them."

Phil swallowed a lump in her throat. "I know how fathers can change our lives. I'm sorry."

Mrs. Toscana took in a rattling breath. "I was fifteen. She was better off with the Hastingses. All the right schools, dances, people. We promised to never tell. They loved her very much."

"But you named her name. Rosalind. Rose. When did she find out?"

"She doesn't know."

"She does, and so does her husband."

"No, it is impossible. No one but Tommy and my parents, but they are both dead."

"Well, they know. And Jarvis is furious with her."

"They will keep it secret if you will keep your mouth shut."

"I intend to unless absolutely necessary, but you should know. He beats her."

"No!"

"I've seen the bruises."

Mrs. Toscana had become so quiet, Phil was afraid she had ceased to breathe. "And someone else knows. Samuel Trout. He's the one who told them, he must be. It makes perfect sense. He's holding it over Jarvis's head, I'm sure."

"That devil," Mrs. Toscana said, in a whisper that sent chills through Phil's blood. "I will kill him. I will kill them both."

"Please, Mrs. Toscana. If you kill either of them, you will go to prison, then who will be there for Rosalind?"

Mrs. Toscana brought her handkerchief to her lips. "I can never be her mother, not even her friend. It would ruin her. When I die, she will be rich, and then it won't matter so much."

"Perhaps she would rather have you living, than your money once you are gone."

"No. Impossible."

"That is up to you and Roz. But just know that if I figured it out and Jarvis and Trout know, people will invariably learn the truth."

Phil held up a preemptory hand. "Not from me. I have no interest in causing either of you further pain. I just thought you should know. I don't expect our paths to cross again. I wish you the best."

On that, Phil turned and left, not looking back.

She'd done her duty. Roz and Mrs. Toscana must choose the rest.

At last, New Year's Eve came. Everything was as planned as possible, though Phil knew full well that the chances of everything going according to that plan were a fool's dream.

Still, the waiting was the hard part. Which was what she was doing now, trying not to fidget as she sat while Lily dressed her hair for the New Year's Eve celebration at the *New York Times* building.

"Madam, are you sure you don't want Mr. Preswick and me to go with you?"

"Absolutely not. I want the two of you to find a perfect place for viewing *la grande descente,* and tell me all about it in the morning." Phil turned her head left, then right. "And now I am perfectly coifed and you must go find your warmest coat and hat. Preswick, too."

At ten o'clock a taxi left her off a block from Times Square. She hadn't taken into account the crowds that had gathered to see the *Times* ball bring in the new year, and she became so impatient that she'd gotten out of the taxi and walked the last block.

She just hoped it hadn't deterred any of the other guests. She had one chance. And if she failed? She wouldn't. Everyone was depending on her.

They were all there when Phil walked into the reception hall. She couldn't have hoped for a better attendance, almost as crowded as Tommy's wake. How fitting that his murderer should be caught—but she wouldn't jinx the situation by predicting its outcome prematurely.

The guests were a veritable who's who of pomp, respectability, and potential criminal intent mingling with the day-to-day employees of *The New York Times.*

The first one she spotted was Sydney, golden boy with the ladies, politicians, and denizens of high-class after-hours clubs—and possible newspaper snitch and real-estate fraud conspirator. He was standing near the entrance—ready to make a run for it?—talking to Imogen Trout and Mrs. Abernathy.

He seemed thoroughly engaged, except for the giveaway flitting of his eyes every time anyone entered the room.

Harriet was back from her holiday, looking as wan as when

she'd left. Eddie stood stalwartly by her side, though Harriet seemed to be purposely ignoring him. Two partners in crime trying to appear innocent?

As Phil watched, Marty stopped to say a few words to them. *Just a few,* Phil instructed silently. *Just enough before passing on.* Marty passed on.

A few minutes later, Phil saw her laughing with Sydney Lord. *Three down.* The three most likely to pass the word on or take the bait themselves.

Samuel Trout was standing with several men who were either politicians or businessmen—any of whom could be privy to the scheme to monopolize the real estate around Union Square. Phil would be keeping a close eye on them all, but Trout especially. And if he needed a nudge, she would be ready.

Atkins was standing with Carr Van Anda, Charlie Miller, and another man she didn't recognize. She gradually made her way over to them to say hello.

They saw her coming. Well, really, how could anyone miss the dress she was wearing, a gold charmeuse with a belted tunic of crocheted net of metallic thread? She was pleased with the effect. It quite made her feel like one of King Arthur's knights, if there had been lady knights. The fact that its light skirt was easily tucked up in the belt if she was required to do any sprinting for her life was reassuring. Not to mention the loaded derringer inside her evening bag.

Charlie Miller took her hand. "Lady Dunbridge, thank you for coming, you look stunning."

He sounded so stilted that Phil was afraid Atkins might laugh. She gave her full attention to the man he was introducing.

". . . our distinguished colleague from Paris. Monsieur Jean Bonheur, editor of *Le Matin.* He's especially interested in seeing our New Year's Eve surprise."

"*Enchanté.*" Monsieur Bonheur—exquisitely dressed and

perfectly coifed, down to his precise goatee—bowed over Phil's hand.

Their eyes met briefly as he straightened.

And Phil marveled at how he had managed it. Did Miller really think he was a French editor, or was he privy to more than Phil was?

And what about Carr Van Anda, the only person she felt was above suspicion, and who kept casting her looks that hopefully would be taken for flirtation because of the wine that flowed and not because they shared a secret in catching a killer?

"We're very excited about this new venture," Van Anda said, just as Samuel Trout came up to the group. Phil prayed that the editor wouldn't be tempted to cast her a knowing look. "One hundred electric bulbs as it gradually comes to rest on the *Times* parapet at the stroke of midnight. It will be seen as far as Long Island and New Jersey. We hope to make it a *Times* tradition."

"Well, I'll be watching from the comfort of the Knickerbocker Hotel," Samuel Trout said. "Champagne, lobster, and central heating."

Everyone laughed politely. Even Phil smiled, though she was thinking, *With any luck, you'll be watching from the back of a Black Maria.*

He turned to Phil, his eyes inviting, challenging. "Perhaps I'll see you there."

"Perhaps," Phil said, practically purring. "But first there's a little business I need to complete after the reception breaks up. It shouldn't take long." She smiled and excused herself, not daring to look back at either Trout or her partners in catching a criminal.

Let them speculate.

Even if Trout came after her personally, she knew the unlikelihood of him being arrested. He could probably shoot her on top of the *Times* building on New Year's Eve with all the city watching and nothing would happen to him. He had the protection of Tammany and of Sergeant Becker.

Perhaps she shouldn't have included Detective Sergeant Atkins in her plan. It could make his life in the police department that much harder if they *were* able to catch the killer.

It might even be dangerous to his life. And what about Phil's own life? Becker was obviously willing to do what he thought needed to be done, as far as she was concerned. And unless she was wrong, Trout was more than willing to see the deed completed.

Not if she moved first.

At eleven thirty, Charlie Miller began to guide the guests toward the elevators. There were only a few stragglers left when Phil began to prepare for her solitary trip to the storage room.

She made a show of looking into her bag. Taking out the key, in case anyone was watching. If the word had leaked out. Though any one of the people she expected to linger had left the room. Hanging out in the shadows or nearby rooms to take her unawares?

She hoped so.

"I still think you should let me go with you," Marty said, coming up to her as she left the reception room.

"We discussed this," Phil said. "Plans only work when they're adhered to." Phil smiled to the Abernathys. "If I don't see you downstairs, happy New Year."

The Abernathys returned the good wishes and joined the others taking the elevator down to the street.

There were only a few people left. She didn't see Sydney anywhere. The Trouts had left earlier, and unless he planned on sneaking back upstairs in the next ten minutes, he would not be giving himself away this year.

Jarvis and Roz had never even made an appearance. Word was that Roz was under the weather and had decided to stay home for the celebrations. *Or was nursing a new set of bruises,* Phil thought, and felt a shot of pure anger.

There were quite a few of the newspaper people still milling about, finishing off the canapés and liquor. Eddie and Harriet seemed to be arguing about something over the punch bowl.

"Go help Mr. Van Anda get them into elevators," Phil told Marty. "And keep your eyes open for anyone who cuts away from the group, but don't confront them."

"I've got it," Marty said. "You be careful."

"Thanks. You, too."

As the last holdouts were herded toward the door, Phil joined them.

In a few minutes all but one of the elevators would shut down. Carr and the "journalist from Paris" had gone down to the editorial floor sometime earlier, and were hopefully waiting to take their positions. Atkins was somewhere about.

It could be any of them, Phil thought despondently. Had she played this too close to home? There was only one way to find out.

As the last of the guests crowded in, Phil took the opportunity to slip away and climb the stairs to the storeroom.

She took in every dark corner, listened for the slightest noise, and let herself into the storeroom with the key she'd just taken out of her purse. Tommy's key was where she always kept it. In her bodice.

She stopped just inside the door, listening, in case the leaker was already inside and waiting for her.

They were. Two of them. Phil froze as two shadows stepped out from the bank of lockers.

They'd beaten her here. How was that possible?

She thought of her derringer, in her purse and totally useless. She stepped back, thinking furiously. Groped behind her for the light switch, hoping to catch whoever it was off guard with the unexpected light.

She felt for the knob, pushed; the light flickered, and Eddie and Harriet stood blinking like two guilty schoolchildren in the sudden light.

Of course. Eddie had a key. But Phil hadn't really suspected these two of being the killers.

For an eon they stared at her, their faces frightened masks.

"Well," Phil said, feeling just as unsettled but hopefully hiding it better.

"We thought you could use some help," Harriet stammered. Phil let out a sigh, not of relief but of chagrin. That's all she needed; two enthusiastic, frightened irregulars.

"Thank you, but you should go." But what if they ran into the villain on his way in? Everything would be ruined, and they might be hurt.

"We want to help," Eddie said. "You shouldn't be here alone at night. Should we hide? I brought a wrench I found in the mail room."

"Okay." Phil looked quickly around. "Go hide behind that row of lockers. Don't come out until I give you the word."

"What word?" Harriet asked as Eddie trundled her out of sight.

"I'll call your name. Until then don't make a move."

There was no time to wait to see them safely stowed away. Phil hurried to the locker and was just unlocking it when she heard the click of the door behind her. She lifted out the packet of notes and turned as the door opened and Sydney Lord stepped into the room.

"You, Sydney." This had better not be another false alarm.

"What? I have no idea what you mean."

"No? You're not here to possibly get a look at these?" Phil held up the packet of Tommy's notes. Sydney's eyes flashed, giving his intentions away. "That's very disappointing, Sydney."

"Just shut up and give me the notes."

The door banged open and Marty burst into the room.

Phil could brain her. Her carefully made plan was unraveling quicker than she could catch the killer.

"Give me those." Marty snatched the notes out of Phil's hands, and Phil had a terrible moment of wondering if Marty and Sydney were in on this together. It only lasted a second.

"Sydney, how could you?" Marty screamed.

"Just give me the notes, Marty. You can have whatever assignment you want, just name it. But give me the notes."

"You're disgusting." She spat out the words and held the notes tighter.

"Look, I need Tommy's notes. I'm in deep to some people. You gotta help me. All I did was sell one measly piece of information to *The Sun*. I just needed a little extra cash. You wouldn't believe what they pay news editors."

"Oh, stop whining. Nobody makes any money in this business. You should have gone into something that pays better and where you don't have to be honest."

"Just give me the papers."

"No." Marty held them out of reach. "You sold out your friends, colleagues, and journalism just to become part of this real-estate extortion scheme."

"I didn't want to. I just needed to make some extra cash. I leaked a few stories. Ran a few errands. Then it got out of hand. They threatened me."

"You killed Tommy, you bastard."

"What? No!"

"You vermin!"

"I didn't kill Tommy. I was just supposed to get his notes and turn them over."

"How?" Phil's voice fell cool and, she hoped, dispassionately into the fray.

Sydney snorted. "From Harriet. Stupid girl, she didn't even know she was blabbing. Then Tommy caught her out. Useless." He lunged toward Marty and the notes.

She tossed them to Phil.

"Please. You're never going to stop these guys. Tammany, the police, they're all in each other's pockets."

"Who?" asked Phil.

"I can't tell. They'll kill me. Please, just give me the notes. No one is going to print them anyway."

"Samuel Trout?" Phil persisted.

Sydney's eyes flashed toward the packet she was holding. Phil stepped out of the way, but Marty wasn't as quick, and he grabbed her and pulled her against him. Held her there with one arm across her chest and the other around her neck.

"Give me the damn papers."

Marty shook her head minutely.

"Or you'll do what?" Phil asked.

Marty opened her mouth and bit his wrist.

Sydney yowled and let go.

"Who killed Tommy Green?" Phil asked.

He was holding his wrist and rocking with pain. "I can't."

"You will," Marty said, and stepped toward him.

He cowered back. "If I tell you, will you give me the notes?"

The door swung open—again.

Now what? Had Miller and Van Anda gotten worried and jumped the gun? No, neither Atkins nor Mr. X would have let that happen.

They all turned toward the door as Jarvis Chandler stepped inside. He was holding a pistol, one much larger than Phil's, which was still in her purse that was hanging uselessly from her elbow. Close, but not close enough.

"What are you doing?" Sydney blurted. "I said I would get them. Did he send you?"

Marty looked as if she were ready to jump him, and Phil silently willed her to stay put.

Jarvis hadn't been at the reception. Had Trout sent him to see what was taking so long? Or had he come on his own behalf? And he'd come armed.

"Where are they?"

"Wait," Sydney said. "What the hell's going on?"

"This . . . is what's going on," Jarvis said, waving the pistol in Sydney's direction.

"You're going to kill me, too? Then Marty and Lady Dunbridge? When is it going to stop?"

"Shut up. Just shut up!"

"You killed Tommy?" Marty said. "Why? Just because you facilitated Trout's real-estate swindle? Nobody would have touched you if you hadn't murdered Tommy. But you did. And now us? And then who? How many people are you going to—"

"Marty, shut up!" Sydney cried.

"Yes, Mr. Chandler. How many?" Phil said. "They say after the first one, it gets easier. How many people have you killed? How many more will have to die?"

"A man can only hang once."

"Or in your case, the electric chair," Phil said.

Marty and Sydney had moved closer together and were staring at Phil as if she'd lost her mind. Perhaps she had. She just needed to get a confession out of him in front of witnesses.

His face crumpled. "No, I'm not like that."

"But you killed Tommy Green. You slit his throat, didn't you?"

Chandler looked wildly around the room. For what, Phil couldn't imagine.

"I didn't have a choice."

"We've heard that before," Marty said. Then clamped her teeth over her lip.

"He was going to ruin everything."

"But not your real-estate fraud against the government? That you could have weathered," Phil said more slowly. "Something a little closer to home. *Your* home."

Jarvis stilled, the gun that had been wobbling steadied. And he glared at Phil with such hatred, she was afraid he was going to shoot her on the spot. It was all she could do not to throw herself behind the nearest row of lockers.

"You. You!" His hand was shaking again, and the pistol was jerking so erratically it looked like a live creature.

"You slit his throat while he sat watching a moving picture at the nickelodeon."

"How did you know that?"

She wasn't about to tell him she was there. Her life would not be worth the fifteen cents it took to get into the theater. He'd confessed and she needed this to end. Her carefully laid plan would have worked if Sydney had been the killer. He would be in police custody by now.

But they were outside waiting for the killer to run with the notes.

She would just have to help him along and hope they all survived.

"Just tell me what happened and I'll give you the notes."

"Phil, no!" cried Marty.

"Tell me."

Sydney snapped. "Jarvis, you fool. I was getting the papers. I was going to bring them to the Cavalier Club tonight and give them to Trout. Now you've implicated us all in murder. You fool."

"I'm sorry. I couldn't wait."

"You couldn't wait," Phil said. "Because you didn't want anyone to see what Tommy might have written, not even your partner in crime, Samuel Trout."

Tommy and Trout and Mrs. Toscana from the same neighborhood, keeping secrets, holding each other in check by the tenuous balance of their determination. Phil wondered if it would hold now.

"Trout already knows; you killed Tommy for nothing."

Jarvis's head snapped from Sydney to Phil, and he turned the pistol on her.

"You—" He straightened the arm holding the pistol.

"No!" yelled Sydney, and lunged at Jarvis. The gun went

off in a deafening report, a blast of fire smothered by Sydney's body, and Sydney fell to the floor.

"Syd!" Marty cried.

From behind the lockers, Harriet screamed.

And in that brief, unexpected distraction, Phil unclasped her purse and grabbed her derringer in an efficient movement that startled her. Jarvis turned toward her, and she fired. The pistol fell out of his hand, and he grabbed his forearm.

For a stunned moment, everyone in the room froze in surprise. Phil was rather surprised herself. She'd actually hit something useful. Those early days of pheasant and skeet shooting must have carried over.

But in her haste, she'd dropped the packet of notes.

Jarvis came to life, snatched up the notes, and ran for the door—and she let him go. After all, there were reinforcements just outside.

"He's getting away." Marty started after him.

Eddie and Harriet appeared from behind the lockers.

"Stay here!" Phil ordered. "All of you. Marty, go make sure Sydney's not going to die on us. We'll need him as a witness."

"Jeez," Marty said, and ran back to kneel beside Sydney. "Is he okay?"

"He's good enough."

"Stay with him and make sure he stays that way." Phil kicked Jarvis's pistol toward Marty, jabbed an imperious finger at Eddie and Harriet to stay put, and went out into the hall.

Jarvis was frantically pushing the elevator call button. One of the problems of trying to kill someone twenty-three floors above the ground: getting away.

The elevator doors opened, but instead of rushing inside, Jarvis stumbled back as Carr Van Anda, the "journalist from Paris," and several other men stepped out.

Jarvis spun on his heel and hurried toward the stairs,

grabbed the rail, and nearly fell as an authoritative voice echoed from the steps below. "Jarvis Chandler, I'm arresting you—"

Phil would know the voice of Detective Sergeant Atkins anywhere.

In a blind panic, Jarvis turned and ran up the stairs to the twenty-fourth floor.

Atkins was right behind him. Phil hiked up her gown and ran after them. She could hear other footsteps behind them, and she only stopped at the top stair long enough to free her skirt.

The observatory sat in the middle of the storeroom roof like the tier of a giant wedding cake. There was no escape. The other elevators had been shut down as soon as the reception room was cleared. He would be stuck in the observatory with no way out.

Jarvis swiveled around. The way down was blocked; the way up led only to the smaller lantern room, where six workmen were at the ready to lower the ball to usher in the new year.

The others were closing in, but instead of surrendering, Jarvis sprinted across the room and pushed open the door to the outside observation deck.

"Stay here," Atkins ordered. "There's only a parapet preventing anyone from falling five floors to the twentieth floor."

Phil ignored his order and followed him outside. She wasn't going to let him go out there to risk his life without her.

Jarvis turned to face them, backed away until he was standing against the parapet. Above them the five-foot ball lit up the sky. Soon it would begin its descent.

"It's over, Chandler. Just step away from the parapet and come back inside."

Jarvis glanced over his shoulder at the black space behind him.

"There's nowhere to go, man."

Jarvis clutched the packet of notes to his chest, but he didn't move.

The other men crowded into the doorway. The "journalist from Paris" caught Phil's eye.

Jarvis took a step back.

Atkins stopped. "Don't do it, Chandler. Thousands of people are watching."

Phil glanced down. Times Square was a sea of uplifted faces. Above her head, the ball, lit with a hundred light bulbs, slowly began its descent.

And there was a swell of voices way below them.

"Ten . . ."

The ball lowered a few feet, jerked, then evened off.

"Nine . . ."

Jarvis stepped back closer to the edge.

"Eight . . ."

"Chandler, stay where you are!"

But Jarvis was beyond listening. His back came up against the marble parapet.

"Seven . . ."

He rebounded slightly, for a moment he seemed to rock forward, then he swayed, his arms waving futilely in the air as his body toppled over the rail.

Atkins lunged for him and managed to grab the sleeve of his jacket.

Phil grabbed Atkins before Jarvis could take him over the side.

"Six . . ." the crowd below chanted as the ball of light came closer and closer, lighting Jarvis's mask of terror.

"Five . . ."

Two of the other men crowded at the parapet, one of them grabbed Atkins to keep him from being dragged over with Jarvis, and Phil quietly moved out of the way.

"Four . . ."

The other man leaned over to grab something but merely came back with the packet of notes. He tossed it to the ground and tried again.

"Three . . ."

"Help us, man, give me your hand."

"Two . . . One . . ."

Jarvis suddenly pushed his feet against the wall, snapping the grip of the three men, who barely kept each other from following him over.

And as he plunged through the night, the ball touched the ground, the electric sign of 1908 lit the side of the *Times* building. The crowd roared "Happy New Year" as a cacophony of noisemakers and horns punctured the night, and confetti filled the air below them.

But on the observation deck, they were all silent. Jarvis Chandler was a mere shadow on the roof below.

Phil stopped Atkins as he ordered his men to the twentieth floor for body retrieval.

He shook his slightly. "I doubt if he survived."

"You'll need an ambulance for Sydney. He witnessed Jarvis's confession. I think he'll 'sing,' I think the expression goes. Are you okay?"

"I'm fine," he said. "Though not the way I would choose to spend a New Year's Eve."

"Nor I," Phil agreed. "And may I just add that I have never in our acquaintance frightened you the way you just frightened me."

"Oh, I wouldn't be so sure of that." Atkins looked around. "Where are those notes everyone is trying to get their hands on?"

Phil looked. She didn't really expect to find them. While everyone was busy trying to save Jarvis Chandler, the "journalist from Paris" had helped himself to Tommy's notes. She wouldn't be surprised if she saw news of some significant arrests in the morning paper.

"I believe they'll find their way to the proper hands," she said.

Atkins beetled his eyes at her. "I don't know what you're up to . . ."

"I'm going across the street to have a glass—or several—of the Knickerbocker Hotel's finest champagne to ring in the new year. One less case of extortion in the city, and one less murderer in the world. I don't suppose you can join us?"

He glanced toward the parapet of the observatory. "Perhaps next year," he said, and ushered her inside.

"Where have you been?" Bev asked when Phil finally managed to weave through the crush to Bev's table at the Knickerbocker. "Were you outside in the crowd?"

"Was I ever. What a crush!"

"Wasn't it the most exciting thing you ever saw?"

"The most exciting," Phil said. Not that she'd seen much of it. A glass of champagne was thrust into her hand, and she took it gratefully.

"Is Marty coming?"

"A little later. She had news to catch up on."

"Well, I hope they finally give her a byline."

"Me, too."

"A toast, Phil. To a happy new year."

Lady Dunbridge raised her glass. "To a happy new year." *And to many more missions to come.*

29

New Year's Day

"This is most interesting," Phil said as she sipped her morning coffee at the breakfast table. There was a stack of morning editions at her elbow.

"Listen to this: 'Real-Estate Extortion Ring Exposed. Leader Arrested.' They certainly didn't waste any time.

"'Last night, as thousands of people thronged Times Square to celebrate the *New York Times* New Year's lighted ball, the offices of Samuel D. Trout were raided in downtown Manhattan. Papers and financial records were confiscated. In the early hours of the morning, Mr. Trout, real-estate broker and a prominent man in New York politics, was arrested at his Manhattan mansion, and his assets were seized. It was a bad night for those involved in manipulating the real-estate market, as there was a tightly coordinated raid at several other businesses, and more arrests were made.'

"I wonder if Marty wrote this? And how did she find out all this information from midnight until this morning? That's quite remarkable."

She turned the page.

"Oh, and this," Phil said, suddenly somber. "'Mr. Jarvis Chandler, Commissioner of Buildings for the City of New York, died from an accidental fall at his home last night.'"

"At his home," scoffed Lily.

"True, but I suppose they didn't want his death associated with what they hope will become a New Year's Eve tradition.

Plus, it will save Roz from certain humiliation and ostracism by society."

His death would be better in the long run for Roz. Men like Jarvis, once given a taste of violence, felt no compunction about using it, and Phil had no doubt that the practice would have continued with his wife.

Bev could teach Roz how to survive widowhood and have a good time while doing it. As far as Roz's relationship with Mrs. Toscana, the two of them would have to figure it out on their own. Phil knew how to keep secrets, and she would keep theirs. Her job was done.

The telephone rang. Preswick wiped his hands and went to answer the call. He came back a moment later.

"That was Mr. Norris, the concierge. A gentleman left a message for you. You're to go to the window and look down at the street."

"That's strange. Did he say why?"

"No, my lady. Just that the man is awaiting your answer."

"My answer?" Phil stood, dropped her napkin on her plate, and went into the parlor, Preswick and Lily following.

She reached the window, looked out. Everything seemed normal. Just a Friend was at his corner. Carriages for hire were lined up along the curb.

"He said to look down," Lily reminded her.

Phil leaned her forehead against the pane and looked down to the street. A maroon Daimler, its gold trim gleaming in the sunlight, was parked at the curb. A chauffeur in full driving coat and cap stood at the driver's side.

He looked up and raised his hand in salute.

"It can't be," Phil said. "Lily, my sable coat and hat. Quickly!"

"But you're not dressed for going out."

"No matter. I shall be in good hands."

She slipped into the coat and shoes that Lily brought. Pulled the hat onto her head. "I'll be back . . . sometime."

He was waiting for her, keys dangling from one finger. "A little late, but I've been busy," he said.

"You have indeed," Phil agreed as she inspected the smooth lines of the Daimler.

"Mine?" she asked.

"Yours. From the powers that be. Would you like to take her for a spin?"

"I would, but first . . ." She gave him a long look. From his immaculate gray-and-maroon braided uniform to his clean-shaven face but for a very tidy straight mustache. The visor hid his eyes, but there was no fake nose or ears that she could tell, no missing teeth.

"Is this the real you?"

"Most of it." He reached up and carefully pulled the mustache from his upper lip. "Now it is." He jangled the keys. "Ready?"

"What's this?"

"Keys. Get in, I'll show you."

Phil took the keys from him and climbed in the driver's seat. He got in beside her.

"Key in there. Push that button."

"Really?"

"That's all it takes."

She turned the key and pressed the button. The Daimler purred to life.

"Amazing."

"It's the future."

"Where shall we go?"

He leaned back in his seat. "You decide."

And Phil was more than happy to oblige.

AUTHOR'S NOTE

Manhattan at any time is a fascinating place. But I couldn't resist the Gilded Age at Christmastime. So many amazing things, places, and people to discover: wonderful things and some not so wonderful. In other words, life.

One I never really thought about was the Black Hand, until one day I was perusing old copies of *The New York Times* just to get a feel for the atmosphere in 1907. (Their online archive is an indispensible research tool and fascinating rabbit hole.) This led me from Christmas trees and the descent of the first New Year's Eve ball from the newly built *Times* building roof to charity balls and food lines at the Salvation Army. I was reading an article about the threat to impose Sunday blue laws on theaters and nickelodeons when my eye caught a mention of La Mano Negra, the "Black Hand." And down the rabbit hole I went.

At the time of Lady Dunbridge's arrival in Manhattan there were widespread incidents of extortion credited to the elusive Black Hand, which held the citizens of several cities in terror. Rumors flourished that residents, mainly Italian immigrants and small shop owners, as well as those of great wealth, were being targeted by a widespread secret crime organization. But though its perpetrators used the same techniques—fires, bombings, kidnappings, murder, and threats signed with a threatening black hand or similar symbol—it was not a well-organized syndicate but a loosely related band of gangsters or individuals feeding on the fear of the populace. In fact, any person with a grudge and who could draw a picture might use the reputation of the Black Hand to frighten his victim. It was not the Mafia, who would take over power in New York a few years later. Nor was it the Camorra. A New York police officer, Joseph Petrosino, headed a squad of Italian-speaking policemen in an attempt to rein in this spate of terror.

Electric Christmas lights were all the rage in the Christmas of 1907. These sets of miniature bulbs were supplied in strings of 8, 16, 24, and 32 lights. They were promised to be "safe, simple, and convenient" and would "avoid all the danger and trouble incident to the use of candles." They ranged in price from twelve to fifteen dollars, equivalent to about four hundred dollars now, more money than many workers made in a week.

The *New York Times* building, which had moved from downtown to the triangle of land between Forty-Second and Forty-Third Streets where Broadway and Seventh Avenue converge, was a largely steel building of twenty-five stories. With an underground shopping area and subway station, it was considered the tallest building in the States. And New Year's Eve of 1907 was the first time a lighted ball descended from the roof, watched by multitudes of revelers in Times Square.

Every year, Mr. William M. Filess really did host an annual newsboys' Christmas dinner, which he and his father before him had been giving for forty years. The celebration took place at the Newsboys' Home on Chambers Street, and consisted of "800 pounds of turkey, 200 pounds of ham, two barrels of potatoes, two barrels of turnips, two double crates of celery, 1,800 mince pies, and 120 gallons of coffee . . . Enough to feed 1,800."

I did take a small liberty with the weather. Now as much as we all love a White Christmas, there was no snow reported for Manhattan during Christmas 1907. So I pulled out my author's license and took everyone to Holly Farm where I brazenly dumped a good few inches of loveliness on our characters.

I hope you will join Lady Phil and friends on her next crime-solving adventure in Gilded Age New York. I hear it's "predicted" that their next case will involve a trip to the newly opened Coney Island.

For directions on how to make paper Moravian stars or Bev's Christmas cocktail, please visit my website at shelley noble.com.

ACKNOWLEDGMENTS

When it comes to thanking all the people who made this story possible, I'm reminded of the final scene from *The Muppet Christmas Carol*. A tight shot focuses on Tiny Tim (played by Kermit's nephew, Robin) joyous over the roast goose. Then widens to show a changed Scrooge, then to the entire Cratchit family and the other guests at the table as they lift a toast. Out the camera pans, past the people peering in at the windows, past the people dancing in the square and filling the streets, until it lifts and soars over the roofs and chimney pots of London to the sky.

That is how my appreciation soars, from those who worked closest on the book, Kristin Sevick, Patrick Canfield, Libby Collins, and the amazing cover artist, Andrew Davidson; to my agent, Kevan Lyon; to my entire Forge team. And finally to those of you who receive it with kindness miles and miles away.

I thank you all.

ABOUT THE AUTHOR

Shelley Noble is the *New York Times* bestselling author of *Lighthouse Beach, The Beach at Painter's Cove, Whisper Beach,* and the Lady Dunbridge series, which started with *Ask Me No Questions*. A former professional dancer and choreographer for stage, television, and film, she's a member of Sisters in Crime, Mystery Writers of America, and the Women's Fiction Writers Association. Noble lives in New Jersey.